Blood
for Blood

Books by S.K. Rizzolo

The Rose in the Wheel
Blood for Blood

Blood for Blood

S. K. Rizzolo

Poisoned Pen Press

Copyright © 2003 by S.K Rizzolo

First Trade Paperback Edition 2008

10 9 8 7 6 5 4 3 2 1

Library of Congress Catalog Card Number: 2002115093

ISBN: 978-1-59058-507-8 Trade Paperback

Poisoned Pen Press
6962 E. First Ave. Ste. 103
Scottsdale, AZ 85251
www.poisonedpenpress.com
info@poisonedpenpress.com

Printed in the United States of America

This one is dedicated to my aunt Mary Simpson, second mom and good friend, and also to my mother, Yolanda J. Pitts, who always encouraged my love of books.

And God shall wipe away all tears from their eyes; and there shall be no more death, neither sorrow, nor crying, neither shall there be any more pain: for the former things are passed away.
　　—*The Book of Revelations*, chapter 21

It will have blood; they say, blood will have blood.
　　—*Macbeth*, Act Three, scene 4

"Come, Miss Julia, no more of your nonsense," said Rebecca as the child pulled away from her grasp to dart behind an urn bursting with flowers. On this early autumn day, the honeysuckle and sweet pea were in full blow, and the grass, crushed beneath Julia's busy feet, was the tender green of promise.

Heart heavy, Rebecca glanced toward the house. Today, with all the blinds drawn, its air of hollowness and decay struck her more than usual. It had been built not long after the reign of the Virgin Queen, and its bricks were black with age. She had overheard the Master, eyes aglow with enthusiasm, speak of rebuilding it one day, but the Mistress had merely smiled, shaking her head. That was some while ago, just after Miss Julia's birth, when it had seemed as if the evil times were ending. They had not, Rebecca had realized even then, for the mark was on them, man and wife, Master and Mistress, and on all their dependents too, she thought. The shadow hovered over them, darkening the brightest of days.

"I'm lost," sang the child. "You can't find me, Nurse. I sh'll go far 'way and leave you. You'll never, never find me!"

Rebecca knelt on the ground and, reaching out, pinched Julia's red-slippered toe visible at the corner of the urn. "You'll not do that, miss. Don't you know how lost *I* should be without you?"

Giggling with delight, Julia hovered briefly just out of reach, then was off again racing toward the sundial at the center of the garden. Rebecca, following, considered scolding the child, yet knew she would not. Not today. As she crossed the open space, a flicker at one of the windows caught her attention, and she paused, feeling exposed, as if somehow caught in the wrong.

It seemed the movement had come from the study where the Master had shut himself up, as he always did. She wondered what he did there all day, alone with his books and papers with only his secretary for company. And the Mistress with her watercolors, poetry books, and endless embroidery, rarely stirring from her own sitting room except to attend to those household duties that could not be left to others. How strange, how endlessly fascinating, Rebecca found them, these beings from another world. She watched, and she pitied them.

Now, shaking off the sensation of being watched, she went and scooped up the child to sit with her, both rather drowsy, on the stone bench in the sun. Time they were going inside, but she felt that today Miss Julia would do better out of doors. She was a sensitive creature, biddable until crossed and subject to violent fits of crying. It was best not to enforce obedience unless absolutely necessary. And Rebecca was tired, for like everyone else, she had not slept much the prior night. Gradually, she felt herself relax, allowing the dreams to drift through her mind like ribbons fluttering in a breeze.

"A word with you, Nurse," said a voice in her ear. Rebecca's eyes flew open, and she jumped guiltily to her feet, startling Julia so that the child set up an aggrieved wail.

"Beg pardon, sir. I didn't see you there." Bobbing an awkward curtsey, she jiggled the child to stop the crying and waited, feeling a rivulet of sweat trickle down between her shoulder blades. She could not look at him, for she was afraid he would be displeased to have found her so nearly asleep—and now to have the child fussing as he looked on. What could be more unlucky? Thankfully, Julia subsided, her head sinking back onto Rebecca's shoulder.

When she came to Cayhill before Miss Julia's birth, the housekeeper Mrs. Dobson had thought her too young to take charge of a child, but oh, Rebecca loved her position, loved living in this house with its grand, shabby furnishings, odd corners, and interesting people. It was utterly different from her family's tiny cottage so packed with humanity that a body's thoughts chased round and round her head with no chance of any solitude to allow them their say.

Seeming ill at ease, the Master had barely glanced at his daughter. "No matter. I only wanted a word."

Rebecca lifted her head, risking a glance, and was surprised to see fresh color in his cheeks. His eyes, too, were the clear, remote silver of a polished coin.

"May I offer my con...condolences, sir?" As her tongue stumbled over the unfamiliar word, a flush of embarrassment crept up her cheeks.

"Yes, thank you, Nurse." He looked faintly puzzled as if for an instant he had forgotten who she was.

After a moment, he went on. "My wife asked me to inform you she won't trouble you to bring Miss Julia to her tonight."

"Yes sir, I figured as much. Poor lady. I'll pray for her quick recovery. To be disappointed when we all hoped that mayhap this time—"

"At least her health is not in peril. It was early days, the doctor says, and the babe not fully formed."

She remained silent, meditating, as she often did on such matters, about the fate of those unborn creatures who did not grow big enough to make their entry into the world, or who spent so few days in it. When once Rebecca had asked Mrs. Dobson, reared in the Romish faith, for her opinion, she had described a place called Limbo where all the unbaptized children were sent to wait till Judgment Day. But Rebecca had also asked her question of Jack Willard, the gamekeeper's son, and he had insisted almost angrily that all such babes either went straight to Old Scratch, or were condemned to wander the earth forever…

"I took Miss Julia to gather hazelnuts today," said Rebecca when the Master seemed to await her response. "She's made her mam a necklace, sir, with nuts strung on a chain for good fortune and fruitfulness. And protection." Hastily, she scrubbed the back of her hand across her eyes and tried to smile, for she was angry at herself for adding to his trouble with her tears. "It was a son this time, wasn't it?"

"What's your name?" he said harshly, intent on her face.

Rebecca stared back, too frightened to break away from that measuring gaze. Now she was sure she had offended him.

Chapter I

February 1812

The crying had continued for hours, a low, throbbing noise that allowed her no peace and sent her stumbling over the rough ground. As she hurried through the trees, a low branch cut her cheek, drawing blood that trickled to her mouth. Her body felt leaden with fatigue, but she knew she must find the source of the sound. It went everywhere, borne on the wind, perhaps just the wind itself.

Ahead loomed a massive oak, its branches silvered by moonlight, leaves a-glitter with a thousand trembling rain jewels. In its shadow, she glimpsed movement and quickened her pace, then halted, confused. The cry intensified, a high note of mourning terrible to the ears.

Penelope awakened. Lifting her head, she looked through the gap in the bed curtains toward the open window. At her side Sarah still slept in the silence that had settled over the house. She could hear her own breathing, quick and shallow, a pulse beating a tattoo at her neck. Slipping out of bed, she crept to the window.

Air, heavy with rain-damp, stroked her skin. Below was darkness, but the sound had come from there, outside in the garden. She stood peering into shadows that she knew concealed trees and barren flower beds. After a time she turned away to slip into her dressing gown, its warmth welcome on this late winter's morning. She lit a candle and went out the door, closing it behind her.

In the library, someone had lit the lamp on Sir Roger's massive desk, around which huddled Timberlake, the butler; the housekeeper Mrs. Sterling, her hair in disarray under a hastily donned cap; and two of the housemaids. A footman, looking oddly unfinished in a loose shirt and no coat, stood at the French window, nose pressed against the glass.

The butler and housekeeper exchanged a glance at Penelope's appearance, Mrs. Sterling's mouth thinning.

"Mrs. Wolfe," Timberlake said, "your rest has been disturbed?"

"Yes, I heard someone cry out. What has happened?" Penelope set down her candle and turned toward the circle of anxious faces.

"You must have keen ears," put in Mrs. Sterling, her eyes coldly appraising. "Sound does not in general carry to the upper regions of the house."

Penelope waited, gazing back at her, then replied in a tone just short of insolence, "My window was ajar, ma'am."

Timberlake spoke. "George and I were on the point of making a circuit of the garden. You had best return above stairs." He turned to the footman. "Where is Dick? Go and rouse him at once, George. Tell him to arm himself with a stout cudgel."

"Indeed, we are only in the way here, Mrs. Wolfe," said the housekeeper, who never lost a chance to put the new companion in her place. "We must see to her ladyship. Would you be so kind as to ascertain that Miss Poole has awakened and gone to her? Lady Ashe may have sustained a terrible shock to her nerves and stand in need of a restorative. George," she added sharply. "You heard Mr. Timberlake. Go at once and fetch Dick."

A strange expression crossed George's face. Turning away, he approached the French window to edge it open a crack. "Listen," he said with an awed horror.

Through the window came a keening moan, alien it seemed, so full of pain and despair that the strangeness of it struck Penelope like a blow. As they waited, paralyzed, the noise repeated.

"What in heaven's name is that?" she exclaimed, striding forward.

The footman had lost so much color that his eyes blazed against the papery white of his skin. "Nothing of this earth, miss," he burst out.

"I beg you will not place yourself in front of the glass, Mrs. Wolfe," said Timberlake. "Who knows but that this uncanny call is meant to beguile us. I will rouse Sir Roger and Lord Ashe."

"Indeed you must, but someone is in great distress. We must go to his assistance at once." Turning to the footman, Penelope gestured into the darkness, her sense of urgency growing. "George, you will go? I will accompany you." The footman started to shake his head, but then nodded reluctantly.

Mrs. Sterling looked her with outrage. "Mrs. Wolfe, you cannot mean to expose yourself thus. You will catch your death of cold, if nothing worse is the result of such foolish and immodest behavior."

The moan came again, fainter, the merest breath of sound. "We must not delay," Penelope said, shivering. "I cannot bear that some unfortunate soul should cry out in need, or perhaps even perish, without we do nothing to aid him."

The housekeeper made as if to block her path, reaching out to grip Penelope's arm. "You don't know who or what it may be. What decent person is abroad at such an hour?"

Penelope did not reply. Deliberately, she removed her arm from Mrs. Sterling's grasp, almost pushing the woman aside in her impatience. Seizing her candle, she pushed open the door and stepped onto the terrace, pausing a moment to get her bearings.

The night faded. What two minutes ago had been impenetrable shadow now exhibited a wavering form, yet a fog lay over the whole. George had followed her out, Timberlake hovering in the rear apparently determined that no mere footman ought to be allowed to shame his manhood.

"Look!" cried George. "I saw movement there by that statue. Someone was there a moment ago, I'd swear it."

"Nonsense." Timberlake looked around uneasily. "It's just the breeze rustling amongst the trees. Mind, Mrs. Wolfe, your candle will blow out."

Ignoring him, Penelope slipped to the edge of the terrace, peering first toward the mist-shrouded shape that in daytime would become a statue of Apollo. Her eyes followed the line of the path that led to the small shrubbery just beyond. She could make out the laurel bushes and the flower beds. Then her gaze paused to linger on a patch of darkness in the middle of the gravel. Wordlessly, she tugged at George's sleeve.

Penelope picked up the skirts of her dressing gown and descended the shallow stairs to the garden. Swiftly, she moved to kneel at the side of a supine form, and with a shaking hand, reached out to touch a shoulder.

"What is it, miss?" George was there, bending over her, his face anxious.

Penelope looked up into his eyes. "A man. He's hurt, I think. Help me to turn him."

Before the footman could comply, the voice of her employer's husband issued from the terrace. "Mrs. Wolfe. May I be of help? Timberlake tells me we have suffered some sort of disturbance."

"Indeed, my lord, for there is someone injured here. Send at once for a surgeon and a constable."

She turned her attention back to the fallen man, and, with George's help, managed to roll him onto his back. In the grayish light she saw he was young and well formed. And as she bent over, she caught the faint gurgling as he gasped for air.

"He's alive," she said triumphantly. "George, go quickly and obtain a blanket, water, and some brandy. George?" She became aware of her companion's rigidity. Biting his lip as if in vain attempt to regain control, the footman stared fixedly ahead, eyes brimming with fear.

"What is it?" Her voice rose in spite of efforts to keep it steady. "There is no time to lose. He will die."

"It's Dick, miss. Don't you recognize him?"

Suddenly, horribly, she did. This was the young man who had pulled out her chair in the breakfast parlor just yesterday morning, the one who had blinked and smiled with his eyes when she thanked him for the fresh coffee.

Penelope stared at him. "You are not surprised to find him here, are you? You knew Dick wasn't in his bed?"

The footman took a shuddering breath. "We share a room, miss. I woke, found him gone, and went to look for him. That's when I heard that ungodly cry that brought Mrs. Sterling and Mr. Timberlake a-running too. But I never thought…what's amiss with him?"

"I don't know." He still wore his silk stockings and black pumps with buckles, but his hair was unpowdered. Then Penelope reached down to run her fingers over the front of his blue and gold livery and felt a dampness. The stain had spread across his chest.

"He bleeds. Go, George," she said through a tight throat. "Get some cloths and inform Lord Ashe of what has happened. Go!"

As the footman backed away, she knelt beside the wounded man, taking his hand. With her other hand she bunched up some of the coat and pressed it against the wound. Her own fingers came back, sticky red. She wiped away the wet and reapplied the pressure.

The early morning birdsong clamored in her ears. Watching the light struggle to pierce the clouds, she thought the new day seemed unnaturally dark and was glad of the candle flickering feebly on the ground next to her. It seemed she waited a long time, dew soaking into the hem of her dressing gown, though it couldn't have been more than a few minutes. Still, it was long enough that she had time to wonder dully where everyone could be.

Penelope could think of nothing to do but pray, bending to murmur exhortations in the man's ear in the faint hope he might somehow respond. His face remained smooth, not so much as a flicker of an eyelid betraying his awareness of her presence, until it seemed he *would* attempt to speak. The horrid gasping intensified, his lips trembled, and he spoke, his voice so low, so thready, that if Penelope were not crouched close to his face she should never have heard him. As it was, she could not be certain she had understood him right, and it seemed to her that his face had grown even more alarmingly pale.

"The sun shall be turned into…darkness, and the moon into blood, before the great and the terrible day of the Lord come." He could say no more, for blood there was, streaming from his mouth and down his smooth chin to stain the white cravat knotted at his neck.

"Help will come." She squeezed his hand. "I promise. It will come." Feeling the wetness of tears on her own face, Penelope put her cheek to his lips a second time, seeking desperately for breath.

She heard footsteps and looked up to see George, gripping a decanter of brandy, accompanied by Lord Ashe, garbed in a rich velvet dressing gown.

"Come away, Mrs. Wolfe," said Ashe. "Assistance will arrive shortly. You can do nothing further here, will only distress yourself to no purpose. George tells me that life yet lingers. Perhaps Dick may survive."

"No. I feel certain he is gone now," said Penelope. She released her grip on the cold fingers, accepted Lord Ashe's proferred hand, and came shakily to her feet.

"You shall have the brandy then," he said, taking her arm to lead her back toward the terrace. But first perhaps you will like to wash your face and change your dress?"

Penelope gaped at him, at first unable to fathom such concern with so trivial a matter as her appearance. But as her gaze followed his to the bloody streaks smeared across her dressing gown, she understood.

Chapter II

Edward Buckler propped his elbows on the balustrade and gazed out over the river, his dog Ruff patient at his side. On winter days the omnipresent London soot mingled with the fog to form a gray pall that blanketed the river, enveloping him in its embrace. Then Buckler could not see the wherries and barges that plied the waters below, though the shouts of the watermen reached his ears as if from a vast distance.

Tasting soot on his tongue, he raised a hand to brush the black flecks from his cheek and nose. He liked days like this, for a man could make his way through the streets to stand on this bridge as if alone in all the world. And when a ray of sun chanced to strike the cloud that hovered always ahead, the atmosphere glowing suddenly golden-orange, the effect was truly beautiful.

He glanced down at Ruff, who looked back with a kind of weary trust that never failed to bring a smile to Buckler's lips. He ought not to keep the dog so long from his breakfast, he thought. But as he turned to go, he saw a figure emerging from the mist and approaching at a rapid pace along the footpath. An arm lifted in a vigorous wave. On Buckler's part, too, recognition was instantaneous even without the aid of the lamps that remained lit at this hour.

"I've been round to your chambers," boomed Ezekiel Thorogood. "Bob told me I'd likely find you here. Fortunate for me as I have a particular desire for a word with you."

"Here I am, as you see." He turned back to lean on the balustrade.

Thorogood chuckled. "That hardly sounds promising, but you will alter your tune once you hear my news. I don't suppose you've any fresh business of your own?"

"I've been pondering the brief Greer sent my way. I'm not so certain I wish to take it on."

"Why not? It's not as if you anticipate a full calendar, Buckler. Never mind that right now. I came to talk to you about Penelope Wolfe."

Buckler was silent, reflecting that of all the topics of conversation, he had not expected this one. Why this should be so he wasn't sure, as he knew the old lawyer was very good friends indeed with the lady. Penelope Wolfe did enter Buckler's thoughts at odd moments, especially when his eyes rested upon Ruff, the ragged companion she had foisted upon him. He felt he had done his duty in helping Mrs. Wolfe to obtain her current position as a lady's companion— and tried not to think much about her otherwise.

"Well? You are not curious? I own I had thought better of you than that."

"I don't suppose you mean to discuss the lady's affairs here. Shall we retire to my lodgings, or would you rather proceed to the Grecian and take some refreshment?"

"Neither," Thorogood boomed again over the din of wheels rumbling on stone. "We must go to my office."

Buckler glanced at him, surprised, and noticed for the first time that the lawyer's long face fairly quivered with a suppressed excitement, and his hat was squashed at an awkward angle on his head. "Not a social visit?"

"Not precisely, no. Let us get out of this confounded fog."

Buckler accompanied him down the walkway and into Chatham Place, where a hackney awaited them. The fog had begun to lift as a sharp breeze flirted among the clouds, blowing, subsiding, blowing again. Finding Thorogood strangely quiet during the short journey, Buckler sank into himself, seeing but not really seeing the familiar scene glimpsed through the coach window.

The streets roared with traffic of all sorts, mud-bespattered carriages, massive lumbering wagons, carts laden with meat or vegetables, the occasional flock of sheep driven by harassed guardians, and, of course, endless, teeming humanity in all its color and stench.

Unlike his friend, who seemed to thrive on the City's jostle, its ability both to feed a man's senses and to spice his life with challenge, Buckler preferred more convivial, eminently civilized surroundings such as his usual haunt, the Grecian Coffee House. It wasn't that he disdained challenge. On the contrary, he liked it well enough within defined limits that suited his temperament. Take fencing, for instance. His Italian tutor was well pleased with his progress, and Buckler enjoyed the choreographed parry and thrust, the footwork, the slow but steady increase in stamina. Not that fencing was a particularly *useful* skill these days, but that was beside the point.

Reining in his scattered thoughts, Buckler looked at Thorogood, who sat opposite, hands wrapped across his expansive waistline. As semi-retired attorney and perennial thorn in the side of established order, he often claimed he'd earned his corpulence and would apologize to no man for any evidence of a healthy partaking in life. *Fruges consumere nati*: born to consume the fruits of the earth.

"You must go at once to Mrs. Wolfe," Thorogood said as if resuming an earlier conversation. "I'd go myself only I don't suppose Lady Whoosit should welcome a visit from a fat old fellow like me."

"The name is Ashe, as you are perfectly well aware. What's the trouble with Mrs. Wolfe?"

"I don't know that anything is." He met Buckler's eyes, his own suddenly serious. "And yet she didn't seem quite her usual self when I saw her last. You wouldn't have thought of that eventuality when you suggested she live there amongst people not of her own kind. What I should like to know is whether or not they are *your* kind?"

"She needn't stay if she doesn't like it," Buckler said, exasperated. "I've not seen Julia Wallace-Crag, or I should say Lady Ashe, in years. Wallace-Crag's estate adjoins that of my brother. I've known the family to speak to my entire life."

"Good. An entry will be useful."

"I think perhaps I should be better off steering clear, if only to save myself a good deal of bother. You do recall the last time?"

"Sometimes, my friend, I can't but think you are a man of sixty clothed in a younger skin. Have you no red blood in your veins, no sense of adventure?"

Buckler looked away, suddenly stung. "As much as any man, I suppose, in so far as the call of business permits."

Thorogood smiled. "Where is the difficulty then? You have no business at present."

They had arrived at their destination. After a brief tussle over who would pay the jarvey, which Buckler won by thrusting coins in the man's hand, they crossed the road at Lincoln's Inn Fields where over two centuries earlier Anthony Babington had been hanged, drawn, and quartered for his role in the Scots Queen plot and where today the goliath plane trees brandished their massive arms.

Entering an old mansion that had been partitioned and sublet to lawyers, they set off down the corridor, glimpsing rows of clerks at work on their high stools. At his own door, Thorogood paused, breathing heavily, then motioned for Buckler to precede him inside. There was a long silence as Buckler's gaze swept round the room.

With its heavy furnishings covered in cheerful red brocade and towering shelves crammed with leather-bound volumes, these chambers had always seemed welcoming. Not today. A chair had been pushed over on its side to spill its innards from a wound in the seat cushion. Some vindictive hand had tossed his friend's treasured books willy-nilly to the carpet. The desk drawers had been upended on the window seat. And, amongst all the debris, fragments of glass glinted like fairy dust.

"He came in through the window," said Thorogood.

Buckler turned to face him. "What's this to do with Mrs. Wolfe?"

❧⸳☙

Seems peaceful enough, thought John Chase as he climbed out of the hackney after the boy. A maid was scrubbing a doorstep as a sedan chair rounded the corner from King Street. A drover passed, guiding two cows toward the park, and across the way, Josiah Wedgwood's china showroom had opened its doors for business.

Chase stood gazing at the elegant three-storied buildings of red brick with stone dressings. In the center of the square, an iron rail framed an equestrian statue of William III, a gallant figure presiding over a large circle of water. Something in the essential character of St. James's Square suggested endurance and safety, hardly surprising, he told himself, for the rich knew well how to create such illusion.

When the message had arrived that morning, he had been abed with no forewarning that the day would bring anything beyond the ordinary round of tracking down pilfered snuff-boxes or serving papers on unlicensed tavern-keepers. Arriving at Bow Street, Chase learned that Sir Roger Wallace-Crag had sent for him by name. And though Chase had questioned the shaken messenger boy during the short journey in the hackney, little information, beyond the barest facts, had been forthcoming.

As he turned to ascend the steps of Wallace-Crag's home on the square's north side, the door opened to reveal the butler, countenance rigid with disapproval, probably because Chase had not rung at the servants' entrance.

"I've brought him," said the boy, pulling at his livery and glancing uneasily at his superior. When the butler merely nodded in dismissal, the boy turned with obvious relief and made his way to the area stairs, disappearing below.

The butler said, "I am Timberlake, sir. Please enter." He held the door wider.

Chase crossed the threshold into Stygian gloom. Pausing to allow his eyes to adjust, he saw that he stood in a vestibule crowded with scores of antique casts and marbles. Candles flickering in brass sconces threw deep shadows.

"Is that the man from Bow Street?" said another voice, and Chase found himself regarded by a slight man with a heavy-lidded, unfocused gaze and a drawn complexion that looked as though it rarely saw the sun. Chase did not miss the look of dislike that crossed the butler's face, but Timberlake said merely, "Yes, Mr. Finch. Will you escort him to the master?"

"Certainly." He bowed slightly. "Owen Finch, secretary to Sir Roger."

Chase said, "I should like to see the corpse first, if you please, then view the spot where Ransom was found."

"That seems a sensible proceeding if you are to report on your observations." Finch glanced at the butler. "That will be all, Timberlake."

When the butler had retreated, Chase went on, "I should also like to speak to the person who made the discovery. I take it you have moved the body? No matter, though my job would be much the easier had nothing been disturbed."

"I need hardly tell you we are not accustomed to doings of such nature in this house, Mr. Chase."

"No? I should imagine not. In any case I shall need to interview the maids and footmen, indeed all of the servants, afterwards. Is there a small anteroom suitable for the purpose?"

"Of course. If you'll come this way."

Chase followed the secretary under an arch into a wide hall. Here more marbles, bronzes, vases, and busts lined shelves on either side. Greek, Roman, Egyptian, there seemed no order to the display. Rusting suits of armor stood guard impassively. Along the graceful staircase rising to the first floor was a series of painted enamel plaques with gilt-framed Italian-looking portraits set above.

Passing several doors, Finch stopped at one, opening it. "We thought it best to carry him in here, sir, until you arrived. The doctor who has been to examine him waits to speak to you. The parish constable also."

"In good time," Chase murmured. He recognized the feeling that had overcome him. Part exhilaration. Part dread. Part a sense of fellowship that makes one keenly regret any loss of human life, be the victim a stranger or not.

Chase stood back politely to allow the other man to enter before him, but Finch shrank back. "I'll leave you to it, shall I, sir? When you are ready, the lady will no doubt be pleased to relate her story."

There was a note in the secretary's voice that Chase did not comprehend. "Lady?" he echoed. Was he to be honored by Wallace-Crag's daughter Lady Ashe, a well-known leader of fashion who, the boy sent to fetch him had confided, resided in this house with her husband? About to articulate the question, he stepped into the room and halted in his tracks. No lady had dreamed up this decorating scheme.

It was like entering a cathedral crypt. Narrow and dark, the chamber featured all manner and sizes of crosses: stone, wood, gold, silver, some bejeweled, others crude and plain. They hung in uneven rows on the moss-green papered walls and clustered on tables and the chimney-piece. Windows bordered by margin lights of blue glass lent an eerie color to the space; incongruously, however, the furnishings were of the conventional style. Chase fumbled in his pocket for his spectacles. Behind him the door clicked shut, and he was alone.

The young man lay on a sofa that had been pushed out of place into a corner. Someone had draped a piece of serge over his form as if in an attempt to preserve the decencies. But there was nothing decent about this death, as Chase saw when he lifted the cloth.

A single clean blow had pierced the man's bloodstained blue coat and embroidered gold silk waistcoat to penetrate the chest cavity beneath. From the looks of the wound itself, the knife had been extremely sharp, but not large. A stiletto?

Interesting that the footman had been fully dressed in livery; clearly, he had not been called out in the night unawares. On that thought Chase slipped his hand into one of the coat pockets. Nothing. But when he tried the other, his fingers closed on something delicate and velvety smooth. Frowning in puzzlement, Chase drew forth a cup-like leaf on which two egg-shaped buds had formed. This he slipped into his own pocket. Then, as he bent over the body to continue his examination, he heard the door behind him open again. Chase turned, expecting to see Owen Finch, and once more was struck dumb.

"I'm so glad you've come," said a familiar voice.

Removing the spectacles, he stared. "Good God. It's Penelope Wolfe."

⁕

"What do you know of this business?"

"Very little," replied Penelope, "though it was I who discovered the body and asked that you be summoned."

Chase studied her. The same thick dark hair, fastened too severely under her cap, the same liquid dark eyes, but without the usual warmth in her cheeks. He suddenly remembered how much he liked this woman, that is when not annoyed by her arrogance or her indomitable naïveté. And he made another discovery. It didn't surprise him in the least to find her mixed up again in murder.

"You needn't remain in the room. I'll finish my examination and come to you presently."

"I shall stay. There will be questions."

He had heard the edge in her voice that told him very plainly to leave be. "Tell me what's happened then, from the beginning."

As she faced him, Chase fixed her eyes, which showed a tendency to stray toward the body. Outwardly, she was composed, but he could see she felt the queer, trembling excitement that often accompanies a shock. She looked utterly out of place framed by the absurd glut of crosses.

It had been two months since he'd last seen her at the attorney Thorogood's Christmas dinner. Chase recalled that she'd asked about his family, and he had actually spoken of his son growing up in America. It was a day he thought of often, one that had seemed to hold loneliness and disillusion at bay. And this celebration had occurred on the heels of the Saint Catherine affair, which Penelope Wolfe had been lucky to survive. He wondered how she'd fared since and whether her ramshackle husband was still missing. He wondered, too, what the devil she was doing in this impossible place.

"At what hour were you awakened?"

"About half-past six, I should think. Time for the housemaids to be at their labors."

"Without the slightest notion what might await you, you went downstairs, leaving young Sarah? Your daughter is with you, I take it?"

She flushed. "Yes. But I wasn't certain what I had heard, only that it sounded like a night cry, and I could not simply go back to sleep. I found the housekeeper and butler in the library." She sat down on a brocade-covered chair and gazed at her clasped fingers.

"Is this cry likely to have issued from the mortally wounded man?"

"I cannot say. It sounded…uncanny. We all heard the moaning. I was certain some poor soul was in torment, and I couldn't bear it. So I went on the terrace, and George thought he saw something move. Then I spotted Dick. I thought at first we might save him." She moved to the narrow sofa where the man lay and gazed down into the face Chase had left uncovered. "He was too young to die."

Approaching to take her arm, Chase steered her toward the door. "Will you take me to where it happened?"

"Yes," she said, smiling a little self-consciously as she looked up into his eyes. "The servants have already declared their intention to avoid the spot. You see, they have long been convinced of something amiss in this house, and Lady Ashe only encourages them in these fancies, I'm afraid, for she dearly enjoys all the romance of a mystery."

"Your employer?"

"Yes, Mr. Chase. I am her companion. I understand the family hails from Dorset. Mr. Buckler recommended me to the position after my landlady decided that a woman on her own with a child did not promote the respectability of her lodgings."

Chase had to restrain a grin at the thought of Penelope Wolfe as genteel companion to a lady of quality. Weren't companions supposed to be little mice whose sole purpose in life was to fetch and carry and to swallow any bullying that came their way? "What of Miss Sarah?" he asked.

"Lady Ashe has kindly assigned a maid to remain with her whilst I am at my duties."

He understood. This was come-down indeed for Penelope Wolfe, raised in affluence in Sicily by an indulgent father, an expatriate Radical philosopher. Yet it was her imprudent marriage to the artist Jeremy Wolfe that had brought her to this pass, and he could not entirely pity her, though he had to admire her courage in facing up to her circumstances.

"This house belongs to your employer's father? Is not Wallace-Crag a Scottish name?"

"Yes. I believe Sir Roger's kin came from somewhere near Dundee originally. His father stayed loyal to King George during the Jacobite rebellion and was rewarded with an estate in Dorset and a baronetcy. Sir Roger was raised in England."

"How large a family?"

"There's just Lady Ashe and her husband. Tragically, her mother died in childbirth when she was quite small."

He regarded her thoughtfully. "I take it neither of the ladies is responsible for the décor?"

Humor sparked in her eyes. "Sir Roger is an antiquary. Overpowering, isn't it? Still, I'm told this is nothing compared to the family seat. When Lady Ashe is able to spare me, I have been helping to catalogue Sir Roger's souvenirs of his travels."

"Any word from Wolfe?" he asked abruptly.

Before Penelope could reply the door opened, and a woman entered. She wore a white gown with short tasseled sleeves and a half train draped over her smooth, rounded arm. An opal necklace lay in two rows round her neck. Her light brown hair was a cluster of delicate curls restrained only by a strip of muslin tied at the side of her head with a bow.

Chase had time to scan her features as she stood without speaking for a full minute and gazed around the room at the crosses, her eyes sliding over the body as if she didn't see it. Her face possessed a piquant sharpness of nose and chin that was by no means unattractive.

"I beg your pardon," she said at last. "I see you are occupied, Penelope."

"This is the man from Bow Street of whom I told you, Lady Ashe."

"Indeed? So this is your police officer. I have always wished to become acquainted with a genuine Bow Street Runner, sir. You will forgive my intrusion and my curiosity?"

Chase bowed. "You would be forgiven anything, my lady." A poor attempt at gallantry, he reflected wryly. "I am sorry to make your acquaintance under such circumstances," he went on. "Ransom's death no doubt has distressed you."

"'Tis a dreadful occurrence, Mr. Chase. Truly dreadful. I need hardly say Lord Ashe and I wish you to do your utmost to get to the bottom of it. We shall put up a reward and pay your fees."

He bowed again, keeping his expression neutral. "Thank you, my lady. Perhaps you will allow me to ask you a few questions. Your footman Dick Ransom, was he in good standing in your household?"

"Oh yes, though he'd not been with us long. Just a few months, I believe." Her gaze fixed unwaveringly on his; her voice was low, a trifle husky. "You may get further particulars from Timberlake, but I always found the young man eager to please and a sober, respectable sort of person."

"As your manservant he must have accompanied you when you paid calls or went out shopping?"

"Frequently, but I noticed nothing out of the ordinary."

"And this morning? Were you yourself roused by the disturbance?"

"No, I heard nothing, for unlike Mrs. Wolfe, I am a shockingly sound sleeper and my window was closed. But it may be we owe Dick an enormous debt. I've very little doubt but that he stumbled upon some villains attempting to gain access to the house and prevented a robbery at the cost of his own life. The villains would have been frightened off."

Chase glanced at Penelope, who had been watching her employer with an oddly veiled expression. There was something definitely amiss there, he thought. Was it that she found this explanation as little persuasive as he did, or was it something more? Lady Ashe's manner did not sit right with him, and he could not for the moment determine why.

"Your butler will be making arrangements for the funeral? There will have to be an inquest, after which Ransom may receive a respectable interment. I shall inquire of your butler if the murdered man has family that will need to be informed."

"Timberlake says he thinks not," broke in Penelope, "or at least Dick never spoke of anyone. He was pleasant enough but kept to himself. One of the maids mentioned he was a Londoner born and bred."

"How clever of you to think of asking the staff, Penelope!" cried Lady Ashe.

When Penelope did not immediately reply, an uncomfortable silence fell. Lady Ashe looked embarrassed, and Chase thought he caught a fleeting expression of hurt in her eyes. He nodded politely. "If you'll excuse us now, perhaps Mrs. Wolfe will show me the garden."

"Yes," said Penelope with alacrity. "I shall join you presently if that's agreeable, ma'am."

She waved a hand. "Take your time, my love. We must do all possible for poor Dick. I know I've no need to ask for your pledge on that score, Mr. Chase." Flashing a quick smile, she glided from the room.

Chase's gaze swept again past the rows of crosses glimmering in the blue-tinged light to rest on the still form on the sofa. "No pledge needed," he murmured. "Poor devil."

Chapter III

Chase squatted down to examine a bloodstain as Penelope stood a little to one side watching. There was blood where the body had lain, but very little along the rest of the path as far as he could see in the gloom. But he spotted areas where the gravel had been displaced when, presumably, the wounded man had stumbled some yards in a futile quest for assistance.

"He spoke just the one time?"

"Yes, those few words only." She kicked at the gravel with the toe of one slipper. "I found the passage. It's a quotation from the Bible. The Book of Joel, a minor prophet who prophesied the Day of Judgment."

"Ransom was preparing to meet his Maker, eh? Probably had good reason to fear the accounting."

"I'm not certain that was it, Mr. Chase," said Penelope, raising troubled eyes to his. "It seemed, I don't know precisely, as if somehow the warning were more general."

Chase half wanted to say something to comfort her but couldn't think what, and in any event offering comfort wasn't really in his line. Instead, he continued slowly up the path a second time, his eyes scanning the close-cropped turf along the border. Several times he paused to slip his hand under a bush or to peer into a flower bed. It was too much to hope for that he would luck upon the murder weapon, yet he had to try.

"You do not subscribe to the theory of a foiled robbery," he said after a minute or two.

She looked surprised. "I don't know why you should suppose I have had the leisure to conceive any theory."

"It was your countenance that told me so when Lady Ashe spoke of the matter."

"I suppose that's true, for I can't imagine why Dick Ransom should have been dressed and out of doors in the first place. How should he realize playing the part of the hero was required?"

"Exactly. Will you come into the shrubbery with me, Mrs. Wolfe? If Ransom came out to meet someone, this part of the gardens would provide some shelter and privacy, I should think."

"Yes. I often walk here when I find a moment to myself."

They proceeded down the graveled path and into the walk lined by hedges and dotted with benches at intervals. Though the air was chill, the close-set greenery did offer some protection from the damp. There was just enough room for Chase and Penelope to walk abreast, close but not touching.

"Are you happy here, Mrs. Wolfe? Your employer seems a tolerable sort of person."

She paused to consider, and he reflected that he had forgotten this trait she had of groping after the honest answer. "No. I cannot say I have been happy here, Mr. Chase, though Lady Ashe has been most generous."

"A generosity that sticks in your throat?" he hazarded.

"Yes, I suppose it does."

Chase thought he understood. She herself had been generous of her time and compassion on behalf of the women of the St. Catherine Society when their patroness Constance Tyrone had been slain, but Penelope no doubt found it a different matter altogether to be on the receiving end. Yet he presumed she actually worked for her daily bread in this house. There could be no shame in that.

"You are fortunate to have found a haven for yourself and your daughter that is both comfortable and secure. Indeed, you are surrounded by every luxury here."

"I do not need you to tell me so."

"I saw your essay about the murder of Miss Tyrone in a periodical I picked up one day. Unsigned, of course, but 'twas obvious who had written it. A pity it won't have sold as many copies as that hack Gander's 'true confessions of a murderer,' despite the fact yours was the far more accurate portrayal."

"You read it?" she said eagerly, her momentary pique forgotten. "Yes. I was proud of that piece, and was, in fact, paid rather handsomely for it."

"Well then. Perhaps you may produce something similar on the life of this Dick Ransom."

"A footman? Somehow I doubt there is as much scope in his history."

He had already turned away, his attention diverted. "Come here, Mrs. Wolfe. What does this look like to you?"

She bent to peer at the gravel next to the bench. Shiny with moisture, the patch was perhaps the size of guinea. "I can't quite see. Oh, it's just a bit of candle grease, but Mr. Chase—"

"Do you walk in the shrubbery after dark?" he said and watched the light of interest and curiosity come rushing back to her eyes.

"Of course, I don't. How foolish of me not to understand you at once."

"Not tallow," he pointed out, rubbing his thumb over the mark. "The dropping is clearly from a wax candle."

"I believe you are right." She was down on her knees in the gravel, heedless of her print cambric morning gown.

"Perhaps Dick sat here waiting for a time," said Penelope. "He set his candle just there on the bench, and because of the incline, the wax dripped from the holder through the slats to the path beneath."

"That is certainly possible."

"Yet I don't know how we shall determine whom he was waiting for, or to what purpose."

"*We*, Mrs. Wolfe?" Though he shook his head at her, he found himself smiling.

John Chase stood in a library that did double duty as an armory, several dozen axes, dirks, sabers, and ornate swords lining its walls. He thought nostalgically of his old navy cutlass, which now reposed at the back of his wardrobe, though of course his cutlass with its plain, thick blade and practical lines was bread and butter to all this cake. Slanting a glance at Sir Roger Wallace-Crag, Chase put his hand to an iron dagger and fingered the curved guard.

"Spanish," said the older man. "Essentially a small sword. A duellist would have gripped it in the left hand, paired with a rapier in the right. See the matching rapier there?"

"Are all the weapons accounted for, sir?"

A robust, high-colored man in his late fifties, Roger Wallace-Crag lounged, quite at ease in a wing chair, legs stretched out to the fire and booted feet crossed. He would have appeared a prosperous country squire, but for the intensity of his glance and the sophistication of his manners.

"The collection is rather haphazardly assembled, you see. Perhaps you should inquire of Mrs. Wolfe, who has been attempting an inventory. My fault for never having made a record of where and when I purchased most of these pieces."

Returning the knife to its place, Chase sat down opposite the older man. Light played over the antiquary's mobile features as he stared musingly into the flames. The man was relaxed. Too relaxed. Chase had seen many reactions to violent death, yet rarely this detachment, this ability to speak so naturally of murder. Granted, the victim was only a servant, but Wallace-Crag hadn't turned a hair when viewing the body.

Deliberately, Chase sat back in his chair. If the baronet wanted to play this as two gentlemen enjoying a friendly conversation, he was willing to oblige.

"Will you describe your work for me, sir?"

"Willingly. I spend much of my time in the country. In fact, I only came up to town for a few weeks to see about arranging workmen for an excavation. There's an old church built over a Druid's circle I've been most eager to explore, but I've had the devil of a time obtaining permission. Had to take matters into my own hands after my fool of a secretary misplaced some important correspondence."

He shot Chase a keen look as if to gauge his interest. "I am compiling a history of Dorsetshire, an attempt to elucidate the lives of its inhabitants going back to the ancient Britons. For me, there is no greater satisfaction than getting at the Truth of the past. Faint though the voices of antiquity may be, they are still audible if one knows how to listen."

Chase smiled. "If I am to discover who is responsible for this deed, I must hope to catch more recent echoes than those of interest to you, sir. It will be necessary to obtain a precise knowledge of events. I've already spoken to your butler and to some of the servants and have examined the young man's effects. But I shall need you to describe your movements last night and this morning."

"I'm happy to do so, sir, not that such information is likely to prove either interesting or useful. Perhaps you will tell me first whether aught has turned up in your inquiry?"

"Very little. I know that the housemaids were turning out the grates at the time of the disturbance, and your cook had busied herself in the kitchen. Some of the lower servants, with the exception of the footman George who had discovered

Ransom missing, were still abed on the attic floor. Your butler and housekeeper had been awakened, of course, but not Mr. Finch."

"I see no help in any of that."

"No, sir, not really. There is also my examination of Ransom's effects. I found very little, no letters, no papers of any kind for all that he is said to have been well spoken. He did, however, possess a Bible."

"I'm afraid I cannot tell you anything further to the purpose, but that is the way of it with servants. The good ones do not intrude upon your notice. Timberlake tells me the young man was not long in service with us."

Chase remained silent, and Sir Roger continued. "As for my own affairs, I dined with friends yesterday evening and retired a trifle later than normal. I'm afraid I never heard a thing in the night and knew nothing of what had occurred until my man roused me."

"Lord Ashe was unable to grant me an interview, but I understand he too was awakened by the uproar this morning. You have discussed the matter with him?"

Some emotion flickered in his eyes, amusement or possibly contempt. "We see very little of each other. He breaks his fast early, about eight o'clock, then shuts himself up with his correspondence." He glanced at his watch. "I am expected at Somerset House in an hour, Mr. Chase. The Antiquary Society has rooms there."

"Thank you for seeing me, sir," said Chase, getting to his feet. "I regret the necessity of troubling you."

"No trouble." Rising, Wallace-Crag held out his hand. "I only hope you may get to the bottom of this matter. And soon."

What was it Wallace-Crag had said about getting at the Truth of people's lives? Chase rather doubted scholarly inquiry yielded anything like pure historical truth, just as his own efforts, even when successful, could provide only a partial grasp of a crime's inner workings.

Which reminded him of the foliage in his pocket. He took it out, saying, "Oh, by the by, this was in Ransom's pocket."

Slowly, Sir Roger reached out his hand for the leaf. "*Corylus Avellana*. The hazel. Note the crimson stigmas at the top of the cluster. Later this bract will become the husk of the nut. That's odd," he murmured.

"Sir?"

"Very likely this is torn from a branch I brought up to town from Dorset. A sort of prop for an engraving of a water diviner dowsing for water with a forked hazel twig."

Chase stared at him blankly. "What value would Dick Ransom find in a bit of greenery?"

"In Avalon the hazel was the Tree of Life at the side of a sacred pool. Only the salmon that lived in the pool was permitted to eat of the hidden wisdom the nuts represent. To the Greeks, the hazel was the rod of Hermes, the messenger, and thus a symbol of communication and reconciliation."

He fell silent for a moment, his expression somber, then said in a lighter tone, "Possibly, the hazel might help one to cross the barrier between the worlds, though how poor Dick should have known such a talisman would be needed, I cannot fathom. Perhaps he felt a premonition. My staff does seem inclined to such foolishness."

"Foolishness, sir?"

"It's my collection, Mr. Chase. They don't like being surrounded by the unusual and the unique. Makes them skittish, I'm afraid. You ought to see what a commotion we have when the housemaids are asked to dust."

"Where is this branch now?"

He shrugged. "It began to appear a bit tattered and browned, so I told Timberlake to throw it in the dustbin. Well, if that is all, sir, do let me know if I can assist further. I don't hesitate to tell you I have the utmost confidence in Bow Street."

When Chase bowed, ready to take his leave, Wallace-Crag stopped him with an upraised hand. "One more thing. It is likely nothing, but I've recalled something Ransom said when he came in with tea and saw the branch. He inquired if I wished him to sweep up the leaves and catkins that had shed on the desk. Then he laughed and quoted an old country saying about a good crop of hazelnuts being a sure sign of disaster, though it may also indicate many babies to be birthed. Another matter entirely."

Leaning over, he deposited the leaf in Chase's palm, then dusted off his hands with a quick, impatient gesture. "Ransom looked down and said, 'Many nuts, many pits.' Pits, meaning graves, Mr. Chase."

❧

Late that afternoon, Penelope found Sarah in the room filled with crosses. The little girl stood at the head of the sofa where Dick Ransom lay, her back to the door. She appeared expectant, her head tilted in a listening position, as if awaiting some signal. One hand squeezed at the fold of her pinafore; the other was slightly outstretched.

Unbidden memory froze Penelope in her tracks. She was a child again at her mother's funeral, clutching at her nurse's calloused, heavy hand. The nurse whispered a steady stream of endearments in Italian and held Penelope so close as to overwhelm the child with the acrid smell of her sweat, stronger even than the heady aroma of flowers and incense. From time to time, Penelope looked up, seeking her father, who stood alone, a few feet away, his face composed in harsh lines. But mostly she stared at the dusty flagstones at her feet, kneeling when directed, or rising again to have her face pressed against the black material of the nurse's skirt.

At length, the woman had led Penelope firmly to the casket, saying softly, "Touch your mama, *cara*, so you will always remember." And, obeying, Penelope had erupted in noisy sobs that set the congregation murmuring and caused the nurse to yank her outside into the courtyard. At that time, she'd been a great deal older than Sarah and was soon heartily ashamed of her behavior. She had been so afraid her father would be angry with her...

Penelope came to herself with a start just as Sarah extended her hand to brush her fingertips lightly over the side of Dick's face.

"Sarah," she exclaimed in horror, "what are you doing?"

Flinching at the sharpness in her mother's voice, the child spun around. "Mama. I wanted to see what he'd do if I touched him."

Penelope swept the child into her arms and hurried into the corridor. "They will take him away soon, but you mustn't go in there again." She pulled the door closed behind them. "Do you understand me, Sarah? You must not."

Sarah looked solemnly into Penelope's face for a long moment, then decided she was aggrieved enough to cry. "You hurt my feelings," she sobbed, drumming her little fists on Penelope's shoulders. "You're mean, Mama."

"I didn't intend to, Sarah," said Penelope, guiltily aware she'd have done better not to overreact. "Where is Mary? Did she put you down for a sleep, love, and you decided to get up on your own?"

"Yes," said Sarah, relinquishing her anger and snuggling into her mother's neck.

Penelope carried her into the library and settled them both into the wing chair by the hearth. Sarah soon dropped off again, but Penelope didn't want to move her. It was comforting to feel the child's warm weight in her arms and to sit thinking of nothing.

Three-quarters of an hour later, Owen Finch entered, dressed in a heavy coat, a blue woolen scarf, and boots. His wide-brimmed hat, slightly too large, covered most of his lank graying hair. Under the hat, his eyes were shadowed with fatigue.

"I beg your pardon, Mrs. Wolfe. I just came to collect my drawing materials. Sir Roger has asked me to go to Leadenhall Street to sketch a Roman tesselated pavement that has been discovered under the carriageway. He said you had agreed to accompany him to view it one day soon?"

"I did, sir. No doubt it will be a fascinating experience." Seeing him glance uneasily at the sleeping child, Penelope added, "You needn't worry about disturbing Sarah. She sleeps like…" She broke off, dismayed.

Finch rushed into speech. "No, no, I should hate to disrupt such peaceful repose, madam, and you yourself so clearly enjoying a bit of quiet. If you'll give me but a moment, I'll be on my way."

Moving jerkily to a cupboard in one of the bookcases, he removed a box of drawing pencils, a miniature easel, and a portfolio, then went back to stand over Penelope. In spite of these encumbrances, he bowed, and a piece of paper fluttered to the carpet.

"You've dropped one of your drawings. May I have a look, sir?"

He gave it to her, it seemed reluctantly. "It's not finished."

"Near enough," she replied as she studied it. The foreground showed a white-bearded Druid in hooded cloak, knee-length tunic, and sandals. At his belt hung an axe and a small bag; he carried a divining rod of hazel in his hand. Ancient oak trees formed the picture's background.

"The Druids were greatly skilled in divination and interpreting omens. They studied birds in flight to perform augury and also divined the future by poring over the entrails of sacrificial beasts."

"You've done a fine job with his expression. He seems utterly clear and confident, though somehow I cannot like him. There is a self-absorption there, as if only his objectives matter. I shouldn't like to be the helpless creature wriggling under his knife." She smiled to take the sting from her words.

He did not return the smile. "The Druids are said to have practiced human as well as animal sacrifice, Mrs. Wolfe. Caesar wrote that Druidic priests preferred thieves and brigands for their ceremonies but would at times seize upon even the innocent. The strong have ever preyed upon the weak."

"Indeed? You are knowledgeable, sir, and no doubt of great use to Sir Roger with his monograph. I believe you have been in his employ for many years?"

His gaze broke away. "You exaggerate my importance. I merely assist Sir Roger. I myself should never care to undertake such a project."

Chapter IV

When John Chase left St. James's Square, he did not at first pay much heed to two men who sauntered in his wake along Pall Mall. He was thinking of Penelope Wolfe in that strange household and of Dick Ransom, who must have been more than he seemed to get himself murdered. Unless, that is, he had simply been in the wrong place at the wrong moment.

And passing the long row of columns that screened off the entrance to Carlton House, the Prince Regent's London residence, Chase wondered idly, as no doubt did many passers-by, what the devil those columns did there, for they supported nothing but their crowning entablature, were only there, it seemed, to spoil the view of the mansion behind. He was not a man prone to metaphor, yet he supposed the philosophers might find food for reflection in those columns, showy and extravagant, but useless. They spoke somehow of the present age.

With such thoughts for company, he nonetheless made sure one part of his mind was fully aware of his surroundings. Any Runner would do the same. It was a matter of expediency, in the event he should later need to recall information, or in case such vigilance might one day be a matter of survival.

As Chase glanced back, the taller of the two smiled slightly. This was a stoop-shouldered man with a thin, sharp face and red, pointy ears. He wore a blue coat with brass buttons and lumpy boots. His companion, heavier-set and considerably dirtier if his execrable linen were anything to judge by, carried a fine Malacca cane with which he tapped out a rhythm on the paving stones.

After Chase had continued up Haymarket and down Panton Street to Leicester Square, the men still dogging his heels, practically breathing down his neck, his irritation flared. Reaching into his greatcoat, he took out his gilt-topped baton, the Bow Street emblem of office, and faced them. "May I be of assistance?"

The man with the cane replied boldly, "Your pardon, sir, but mayhap you can. We thought as since you been to inquire about the goings-on in St. James's Square, you might have a word or two for us."

Journalists already? But neither of these blokes ran true to type, he thought, nor were they flourishing their inevitable notebooks. "Who are you, and why do you want to know?"

Pointy Ears answered this time. "A friend of the late lamented sent us, sir. Quite broke up by the news, he is, and couldn't come 'imself. He'll be glad to know what's what. And there's the matter of some property as was lent to the fellow as has turned up his toes. Our friend is anxious for its return."

"Property? Of what sort?"

"I couldn't say exactly," said the shorter, dirty one, taking his turn. "Papers, I should think, or something of that nature. You find anything out o' the way amongst this Ransom's effects?"

"Who are you?" Chase repeated. "Give me your names and direction and that of your friend. I'll deal direct with him."

The two men looked at each other. "Afraid that ain't possible," said Pointy Ears at last. "Not to worry. He knows where to find you."

"Bid you good day then, sir," said the other, and bowing, gave a toothy smile and a jaunty lift of his cane.

Before Chase could respond, they had stepped around him and set off down the street at a rapid pace, almost colliding with pedestrians in their path. Chase was after them in an instant, waving his baton and shouting as he went. "Stop, you hedge-birds! You filthy knaves!"

Pointy Ears glanced over his shoulder. Seeing he was being pursued, he tugged his companion's arm. They broke into a run. Chase followed grimly as his old knee wound sent agonizing shafts of pain up his leg and spine. Still, he managed to keep them in view as they traversed several smaller streets. But when they turned up Long Acre and put on a burst of speed, he quickly lost them.

Cursing, he paused, undecided. This area was crowded with coach-builders as well as furniture makers. All around him, workmen went about their trades, and patrons alighted from carriages to conduct their business. Chase stopped one carpenter walking with his tool-bag slung over his shoulder, but was rewarded with a stony stare when he tried to describe the men. All up and down the street it was the same. No one had seen, or would admit to having seen, the two men.

Finally, giving up, he returned to Bow Street police office, where the magistrate on duty was Mr. Graham, who had proven himself a constant friend. It was he, in fact, who'd helped Chase to become an officer after an initial assignment to the foot patrol. Chase had known Graham's son in the Navy, and when Chase had found himself in London after resigning his own commission, he'd looked up his old friend's father. That had been a decade ago.

Although the court was deserted, Graham still sat at the table behind the bar. At Chase's entrance, he pushed aside his paperwork. "You're late."

"You received my message about the murder inquiry, sir?"

Graham's eyes sharpened, but when he spoke his tone was mild. "What's the world coming to when murder occurs in St. James's Square of all places? I don't doubt we'll be hearing from the Home Secretary in the morning. He'll want to know an arrest is imminent. Shall I be able to so inform him?"

"No, sir." Chase had spent the day talking to Sir Roger's servants and the square watchmen. No one had noticed anything out of the ordinary, though a portrait of the slain footman had emerged: well-spoken, courteous, and sober in mien.

"Humph. No doubt you'll be pleased to inform me as soon as matters do take that desired turn?"

"Yes, sir." He was grateful he was not the one to contend with official shilly-shallying and thick-headed interference. No, John Chase just did his job, alone for the most part.

Graham was studying him closely. "Well, what do you make of it? Robbery?"

"Possibly, sir, yet nothing is missing from the house, nor is there any sign of forced entry. Moreover, this young man was reputedly of good character."

The magistrate nodded. "Any known enemies? Love affairs gone sour? Family problems? Financial reverses?"

"Too soon to say. No one seems to know much about his background. He was quite close-mouthed. One curious thing, sir, the servants all agree Ransom was a Londoner, but Wallace-Crag has reported an exchange he had with the man in which Ransom quoted a bit of country lore about hazelnuts. I should add I found a hazel leaf in the dead man's pocket."

Graham frowned. "If this is intended as some sort of message, what are we to understand by it?"

"I don't know. Sir Roger seems to think Ransom may have had an omen of disaster and taken the hazel to protect himself or possibly to assist in crossing between this world and the next. Or perhaps the murderer placed the greenery in the dead man's pocket."

"Come, Chase, this begins to seem a fairy tale. Whoever committed the crime had a serious purpose, however many maygames he thought to confuse us with. Sir Roger Wallace-Crag? I know of him. He has a beautiful daughter who got herself married off to Viscount Ashe. I understand he's a bit of a cold fish. Ashe, I mean."

"I'm to see him at the House of Lords tomorrow," said Chase. "Purely as a matter of form."

"Get on with it then, but be careful. I hear the man is jealous of his dignity. See that you don't raise any hackles." He turned back to his papers, and Chase was able to take himself home.

Having missed his dinner, he would have to make do with cold meat and bread in his room, though Mrs. Beeks, his landlady, would have held the meal for him had he not given strict instructions to the contrary.

When he entered, Leo was lurking on the stairway. A fair-haired, sweet-faced boy with terrifying courage and a staunchly independent mind, Leo had once tended to make a hero of his mother's lodger, an actual Bow Street Runner. Lately, however, Chase had noted a slight lessening of the glow, as if the boy had begun to realize that a man over forty, graying and somewhat shabby, who tied a poor neck-cloth and slurped his soup, wasn't entirely suitable material for adoration. Chase was relieved.

"Evening, sir," said Leo, popping down the stairs. "I was wondering when you'd come in. You missed dinner!"

"So I did. I trust you had a good day?" He'd been making an effort recently to be more forthcoming with Leo and his brother William after Mrs. Beeks had tearfully confessed that the boys were sometimes hurt by his seeming coldness.

"Oh dreadful dull, sir. Nothing much ever happens around here."

Chase regarded him a moment. "Be glad of it." With a nod, he limped toward the stairs.

"Leo," came a voice from the kitchen below. "Is that Mr. Chase, and you keep him talking after a long day? Ask him what he fancies for his supper."

"Yes, mum," Leo shouted, then spoke quickly to Chase in a low tone. "One of my chums said some of the Runners ain't above laying a trap for a man just so they can collect the reward for his conviction. I didn't believe it for an instant, but I knew you'd tell me true."

Chase suppressed a groan. It was certainly true that honesty was a somewhat rare commodity amongst his colleagues; the system itself discouraged this virtue. Not that he was about to admit that to Leo or tell him about the persistent rumors dogging certain of the Runners…

"It rather strains credulity that the magistrates would permit such villainy. Those of Bow Street are much respected and have a reputation throughout the land to uphold. Tell your friends so, Leo."

"Leo!" Mrs. Beeks cried again, sharp with impatience. "Did you give Mr. Chase his letter, and what about the dinner?"

Looking sheepish, the boy darted to the hall table and put the letter in Chase's hand. It was from Abigail in Boston, and Chase suddenly found he could neither speak naturally, nor endure the sudden curiosity in Leo's eyes. Bidding Leo goodnight, Chase continued up the stairs and into his room, shutting the door behind him.

It wasn't till much later, after dining on the meal Mrs. Beeks had insisted upon providing, that he took his seat by the fire, donned his spectacles, and opened his letter, his left hand cupping a glass of brandy, which he drank slowly to savor the heat. His eyes went first to the bottom of the page, where eleven-year-old Jonathan had added his bit to his mother's letter:

> *Dear Father:*
> *I hope this finds you well. We are fine, though Mother says she fears Spring will forget all about us here in Boston. My schoolmaster believes our two countries may soon go to War. Would that mean we could not receive your letters?*

I told Mother I should like to go to sea and defend our right to trade freely. But she asked me if I would care to fire on my father's countrymen, and I had to say no. Still you were in the Royal Navy when you met Mother, weren't you? I know you would understand.

Yes, he would, Chase reflected, proud of his son. The letter concluded with the usual wishes for his continued good health, then came Jonathan's postscript: *May I travel to England to see you one day?*

Good question, he thought, stretching his legs to get more comfortable.

⋘⋙

"What will you wear, mum?" said Maggie, standing at the wardrobe, a doubtful expression on her face.

She knew as well as Penelope that only three choices presented themselves: a well-worn gray wool, a staid navy silk, and a creased light muslin in which the wearer would freeze in the drawing room drafts.

"The silk, I suppose, Maggie," said Penelope absently, her attention focused on Sarah at the window. What made the child so intent? Was it her own reflection in the glass, or something else? The slump of her shoulders and a certain air of dejection gave Penelope pause, made her heart sink with a vague dread. She crossed the room to Sarah's side and brushed a hand over her hair.

"What do you see, love?"

Sarah pressed her nose against the glass. "Rain, Mama. Does the rain fall where Papa is? He will be wet through if he is out of doors."

"No, love," she said with forced cheer. "Don't you remember he is in Dublin teaching little girls like you to draw? He has his umbrella, of course, or he is warm by the fire as we are. You need not worry."

Sarah nodded, and Penelope looked up to find Maggie watching them gravely. Upon Maggie's arrival, Penelope had informed her of Dick Ransom's death in a hurried undertone. And after the incident in the cross room, Penelope had had to explain more of the facts to Sarah too, not that a four-year-old had any real understanding. But she had observed the doctor coming to make his examination, followed by the woman responsible for the washing of the corpse. The maids went about their work, red-eyed, and Timberlake and Mrs. Sterling were grim-faced.

"If Dick has gone to Heaven, why's everyone so sad?" Sarah had asked.

Penelope knew it was her daughter's nature to brood for days if not given a satisfactory answer, yet what could she say? "It's…it's just that it was unexpected, love. We shall all need time to grow accustomed."

So much change and loss in one little girl's life. The absence of a father. A mother forced to work for her bread in a stranger's establishment. And far away in Sicily, a grandfather Sarah had never met.

Penelope hurried across the room to Maggie's side as if the wardrobe question were suddenly paramount. As indeed it seemed these days, for she was often at her wits' end as to how to handle the continual dressing and undressing that took place in a fashionable London establishment.

Raised under a rather sterner philosophy, Penelope found herself quite unable to account for this penchant for wasting so many hours of one's valuable time. Lady Ashe came down to breakfast *en déshabillé*, wore morning dress for shopping excursions, later donned afternoon dress, and finally blazed forth in full dress for evening parties.

Penelope had hoped her humble position as companion would exempt her from such requirements, but she had found that her employer, in a misplaced spirit of kindness perhaps, wished to treat her more as honored guest than as dependent. Delicately, Lady Ashe had even intimated that Penelope might wish to try some of her own garments that no longer quite "suited," a temptation so far stoutly resisted.

"Let me help you, mum," said Maggie, pushing Penelope on to the rug by the hearth and starting to unfasten the buttons at the back of her dress. "Let's see…your hair. Shall I dress it in a high knot with some curls about your face?"

Maggie so loved to play at being a lady's maid that Penelope could not discourage her. The directress of the St. Catherine Society, where Maggie was employed, seemed to feel she owed a debt of gratitude to Penelope for having helped to secure the philanthropic organization's funding; thus, she did not object if Maggie left her two children and slipped away of an evening to spend a hour or two with Penelope. And Penelope always gave Maggie a few shillings to eke out her meager income. For Penelope, the hour spent in Maggie's company was often the only time in the day she felt truly comfortable.

"Murder," said Maggie now in a low voice as she pulled the silk gown over Penelope's head. "I can't say I'm surprised, mum."

With a quick glance at Sarah, who now knelt by the fire whispering to her doll, Penelope replied, "What can you know of the matter?"

"Why once when Mrs. Sterling was so kind as to offer me a cup of tea in the kitchen before I took my leave, I met this Dick Ransom. I noticed him right off. There was something about him."

"I can't agree. I thought him the usual sort of footman. Young, tall, and fair of face. He knew how to blend in, Maggie. I don't believe I ever exchanged more than a handful of words with him."

"No more you should. It's different for me, not that he paid me any heed, mind. All the same I saw what I saw, and you mark my words, mum, Mr. Chase will discover I'm right."

"About what?" said Penelope, exasperated.

"Just this, mum. He thought too much of himself to be a proper servant."

There seemed little to say in response, so Penelope turned back to her ablutions. A quarter hour later she sat at the little rosewood vanity table, applying the finishing touches with the haresfoot and powder. "You've done well." She smiled into the other woman's anxious freckled face in the glass. "I look quite the fine lady, and I thank you."

Maggie beamed. "You look lovely, mum." Reaching out, she fingered the strand of pearls around Penelope's neck. It had belonged to Penelope's mother, and its constant use of late had lent the pearls a deeper luster.

"Mrs. Pen," Maggie said after a moment, "do you ever think of what might be if things was better managed with your wedded man? A house to be mistress of, a maid or two for the heavy work. Nothing on this scale, of course, but 'twould be your own."

Penelope was silent, recalling all the lonely nights she had endured this past winter.

Chapter V

"Won't you sit down, Mrs. Wolfe?" asked Sir Roger, bowing her into a chair.

They were in the drawing room, a dim chamber with a fireplace that smoked, old-fashioned heavy furniture, several darkened portraits, and an enormous curiosity cabinet of specimens from Wallace-Crag's foreign tours.

Finch came forward to greet her, twitching at his shabby black coat to straighten it. "Good evening, ma'am," he said, but almost before she could frame a polite reply, the secretary had again retired into the background.

Sir Roger sat opposite, eyes fixed on hers. "They hold that the soul of a dead man does not descend to the silent, sunless world of Hades, but becomes reincarnate elsewhere. If they are right, death is merely a point of change in perpetual existence."

"Lucan, sir?"

She recognized the quotation from her reading. Her budding interest in the ancient history of Britain had pleased Sir Roger, for she had been more than willing to offer her services since the duties Julia required were so light. In any event, the task of cataloguing Sir Roger's vast collection was a pursuit much more to Penelope's taste.

He nodded with approval. "Fascinating, isn't it? According to Lucan, the Druids believed a soul was transferred to another person after death. However, Mela and to some extent Diodorus imply something rather different—"

He was interrupted by the door opening. Ashe came in, dressed meticulously with his usual understated elegance, making Penelope think not for the first time how out of place he seemed in this eccentric household.

"Good evening, Sir Roger. Mrs. Wolfe." He nodded at Finch, who offered a deep bow.

Wallace-Crag nodded genially. "Ah, Ashe. Mrs. Wolfe and I were just discussing the transmigration of the soul. A fascinating topic, would you not agree?"

The viscount did not at first reply, his glance flickering over Penelope. "You're in looks tonight, Mrs. Wolfe, in spite of your dreadful shock this morning. May I tell you how sorry I am such a thing should happen to you in this house?"

"No need, my lord. It is rather poor Dick who deserves our pity."

She was never sure what to make of Lord Ashe. His demeanor to her varied between flirtatiousness and cold formality, as if at times he disapproved of his wife's choice of companions, though occasionally, as now, he seemed human, almost likeable. In his late fifties, he was yet a handsome man. Penelope could not help wondering about his relationship with his volatile wife. She had heard the whispers that between them Sir Roger and Lord Ashe had cooked up the marriage, the one side to provide pots of money and a youthful bride, the other a title and an ancient name. A common enough arrangement, Penelope supposed.

Ashe turned to Sir Roger. "I'll see that fellow from Bow Street tomorrow. He's to report to me after the inquest. I don't know that there's anything further we can do."

"Nothing I know of except that we'll need to make a push to find the young man's family and arrange for a proper send-off."

Finch broke in. "If you'll excuse me, Sir Roger, I must say I don't think the manner of 'send off' truly signifies. The fact is that Ransom has put off his earthly corruption to become Spirit. Nothing can touch him more."

"Nonsense," said Ashe. "The funeral service is for the living, not the dead, and is necessary to preserve the decencies."

"Stop your bleating, Owen, unless you wish to appear more the sapskull than usual."

"As you say, Sir Roger." The secretary retreated behind the cabinet.

"Where the deuce is Julia?" said Sir Roger. "I hope she does not intend to keep us waiting for our dinner again."

"She'll be along."

Penelope noticed that a frown had descended upon Ashe's brow at the mention of his wife's name. Fortunately, Julia entered upon his words with Timberlake on her heels to announce dinner. At the sight of her, resplendent in white satin and a silk shawl, the frown in Ashe's eyes only deepened.

"You're just in time, my love."

She kept her gaze averted. "That is fortunate. Poole would fuss and scold, no matter what I said."

"Ah, but the result is surely worth it." As Ashe lifted her hand to his lips, Penelope was amazed to see her snatch back her hand, her face twisting in anger.

But the moment passed nearly unremarked, for Sir Roger had already stepped toward his daughter for the nightly procession to the dining room. It was a ritual Penelope rather dreaded when there was no company to dine, as she could not imagine why Lord Ashe should wish to give his arm to his wife's companion while Sir Roger took in Julia, Finch trailing behind.

At table, as Sir Roger and Lord Ashe upheld a flow of easy conversation, Penelope kept her attention on her plate, finding that the rigors of the day had made her hungry. And the delicate balance between being conversable yet not putting herself forward in any unbecoming way, difficult at the best of times, seemed beyond her tonight.

Julia too seemed oddly withdrawn, barely responding to the remarks her husband addressed to her. She drank glass after glass of wine, refilled by a hovering George, her hands trembling visibly as she lifted the crystal to her lips. After a while, Ashe abandoned his attempts to engage her in conversation, but Penelope saw that he watched his wife from the corner of his eye.

Relieved that the interminable and uncomfortable meal approached its end, Penelope was just scooping up the last of a fruit tart when Ashe addressed her, his voice suddenly very smooth. "By the by, Mrs. Wolfe. I understand it was Mr. Edward Buckler we have to thank for your presence here. Did he not provide your character?"

Penelope sat up straighter. "That is so, sir," she replied politely.

"I hope you have remembered me to Mr. Buckler," said Sir Roger. "I've always liked that young fellow, not that he ever had much to say to a musty fellow like me. Still, I have often noted that he possesses a fine mind and a sturdy integrity."

Finch gave a small cough. "You speak of the barrister Mr. Edward Buckler? Lady Wallace-Crag always thought well of his family." He looked at his master as if to ascertain how this mention of Sir Roger's dead wife and Julia's mother went over, then at Penelope. "Mr. Edward Buckler's brother holds the neighboring estate in Dorset. Both Mr. Bucklers are most fine gentlemen. In point of fact, Lady Wallace-Crag used to say—"

"In point of fact, Mr. Edward Buckler's brother is a baronet, not a mister, Finch. Not that it truly signifies," said Sir Roger.

Finch fell silent, and Sir Roger turned again to Penelope, saying, "Perhaps you'll tell us, Mrs. Wolfe, how it was that you made Mr. Buckler's acquaintance. Your families know each other, do they?"

"No, sir. A mutual friend, Mr. Ezekiel Thorogood, presented me." She certainly wasn't about to tell him the circumstances of that first meeting, when she'd employed Buckler to defend her husband on a possible murder charge.

"Thorogood? It was he you went to dine with the other day, Penelope," broke in Julia. "An attorney, didn't you say?"

"Oh indeed," said Sir Roger, losing interest, but Penelope, noticing that Lord Ashe was staring down his nose at her, a smirk on his lips, felt hot words rise to her lips. She opened her mouth to make what would likely have been an ill-judged remark, but was forestalled by the entrance of Timberlake.

"I beg your pardon, Sir Roger," he said, struggling visibly to speak in his usual sepulchral tones. "One of the grooms has apprehended a woman in the garden. She was peering through the window. God only knows what mischief was intended."

"Have her arrested at once," said Ashe.

Timberlake hesitated. "Of course, my lord. But I'm afraid she is queer in her attic. The men can barely hold her she struggles so fierce."

Sir Roger pushed back his chair. "We had best go and see for ourselves, Ashe. Julia, my dear, you will remain here with Mrs. Wolfe."

Julia regarded him with an unblinking gaze that held more than a hint of challenge. "I think not, Father. I will accompany you. Surely you do not mean to leave us here on our own with just *him* for protection?" A contemptuous wave of her hand dismissed Owen Finch.

Timberlake again addressed Sir Roger. "I am sorry, sir, but Mrs. Wolfe had better accompany you. In the flurry of the moment I neglected to mention that we found her young one out of doors. Apparently, the child has strayed from her nurse."

"Why didn't you say so at once?" demanded Julia. "Penelope, you must take my shawl."

"Sarah?" said Penelope, nearly dropping the wrap as her fingers did not obey her.

"Not to worry," said the butler. "The child is unharmed."

"Finch!" snapped Sir Roger, catching sight of his secretary hovering around the door. "What the devil do you think you're doing?"

"I...I thought you would wish me to summon the authorities."

"Go then. And let the rest of us proceed to the garden and get to the root of this insanity."

They surged down the corridor, into the library, and out the French doors. It was a calm evening, hushed and expectant, as if nature, sensing the nearness of spring, no longer found it expedient to bluster and storm. The voices carried clearly on the crisp evening air.

A group had clustered around a woman who thrust her body first in one direction, then another as if engaged in some obscene dance. Two grooms held on grimly while the coachman called out advice and warnings. Sarah, a tiny, huddled figure, looked on, unnoticed.

"Watch it, lads," the coachman called, "she's a proper handful. She'll bite you if you're not careful. You'll have to plant her a facer before she be giving over."

Sir Roger called, "No, do not strike the woman. Let us first see if we can reach a glimmer of reason."

Reaching Sarah, Penelope scooped her up in the shawl.

"Is she all right, Penelope?"

"Just chilled, ma'am." She whispered to Sarah, "What are you doing out here? Mama was so frightened."

Sarah burrowed her face in Penelope's neck. "I saw her from the window earlier, just standing there in the rain. She looked so sad. So I came to see what was wrong. I thought I'd find you and tell you."

Penelope struggled to keep her voice even. "You've found me, sweetheart, but you must never come out of doors in the dark again. Come, we will get you back to bed."

Without another word, Penelope hurried into the house, where at the foot of the staircase she encountered the nursemaid.

"I thought she was in bed, ma'am," the girl burst out. "She slipped out when I wasn't looking, and I'm sure to lose my place!"

No more than you deserve, Penelope wanted to tell her, but as she gazed into the stricken face, her indignation faded. "You must be more careful in future, Mary. Anything might have happened. Her voice trembled as she put her deepest fear into words. "What if that creature out there had picked her up and borne her away? Look, she is nearly asleep. You may take her."

Returning to the terrace, Penelope was in time to hear Sir Roger say sternly, "Calm yourself at once. You must tell us what you want."

The woman twisted away. She was covered in a voluminous cloak, but now her hood fell back to reveal a countenance ravaged by fear and desperation, hair straggling over gaunt cheeks, eyes rolling so that the whites gleamed in the torchlight. Penelope heard Sir Roger's breath hiss between his teeth; he seemed frozen. Julia reached out to clutch her father's sleeve, but when the woman lurched in her direction, she shrank back into the shadows with a little cry.

Penelope stepped into the torchlight. Becoming aware of her presence, the woman extended her hands. "Please. Help me. I must find…"

"Find who?"

The eyes rolled again. After a moment, Penelope tore her gaze away to glance down at the woman's hands, still held out in appeal. In the flickering light, she saw faded reddish scars crisscrossing her wrists.

As if the spell holding him in place had shattered, Sir Roger pushed forward. "She's naught but an old Bedlamite. Perhaps she merely wanted to pay her respects to Ransom, having heard of his passing. For pity's sake, we will let her go."

Everyone gaped at him, and Ashe growled, "I do not think that would be wise, sir. Let her go so she can come back later and roust us from our beds? Or worse, murder us in 'em. No, she wants locking up."

"She was trying to open the French window, Sir Roger, when I come upon her," gasped one of the grooms as he subdued a flailing arm. "I saw her rattle the handle."

"Perhaps she did wish to pay her respects," said Penelope with some doubt. "The word will have spread by this time. I believe the people often feel such curiosity."

A look of confusion crossed the baronet's face, and it seemed he would address the woman, whose resistance had finally begun to diminish from sheer exhaustion. Instead, he turned away. "I suppose you are right, Ashe. There's a chance, I suppose, that this pitiful creature is dangerous. We must leave it to the authorities."

On cue, Timberlake bustled onto the terrace, escorting the Watch and several parish constables.

"Here, what's this?" blustered the head constable as they came up. He glared at Sir Roger. "Evil doings, sir, but we'll manage this little problem, all right." He gestured to his companions, who moved forward to seize hold of the woman. She had gone limp, having utterly divorced herself from her surroundings.

"Where will you take her, constable?"

Surprised, he turned his frowning glance Penelope's way. "No need for concern, ma'am. She'll cool her heels in the watch-house with the other drunks and half-wits. In the morning, we'll find out what's what."

"You will send a message to Mr. John Chase at Bow Street?" insisted Penelope. "He will need to question this person."

It was the wrong thing to say. Exchanging a speaking glance with his companions, the constable drew himself up. "I'll warrant Mr. Chase of Bow Street well knows his duty, madam, as I most certainly know mine."

Julia thrashed, flinging out one arm. Sighing, Rebecca bent to replace the bedcovers. Would the child never settle? The long-case clock in the corridor had long since chimed the hour, and she was very late.

Holding her breath, she waited. Then when Julia did not stir, she tiptoed away over bare floorboards, stepping gingerly to avoid the creaks. She'd always found it strange that so rich a family should permit a daughter to live in such cheerless surroundings. The nursery did not have the thick, soft carpets that warmed the other bedchambers at Cayhill. The room was furnished in castoffs from other parts of the house so that Miss Julia's table and chairs were absurdly large for her.

Pausing at this table, Rebecca picked up her shawl and wrapped it over her head and shoulders with hands that trembled with fear and a deeper excitement that roiled just below her awareness. She told herself it was the cold. The November nights were chill, draughts whistling through the old house like tiny spirits seeking their rest. Sometimes, when Rebecca was abroad in the night, she fancied these spirits accompanied her, nipping at her ankles, whispering warnings in her ear. She did not heed the spirits.

She glided to the door, opening it. Outside, the corridor stretched away from her, dimly lit by occasional wall sconces. The Mistress would have retired, for her routine never varied, especially when she was breeding, which according to belowstairs tattle she was again. After dinner, she sat in her sitting room while the Master's secretary read aloud to her from improving tracts until the tea-tray arrived. By now, she would be asleep and everyone else, too, except for *him*, and he would be waiting.

One hand clutching the shawl, she made her way to the back stairs and began to descend, gripping the banister hard, for here the darkness was complete. But Rebecca knew the way. A curious weightless sensation overcame her as she began to move faster. Her hand skimmed along. Her feet beat out the rhythm her heart echoed. *He is waiting. He is waiting.*

Reaching the landing, she collided with something solid. Arms came out to bite into her flesh. She was shaken roughly so that the shawl slipped from her head, exposing her face and the hair that tumbled about her shoulders.

"I've been waiting for you, girl."

"My lord?"

Faint light from the corridor lined his tall figure, but she could not see his expression. She knew the voice, however.

"Miss Julia has the toothache," she babbled when he didn't at once speak. "I'm going to the kitchen to fetch a clove. I thought it might give her ease."

He shook her again. "You lying little slut," he said, and his mouth crushed against hers.

Rebecca gagged as she felt his tongue force itself between her teeth. He had her pressed against the wall in the narrow space, hands wrapped around her hips, bruising her. He'll leave marks, she thought with horror, and tried to twist her head away. He forced her back.

"I know all about you, pretty maid," he hissed, low and taunting. "I've heard you sneaking about in the night, and I know where you go. Don't think you're too clever for me with your modest down-turned eyes and demure face. You stupid bitch."

His hands, cruel and punishing and insultingly thorough, moved down her body; then, abruptly, he pushed her aside so that she slumped against the railing. "Don't you ever turn me away again, or I swear I shall tell everyone what you are. Remember that, Rebecca."

At first she could not fathom his meaning, but suddenly she understood. He had come to the nursery the other day to see Miss Julia, had wanted to take the little girl out to try her pony. But Rebecca, knowing how the child felt about her father's friend and fearing another of the tantrums that occurred with alarming frequency these days, had intervened. She had said Julia was sickening for something and should not go.

"What do you want?" she whispered.

He was gone, leaving her alone in the dark. Clinging to the banister, Rebecca swallowed convulsively, willing herself not to faint. Her head swam, and tears of humiliation and anger dripped down her cheeks unheeded. She knew she should return to her room, yet couldn't bear the disappointment. She told herself she would inform the Master and he would protect her, but she knew it wasn't true. She would never tell.

When she had herself under control, she made her way down the stairs to the ground floor and crept ghostlike through the green baize door into the main part of the house. The Master's study was at the rear just beyond the music room. She met no one, and reaching the door, was relieved to see light gleaming underneath.

He had told her never to knock but to slip in, so she turned the knob and entered, her palms slick with sweat, her breath so shallow she felt as if the air were being squeezed from her lungs. Already, she had half forgotten the encounter in the stairwell. It was a nastiness, pushed to the back of her mind, to be brooded over in the day, but not now in this strange otherworldly time when there was nothing but the two of them, bodies and hearts straining together.

The Master sat at his desk, leaning on his elbows, a book propped against the decanter. His candle had guttered low so that, without realizing it, he had to bend closer. His spectacles perched halfway down his narrow nose, the nostrils flaring slightly as they always did when something excited him. Her eyes took in his heavy, capable forearm, relaxed on the desk, and lingered over thick, workmanlike fingers cupped around a forgotten snifter of brandy. In the instant before he noticed her, his image was branded on her eyes forever.

He looked up. "There you are at last," he said softly. "Come here."

Rebecca ran into his arms.

Chapter VI

Buckler had last seen Julia Wallace-Crag when she was seventeen and about to embark upon her first London season. She'd been so alive, so full of joyous expectation, so certain the world would offer her everything. He wondered whether the world had delivered. Certainly, in one sense it had, he thought, gazing around the morning room with its silk hangings and fine French furniture. The rest of the house had struck him as gloomy and oppressive, but this was clearly a woman's domain.

"Mr. Buckler. It has been years." Smiling, she came forth to give him her hand. "I know you've come to call on Mrs. Wolfe, but you will allow me to make my own greetings first."

"A pleasure, ma'am." He allowed her to draw him over to a grouping of chairs covered in straw satin.

"I'm glad you've caught me alone. A rare occurrence, I must tell you. Let me ask at once. I understand you have made a name for yourself in your chosen profession, and I've been expecting these five years to be presented to your wife. Surely a pretty little wife and a few babes would round things out most delightfully?"

He laughed. "Making a name for oneself is slow going in the legal world, ma'am. A good thing I have independent means else I might well have starved to death."

"You might go into Parliament," she said, eyes wide, as if his reply meant all to her.

"Perhaps one day." He felt himself flush as this secret ambition of his was put into words. "What of you, Lady Ashe? You have done very well indeed for yourself."

"Oh, really, must you call me that? When we were children, it was always Julia. Won't you call me so now while we're on our own? How can it be otherwise when I was the one to witness the thrashing you once got from the black-smith's boy?"

Buckler laughed. "All right then—Julia. But you must answer my question."

She looked away for the first time. "You see for yourself. Only the truth is no one sees, not even the oh so admirable companion you sent to me. Oh, don't poker up," she added as she saw him stiffen. "I mean no criticism of Mrs. Wolfe. It's just I am quite certain she thinks me a foolish sort of creature with more hair than wit. Certainly, she does not honor me with her confidence."

"She has been used to being on her own," replied Buckler, profoundly uncomfortable.

There was no time for more, for the butler entered to announce several other callers, two young gentlemen, both dressed in the height of fashion, and a bustling, hard-faced matron. On their heels, Penelope came into the room, and, not seeing Buckler, made as if to draw back.

"No, no, Mrs. Wolfe," said Julia gaily. She went to take Penelope's arm. "You will not escape so easily." Keeping Penelope half turned away from Buckler, she introduced her to the gentlemen, who bowed languidly, and to the matron, who put up her brows, just inclining her head. Penelope bore it well, Buckler thought.

"Now, a surprise," cried Julia and spun around. "Look, Penelope. I know you will be glad to see Mr. Buckler." She went on to introduce Buckler to the others, then drew the other callers across the room to some sofas, leaving Buckler and Penelope alone by the window. It was masterfully done, but Buckler saw that Penelope looked embarrassed by these tactics and felt some warmth in his own cheeks.

When he realized he had been standing stock still, holding her hand too long, Buckler dropped it and smiled at her. In spite of what Thorogood had said, he thought she looked well in these surroundings, for she possessed the breeding to carry them off. And yet, the old lawyer was right; she also looked...unsettled, he supposed, as if she had eaten something that didn't quite agree with her. There was also a bruised look about her eyes.

"I am pleased to see you, Mr. Buckler," she said, mindful of possible listeners. From across the room, the younger of the two gentlemen smiled ironically at Buckler and gave a barely perceptible wink. Buckler turned his back.

"Sarah? She is well?"

"Indeed, sir, though she has reached an age when the forbidden is ever beckoning and thus requires careful watching. But I am glad of an opportunity to thank you for recommending me to this position."

"It was nothing. Anytime I can be of service." He was aware with surprise that he meant it.

Gathering his wits, he went on quickly, "Thorogood asked me to call today, Mrs. Wolfe. He wishes to be assured you find yourself comfortably situated. You see, something rather worrisome has occurred, and he fears—Why, what is it, ma'am?"

"Comfortably situated? You haven't heard then. A footman in this household, one Dick Ransom, has been stabbed through the heart, Mr. Buckler, and it was I who found the body yesterday morning."

Buckler felt a deep pang of foreboding. "Murder? How extraordinary. I wonder, what is the connection? I cannot understand this at all."

"Connection to what?" demanded Penelope, moderating her voice with difficulty. "Has something occurred to alarm Mr. Thorogood? I was just with him in Lincoln's Inn Fields two days since."

"You might say so. The matter of a letter addressed to you and delivered by an old street woman just as you departed after your visit. When he was unable to catch your attention, Thorogood meant to have it sent on to St. James's Square, only his office was ransacked. The letter seems to be the only item missing. It was in plain sight on the desk, so we can only assume the intruder disarranged the room to muddy matters."

She stepped closer, her eyes gleaming. "Street woman? The parish authorities apprehended such a person, a trespasser, in the garden here last night. Perhaps she is your delivery person, though I've no notion who might have sent her, nor why she should wish to communicate with me."

"There's more," he said grimly. "Thorogood believes she was lurking in the street, probably hoping to address you when you emerged. But Lady Ashe's carriage arrived, and this footman—I presume it was the same one—had jumped down to summon you."

"Heavens yes, I had forgotten Dick was there! There *was* a beggar woman on the pavement when I stepped outside. Dick took one look and pushed her away. I wanted to protest, but he hustled me into the carriage. I never saw her face, for it was wrapped in a shawl."

"A curious thing. When Thorogood, intending to give her a coin or two, helped her to her feet, she thrust the letter at him and took to her heels. He saw it was directed to you, Mrs. Wolfe, so he held it up and waved. He says Sir Roger's footman turned round on the box and looked right at him. He must have realized Thorogood was trying to attract your attention, yet the coachman drove on."

A burst of laughter from across the room startled them both so that they jumped like guilty conspirators. Glancing up, Buckler saw that the young gentleman was now observing them through his quizzing glass.

He gave the fellow a haughty frown and turned back to Penelope. "Odd that Lady Ashe did not mention this Ransom's death to me." He paused. "I cannot like this situation, for it seems this footman had embroiled himself in some nefarious business. If indeed he glimpsed the letter in Thorogood's hand, it's possible he did intend you should receive it, Mrs. Wolfe."

"But why?" said Penelope, chewing her lip thoughtfully. "It cannot be coincidence that he should turn up dead the very next morning." She put a hand on his sleeve. "What do you intend to do, sir?"

He looked at her blankly. "Do?"

"You might go round to the watch-house and discover what's become of that poor, witless creature. I'm not convinced she meant any harm. If she were loitering in the area on the night of the murder, might not she have been a witness?"

"Why not tell Chase? Surely he could do more than I."

She smiled. "I've not seen him today. Anyway, a visit from a bona fide barrister would no doubt terrify the authorities into good behavior. And a little kindness might go further to convince the woman to speak."

Buckler bowed over her hand. "I don't suppose you've considered that she herself might be guilty of the crime. You have heard of murderers compelled to return to the scene of their infamy?"

❧❧

At dusk in St. James's Square the great houses were illumined as the inhabitants dressed for sumptuous dinners followed by a night of pleasure, debauchery, or both, depending on tastes. Soon the streets of Westminster, quiet at this hour, would come alive, clogged with carriages and shrill with voices.

The usual observation was that people of this stamp were largely unaware that a stone's throw away a different London scrabbled and toiled and plundered its victims. John Chase thought that nonsense. The inhabitants of St. James's and of all the leafy, elegant squares of the West End knew perfectly well that accidents of birth and geography brought everything that mattered in this world, and the only worthwhile endeavor in life was to cling tenaciously to those things and to act like they belonged to you and your descendants by God-ordained right. In their position Chase would probably do the same.

After attending the inquest and talking to some of the servants in households around the square as well as to the local tradesmen, he was on his way to have a word with Penelope about an intriguing development in the Ransom case. Attempting to call upon Dick Ransom's former employer, a Mrs. Janet Gore of Bruton Street, a supercilious maid had informed Chase that no lady of that name had ever resided at that address, nor had anyone in the household heard of Dick Ransom. It seemed, thus, that Ransom had falsified his character.

Setting off down the pavement, he was brought up short by approaching footsteps. Even in the dimness, he recognized the man as Edward Buckler, the barrister. Chase waited, not speaking until Buckler was almost upon him. "Good evening, sir."

"Mr. Chase. This is most opportune. Now you may accompany me."

"Where to?"

Buckler thrust out his hand. "On an errand of compassion, sir. I own I shall be glad of your company."

Chase shook the hand, but kept his inquiring gaze on the other man's face. Buckler said, "A poor woman, Mr. Chase. Last night she was apprehended trying to enter Sir

Roger's house. Apparently, she made a rumpus, interrupting the family at dinner. You hadn't heard?"

"Where is this female now?" Chase said curtly.

"At the local watch-house. Mrs. Wolfe was not at all taken with the constable who appeared on the scene. She thinks we ought to ascertain if the woman has been treated justly and attempt to solicit her knowledge of Ransom's murder." He described the events in Lincoln's Inn Fields.

Chase swore. "What business could this creature have with Mrs. Wolfe? Had this not been the one time the blasted parish authorities took their duty seriously, Mrs. Wolfe may have learned more of the circumstances. And I suppose it never occurred to the dolts that I might want to see this woman myself."

"I don't suppose it did."

"I'll be off then. You needn't come, sir." Chase strode off up York Street.

The barrister stayed with him, however, after a moment saying somewhat breathlessly, "Slow up. I promised Mrs. Wolfe I would go myself."

With a lift of his brows and a skeptical grunt, Chase did not pause to comment. Heavy shadows lay across the cobbles now, a pervasive chill seeming to rise from the stones to permeate even stout boots. Well used to London damp, Chase ignored it, his mind sifting through the fragments of this murder inquiry, assembling, tearing apart, assembling again in new forms. He had yet to piece together a mosaic that satisfied.

As the clock chimed the hour, they passed St. James's church then crossed Picadilly. Just ahead on Little Vine Street was the watch-house, a squat, mean-looking structure.

※ ※

Edward Buckler had never before entered a watch-house, or roundhouse as they were often called. This one was faintly ramshackle with peeling walls plastered with notices and schedules for the watchmen's rounds. The wooden floorboards had splintered in places.

In one corner of the room sat the Night-Beadle at a scarred deal table. This individual had reclined his chair against the wall and sat staring upwards as if to ponder some message set in the air above his head. He appeared to be paying no attention whatever to the thumps and scattered moans emitting from the cellar below, nor did he immediately look up upon their arrival.

"A word with you, sir," said Chase.

The beadle slowly lowered his gaze from the ceiling. "Of a certainty, you may have it," he pronounced. Again very slowly, he got to his feet, picked up his staff of office, and settled his cocked hat on his head. This was an archaic specimen with three corners, a turned-up brim, and gold lace. The man himself, bony and sharp-featured, was about sixty years old.

"You are Constable of the Night here?"

"Who asks?"

"John Chase, Bow Street."

From below, the cries rose in a chorus. The Beadle reached out with his staff and tapped gently on the grating. "Bit restive tonight," he remarked.

"How many do you keep down there?" asked Buckler. These would be disorderly drunks, vagrants, prostitutes, or pickpockets who were confined for up to forty-eight hours until they could be brought up before a magistrate.

The Beadle turned a limpid gaze on him. "That all depends, sir. Things get pretty lively."

"I need to speak to one of your inmates," said Chase with obvious impatience. "A female brought in last night, she who was caught trespassing in Sir Roger Wallace-Crag's garden."

"The one as wanted a peep at the corpse? A bad business that. You fellows best nab the one as done the footman right quick. We can't have the swells troubled by such goings on."

"The woman?"

"I'm sure I don't know why Bow Street has an interest in *her*." The Beadle rubbed a hand over his unshaven, pimply cheeks and eyed Chase right back. "It makes no matter anyhow. She ain't here."

"Brought up at the police office?"

"No, sir."

A silence fell in which each man proceeded to take the other's measure. While Chase was curt to the point of rudeness, there was no real heat in his tone. Similarly, the Beadle was determined to offer not one word more than necessary, but he too seemed unruffled, even faintly apologetic, as if wishful to convey he bore no one a grudge in the execution of his duty.

"Released?" said Chase at last.

The Beadle looked away for the first time. "There was someone what vouched for her. She was judged fit to be set at liberty."

Buckler said, "You let her go without so much as a by-your-leave from your superiors? I suppose any malefactor may look for such generous treatment?"

"I wouldn't say so. No, not at all."

Chase sighed. "It's no use going that road, Buckler." He fixed the watch-house keeper with a frown. "Who?"

"Beg pardon, sir?"

"You said someone vouched for the woman."

The Beadle took a few steps, swung his staff, and tapped again on the grating. "Ripe for Bedlam, that one, but the lady said as the poor thing were just curious, wouldn't hurt a living soul despite being more than a little simple in the head. Said as the old half-wit used to be her nurse and promised to see her safe home."

Buckler turned to Chase, exclaiming, "There's a bit of luck for you. Now you may interview this good Samaritan who may well be able to give a better account of our corpse peeper, than, I dare say, she could give of herself."

But Chase, still regarding the watch-house keeper, said, "I think our friend here is about to tell us he neglected to solicit the lady's name—or direction. That right?"

"That's about it," the Beadle said primly. "For all she wore a veil to shield her countenance, I pegged her soon as she opened her mouth. She were the real article, gentlemen. 'Twouldn't have been seemly to press a fine filly out to do her bit o' good."

"No doubt. We'll bid you good evening then," cut in Chase over Buckler's protest. He tossed a coin on the desk. "For your trouble, constable."

The Beadle made no move to pick it up. "Thank you, sir."

Buckler waited until they were outside, then burst out, "That scoundrel took a bribe to let his prisoner go, no questions asked. You know it will be impossible to trace her or her benefactress with such paltry information, if that's what you have in mind, Chase. Don't they keep better records of transactions? And why the devil did you give that fellow a gratuity?"

Chase put up a hand to stem the flow. "Calm yourself, Mr. Buckler. I'd not last three days in my job if I allowed incompetent fools to stop me for long."

⁂

When Chase arrived at the House of Lords, a bloodless, girlishly handsome youth had risen to address the chamber. Standing near the entrance, Chase paid no attention at first until gradually the words penetrated, and he began to listen.

"But while the exalted offender can find means to baffle the law, new capital punishments must be devised, new snares of death must be spread for the wretched mechanic, who is famished into guilt. These men were willing to dig, but the spade was in other hands. They were not ashamed to beg, but there was none to relieve them. Their own means of subsistence were cut off, all other employments preoccupied.

And their excesses, however to be deplored and condemned, can hardly be subject of surprise."

A quick glance around told Chase that most of the other peers lounging on the red cloth covered benches remained unimpressed, not that they talked among themselves or did anything overtly rude. Still their expressions were disdainful, though there were a few looks of pleased surprise and interest to be seen on the opposition side.

At Chase's back the friendly yeoman usher who had admitted him to the gallery whispered, "As I told you, sir, we've no accommodation for visitors. As you can see, we're full up. Should you like to await Lord Ashe in the lobby?"

"No, thank you. I've served guard duty in the Commons on occasion, so I am quite familiar with it. This is the first time I've had occasion to visit the Lords."

"Usually rather less fire hereabouts, sir, present instance excepted. Of course, we need to make allowances being as this is the young gentleman's maiden speech."

"Who is he?" Chase murmured as the young lord gestured energetically and launched into still more impassioned rhetoric.

"Lord Byron, sir. Not a very distinguished or prosperous barony, though I understand he's the sixth of the title. He's talking of the Luddites. The bill under debate today seeks to make framebreaking a hanging matter."

Byron drowned him out easily. "I have traversed the seat of war in the Peninsula. I have been in some of the most oppressed provinces of Turkey. But never under the most despotic of infidel governments did I behold such squalid wretchedness as I have seen since my return in the very heart of a Christian country."

It seemed to Chase that these words dropped from the speaker's mouth only to fall into a curious void. Certainly, they were incongruous here in this elegant room packed with the cream of the nation's aristocracy, themselves surrounded by walls lined with rich, old tapestries depicting England's glorious defeat of the Armada. At the chamber's upper end sat a throne, gilded and spread with red velvet. It was surmounted by a canopy, also of crimson velvet, bearing the imperial crown at its apex. A seat for a monarch whenever he or she should choose to take it.

The ever helpful usher whispered to Chase again, pointing out the Lord Chancellor, the Lord Chief Justice, and the Master of the Rolls, who observed the proceedings from broad, backless, uncomfortable-looking seats below the throne. To one side were benches for the lords spiritual, the archbishops and bishops, who also sat stiffly, staring straight ahead.

At length Chase was able to pick out Ashe on the government side. And if the sneer on his thin, aristocratic mouth were anything by which to judge, he too did not approve of what he heard. The North seethed with unrest these days as workers raided the mills to smash the new shearing frames they claimed were a threat to their livelihoods. Widespread wage cuts and astronomical food prices had made the Luddites, as they called themselves, so desperate as to have nothing to lose. Not that Chase supposed men like Ashe cared to concern themselves beyond passing an act that would be sure to infuriate the rebels even further.

Young Byron thundered on. "Is there not blood enough upon your penal code, that more must be poured forth to ascend to Heaven and testify against you? How will you carry the bill into effect? Can you commit a whole country to their own prisons? Will you erect a gibbet in every field and hang up men like scarecrows?"

Gazing around at the sea of implacable faces, Chase was certain he knew the answer to that question.

Chapter VII

"A satisfied stomach makes unpleasant business the more palatable, wouldn't you agree, Mr. Chase? Tell me, sir, how do you find your repast?"

Chase could find no fault with the steaming pigeon pie and excellent wine in this Old Palace Yard chophouse. The invitation from Ashe, however, had surprised him. "Delicious, my lord. You are most generous."

He waved a dismissive hand. "Since I was unable to give you the meeting in St. James's Square, it seemed the least I could do. I understand from Mrs. Wolfe you are just the man to get to the bottom of this matter. I shouldn't be surprised if you discover this manservant was in league with a nest of vipers who turned against him. Thievery, perhaps?"

Interesting that both Lady Ashe and her husband seemed to wish to nudge his thinking in that direction, though Lady Ashe's was the more charitable of interpretations. "I have no such evidence at present," Chase said carefully. "Your butler has given the servant a good character. No signs of forced entry, nor is there anything missing from the house so far as I have been able to ascertain."

Ashe looked as if he didn't much like to be contradicted, but his tone remained genial. "You would know best, though I am at a loss to understand what could have befallen the fellow. One hardly expects to find a man stabbed to death in one's garden."

"When he entered your father-in-law's employ some two months ago, Ransom provided a testimonial from a woman called Mrs. Janet Gore. I attempted to verify this reference, but there seems to have been some error. No such person as Mrs. Gore resides at that address, nor had anyone there ever encountered Dick Ransom."

"Ah, we see how such testimonials may easily prove forgeries. Clearly, Ransom played some deep game, sir, not so terribly surprising in these unsettled times. You will oblige me by not speaking of the matter to my wife. I do not want her disturbed."

"Yet, like your butler, Lady Ashe has spoken well of the dead man."

Ashe put down his fork with a clatter, his brow contracting. "My wife? What the devil do you suppose she knows about it? She rarely concerns herself with domestic arrangements."

"No doubt social engagements occupy her time?"

"Naturally."

A trifle touchy on the subject, it seemed, reflected Chase, thinking of the rumors that Lord Ashe had wed his lady for an heir—and her money. He went on smoothly, "The coroner's inquest was held this afternoon, my lord. I arranged that only your butler and one or two of your other servants were asked to testify."

"We thank you for that, Mr. Chase. The verdict, I suppose, was a foregone conclusion?"

"Murder against person or persons unknown. There is, as yet, little more to go on. The body is to be released for burial." Chase paused. "If I may inquire, my lord, what brought you downstairs yesterday morning?"

"I don't claim to have heard the uproar as Mrs. Wolfe did, but I had awakened nonetheless. Can't say why really. I often rise early to work, and that was my intention."

"Lady Ashe was not disturbed?"

His eyes fixed coldly on Chase's. "I believe not. If you are quite through, sir, I must be getting back." Shoving his plate away, he made as if to rise, but Chase held up one hand to restrain him.

"The female intruder has eluded us for the present, as she has been discharged by the parish authorities. But it is possible she is connected in some manner to Dick Ransom's death. Did anyone in your household recognize her, my lord?"

"No, I'm sorry."

"A lady, an *incognita*, vouched for the woman and secured her release. She told the watch-house keeper the female had once been her nurse."

"A pretty story," replied Ashe, shaking his head. "You must hope then that this 'lady' will lead you to the others. One of a gang, I should imagine, perhaps from the King Street rookery just off the square."

Chase wiped the crumbs from his mouth, tossed aside his napkin, and got to his feet. "By the by, my lord, what did you make of that speech about the Luddite business? Have you any fears the disturbances will spread? Till now they been confined to the Midlands and the North."

"Byron? Parcel of nonsense. He ought to know that such lawlessness respects no boundaries. Indeed, it spreads like some dread disease. I am afraid sometimes the scoundrels will be satisfied with nothing less than the destruction of what makes England great. The stability and proper respect which governs relations among the classes. The mighty wealth and commercial prosperity that is our reward for each playing our part. They cut off their noses to spite their faces did they but know it."

"You mean the destruction of machinery only hurts everyone, man and master alike?"

"Of course. Consider the nightly depredations in Nottingham over the past few months. The Government has been forced to deploy thousands of soldiers so that peaceable individuals should not be afraid to retire to their beds. How many shearing frames—valuable property, mind—do you suppose the rogues have dared to destroy?"

"A vast number, I should imagine."

"Over three hundred in January alone. And the ne'er-do-wells will only grow the more brazen unless firmly checked. I tell you we must put them down."

"So you believe the threats are to be taken seriously? I would not be surprised should they dare to threaten even the Regent."

Ashe spread his hands. "What else can I believe? The sentiments are explicit enough." He waited a moment, then dropped his next words very slowly into the silence. "Blood... for...blood."

"I know you. You'll walk a few paces and expect me to carry you the rest of the way."

Sarah's brows drew together. "I won't. Besides, you promised me a sweeting, Mama."

When the misspelled, crumpled note, addressed to the "kind lady muther of the littel girl" had arrived this morning, Penelope's first impulse had been to turn the matter over to John Chase. But the letter required her presence, and the instructions seemed straightforward enough. She was to see the knife-seller in Covent Garden Market for a message, and Penelope was certain she knew who had sent it.

Though she doubted the wisdom of bringing the child, Sarah would never give up without a battle, one that might not be in a parent's best interests to wage. And she herself might not have another opportunity to get away for days. Lenient mistress though Julia undoubtedly was, she was just as apt to demand her companion dance attendance on her for hours as she was to ignore Penelope's very existence. One could never be sure.

As she laid aside the note, Penelope had asked, "The woman in the garden didn't threaten you? I mean, did she frighten you?"

"I didn't like it that she cried so and wouldn't stop."

An idea occurred to Penelope. "Had you seen her before that night, my love, perhaps when Mary took you out for your walk?"

Sarah put down her spoon, always glad of an excuse to avoid eating the detested porridge. "Yes, I did see her. I wanted to give her my penny, but Mary had bid me throw it in the basin. I couldn't ask Mary 'cause she was busy talking to the groom from the house across the way."

Seething, Penelope forced herself to ask cheerfully, "When was this, love? Did she try to speak to you?"

The child paused, and her face fell, eyes filling with tears. "I don't think so. I don't remember exactly when it was."

Penelope lifted her into her lap. There was no point, she knew, in pressing for more. "Never mind, darling. If you remember, you can tell me later."

Now, trying to ignore the stiff breeze that whipped at their cloaks and stung their cheeks with color, Penelope came to a decision. "All right then. We'll walk in that direction, but you mustn't give me any trouble, mind."

"Oh, I won't, I won't," sang the little girl joyfully.

She took her mother's hand, and they set off, Sarah giving occasional hops to avoid the muck on the pavement. The day was overcast with fat, sullen clouds suffocating the earth and a wind so sharp it made the ears ache. Hardly a good day for an excursion; still they needn't stay long, whether or not Penelope's business came to anything.

A brisk walk brought them to the Market, and none too soon, for Sarah, inevitably, had begun to whine and drag her feet. Stepping gingerly over discarded leaves and walnut shells, they threaded their way through stalls piled high with brightly colored carrots, cabbages, cauliflower, and oranges.

Women carrying baskets on their heads wove gracefully among the crush of hampers, carts, and donkey barrows, even as the wind buffeted their skirts. Aproned greengrocers called out the virtues of their produce to passing customers. Ragged, grimy costers swarmed from shop to shop seeking the better price.

Crowded against St. Paul's, Covent Garden, the Market brought choking traffic into the area, inciting endless complaints from residents. It was a frenzied, ill-organized tangle offering far more than the original roots, herbs, flowers, and fruits. One could purchase slippers, baskets, combs, crockery, and poultry. Even the dealers in knives and old iron had elbowed their way in as if to serve notice that a new era had arrived.

"Stay close, Sarah," she warned, reaching down to grip her shoulder.

Sarah shook her off. "Look, Mama. What's he doing to that chicken?" She pointed to where a homely, slit-eyed man stood gripping a chicken by its neck. Apparently, he had just purchased it from the poulterer's stall, for at his back a confusion of white-feathered birds fluttered and squawked in their cages. The chicken in the man's hands, however, hung mutely between his powerful thumbs, perhaps already dead.

"What's he doing? I want to see." She started forward.

"Sarah." Penelope made a grab for her and missed. The child stopped a few feet away, one knuckle in her mouth.

"Mama. It doesn't move. What's wrong with it?"

She didn't sound particularly distressed, but that was Sarah's way. Her first response to something outside her experience was always an intense desire to know more. She internalized it, pondered it, and only then expressed amusement, sadness, or bewilderment. Penelope knew they'd be talking about that blasted chicken for days to come.

"Let's go look at the apples, shall we? Would you like one to eat on the way home?"

She stepped closer, intending to propel her daughter in the opposite direction, but found her attention caught by the slit-eyed man again. Starting to move away through the crowd, he swung his fowl back and forth in ever-widening circles as if preparing for some show of athletic prowess. People stared and shoved at him resentfully, for he seemed not to care whom he struck. Loud complaints erupted.

Several feet on, he encountered a stall where he jarred a patron rudely, earning another curse before he finally lost himself in the throng. Sarah turned away. Penelope, however, remained transfixed.

She reached for Sarah's hand. "Come on."

They went briskly across the piazza to the stall, where the proprietress was still busy serving her customer, a plump housewife come to have her knives sharpened. The knife woman wielded the whet stone with deft fingers, the blade turning and flashing in her hands.

Sarah pulled at Penelope. "I want my sweeting."

"Just a moment. Mama needs to speak to this woman."

When the housewife had departed, Penelope said to the vendor, "A word with you, if you please."

Her voice sounded more peremptory than she'd intended, probably because the knife-seller kept her eyes averted in what seemed a pointed rudeness. Thin, but not gaunt, she wore a clean woolen gown. Her face, above a frayed and heavily darned lace collar, might have been forged from the same metal as her knives, all hard edges. She could have been anywhere from forty to seventy years old.

"Yes, missus?" She thrust swollen, bony fingers into a display case and began to adjust her merchandise.

Loosening the strings of her reticule, Penelope drew out the note. "I believe you sent this. You have a message for me?"

After a short silence, the vendor said, "I might."

Her fingers continued to roam over the knives in their tattered velvet casing like some enormous, restless spider.

At Penelope's side, Sarah began to squirm. Market cries rose and ebbed on the wind.

"Who from?"

This time the pause was even longer before the woman replied, "I seen her yesterday, but she been around before. In a state, she was. Said as how you might be willing to help, that's all." Turning away, she called out in a heckling tone to another potential customer, who had hesitated over a pile of rusted iron locks.

Penelope spoke louder. "This woman is connected to an establishment in St. James's Square?"

The woman looked her full in the eyes for the first time, a dark, heavy gaze rather like the reflection cast by her knives. It revealed nothing of her thoughts. "What's it to me if she were?"

Was she fishing for a bribe to loosen her lips, Penelope wondered, bewildered. Would such an offering be an insult?

"Let's go, Mama," said Sarah, tugging insistently.

"Hush. I'm not finished." Penelope pulled her hand away and fumbled in her reticule for a coin. She held it out. "Here. Perhaps this will help."

The knife vendor took the coin, biting it absently. "Thank ye kindly. Truth is, mum, the old half-wit give me something for you. Probably worth at least ten quid, I'd say, but I'll let you have it for five."

"Five pounds? I don't have that kind of money. Besides, I'm sure she meant for you to give it to me."

The woman shoved so violently at one of her trays that some of the knives tipped from their slots. "That I won't do. Get off with you then."

When she straightened, her expression was so ugly that involuntarily Penelope shrank, tightening her hold on Sarah.

"Get off," the woman repeated shrilly. "I won't be cheated. You don't belong here. You take your pretty baby and go on home before something happens."

"There's been a terrible crime committed in St. James's Square," Penelope said coldly. "Unless you want to be held accountable, you'd best be a good deal more forthcoming. I can tell you that matters will go hard for you if it's thought that you are withholding evidence."

"You got windmills in your head, lady. That beldame ain't done nothing. Ain't a thought in her head that someone else didn't put there."

"You won't mind at least showing me what she gave you."

The woman trained her unreadable stare on Penelope's face. A fragment of conversation reached them, then laughter, shouts, and singing, but they might have been alone.

Penelope opened her reticule again and poured out the remaining coins into her palm. "Will you show me—for this?"

The woman's gaze narrowed. "All that just to lay your peepers on it? Not to keep."

"Done." Penelope's heart hammered against the side of her neck, making her feel slightly breathless. At her side Sarah was held motionless by a tension that was thick as syrup.

The woman held out her hand for the money. Then, she half turned away, reaching down into an inside pocket of her dress to draw out a package, narrow, about half a foot long, covered in plain brown paper and fastened with twine.

"Do you know what's in there?" asked Penelope as the woman's fingers started to work the wrapping loose.

"The old beldame told me, but she run off before I could get a glim of it."

"You don't know her name or where she comes from?"

"Naw. She dosses down under the stalls at night with the vagabond children sometimes. That's why she give me this here. She said it'd most like be stole off her anyway, and she didn't want no nonsense about it. She said you'd know what was to be done."

The woman ripped off the last bit of twine and reached inside the paper to pull out the object. "There. You satisfied, lady?"

She held up a lovely, slender dagger of solid gold. The hilt was formed by twin serpents entwined so that their heads formed a hand grip, their eyes marked by tiny rubies. The blade itself was etched with more snakes and delicate bejewelled wheels.

"Gawd," breathed the knife vendor reverently. "She said it were just a little knife."

Penelope was frozen with shock. The last time she had seen the dagger was in its place on Sir Roger Wallace-Crag's desk. He had designed it himself, she knew, and had used it to break the wax seals of the numerous letters he received. Sir Roger was immensely fond of his tiny dagger, always careful not to misplace it.

Which meant the old woman must have been in Sir Roger's study. Which also meant she could well have dispatched her victim with this very knife and carried it away for disposal. For a moment a blank horror kept Penelope silent.

"Well, you've seen," said the woman, setting her prize back in its package and glaring. "Get on with you."

"Let's go, Mama," Sarah whispered, a catch in her voice.

Penelope paused, uncertain. The letter opener was vital evidence John Chase must have. But this woman would undoubtedly take the first opportunity to sell it, and it might never be recovered. And Penelope had no more money with which to offer a bribe.

As the woman watched her with increasing suspicion, Sarah whimpered a bit in discomfort, or fear. A fierce gust of wind rippled over the wrapping paper. Balanced precariously, the dagger teetered, slid over the edge of the stall, and landed in the sawdust and fruit debris at Penelope's feet.

She reacted without thought. Snatching it up, she tossed it in her gaping reticule, hoisted Sarah in her arms, and ran. She heard the knife vendor's hoarse shout of rage, but no sound of pursuing footsteps. She could only hope the woman would not want to leave her stock unattended.

"Thief, thief, thief! Stop her!" came the almost incoherent howl, somewhat muffled by increasing distance and the thick crowd.

Forced to slacken her pace to avoid a heavily loaded dray, Penelope struggled to get her breath. She felt as if everyone in the vicinity must know of her transgression by now. Hands would seize her, haul her up before the magistrate. She could not imagine the humiliation of such a moment. Then Sarah whimpered in her arms, and Penelope knew that possible embarrassment was the least of this affair's repercussions.

"Hush, love, it's all right," she gasped, trying desperately to regain some semblance of calm.

They had reached the edge of the square, and just ahead was a gate that led to a side street. Overwhelmed with relief, Penelope moved toward it deliberately, trying not to attract attention.

She was reaching out her hand for the latch when a hand descended on her shoulder and a voice growled, "Here now. You wait just a minute."

Slowly, she turned to confront a broad-nosed, wide-mouthed, greasy-haired man wearing a calf-length apron luridly streaked with vegetable stains. Penelope's heart dived to her boots.

"Yes?" she faltered.

"The knife-seller says you got something what belongs to her." His eyes bore into hers. "Give it here."

For one panic-stricken instant, she held his gaze, then whirled and fled into the street. She thought for certain he would follow, but when she glanced back over her shoulder, he remained by the gate, watching her, arms folded across his stomach. Penelope pressed on. Her one thought now was to get home and relinquish her discovery to John Chase.

Sarah lifted her head. "Put me down, Mama," she said, squirming hard until Penelope was obliged to set her on her feet. The little girl smoothed her cloak and stamped her feet to get the blood moving. She took one step and paused.

"We have to go. Take my hand," said Penelope urgently.

Sarah looked up, her eyes serious. "Did you do something bad, Mama?" She was quiet a moment, thinking; then her face crumpled. "I didn't get my sweeting!"

"Go on then. They're waiting for you," said the Master's secretary, who had opened the door to find her hesitating in the corridor. His tone was not unkind, but to Rebecca, the pity and contempt were clear. Lifting her chin, she stepped over the threshold.

Greeted by a blaze of light from the tall windows that overlooked the garden, she was for an instant dazzled. In these last days of summer, the heat had been considerable and the temperature stifling. The assorted smells of the people in the room, perfumes mixed with sweat and the reek of gloating triumph, assaulted her senses. Slowly, the faces came into focus, and Rebecca's heart jumped when she saw that the Master was present, leaning against the mantel. She sent him no more than a glance, but he was staring at his boots, his expression preoccupied.

Besides the Master and Mr. Finch, there was Mrs. Dobson, a black-garbed figure hovering over the Mistress, who sat in her favorite chair, her spindly legs propped on a needlework footstool. Rebecca thought the Mistress appeared more sallow, more loveless than usual, despite the richness of her green silk gown. She had lost a great deal of flesh since her last miscarriage earlier in the year.

"Come in, Rebecca," she said in her soft, weary voice, and Rebecca went to stand in the middle of the carpet, arms behind her back and belly outthrust. She knew the Mistress was studying her and was suddenly, fiercely, glad. Let her look her fill.

There was a sharp silence; then the Mistress said, "Mrs. Dobson tells me she has spoken to you, but you are disposed to be obstinate. You know that in any other household, you would have been turned off long since."

Rebecca bowed her head, her heart rebellious. Why should they say such things to her? She gazed down at her crisp white apron and willed herself to be calm. She knew she looked well, had taken great pains with her appearance. She knew also that she had done nothing of which to be ashamed.

"We have kept you on," the Mistress continued, "not because we credit for one moment this absurd tale you tell to cloak your sin, but because we are a Christian household. If you would only tell the truth, it may be that we can persuade the man to marry you and give your infant a name and you a respectable future."

Rebecca raised her face to the afternoon light that seemed to caress her skin in reassurance. "My child *will* have a name, the highest that can be bestowed. The Lord will not forsake His own. He has sent this babe to me for His own purposes which shall be revealed in due course."

"You blasphemous, wicked girl!" exclaimed Mrs. Dobson, but she was staring in half-horror, half-admiration, as if nothing Rebecca did would be a surprise.

So it seemed to Rebecca herself these days. Nothing surprised her. The lie, a tiny seed buried in her soul, had grown into a vigorous, sturdy sapling that one day soon would erupt in bloom. The seed itself mattered nothing, and indeed, Rebecca had half-forgotten its origin as her life was taken up to be directed into new channels. And yet, seeing the Master now, she felt the tug of the old weakness, the old yearning. She wished he would look at her.

Stifling that thought, Rebecca said, "I speak the Truth. What do I care for your threats?" She stepped closer to the Mistress. "Can you afford to spurn this mark of the Almighty's favor? You ought instead to ask yourself why your house should have been chosen for this honor."

The Mistress swallowed audibly. "You mustn't say such things, Rebecca." Her hand rested on her own flat abdomen before she continued. "If you are not going to tell us, I'm afraid—"

"Yes, madam. You are afraid. But God hears your prayer, and it may be that He will grant it. You must take heart. You must believe."

The eyes still fixed on Rebecca's filled with tears, and the Master cleared his throat. "My dear, I believe we've heard enough." He squeezed his wife's shoulder. "The girl must go."

Rebecca stared at him in disbelief. He had not once met her gaze, yet she knew him well enough to read profound discomfort in the set of his mouth and the tension in his shoulders. How could he betray her thus? For a moment, the shame, a thing of darkness, nibbled like a rat at her gut.

The Mistress spoke, voice sharp with repressed anguish. "Turn out mother and child to starve or, worse, to fall deeper into the pit of lust and debauchery. No indeed. I cannot reconcile it with my conscience, Sir Roger."

"My dear!" he expostulated.

"Sir Roger is right, ma'am," broke in Mr. Finch eagerly. "There are foundling hospitals to care for such children so that their mothers may be set back on the path of virtue. Allow me to make the arrangements."

A look flashed between them: his a question, hers a tiny shake of the head. The secretary's shoulders slumped in defeat, and he said no more, though he kept his mournful gaze on Lady Wallace-Crag as if awaiting a summons to her assistance.

Rebecca drew herself up. "Do not fear for me. I have only stayed with Miss Julia out of love and fear for her safety. Her fits grow worse lately. Do you never ask yourselves what could be amiss?"

"I have not the slightest notion what you could mean." Two spots of color now appeared high in the Mistress' cheeks.

"My lord Ashe," replied Rebecca, hating them. "He is evil. He says he wishes to teach the child to ride her pony, but I believe he seeks to…interfere with her. Why else should a man grown, a bachelor, dance attendance on a mere babe who detests the very sight of him?"

The color ebbed from the Mistress' face, and, shooting Rebecca a burning look of reproach, the secretary went to kneel by her chair, offering her the cup of water from the table at her side. She took the cup with a nod of thanks and turned to look over her shoulder at her husband.

"Well, sir? What do you make of this terrible accusation against your friend?"

"Pure nonsense. The girl is obviously over-wrought and proclaims these stories to divert attention from herself. We need not regard anything she might say." He paused, then added, "Charity is all well and good, my dear, but you cannot allow her to corrupt the other servants. Let her be sent away."

At his words, a shutter came down in Rebecca's mind, and her knees began to buckle, the rat gnawing at her vitals. Then she remembered she was not alone and had only to look toward the light.

Chapter VIII

John Chase stood in front of the Tower of London, a grim, massive pile overlooking the River Thames. So many had met their fate at the headsman's axe here that even the thickest of visitors must surely sense far-off echoes of pain and terror. To Chase, the Tower suggested the implacable power of the State that no puny individual would do well to bestir. Far better to let the leviathan slumber, or preen itself, in the sun.

Chase's business would not take him beyond the outer ward of this vast fortress that was also garrison, arsenal, palace, and state prison. Entering from the west through the Lion Gate, he saw ahead, rising from the center of the smelly, unsanitary moat, the Middle Tower with its double portcullis; beyond that, the Byward Tower, even more formidable, and guarded by both soldiers and warders.

However, Chase turned right to the Lion's Tower, the outermost of the three bulwarks of defense and home of the Tower Menagerie. As if to herald his arrival, the roar of a lion and the shrill laugh of a hyena rose in chorus round the courtyard.

He rang a bell, soon answered by a man dressed in the warder's uniform of scarlet coat and skirt. He was of nondescript age, hunch shouldered and hairy, well suited to his position as keeper of the beasts.

"A shilling to view the animals. Though this time of year they be unduly lethargic."

As instructed, Chase replied, "I've come for a special showing."

Glancing back over his shoulder, the keeper lowered his voice and drew closer. "Two shillings then."

Chase produced the coins and followed his guide toward a series of tall archways set in a semi-circle. Within each arch was fixed an iron grating behind which animals sulked in murky dens.

The pens appeared tidy and commodious enough, despite the keeper's grumble that the menagerie had been sorely neglected during the war with France. They were built in two stories with the bottom allocated for the animals' daytime use, the top for sleeping. In one cage Chase made out the dim form of an old tiger curled in the shadows. In another, two leopards watched him with coal-ember eyes. A wolf lurked in a third.

"Take care to stay back, sir. Lethargic or no, these beasts ain't nothing to trifle with." The keeper paused, then added reflectively, "It's a funny thing, but the ones as were whelped here in the Tower are more vicious even than them taken wild."

As he spoke, he approached one of the dens and fumbled with his keys. A click, and the iron gate creaked open. "In here, sir. I'll return presently."

Chase stepped into the gloom, finding himself in a vacant half-moon shaped chamber. A musty animal smell assailed him. Uncertain, he gazed about until he saw that a glow flickered from the upper story. He approached the stairway, but hesitated upon the thought that this could be a trap. Then a voice he knew whispered from above.

"Come on up, Chase."

The upper room was low and cold. A tallow candle set on a low stool provided the only light and warmth. There was no other furniture in the room save for a thin mat tossed over a pile of straw.

"Nice crib, Packet," said Chase.

"My own little bit of paradise. I'll move the glim so you can sit. I wouldn't want you to spoil your pretty trousers." Noah Packet took the candle and lowered himself to the dusty floor.

Taking the offered seat, Chase stared down at his companion. Packet looked drawn and ill, his deep-socketed eyes blinking in the light. Streaked with dirt, his black suit hung in enormous creases on his slight frame as if it had been slept in more than once. But he was not the sort to squirm under scrutiny.

"What did my friend the keeper relieve you of?"

"Two hogs," said Chase indifferently.

He smiled. "Worth every penny?"

"That remains to be seen. What's amiss, Noah? Why the deuce did you bolt to this hole?"

He didn't really expect Packet to tell him. While the two were friends, they met purely in the course of Chase's work. A small-time thief who earned a bit on the side in trading information, Packet continually astounded Chase with what he was able to glean from his always unnamed sources. Chase suspected that, in addition to having an excellent ear for servants' tattle, Packet was not above delving in rubbish heaps. But if he could come up with gold this time, even while in hiding, that would be talent indeed.

Packet said, "Let's just say I'm here on account of a small misunderstanding. I'll manage. In the meantime, 'tis best to play least in sight. I got your message, however, and it may be I can help you some." He paused. "I ain't seen you much of late, Chase. You been busy larking with that gentry mort what's aiming to make a civilized man of you? Mrs. Wolfe, was it?"

Chase grinned. "No, I haven't seen Mrs. Wolfe, at least not until the other day. Once again it's a matter of business, if you catch my meaning." A long, low wail cut through the darkness, sending shivers up his spine. "Good Lord, Packet."

"Just an animal, or maybe a ghost?" He gave a croak of a laugh. "Ain't always easy to tell the difference."

"What's being said about the killing at Sir Roger Wallace-Crag's house in St. James's Square? I saw the victim buried today."

Packet ruminated, eyes sliding up the stained, damp walls, then sweeping back to Chase's face, only to flit away again. "I ain't heard much. Just that the poor sod was found in the garden with a knife sticking in his chest."

"Actually, the knife was gone, but, yes, you're correct. Any whispers about who's responsible?"

"Nothing prigged? No cracksman then, not that any I know of would try their lay in that part of town." Packet cleared his throat and rubbed his hands together. "This fellow get on well with his employer?"

"As far as I can tell, yes. There's also Sir Roger's son-in-law, Lord Ashe."

"I hear he ought to be one satisfied man with so young and beautiful a wife. They say she's an heiress too."

"A happy couple?"

Packet laughed. "What should I know of the nobs and their doings? Besides, they're wed, ain't they? Here I was thinking the rich got their scruples."

"Noah. Answer the question."

After a few more chuckles, he said, "All right, all right. Naw, I ain't got nothing on Ashe. You've put me in mind of something though. A bit o' servants' talk about the lovely lady's papa.

"Seems a few years back Sir Roger invited one of the kitchen maids, a pretty young thing, to his study. He said he wanted her to pose for a picture in his book. Of course, she thought he had something else in mind and must've thought she could earn a bit on the sly. Only it didn't come out that way."

"What happened?"

"She said something to let him know she's willing like. Then he flew out at her like she were a she-devil. He cut up savage till the poor girl was nigh hysterical."

"Odd. What of his picture?"

"Oh, they took care of that afterwards, he dressing up like some sort of barbaric priest, she playing the part of nun or some such while another bloke took down the whole in his sketch book."

"Packet, what do you know of a woman called Rebecca Barnwell?" he said, obeying an impulse.

Chase had heard Barnwell's name from the footman George as they faced each other across the table in a local pub. George had been more forthcoming than Chase had expected, and Chase was glad he'd thought of conducting his interview away from the square. Well worth the price of a few pints.

"Dick?" George had said, taking a long pull from his mug and replacing it carefully on the table. "I can tell you one thing I noticed, sir. He was right anxious to go along with Lady Ashe when she did her shopping and morning visits. He promised he'd make it up to me if I let him be the one."

"Did he tell you why he wished to accompany her?"

"I thought it was on account of her being so…you'll forgive me, sir, I mean no disrespect."

"You thought he admired her beauty?"

"Yes, sir, that's just it."

"What else, George? Don't be afraid to speak up, no matter how unimportant you think it might be."

Chase had waited patiently while the young man hesitated, clearly uncomfortable. At length, George said, "There was a time or two when Dick asked me to cover for him for a few hours. You'll think me a paltry fellow when I tell you I didn't ask why. You see, I liked him, sir, and thought we ought to oblige each other when possible."

"A shame. I shall have to seek elsewhere to discover what Ransom's lay may have been."

George flushed. "I'm sure poor Dick was honest, Mr. Chase, but I admit I wondered. He dropped his purse one day, you see, and a wad of notes tumbled out. Where's a servant to get that kind of blunt?"

Chase digested this. "What makes you so sure he was honest?"

"He was God-fearing, sir. He used to pray on his knees every night before bed and read his Bible. Hours and hours sometimes, he'd be that troubled in his mind. Dreams too, thrashing in his bed all night long. Then there was the seal."

"Seal?"

"You've heard of that west-country prophetess Rebecca Barnwell? He had one of them seals of hers which he used to mark his place in the Bible."

Chase had heard of Miss Rebecca Barnwell and her ministry. Had Ransom been after his own little piece of salvation? If so, he was not alone. It was said that thousands followed the prophetess, daughter of a West Country farmer. But who had removed Ransom's seal and why?

"I found no seal when I examined Ransom's Bible, no loose papers or inscriptions of any sort." He whistled softly. "Did Dick have a particular reason to fancy himself in need of salvation?"

George's eyes were sad. "Don't all mortals hunger for that promise?" He slammed down his mug, wiping off his mouth, and Chase knew he'd gotten all he could.

Now, Packet, his face wearing a curiously arrested expression, groped in his coat. "You mean the preacher lady?" He pulled out a piece of paper, unfolded it, and handed it to Chase. It was a sort of certificate, bearing these words inscribed inside a circle:

> *The Sealed of the Lord*
> *The Elect precious*

Man's Redemption to Inherit
The Tree of Life.
To be made Heirs of God and Joint
Heirs with Jesus Christ.

At the top someone had scored through the original recipient's name, substituting Packet's instead. The signature at the end of the inscription, though an untidy scrawl, was clear enough. Rebecca Barnwell. Chase flipped over the certificate. On the back was a piece of broken sealing wax, imprinted with the initials "IC" and two stars. *Iesus Christus.* Jesus Christ.

"Where the devil did you get this?"

"They cost a pretty penny. It's a ticket to heaven or so they says."

"You believe it?" Chase studied the seal in the candle glow. "Are these people capable of violence?"

"Bible folk out to save the souls of the poor? Could be. Maybe they think it's their duty to rid the world of a few sinners." He stopped to consider. "Though it hardly makes sense if you think the world's about to end anyway. Why not let the Almighty do the dirty work?"

"You have yet to explain why you have one of their seals, Noah."

Packet folded up his document and restored it to his coat, giving his pocket an absent-minded pat. "Ah well, when you play the long shots of the game like I do, it's best to cover the odds. Who knows what a small bit of forethought might do?"

Chase shook his head. "You prigged it, didn't you? Doesn't that make a difference?"

"Nah. I don't suppose them at heaven's gate has time to check the signatures so careful. Too crowded like."

"What of this Dick Ransom? He forged the character he gave Timberlake, the butler, and I've not been able to discover any trace of him prior to his employment in St. James's Square."

"Can't help you there, but since you mention Rebecca Barnwell and her minions, I do know a titbit that might interest you, especially since I know how you feel about them as wear the mask of godliness."

Chase thought of his own father's terrible Christianity that softened not a whit even in the face of loss and grief and of his mother who had dutifully borne him twelve children, of whom five had lived. He nodded.

Packet went on musingly, "There's some that say you don't need no sackcloth and ashes if your faith be pure. Seems like a fine bargain to me. Give your heart to God—and do what you will with the rest."

A rattle at the lock below announced the arrival of the keeper. "Time for you to go." Rapidly, Packet recited the rest of his information, his eyes avoiding Chase's face, his voice low and hoarse.

As he listened, Chase's excitement grew. At last a solid lead to pursue. Getting to his feet, he slipped a few shillings into his friend's outstretched palm. "Noah, if there's anything I can do…"

Packet's eyes flitted around the den, but he gave a philosophical shrug. "This'll buy me some warmth at any rate," he said as his fingers closed convulsively around the coins. "Anyway, I've got my salvation seal to give me a lift if matters get desperate."

Chapter IX

Somehow the girl called Belinda looked familiar, like the stranger on the street who tantalizes one with haunting recognition, a memory only obtained, perhaps, in a dream. She was carefully and expensively dressed in fine muslin of *ingenue* white. Loose hair framed an artless face dominated by wide eyes and delicate brows. Her only ornaments were a tiny pearl ring on her right hand and a locket around her plump, white neck. At first glance, John Chase felt her fascination.

"Don't look so worried," he told her. "I mean you no harm."

"You may not intend wrong, sir, but if the Mistress knew you were speaking to me...how did you get in here?"

"Greased the porter's palm, miss. I am a Bow Street officer, and he didn't want any trouble for himself or this establishment."

She shuffled her feet in their tiny kid slippers. His eyes traveled around the room. A thick Aubusson carpet overlaid polished floorboards, the room well warmed by the coal fire in the grate. Delicate watercolor paintings of St. Paul's Cathedral and other London scenes adorned the walls. A mahogany wardrobe and dressing table glowed with cleanliness, as did the nightstand upon which sat an open Bible.

There was the bed, voluptuously large with enormous pillows and a green silk counterpane, next to which stood the girl. As his gaze fell on her again, he saw the birch flagellation rod she had been attempting to thrust out of sight with her foot. It had blended well with the greens and browns in the carpet, but now his gaze fastened upon it— and held. Noticing his interest, she stopped her furtive movements.

"I seek word of a man called Dick Ransom," he said curtly. "Your doorman seems to think you may be able to help."

She looked confused. "Why ask me?"

"He's dead, you see, and I am investigating his murder. I have reason to believe he may have been known here. A client possibly?"

"He's dead, you said?"

"That's right, miss."

Her hands twisted together. "I know nothing, sir! He was not our…client. We welcome—"

"Rich men, I think. Town swells, members of parliament, a judge or two? No, Dick Ransom was only a footman from a house not far from here."

"Footman?" she exclaimed with some relief. "Dick is not a *servant*. There has been some mistake, I thank God for the sake of my poor Mistress."

"You must tell me what you know of this man, miss. What is he to your Mistress?"

He willed her to look up and meet his gaze, and after a moment she did. To his surprise, he saw genuine regret etched on her face.

"I am very sorry, Mr. Chase, but you have no right to question me thus. I know Mrs. Gore would not like it. Let me take you to her." She slipped gracefully toward the door which he had closed upon his entrance.

"Gore?" he echoed. That was the name Ransom had given with the false address for his character.

Turning, she blinked at him. "Yes, she is mistress of this establishment."

"Belinda," he said, using her name for the first time, "you will do her a very great favor by speaking out. I could make matters most unpleasant for you all, as I'm certain you realize."

She debated a moment, then said, "Our Mr. Ransom dines here on occasion with a group of other gentlemen. Some sort of debating society, I was told. No ladies permitted, and Mrs. Gore doesn't like us to mention it to the regular clients."

"Were you yourself friendly with Ransom?"

A blush spread over her face and neck. "I am acquainted with him, sir," she said with dignity and stood with head bowed like a child awaiting a parent's punishment for some misdemeanor. Chase felt a surge of emotion, equally compounded of anger, frustration, and disgust. He told himself he pitied her, but knew that wasn't quite true. He wanted to believe himself immune to all she represented, but knew that too was a lie. The mask of godliness, indeed.

"That would explain why the doorkeeper sent me to speak to you, miss," he said finally. "He didn't seem to think your mistress would care to encounter a police officer." Chase gestured at the Bible. "You're fond of the Good Book, Miss Belinda?"

"I...I suppose," she said in surprise. "There's one in every room here, and we have prayers morning and evening in the parlor downstairs."

Chase digested this. It fit, of course, with what he'd learned of the murdered man thus far. But just who was Dick Ransom, and what sort of rig had he been running? He wondered too what the purportedly religious Ransom had made of this place and especially this girl. Apparently, he had not objected to her company. Nothing's simple in this life, he reflected wryly, especially when a whore looks like someone's young sister. Or a Raphael Madonna.

"You ever hear of the prophetess called Rebecca Barnwell?" he said conversationally.

"Why, yes. Like I said, my mistress is a devout woman, and I believe Miss Barnwell is a friend of hers. There's really nothing more to tell, sir. Mr. Ransom is a gentleman, always courteous and well spoken, but I don't know him, not really. We've spent an evening or two in one another's company, that's all. Now, you must go, or you will land me in difficulties."

"No harm done, miss. I've no doubt Mrs. Gore guards her treasures most carefully." He kept his eyes on her face. "And yet perhaps Ransom was one of the few men in the world who could be trusted to be alone in a room with someone like you?"

A tiny smile curved her lips. "I wouldn't be so certain about that, Mr. Chase."

Thanking her, Chase opened the door and stepped into the deserted hallway, glad to escape the closeness of the chamber and its occupant. As he descended the staircase, he caught the sound of voices and the chink of silver and glassware coming from the dining room. He'd timed his visit well, and now, if luck would hold, he could be on his way with none the wiser. He would be back, but it suited him to postpone his interview with the madam for now.

❧

In the entry, he nodded pleasantly to the doorman, pressed another coin in his palm, and waited while he opened the door. Emerging into King's Place, he strode down the street, scarcely noticing the light rain that trickled from a lowering sky.

Turning his thoughts to the dinner he had missed again, and to his bad knee that always ached in the damp, Chase pondered the evening ahead, sighing, though he enjoyed the company of a fire and a good book as well as any man. Then, from behind, rapid footsteps approached, and Chase glanced back, glimpsing two familiar figures, one tall, one shorter, carrying a cane.

When they saw him looking, the taller man cried out, "Mr. Chase! Hold a moment, sir."

He stopped, waited for them to draw level. "Here you are again, gentlemen. This time let us hope you will linger long enough to make your business clear. How do you know my name?"

"The porter of the house you just visited told us," gasped the taller man, whose ears, like the last time, were pink with the cold. "A friend of ours wants a word with you, so if you'll come with us—" He stepped closer.

Chase felt a prickle of unease. "I don't think so," he responded politely. "You see, I am late for a dinner engagement. Perhaps another time. If you will provide your card, sir?"

For an answer, the man reached out to grab Chase's arm. Chase wrenched away and shoved him to one side. He came back, fists swinging, catching Chase a blow to the side of his face. For a moment, his vision blurred, just long enough for the man to twist Chase's arm behind his back, cruelly twisting his wrist.

In response, Chase lifted his heavy boot and smashed backwards, catching his attacker's shin. Off balance, the man loosened his grip, and with his other hand, Chase was able to fumble for the pistol in his pocket.

But as his fingers started to pull it free, the other man stepped forward and raised his cane. His first blow caught Chase square in the kneecap; the second struck him across the temple.

❦

As Chase's assailants dragged him down the street and thrust him into a waiting carriage, he was dimly aware of everything that happened to him, the pain in his knee like some ferocious fire licking at the doors of his mind. On the other hand, he was not there at all, but instead stood on the deck of a ship on his way across the Atlantic to see Jonathan and Abigail, watching the rise and fall of the black waves which somehow got all mixed up with the swaying and painful jolting of the coach.

After a time, he realized that the blackness in front of his eyes was not the sea at all, only a bit of cloth tied around his eyes. Then he heard someone say, "My God, look at him. I didn't think I hit him that hard."

"Not bad for a little rat like you, eh Dobbin?" said another voice.

"Shut up, the both of you," said a third man in amused, far more cultured tones in which Chase thought he detected a faint Irish lilt. "No names, as I told you. He will wake soon." Chase strove to keep his face blank, though he must have made some sign, for the gentleman said after a moment, "Ah, I do believe he has returned to us. Help him up, and offer him this."

Rough hands pulled him to a sitting position against the luxuriously soft cushions. A flask was thrust under his nose, and a fiery liquid trickled into his mouth. Coughing, he reached up to try to push aside the blindfold, catching in the process one fragmented glimpse of a high-colored, handsome countenance. He felt stale breath on his face as he was shoved back roughly, his blindfold tightened, his hands bound with a rope, tightly, so that the sensitive skin on the inside of his wrists burned in protest.

"I do apologize, Mr. Chase," the voice said softly. "I'm afraid these two oafs misunderstood my instructions. No bones appear to be broken, though you will likely find yourself a bit bruised. Are you better now?"

"The blow has aggravated an old navy injury," he croaked in reply and gingerly straightened his leg, relieved to note that the pain had receded to a more manageable level.

"I am the more sorry then. Give him some room, fools." To Chase's relief the hot breath withdrew.

Chase said, "I think you had best explain yourself, whoever you are, and remove these bonds. No coercion is necessary, you know. I would have been most happy to speak with you."

"Let's just say it was necessary that we make assurance double sure. These men are officially employed, Mr. Chase. On special assignment, actually, though I'm not really at liberty to provide all the details. I am privy to only a few of them myself."

Chase was suddenly very wide awake indeed. "Who are you, sir? What do they, and you, want with me?"

"You've been very clever in the Ransom matter thus far, Mr. Chase. More clever than expected. But I do believe we should prefer you forgot you ever found your way to that brothel. Truthfully, you have stumbled upon a matter of grave importance to us all, to every true-blooded Englishman, in fact."

"You've acted quickly, sir. How did you happen to be on hand to intercept me?"

"We've been watching the house, of course. It was luck, I suppose, that there was time to fetch me so that I could deliver my little warning in person. Now, you must be content to leave this business to those who have it well in hand. I am certain you can understand the danger of a feint in the dark?"

"I can. Which is why I must insist that you illuminate the matter for me. I seek only to do my job, sir, the job for which I am paid."

"A duty you have performed well." Chase heard the rustle of the man's clothing, a distinct click, then the chink of coins.

Rage obliterated his discomfort and fear. "Do not think to bribe me. I take blood money from no one. No matter who Dick Ransom truly was, he deserves that his murderer should be found—and punished."

"You are a stubborn man and, as I said, a clever one, Mr. Chase, but you've got the shoe on the wrong horse. Poor Dick's death was most unfortunate, but there is far more at stake here than you realize."

"Dick? You knew him?"

"Oh, very well. We were good friends, and no one can regret his loss more than I."

"Sir!" cried the one called Dobbin.

"Not to worry. Our friend of Bow Street does not understand, and I see it will take a little more to satisfy him. Mr. Chase, I feel confident that His Majesty's government can reply upon your discretion. Let me remind you again that these are uncertain times. We believe there is a scheme brewing that may well be poisonous, fatal, to us all. There are dangerous men anxious to stir the broth. I can put it no more clearly than that."

"Men like Dick Ransom?" he replied, trying one of his feints in the dark.

Chase's ears caught the indrawn breath. "You are unwise, Mr. Chase. You must realize that the villains will stop at nothing. They've murdered Dick for all that he was a friend to them."

"What is this danger, this conspiracy of which you speak?"

But his captor had apparently yanked the pull to alert the driver, for the carriage came to an abrupt halt. Hands plucked Chase from his seat, and he felt the cold air on his face. He was sent sprawling to the pavement.

The soft voice floated out after him. "Remember, Mr. Chase. You have been warned."

⌘

Chase lay in his bed, so angry he couldn't rest despite the fact that his bruised body desperately craved sleep. He had managed to eject Mrs. Beeks after allowing her to fuss over him for several hours. She had bathed the scratches on his face and arms and smoothed foul-smelling ointment all over him, but he'd growled and pushed her away with a harsh word once she turned her attention to his viciously swollen knee. He had also refused her laudanum, which still sat on the table within reach, calling him.

He felt sorry for his rudeness now, sorry too that he had not let Mrs. Beeks summon a surgeon. He remembered the last time his knee had been hurt like this, when Abigail had tended him after the battle of Aboukir; she had saved his leg, he always thought. Then she had loved him, bedded him, and become pregnant with his child, refusing nonetheless to marry him when the idyll ended. Well, she wasn't here to help him now.

The knowledge that he would be lying here for some days was bitter, for he was certain that had been the intention of those men, to tie him by the heels until his ardor should have cooled, until he returned to work no doubt to find new and more pressing business awaiting him. Why should he care then to pursue the death of a mysterious footman, especially since he'd been instructed to leave the matter in other, more capable hands?

Ah, but they had miscalculated, did not really know him. The mysterious footman interested him more than ever, his death of far greater moment than the domestic affair or robbery he had first envisaged. Chase knew he must discover what Ransom with his reputed criminal connections had been doing in St. James's Square, that respectable bastion of the aristocracy.

Recalling the conversation about the hazelnuts Sir Roger had reported, Chase wondered if Ransom had meant to deliver some sort of threat. But of what? There was also the lovely Julia, Lady Ashe, of whom Ransom was said to have been enamored, wed to a much older husband. And the female intruder, fortuitously released from custody, who might or might not possess knowledge of the crime. And finally the prophetess Rebecca Barnwell—what role did she play in this drama? Surely, it would not be difficult for Chase to locate a public figure such as she.

The man called Dobbin had been right that his master had spoken too freely, for if there were some foul conspiracy afoot, John Chase was not the man to turn away from it.

❧ ❧

March slipped by, and still Mr. Chase did not come to St. James's Square. Penelope had wrapped up the little dagger carefully and put it in her drawer to keep it safe. She did not mention the matter to Julia, nor to Sir Roger, though she watched the baronet surreptitiously and wondered why he had never spoken of the loss of his property.

In truth, Penelope watched everyone in that strange household, feeling herself like a bit actor set down in the midst of a play for which no one had bothered to give her the script. It was hard not to be aware of the whispers, for the society women did not scruple to gossip behind their fans even when Lady Ashe's companion was within hearing. Julia took too much wine, they said, laughed too loudly, flirted too outrageously, angered her husband with her enormous gambling losses and, worse, her inability to produce an heir after six or seven years of marriage.

Julia and her husband often went days without seeing one another, which was not unusual in their station. On occasion, both would dine at home, and then Ashe would make everyone uncomfortable with a series of barbed comments, masked as pleasantries, aimed at his wife's extravagance, her "French" volatility, her forgetfulness.

Or Julia would dress herself in her prettiest gown to seek out her husband's company, then flounce back an hour later and spend the rest of the day alternately crying how she loved him and raving about his coldness toward her. Once, entering the sitting room, Penelope came upon them, Julia sitting on the carpet at her lord's feet, arms clasped about his knees. As Ashe looked up to meet Penelope's gaze, he lifted one finger to his wife's cheek and stroked downward, his eyes empty.

There were also times when Julia would abandon high spirits to turn abruptly mumpish and solitary, deciding at the last moment not to attend a much-anticipated party in favor of an evening spent nursing a headache in her bedchamber with orders she not be disturbed. Penelope could not comprehend her.

So it went on until an encounter in the Park which only strengthened Penelope's determination to leave her situation. She met her cousin Gideon Sandford, a man she'd never met but whom she recognized immediately from his resemblance to her father. Tall and rather spare with an ascetic face and heavy-lidded blue eyes, he had approached to greet Julia's companion, a Mr. Ogden. Their conversation complete, he turned toward Penelope, apparently having caught her startled eyes on his face.

"Ma'am?" he said, bowing.

Mr. Ogden performed the introductions, a little vaguely for Penelope could see he didn't quite recall her name. Afterwards, obeying an impulse she feared she might regret, she found a moment to say quietly to Mr. Sandford, "I see you do not know me, and there's no wonder, sir, for we have never met. I am Penelope Wolfe. My father is Eustace Sandford, you see, which makes you my—"

"Cousin," he broke in, a smile spreading over his face. "My father has often spoken of yours and regretted the rift between our families. But I suppose the distance…may I hope your father has at long last returned to his native shores?"

"No, indeed sir. I believe he intends to make Sicily his permanent home. I myself only came to England after my marriage. My husband is fixed in Ireland at present, so I am fortunate enough to find a place as Lady Ashe's companion and a home for my young daughter." Stumbling a little over the words, she felt the heat mount in her cheeks. She might have added that she had received only two letters from her father in the prior twelve-month and missed him terribly, especially in Jeremy's absence.

"I see," Mr. Sandford replied after a short silence. He glanced toward Julia, who had her hand on Mr. Ogden's sleeve and was smiling into his face and chattering away. Her voice carried that note of desperate gaiety that always made Penelope wince.

Mr. Sandford looked grave, seeming to debate with himself. All he said, however, was, "My father and mother rarely leave the country these days, but you must come and see me and my wife in Brook Street, Mrs. Wolfe. We should be most pleased to welcome you, I hope for a visit of some duration. And, of course, you must bring your little girl if you are not afraid to trust her amongst our wild brood." Smiling, he took her hand again, but there was no time for more, for Julia, not seeming to notice Penelope was engaged, had allowed the groom to assist her to mount into the driving seat of her stylish phaeton.

Julia continued to insist Penelope accompany her on these excursions into society, for the Season was in full swing now with a bewildering round of balls, routs, assemblies, and visits to the theatre or opera. Wrestling with her pride, Penelope told herself it didn't matter a snap if perfect strangers saw her dressed as a dowdy. She was the companion, after all, and therefore blessedly invisible much of the time.

In any event, no matter where they went these days, the name on everyone's lips, the focus of everyone's attention, was Byron, the young, compellingly handsome nobleman who had just published the first two volumes of a poem called *Childe Harold's Pilgrimage*.

Penelope stayed up into the night reading Julia's copy and found much of exotic color and whimsicality in the poem's exploration of the East. Nor could she deny the appeal of the hero, the world-weary outcast, the fallen angel, racing toward perdition as if all the hounds of hell were on his heels. Yes, both the poet and his creation intrigued her, though the swooning girls and predatory hostesses scheming to get the newest sensation into their drawing rooms filled her with disgust.

Entering her chamber one evening to fetch a shawl, Penelope found a gown laid out on her bed. It was of pale green sarsenet, shot with white, and of walking length. The bodice and back were of white lace, the three quarter length sleeves also trimmed in lace, and a band of blue embroidered ribband encircled the waist. Next to the gown, wrapped in tissue paper, were white kid gloves and a pair of slippers. A card was included which read, *"I beg you will accept these trifles with my sincere friendship and appreciation. Julia."*

Penelope stood for a long time, gazing down at the dress. It had been so long since she'd possessed anything new, anything this fine. For a moment she was back in Sicily, a young lady again with an armload of dresses and no more taxing duty than serving as her father's hostess at his famous dinners. Then as Julia entered the room, Penelope turned, blinking back the tears that had sprung to her eyes.

"Do you like it?" Julia said, her face eager, full of hope.

Penelope opened her mouth to tell her of course she liked it, but she really couldn't accept anything so expensive. Instead, she found herself saying, "It's lovely, ma'am, and I thank you."

"Come, you must try it on." In no time, she had Penelope stripped to her shift and stockings. Pulling the gown over her head, Julia smoothed it down, then unceremoniously swung Penelope around to fasten the row of tiny white buttons at the back.

"I think perhaps a looser hair style," she said thoughtfully, studying their two faces in the dressing table mirror. "You know, you have the most delicious brown eyes I have ever seen. Your hair is pretty too, such a rich color, but you really mustn't scrape it back like that."

"I don't like it to flutter about."

"No?" Her hands brushed up and down Penelope's arms, which looked quite brown in contrast to my lady's fairness. Feeling the gooseflesh rise on her skin, Penelope felt a strange lassitude. How pleasant it would be to live like this always, she thought dreamily, the scent of Julia's perfume overwhelming her senses, the soft embrace surrounding her.

Julia smiled at her in the glass, then dropped a light kiss on her forehead. Standing back, she clapped her hands. "Let me look at you. Famous! You may wear the dress tomorrow to Lady Caroline's morning reception at Melbourne House to practice the waltz. Give me no nonsense about not knowing the steps, for that is why we go, to practice. And who knows, perhaps we will be so fortunate as to meet *him* there."

"Surely Lord Byron does not dance," was all Penelope could find to say.

Chapter X

The boiled beef was tough, the mutton not much better. The port wine was passable, but always in short supply as someone invariably consumed more than his fair share of the allotment. And while once Buckler might have deemed it quaint to dine on wooden trenchers and sip his wine from green earthenware pots, he now thought the whole business a confounded nuisance.

Add to these discomforts that the ancient refectory of the Knights Templar was draught-ridden and smoky, the louvres above the massive hearth in the center of the Hall providing only imperfect ventilation. In inclement weather, the wooden bell cupola let in the rain. Worst of all, Buckler often wondered if the high roof supported by pointed and heavy timber arches might one day tumble about their ears. He could just imagine a Bencher rising stoically from the rubble to exclaim, "Gentlemen, I represent to you that the repair and renovation of this Hall must henceforth be our chief concern."

Such was "keeping commons" in the Inner Temple: students of the law dining at least a fortnight of each term in Hall, eventually completing twelve terms to become eligible for the Bar. As fully qualified barrister, Buckler was not strictly required to attend, but often did anyway. Dimly, he sensed that participation in this communal activity was good for him, for the conversations, occasionally thought-provoking, often trivial and irritating, brought him out of himself.

On this particular evening a dialogue of the latter variety had erupted of which Buckler found himself the unwilling focus. It was begun by Leonard Crouch, a barrister who could be counted on to serve up the latest gossip at table with all the skill of a blunt-axed executioner. Buckler had no doubt Crouch believed it his duty to enliven the proceedings; still he wished that the man's entertainment might be got at someone else's expense.

"You've nothing to say, old boy?" another man named Rutherford said after a time. "That, of course, lends rather more credence to this foolishness than it might otherwise have had. Surely, you'll tell *us* the whole."

"That he won't do," said Crouch, grinning evilly. "No true gentleman ever tattles. But as far as I'm concerned, silence is an admission of guilt. Anyway there were several witnesses…"

Rumor of his visit to Penelope Wolfe in St. James's Square had reached the Temple, via one of the other morning callers, who, unbelievably, was some sort of relation to Crouch. Now Crouch amused himself and anyone within earshot with a series of broad references to a certain coy lady and her "willing" soul that needed only a little more encouragement. The bastard was literate, you had to hand him that, damn him. *And while thy willing soul transpires/At every pore with instant fires,/Now let us sport us while we may…*

Another voice broke into Buckler's thoughts. "You're a sly one, sir. I wouldn't have figured you for the type."

"According to hearsay, the pretty, little er…widow had eyes for no one else in the room," remarked Crouch with arch disapproval. "Got your blood up, Buckler?"

Buckler ignored them, turning instead to strike up a conversation with his neighbor on the other side, an earnest, fresh-faced young man, newly called to the Bar. This served for a time, at least until the replies to Buckler's polite queries became monosyllabic as the younger barrister addressed himself to his beef.

Having bided his time, Crouch broke in. "Buckler," he said, "I must counsel caution. I understand the lady is no widow at all but rather a deserted wife whose husband can be counted on to spoil the fun one fine day. Perhaps you will favor us with your opinion of the relative merits of swords versus pistols? Fighting with a blade must be thought sadly old-fashioned, but it does have a certain cachet that blowing a hole in one's opponent quite lacks. Do you not agree?"

Buckler took a frugal gulp of his port before replying. "As I'll never have to make such a decision, I couldn't say, Crouch. You may know better."

"I?" he said, throwing a glance around the table. "You do me too much honor, sir. I have never yet been out, nor am like to. I fancy myself a peace-loving sort of fellow and have no need to prove my mettle thus, I assure you. Not to mention that I have far too much respect for the sacred bonds of matrimony ever to come between a man and his wife." He gave a cringing, unctuous laugh.

Buckler felt his face grow hot, but he fought to keep his anger from showing. The gibes didn't bother him on his own account, but he found that he did mind, terribly, hearing a crass fool like Crouch bandy about Penelope's name.

He let the expectation deepen, then said, "I never supposed you'd actually participated in an affair of honor, much less one inspired of passion, Crouch. Despite your obvious talents, I should imagine that passion is not a challenge to which you would ever *rise*."

Cracks of laughter greeted this sally, and several of the Benchers looked over curiously from their table. Crouch was, for the moment, silenced.

Finally, the meal wound to a close, an under-butler bringing out the bowls of rose water the diners used to wash their hands. A few minutes later, Buckler made his way to the exit, but paused in the doorway to exchange a few words with a colleague. Crouch soon joined them.

"Stopping to admire the Rysbrack?" he asked jovially. "A fine piece, what?" He pointed above the doorway at the white marble carving of the Pegasus, the Inner Temple's perennial symbol.

Buckler's companion gave Crouch a blank look, blurted an excuse, and moved away. With a sigh, Buckler said, "Well?"

"One further word with you, sir. It is ever my way to beguile the dinner hour with pleasantries. I trust you've not taken my wit amiss?"

Buckler lifted his brows, forcing a smile. "Think nothing of it."

"It doesn't do, you see, to set someone's back up to no purpose. One never knows when an acquaintance may prove an asset in some matter of business."

"Long-headed of you, I must say," replied Buckler, not troubling to disguise the irony in his tone. He went down the stairs and out into early evening with Crouch on his heels. The day lingered, and the ancient round church near the Hall glowed serenely in the last of the golden light. Catching sight of his master, Ruff lurched to his feet, shook himself violently, and fawned at Buckler's feet.

"Hello, old chap," he murmured and bent to pat the dog, turning his back on Crouch with relief and forgetting him almost at once. Buckler's momentary anger had evaporated, and he was left instead to ponder, with some dismay, why putting a bullet through the elusive Mr. Jeremy Wolfe had not seemed so unreasonable a course of action.

❧ ❧

As Edward Buckler's notoriously unreliable long case clock chimed the hour, he surveyed his chambers with a discontent that had little to do with faded upholstery and dusty books, though he vowed silently once again to give the old place a good turning out before the month was out.

"Listen to this, Buckler. They've placed an advertisement as they don't wish to impose upon the Publick." A plume of smoke from Thorogood's pipe rose up from behind the newspaper he held before his face. His toes were stretched to the fire, a glass of punch gently steaming on the table next to him.

Buckler's clerk, Bob, set aside his quill. "'Tis said a lady of rank has given Miss Barnwell a crib costing two hundred pounds. Satinwood ornamented with gold and gilt lattice work. There's a cloth at the head bearing a celestial crown of gold and a blue satin canopy."

"Good Lord. They've all lost their wits, the so-called prophetess most of all."

Thorogood lowered the paper to reveal a face full of mischief. "*Nullum magnum ingenium sine mixtura dementiae fuit*, my dear Buckler. There has been no great genius without a touch of insanity. You see, she has it on the good authority of her guiding Spirit that this year, in the forty-seventh year of her age, she shall give birth to a Son who shall be called Shiloh. He's to be a sort of king, I take it, to prepare the world for the Second Advent."

Buckler had to laugh. After Leonard Crouch's version of dinner table conversation, his friend's company was welcome relief. Still, he knew it was only a matter of time before Thorogood came to the real point of his visit, which, Buckler well knew, was to determine if the promised visit to Mrs. Wolfe had been paid.

"When is this miraculous babe to make his appearance?"

"Soon," said Thorogood. "The lady, of 'obscure and humble origins,' we are informed, has gone into seclusion to prepare for her accouchement. Listen. The *Times* has printed a letter from a clergyman recently converted to the cause. He feels a strong conviction that great events will soon sweep the face of the earth. After the period of bloodshed and chaos already upon us, a time will arrive when all mankind will live in peace and brotherly love, 'the sword to be turned to a ploughshare, the spear to a pruning hook, and the poor man to get his bread without the sweat of his brow.'"

"I like the sound of that," said Bob, putting down his pen again and giving the pile of papers on the desk a contemptuous push.

"Vastly overworked, aren't you, Bob?" said Buckler dryly. "Perhaps I ought, in all justice, to release you from this servitude."

"Or increase his wages." Thorogood lifted the paper again, continuing a moment later, his voice rather muffled. "So, Buckler, speaking of servitude, you've yet to tell me how you found our friend Mrs. Wolfe. She is well, I trust, and not beating her wings against the bars of the gilded cage?"

"What makes you think I already paid the call?"

He snorted. "I knew my proposal would prove irresistible. What did you discover?"

"More than you had anticipated, old man. Of that I am certain." Describing the murder and subsequent events in St. James's Square, Buckler was human enough to enjoy the expression of pure astonishment on his friend's face.

"Just today," Buckler went on, "I received a note from Mrs. Wolfe. In some questionable manner, she has managed to obtain a little dagger she thinks may be the murder weapon, and apparently John Chase has been making himself scarce."

"Penelope knows how to look after herself, never fear. Nonetheless, I suppose you should pay her another visit. And someone ought to make a push to locate this female with her wits gone a-begging."

"She may have thrown herself in the river for all I can do about it, what with the world coming to an end and all that. Seems a popular enough idea these days."

"I never took you for a millenarian, Buckler."

Buckler drained his punch and gazed into the fire, suddenly thoughtful as he recalled the restraint marks Penelope had reported seeing on the old woman's wrists.

"The world ends for someone every day, every hour," he said at last. "But unwilling as I am to admit it, you've given me an idea. Where, after all, does one go to seek a mind diseased?"

Pausing in front of the iron gates, Buckler contemplated the two recumbent stone figures atop the piers, one in chains to represent raving madness caused by an excess of blood and yellow choler, the other melancholy, the result of too much black bile. He supposed it said a lot about a man's character as to which form his madness might take.

The porter who waited at the small side entrance watched him incuriously, then lowered his head to examine the paper, signed by one of the governors, that Buckler had presented.

"If you'll follow me, sir," he said when satisfied.

Buckler stepped through the entrance and accompanied the man up the sweep. The palatial building of stone and brick stretched out before them, a long frontage with a protruding wing at either end, the whole embellished with foliages and decorative work. Buckler recalled that the structure was modeled on the Tuileries in Paris, an insult which Louis XIV was said to have felt keenly. As they approached, however, it became clear that the Hospital of St. Mary of Bethlehem, popularly known as Bedlam, found itself in a ruinous state, made obvious by the presence of scaffolding, fractures, uneven walls, and areas of settlement.

"We'll be moving to St. George's fields as soon as the new hospital can be built," said Buckler's guide, having read his thoughts with accuracy.

Buckler forbore to comment, for as they entered the hall, a man came forward to greet them. In his late forties, he wore the dress of a gentleman and carried himself with a swaggering sort of authority. "Good day, sir. Our steward is otherwise engaged, so I shall myself inquire as to your business. I am John Haslam, apothecary here."

"Good day, Mr. Haslam. I am Edward Buckler." He held out his hand, which the apothecary took rather warily, then offered his piece of paper. "Here is my letter of introduction from one of your governors, Mr. Justice Burns. I am seeking a poor, mad woman I had hoped might have come in your way."

"'Tis usual for a governor to accompany you himself on any visits to the Hospital. We cannot allow outsiders to disturb our routines or upset our patients," replied Haslam, his eyes still on the letter.

Buckler bowed. "I shall not trouble you for long, sir. Perhaps you might just check your records. To tell you the truth, there's so little to go on it is unlikely you will be able to assist me."

"Who is this woman you seek, and why do you seek her?"

Why indeed? When Buckler had broached the notion of this visit to Bedlam, he had sensed Thorogood's unease. And although the old lawyer was too wise to express his misgivings, Buckler had understood it all. Thorogood deemed Buckler's mental state too fragile to sustain a visit to the madhouse. In the last year Buckler had suffered several bouts of melancholy that had confined him to his bed for days at a time. He himself could not fathom the origin of this misery, for there was nothing particularly awry with his life other than a moribund career and a persistent feeling of separateness from his fellow creatures that often threatened to overwhelm him with its bitterness.

Now, studying the apothecary, who awaited his answer with obvious impatience, Buckler realized how foolish he had been to come. The chances of learning anything to the purpose were practically non-existent. On the other hand, as he looked around the sunlit, spacious hall, he was relieved to note that no thought of the hospital's hidden horrors disturbed him. He might look upon the wretches who lived out their lives between these walls with no deeper emotion than pity.

He smiled at Haslam. "I dare say I have come on a fool's errand. I am a barrister of the Inner Temple, sir. The woman I seek is poor and plain and very likely deranged. She bears the marks of restraints on her wrists, from which I have deduced she might once have been confined in a place such as this. The authorities believe she may have knowledge of a murder."

"How do you come into the matter, Mr. Buckler?" Haslam inquired, his interest sharpening. "I have had occasion to testify at criminal trials, offering up my years of experience earned in the field of mad doctoring. Is that why you are here? Are you employed in the defense of some unfortunate lunatic?"

"No, sir. I am here in no official capacity. The murder occurred in the home where a friend of mine currently resides. I merely follow a hunch to satisfy my own curiosity and to lend whatever assistance to my friend that is practicable."

After the apothecary had studied him in silence a moment, he seemed to come to a decision. "As it turns out, you may be in luck, sir, though I promise nothing, mind, and it may just be a rather odd coincidence." He laughed once, scornfully, at Buckler's mystified air and motioned for him to follow.

They ascended the stairs, Haslam saying over his shoulder, "I am sure you will not be disturbed by a bit of a rumpus, sir. The inmates do tend to drum their feet and sing and halloo. We restrain them only as necessary to prevent them from committing any violence. I can truly declare that by gentleness of manner and kindness of treatment, I have never failed to obtain the confidence of insane persons."

Passing through an iron grate into the female gallery, they were indeed buffeted with a din which Haslam ignored, though Buckler shivered with his first apprehension at the unmistakable sound of chains rattling against the floorboards. They continued past an open chamber where he had a clear view of about ten women, each chained by one arm to the wall, some standing, others slouching over a bench that permitted them their only rest. He caught a glimpse of heavy breasts spilling out of the blanket covering one woman wore and saw her mouth contort in a grimace as she noticed him looking in her direction.

At the entrance to one of the cells, they meet a keeper, a burly, hard-eyed man, carrying a bucket of water.

"How is she today?" inquired Haslam.

"About as usual. I've given her a bit of a wash, sir, and done her feet. You mean to vomit her?"

"Not today. We'll just go in and have a word."

A naked woman, dark haired and plain, lay chained to a pallet in a corner of the room. Haslam motioned Buckler forward and went himself to kneel at the woman's side. He picked up her blanket gown and threw it over her as she twisted her head away and closed her eyes. "I know you can hear me, Dora. I've brought someone to see you. Sit up now and make your greetings."

"A visitor?" she quavered. The straw rustled as he pulled her to a sitting position. She opened her eyes, her gaze flying to Buckler, who had lowered himself next to the apothecary. "Can it be possible? Oh, sir, are you of the nuptial party come to fetch me?"

Haslam sighed. "She believes she is to be wed to Jesus Christ, who will arrive with his prophet Isaiah and raise her to His Kingdom. I had hoped we might reach some remnants of reason, but I fear not. Answer her, sir, calmly and firmly. There are still moments when sense returns to her."

Buckler found himself taking the hand she stretched out toward him, a profound pity choking his throat. "No, Dora. I am not the person for whom you wait."

Her eyes closed again, tears trickling down her lined cheeks. "I know I can never be worthy for all that He is so good to me."

Haslam said, "You had a visitor not too long since, Dora. A woman, was it? I recall the keeper mentioning the matter. She was not permitted to see you, but she did charge us with a message for you."

There was a long pause before Dora said dully without looking at them again, "Yes. My friend." Withdrawing her hand, she began to rock back and forth, dragging her chain across the straw as she swayed.

"I cannot tell you if this female is the woman you seek, Mr. Buckler, but she did fit your description, the scarring at the wrists and all, so I thought it worth a try." Haslam reached forward to shake her and went on more sharply, "Dora, tell the gentleman about your friend. Did you make her acquaintance at the school where you were once employed, or perhaps at the other asylum?" He turned to Buckler. "Dora came to us from a private establishment in Islington. Her family was no longer able to pay the piper, I understand, as is often the case. I don't believe she will answer us, sir."

"Leave her."

He wanted nothing so much as to depart this place and had risen to his feet when Dora suddenly looked at him again, smiling through her tears. "Oh, she is far more worthy than I to be espoused to Our Lord. And she brought news. At long last there is to be a child!"

Throughout the morning, Rebecca had managed to ignore the nagging ache in her back as she and the Mistress knelt together, raising hearts and voices to God. Rebecca studied her companion with satisfaction. Lady Wallace-Crag's sallow cheeks were flushed, her eyes glowing, for it was clear the power of prayer had allowed richer, more nourishing blood to flow through her pallid veins.

Reaching out to Rebecca, she said, "Thank you, my dear. You have done me good as usual." She bowed her head over their clasped hands, then looked up, saying with a forced smile, "I must tell you my monthly courses arrived this morning. The Lord has not seen fit to answer me."

"He will in His own time, madam. It is not for us to question."

"Yes…well, you are right, of course, but it is hard all the same to endure my maid's pity and Roger's questioning looks. Do you think if we—"

At the sound of a knock on the door, she broke off in annoyance and rose stiffly. "I told them we were not to be disturbed."

Rebecca stood too, swaying a little on her feet. She felt the baby give an odd little kick. "No matter, ma'am. I must return to my chamber and pursue my meditations."

And rest, she thought. These days she had no real duties, other than acting as spiritual advisor to the Mistress and certain of the maidservants who crept up to her new attic room to consult her in secret. Rebecca found that she relished the role and had grown almost to love Sir Roger's wife, though she was vaguely troubled by the implacability of the shadows that surrounded this rich yet unhappy woman. Rebecca did her best to banish them, but they were strong and full of impending doom, like death with no hope for resurrection.

Rebecca was more at ease about Julia, who had a bright-faced new nursemaid. While she missed the child, she did not mind doing without the constant demands on her own time and energies. Lord Ashe continued to be a frequent visitor, but the Master must have dropped a word in his ear, as Rebecca had been told that he kept his distance from the nursery. Once, when she had encountered Ashe in the corridor, he sent her a black look that promised retaliation if the chance ever presented itself. Secure in the Mistress' favor, she had told herself not to regard him.

Entering the room, the secretary Owen Finch gave a respectful bow. "The Master asks that you have a word with Mrs. Dobson about the dinner, ma'am. Lord Ashe will be staying, as will Sir Roger's man-of-business from London."

"Thank you, Mr. Finch." Sighing, the Mistress turned to Rebecca. "Return to me this afternoon after dinner, if that will suit."

Rebecca inclined her head. "Of course, madam." As the Mistress went out of the room, Rebecca stooped to snuff the candles burning on the low table that served as their altar. Picking up her Bible, she turned to go, but Finch blocked the doorway.

"I've a message for you as well. You are to pack your things. A carriage will arrive for you after nightfall. There is naught to fear. The Master has made arrangements for your care."

"I'll not be sent away like a thief in the night."

"You must go willingly," Finch went on, his voice pleading. "Surely you see the necessity. My lady would be humiliated if she knew the truth, and you could be hurt if you are not careful."

"I'm sure I do not know what you mean, sir. If you will excuse me." She moved toward him, intending to brush past and make her escape, but he did not budge.

"That is not all. If you refused to see reason, Sir Roger bid me say he would speak to you in private. There are too many listening ears here. He would like to take you up in his carriage for a short drive, say about six o'clock? Meet him in front of the gatehouse."

She gave a scornful laugh. "I am to venture abroad in my condition? I think not, sir. Let him come to me here at Cayhill if he so desires."

"Six o'clock," repeated Finch.

At the appointed hour, Rebecca waited, wrapped in a cloak against the chill. The ache in her back had intensified, and her eyes burned with fatigue. She had not been able to sleep, nor had she eaten any of the dinner sent up on a tray.

Telling herself she now belonged to God, she had nearly disregarded the Master's summons. And yet she was conscious of a treacherous gladness at the prospect of seeing him alone. She knew he should have been her champion, not his wife. He had failed her, but for all that the heart does not so easily withdraw its tenderness.

From here, at the head of the drive lined by massive oaks, she could not see the house. The gatehouse keeper, an old man, deaf and somnolent, was likely dozing by his fire, and the whispering of the trees filled her ears. Then she heard the rumble of wheels on gravel.

The coach jerked to a halt, the horses' breath steaming gently in the luminous early evening air. As if embarrassed, the driver kept his face turned away. With a prickle of unease, Rebecca studied him. He was the wrong shape to be John Coachman, and the carriage itself, mud-bespattered and shabby, looked strangely wrong too. Before she could pursue this thought, a figure leaped out of the trees at her back to seize her.

"Come, girl," a man's voice snarled. "You're to take a journey." Plucking her up as if she were a feather-weight, the man threw open the door of the coach and tossed her inside. "That's for your cursed impudence," he said as the door slammed shut. Rebecca lay against the floorboards, stunned.

The carriage moved off, and slowly, painfully, Rebecca struggled to lift herself. She had felt something shift within her, had felt the hot liquid gushing out between her legs, soaking into her skirt. She moaned as a terrible, wracking pain convulsed her frame.

And there appeared a great wonder in heaven; a woman clothed with the sun, and the moon under her feet, and upon her head a crown of twelve stars. And she being with child cried, travailing in birth, and pained to be delivered...

For a time the jolting over the deeply rutted track so beset her that she could do no more than brace her hands against the seat and chant an incoherent prayer. The pains came faster, harder, the evil swirling around her, a miasma that made it difficult to think or breathe. Demons howled in her ears, poked her, prodded her, laughing maniacally as she sobbed her fear. Rebecca sank into a stupor, only rousing when a short time later she heard a loud crack and the carriage wrenched to the left.

When her most recent spasm had passed, Rebecca held her breath, listening. The demons were silent now, but she heard the man curse. Crawling to the lower of the two windows, she peered out to see that they had stopped in the middle of the narrow track, the coach leaning drunkenly to one side. A wheel had broken, she judged. Perhaps God had answered her, after all, for the coachman would be occupied with his predicament, and she might have a chance of slipping away through the trees.

Rebecca opened the door to peer through the gap. Craning her neck, she glimpsed two dusty booted feet near the horses' heads, and again, she heard the coachman, murmuring reassurance to the beasts that whickered and tossed their manes. She did not wait. Gingerly, she thrust the door wide and lowered her body through the opening, her feet finding the ground below. Heart in mouth, she fled across the track and into the forest, rewarded by no pursuit in her wake.

But a few yards farther, the pains came upon her again, and she fell to her knees in the undergrowth, scoring face and hands on a thorny shrub so that a trickle of blood traced a pattern down her cheek. The solid world faded. She was afloat in a sea of pain, the demons back to torment her with their taunts and jabs and hideous cries. And they were not alone; their master had joined them. She sensed his presence, vast and black, lurking just beyond her range of vision. He wanted her child, she realized with a shiver of pure terror.

> *And there appeared another wonder in heaven; and behold a great red dragon, having seven heads and ten horns, and seven crowns upon his heads. And his tail drew the third part of the stars of heaven, and did cast them to the earth: and the dragon stood before the woman which was ready to be delivered, for to devour her child as soon as it was born...*

Heedless of the thorns, Rebecca grasped the shrub and hauled herself upright. Panting heavily, one hand clutching her stomach, she ran, frantically slapping away the branches that reached out to hinder her progress. The demons howled in anguish and gave chase.

Stumbling out of the wood, she found herself on an open plain. Just ahead she beheld several yew trees, black against the darkening sky, with a smaller copse of hazel in their shadow. She moved toward the hazel shrubs that gleamed whitish red, beckoning her. At this season, the nuts were ripe for the picking and eating straight from the tree. Rebecca's hand shot out. It was the work of a moment to grab a handful, which she slid into her apron pocket. For protection, she told herself, recalling the hazelnut necklace she had helped Miss Julia fashion for her mother.

Just as the pains took her again, the demons were at her shoulder. Their hot breath scorched her ear, and their cruel claws dug into the tender skin at the back of her neck. They meant to hold her until *he* arrived. With a cry of determination, Rebecca ripped herself free. She knew she must keep moving or she would be lost, but the pain was pulling her in two. She managed a few steps and thought she could not go on. Then, looking up, she saw the old ruined church and realized for the first time where she was.

People called this an accursed place, and yet what choice had she? It was shelter of a sort, despite its bare, roofless walls, and perhaps something of God's power lingered in the very stones. Rebecca kept her eyes fixed on the crumbling tower as she pushed herself the last few paces. Once inside, she found a corner, spread her cloak, and lay down, giving herself to the agony of birth.

Outside, the demons roared their disapproval, but Rebecca scarcely heard them. She knew they would rouse their courage and come inside to torment her soon enough. She hoped the babe might come first.

After that, everything became confused. It seemed she battled the demons, at first one by one, then in hordes. Their master watched from a distance, amused, biding his time. Somehow she beat the demons off, growing weaker and weaker. The pains wracked her, split her open like over-ripe fruit. Sure she was going to die, she summoned her will one last time to push. The demons faded. Rebecca thought she heard music, angels singing, and then the faint, mewling wail of an infant. Gasping, she subsided onto her hard couch.

And she brought forth a man child, who was to rule all nations with a rod of iron: and her child was caught up unto God, and to his throne...

Much later, she awoke to a familiar face bending over her. "The Lord save us from all evil," said Jack Willard, the gamekeeper's son. As his hands moved down her body to tug down her skirt over her nakedness, his features contorted in a grimace of disgust.

Pushing him aside, Rebecca sat up and gazed around wildly. "Where is my child?"

Chapter XI

"You must come along and dance with Penelope," said Julia the next morning to Edward Buckler, whom they encountered in the hall as they were on the point of setting out for Melbourne House.

"I wouldn't think of it." Buckler avoided Penelope's gaze, retaining a grip on his hat, of which the butler had been attempting to relieve him. "I wanted a word with Mrs. Wolfe, that's all. I shall take myself off and hope to find you in another day."

"That won't do, sir," Julia returned smilingly. "We have need of your escort. You will find, Mr. Buckler, that no one in that house will look askance at an unexpected guest. I should be very much surprised, in fact, if your presence is even remarked upon."

After a few more protests, he was driven to bow his compliance, though Penelope saw his unease and wanted to throttle Julia. Edward Buckler was of good family, she knew, but would not aspire to such heights as Melbourne House, despite Julia's blithe assurance that Lady Caro's husband had himself been called to the Bar before turning to politics upon the death of his elder brother. Still, Penelope doubted Buckler would be acquainted with a soul there.

Julia kept up a flow of conversation during the short drive to Whitehall, and soon enough they were deposited in front of the massive pile of rusticated stone that was the London mansion of the aristocratic Lamb family.

As they proceeded through the portico and into a large rotunda to mount the steps ascending to the drawing rooms above, Penelope felt her palms moisten despite the comfort of her new gown. Hearing the music, voices, and laughter, she wished, fervently, that she had braved Julia's displeasure and remained at home.

But this proved to be an informal gathering, their hostess a laughing young woman, golden-haired and slight as a boy, who flitted from one end of the three interconnected rooms to the other, bantering daringly with her guests. Julia managed to detain her long enough to effect an introduction.

"A pleasure, Mrs. Wolfe," Lady Caro drawled. Seeing that her hostess' large, dark eyes had already wandered, Penelope curtseyed again and stepped back.

They were in the salon set aside for dancing, where some two dozen couples whirled about the space that had been cleared by furniture pushed against the walls. Penelope followed Lady Caro's restless gaze to a young man who leaned against the wall, observing the dancing.

"Who is that?" asked Buckler in a low tone.

Penelope studied him. His skin was of marble pallor, hands beringed, hair a mass of dark reddish curls that tumbled over his forehead. His lips revealed a disdain he often sought to hide, it seemed, by raising a hand to cover his mouth. He was strikingly handsome, but a little petulant.

"I fancy that is Lord Byron."

"The poet? He looks as if he has the indigestion," said Buckler indifferently. "Mrs. Wolfe, I'm sure you are wondering why I called. It's about that woman, the one apprehended in Sir Roger's garden. I may have word of her."

She turned to face him, realizing in that instant that she hadn't truly looked at him today. He too was handsome in his morning dress of buff trousers, blue coat, and top boots, a man, she suddenly realized, not a boy. He was studying her, eyes bright and amused.

"Tell me at once. Have you informed Mr. Chase?"

"I did send a message to Bow Street but have received no reply."

Before she could answer, Julia swept up, her arm tucked in that of her latest cavalier, some gentleman Penelope did not recognize, not that it mattered for they were all essentially alike.

"You do mean to dance with Penelope, sir?"

Buckler grinned. "Of course, ma'am, if she will so favor me." He bowed to Penelope, adding in an undertone, "That is if that poet fellow will cease his glowering in our direction."

"He does not appear to approve of the pastime," Penelope agreed, observing the way the poet's eyes followed their hostess as Lady Caro slid into the arms of her partner. The poet was said to be lame and presumably could not dance himself, so perhaps that accounted for his frowning looks. Penelope would not regard him.

Suddenly lighthearted, she placed her hand in Buckler's, allowing herself to be led to the floor. She did not know the steps of the waltz, but, watching the others, had seen that it was nothing so very difficult, after all. The blood sang with the tempo of it; the body moved almost of its own volition. After a moment or two of awkwardness, she and Buckler were gliding smoothly, Penelope feeling the warmth of his arm at her waist, his hand clasping hers.

She sensed no real danger, was merely enjoying herself thoroughly, until she looked up. There was no trace of the earlier amusement in his eyes but instead a kind of raw intensity that made her begin to tremble.

For a moment Penelope couldn't speak as they stared at one another. Through a tight throat, she said, "What of the woman, sir? You were about to explain when we were interrupted."

His grip tightened. "Later, Mrs. Wolfe. I need to mind my steps."

As Buckler led Penelope from the floor, she saw that Lord
Byron, looking faintly bored but willing to play his part,
was now engaged in conversation with Julia. In contrast,
Julia's face was alight with mischief, and, as she leaned over
to address the poet, her plump breasts strained against the
diaphanous material of her gown. She seemed to have
forgotten her earlier escort, who, Penelope imagined, would
have been relegated to a corner to watch.

As Buckler and Penelope passed, she broke off in mid-
sentence, calling out, "I see you enjoyed your dance together."

Buckler bowed. "Thank you, yes." He would have
continued on without intruding further, but Julia motioned
them over in a friendly fashion.

"Mr. Buckler is a barrister, sir, and a friend of my companion, Mrs. Wolfe." Gracefully, she completed the introductions.

Curtseying, Penelope slanted a glance at the poet. Up
close, he seemed less the sulky little boy. She thought there
was obvious intelligence in his eyes as well as a kind of wry
self-mockery. "I have enjoyed reading your poem," she said,
"and I can well understand the appeal of your hero for those
who have no intention of attempting new experiences. All
the benefits without the risks."

Byron's eyebrows rose. "I take it you do not class yourself
in that category, ma'am."

⟋⟍

"Steady. Give me your left foot," said Sir Roger from below.
He grasped Penelope's ankle and guided it to the rung of
the makeshift wooden ladder.

"I've got it now. Thank you." Embarrassed, she maintained her grip on the flimsy ladder while her other foot
dangled rather unpleasantly over the ten-foot hole in the
pavement and hoped that she wasn't giving him an immodest
view. After a moment, her foot found purchase, and the rest
of the journey down was easily accomplished.

Wallace-Crag beamed at her. "Brava, ma'am. Now, shall we have a look? We'll never have a like opportunity. They'll break it to pieces when they take it up, you mark my words."

He turned away without further ado to busy himself on his hands and knees. Penelope noticed that he first spread a wide handkerchief on which to kneel so that he wouldn't soil his trousers. Amused, she noticed too that he spared no thought for how she would manage, for he was mysteriously unafflicted by the inborn gallantry of the gentleman. He ignored her, in fact.

She lowered herself to an awkward crouch, lifting her dress with one hand. And immediately the sense of being enclosed intensified as she gazed up dirt walls stretching toward a sky that seemed a long way off. They were in a large space, perhaps thirteen or fourteen feet square, below the carriageway. The traffic from Leadenhall Street murmured softly as if the bustle of people about their business had no place down here. The hole was bitterly cold and damp. Penelope huddled closer into her pelisse.

"Quite, quite wonderful." He glanced toward her with another brilliant smile. "Come here, Mrs. Wolfe."

She straightened and moved nearer to him. They were looking at a large piece of Roman tessellated pavement that workmen had discovered in digging for a sewer opposite the East India House portico. And her companion was correct: the mosaic *was* awe-inspiring.

Inside the design's central circle an exquisitely rendered figure of Bacchus reposed on a tiger's back. He wore a wreath of vine leaves on his head and a mantle of purple and green over his shoulder. From one hand dangled a drinking cup; the other gripped his thyrsus, a wand tipped with a pine cone.

"How did the artist achieve the coloring, sir?"

"By the use of about twenty different tints. Most of the mosaic is composed of baked earths, but the more vivid colors, such as those in Bacchus' mantle, are glass."

Wallace-Crag took Penelope's fingers in a quick, impersonal grip and brushed them lightly across the surface. "See how noble his bearing, how serene his countenance," he went on in the same exultant tone, his ruddy complexion more flushed than usual. "Bacchus has displayed that precise expression for over fifteen hundred years whether there was anyone to look upon him or no. He cares nothing for our paltry response to his magnificence."

"No more he should," replied Penelope softly. "But one does not usually associate serenity with Bacchus. Was he not a rather riotous god who encouraged free indulgence in wine?"

"And in other things. Yet he also has a more serious aspect. As Dionysus he is associated with the goat ritually torn asunder to ensure the land's fertility. The people used hazel twigs to bind the vines sacred to Bacchus to stakes. Any goats found feeding on the god's vines were to be captured and sacrificed."

"These people must have had a profound belief in the efficacy of their ritual."

"Oh, they did, Mrs. Wolfe. You are wise to view it in that light. Most today shun the very thought of religious ecstasy, at least in England. When my wife died, I recall being struck by the aridness of the pastor's eulogy. Our clergymen never dare to ride the tiger—" He broke off as if he'd said more than he intended.

"I understand completely," said Penelope with warm sympathy. "When my mother died in Sicily, her memorial was conducted by a Catholic priest. My father said it was a far more moving and fitting occasion than would have been usual here." She hesitated. "How unfortunate to lose your wife so young. I am sorry, Sir Roger."

He ran an absent hand through his short, graying hair. He was still an attractive man, Penelope thought, his features smooth and appealing, his eyes radiating an intelligence that was fluid and flexible, yet also detached.

"Every man has a time in his life when the darkness is absolute, and that was mine. I had such hopes of an heir."

She looked at him curiously. What of the woman herself, she thought. Had he mourned her loss? "How dreadful. Have you never considered marrying again, sir?"

"No, for you see, I have my books and my work to occupy me, and I suppose I have grown accustomed to my own company. It was all a very long time ago, even if not quite so distant in time as the creation of this lovely treasure." His voice dropped. "I had hoped Julia would give me a fine grandson of my own blood, but perhaps…"

Shaking his head as if to rid himself of unpleasant thoughts, he turned back to his examinations. Penelope said, "Sir Roger, to speak of a treasure, I've been meaning to ask you about your little Celtic knife. I noticed you've been using a different letter opener. Have you lost the knife?" She was aware of how odd and abrupt the question sounded.

"I must have misplaced it."

"We should consider the possibility that whoever murdered poor Dick may have taken your knife to use as a weapon. If that is so, this villain must have had access to the house." Glancing at him from under her lashes, she surprised a flicker of dismay followed by a mask of determined nonchalance.

He said lightly, "I believe, ma'am, you would do well to confine your curiosity to the past and its glorious secrets. I would not wish you to alarm Julia."

"Did you note any other signs of disturbance, sir? Perhaps Mr. Chase observed something?"

"I did not tell him about the knife. Mrs. Wolfe, I ask you again to leave it alone."

"Today, Lady Ashe and I attended a waltzing party in the company of Mr. Edward Buckler. He has interested himself in the matter of Ransom's death and has hit upon the theory that the woman who trespassed in your garden is one Rebecca Barnwell, a female prophetess. It seems—"

"You don't understand, or you would do as I ask at once. There are reasons, my dear, that I won't trouble you with just now. Look here, there are details in the pavement you simply must not miss."

Unwillingly, Penelope allowed herself to be guided through an examination of one of the borders around the central circle that exhibited a sinuous serpent, black with a white belly. Sir Roger removed a diary and pencil from his pocket and began to make notes and a rough sketch as if their conversation had never occurred. And yet she had been watching his face as she spoke and knew she had not imagined the apprehension that had overcome him at the mention of Miss Barnwell.

After a moment, he spoke. "Since I leave for the country in a few days, I shall commission Finch to come back here and make another drawing for the engraver."

"You truly think the mosaic will be destroyed?"

He shrugged. "I am told the Company intends to place it in its library. Let us hope the extraction is handled with delicacy."

A few minutes later they stood above ground. Clerks swarmed in and out of the enormous sprawl of East India House. A man walked by with a bag of game purchased at nearby Leadenhall Market. Several Jews in long, black coats and wide-brimmed fur hats passed on their way to the synagogue down the street. Penelope drew in great lungfuls of air, finding herself glad to be up in the world again.

Sir Roger offered his arm. "Would you care to view an altogether different sort of tiger?" he inquired with a mischievous grin.

"That must depend on the sort you mean and its relative proximity."

Chuckling, he led her toward the entrance to East India House. "Since we're here, it would seem a shame for you to miss the Oriental Repository. It contains artifacts the Company has collected in India over the years such as weapons, musical instruments, a silver howdah, and, of course, its chief attraction, the Man-Tiger-Organ."

"That sounds distinctly ominous. No doubt it will give me nightmares."

His keen eyes swept her face. "I shouldn't think so. You seem to be made of more resilient fiber than that. The Man-Tiger Organ is a mechanism created by an Indian called Tippoo Sahib, who was killed during the capture of Seringapatam. He abhorred the British."

"I suppose the tiger jumps out at one or something similarly horrid?"

"No. The mechanism presents the sounds and sights of a tiger making mincemeat of a red-coated Englishman. From the Indian perspective, that is highly appropriate, even profound. Here, however, it degenerates to absurdity. Which, of course, is why we're going to see it."

Penelope lifted her brows in question. "After admiring an ancient Roman mosaic, you feel the need for tomfoolery?"

He nodded, his eyes suddenly serious. "Ah, but that is just the point. A wise man always follows the sublime with farce."

⊱⊰

Penelope found Timberlake in the butler's pantry, a narrow stone-flagged chamber furnished with an enormous press that housed the establishment's collection of plate, glassware, and silver.

After a stiff exchange of greetings, she said, "Did you know that Sir Roger's letter knife has gone missing?"

The silence lengthened as he stared down his nose at her, his nostril hairs fluttering as he exhaled. She wanted to shake him. Penelope got on better with Timberlake than with Mrs. Sterling, but it irked her when he hid behind his stately exterior. The closest she had ever seen him come to a purely human response was in the aftermath of Dick's murder.

"May I inquire why you should concern yourself with such matters, Mrs. Wolfe?"

"I must say I feel uneasy at the thought of a murderer in the house. 'Twas bad enough that whoever it was attacked poor Dick in the garden outside my window. I still have nightmares about it."

"Not to worry," he replied, seeming to appreciate this show of feminine sensibility. "I have added new bolts to the doors and many of the windows. Not that there's any reason to fear further disturbance, but it pays to be careful. You may rest easily, ma'am."

She opened her eyes wide, fixing them on his face. "But what if the villain is someone yet within these walls?"

"Stuff and nonsense, ma'am. Who do you imagine it can be? It's plain as day that Ransom had taken up with ill company. He and his cohorts planned a robbery, and you see how the scoundrels repaid him. They would not dare to return."

"What of the knife, Mr. Timberlake? Nothing but that was missing."

He held up a silver ladle to the waning light. "You have no proof the letter opener was stolen, ma'am. You know how forgetful Sir Roger is. Perhaps he has merely misplaced it."

Penelope considered, then rejected, the notion of telling the butler about the incident at Covent Garden Market. Instead, she said, "Why should Sir Roger keep silent about the loss of his property? When I inquired, he seemed…reluctant to speak of the matter, especially after I mentioned the woman apprehended in the garden."

From the doorway, Mrs. Sterling suddenly spoke. "No doubt he has his reasons."

Starting violently, Penelope wondered how long the woman had been standing there. Her little cat feet went everywhere in this house as she delighted in terrorizing the maids. Penelope had to force herself to nod pleasantly. "Good afternoon, ma'am."

The housekeeper approached with a rustle of her black bombazine skirts. "You refer to Sir Roger's little Celtic letter blade? Well, that is interesting. But he is a gentleman, after all, Mrs. Wolfe, and a true gentleman always keeps mum when it comes to protecting a female in his charge. 'Tis a trait bred in them from birth."

Timberlake cleared his throat. "You will excuse me, Mrs. Wolfe? I have much to do to prepare for dinner this evening, and I am sure Mrs. Sterling likewise has duties that await her."

"Indeed I do. You are quite right, Mr. Timberlake." She glanced around as if seeking some excuse for having entered the room and, finding none, took a step toward the door.

"Mrs. Sterling," said Penelope. "I must beg you to speak your mind plainly. It has long been evident to me that you are no friend to Lady Ashe, but this sort of innuendo is the outside of enough."

The older woman swung back to face Penelope, the strings of her cap a-quiver with indignation, her cheeks reddening. "How dare you speak to me thus. You are no better than she, and the good Lord knows that is bad enough. Don't you play off your fine lady airs on me, ma'am." She glanced at the butler, who was shaking his head. "No, Mr. Timberlake, I won't be gainsaid. There's wickedness afoot in this house, and I won't be a party to it, not even if it costs me my place."

"You believe that Sir Roger is protecting his daughter?" said Penelope slowly. "What is it you imagine she's done?"

"Imagine? I imagine nothing. Ask her ladyship's abigail. She'll tell you. Lady Ashe was not safe tucked up in her bed that night or many other a night either. You ask Miss Poole about the cloak she found stuffed under the counterpane where it had no business to be. Damp it was. You ask her how the mistress cried herself to sleep for days after that low footman died. Don't tell me I imagine *that*, Mrs. Wolfe."

For a moment Penelope was too appalled to respond. The virulence of this woman's spite was something altogether beyond her experience, yet Penelope could not help but believe the housekeeper spoke the truth as she saw it. She was ignorant and hateful, but not false. And what she said made a horrible kind of sense.

Penelope groped for words. "What precisely are you saying, Mrs. Sterling—that Lady Ashe went out that night to meet Dick?"

She gave an angry shrug. "How should I know? But he was trouble long before he turned up dead. Oh, he played the servant well enough, but he got above himself. If you ask me, he seemed a deal too curious about his betters, always asking questions about the family."

Penelope would have liked to press further, but Timberlake looked like he was about to have an apoplexy. Quietly, she said, "You need not fear I will convey your accusations to Lady Ashe. Your place is safe, so far as I am concerned. But I must ask you not to repeat your charges to anyone else, ma'am. You take your bread of this family, and I'm sure you would not wish to be unjust."

At that, Penelope hurried from the room and went upstairs to fetch her wrap. Though there would be little daylight left, she suddenly felt she would go mad if she did not escape. Once outside in the shrubbery, she marched up and down, moving briskly to keep warm. Could it be true? Had Julia and Ransom been lovers? Had she slipped from her chamber to meet him that night, perhaps here where the candle grease had been found? Then who had murdered Dick? Surely the culprit could not be Julia, who seemed to mourn him truly. But then Penelope recalled the look in Lord Ashe's eyes as he stroked his wife's cheek and shivered.

Finding after a while that her thoughts gave her no peace, she hurried through the shadowy garden and in the side door. She would go up the servants' stairs to avoid encountering any of the family and play a while with Sarah before dressing for dinner, though how she was to sit at table with these people without revealing her doubts and fears, Penelope had no notion.

In the corridor outside her room, she met Sarah accompanied by the nursemaid. "There you are ma'am," she said cheerfully. "Miss Sarah and I have been down to the kitchen for a bit of gingerbread and a chat with Cook. She fair dotes on the child."

"Thank you, Mary. I'll take her now."

Sarah had bounded inside to be met by a glow of warmth. Apparently, the upstairs maid had already been by to tend the fire, which was not enough, however, to banish the gloom. Penelope lit some candles, then carried the candelabra over to the table to light several more.

Dancing over to the bed, Sarah exclaimed, "The maid has laid out your dress for you, Mama. Oh, it's your pretty one. Oh no, Mama. Look!"

Penelope moved swiftly to her side. "What is it, darling?"

One glance told her the tale, for someone had taken scissors or a knife to the green sarsenet, slashing in long, uneven strokes down the front of the skirt. The beautiful lace bodice, too, was cut to pieces.

Chapter XII

One of Wren's churches rebuilt after the Great Fire, St. Matthew's was a plain structure of modest proportions on Friday Street near St. Paul's Cathedral. In the west a low brick tower nestled against the skyline; the east end fronted the street where John Chase stood. He saw that the book-seller's stall still sat near the church, not far from the more prosperous establishments that congregated in St. Paul's churchyard.

The proprietor watched Chase approach. About Chase's own age, he was a harsh-featured mulatto, a stocky figure in nankeen trousers, a blue coat with anchor buttons, and an old leather hat. In addition to the seditious tracts, broadsheets, and bawdy prints spread over his table, he offered a pile of old clothes. A small sign advertised his services "however trifling" to any passerby in need of a patch or a darn.

The son of a Jamaican sugar plantation owner and an African-born house slave, Abel Purcell had served under Chase in the West Indies. Afterwards, Purcell had joined the ranks of other former sailors scrambling, often unsuccessfully, for a living. As to what had reduced him to street peddling, Chase had no clue, but he was hopeful that someone of Purcell's much vaunted political views might be of help to him now.

"Good day, Purcell. You will remember me, I believe."

Purcell's gloom did not lighten. "I do at that, Mr. Chase of Bow Street, though it's been some years since you happened by. One does not forget an old navy man, however. Your injury, sir? Seems that leg is yet a mite stiff."

Chase shrugged. "I get on. And you?"

"Well enough for the present." He had been leaning against the wall. Now he straightened, and Chase glimpsed for the first time a chalking on the church wall behind him: *No Orders in Council, No King, No Parliament. Bread or Blood.* And under that, in another hand, was scrawled: *Prince Regent damd Raskel We have his life before long.*

"Your work?" said Chase sternly.

The ubiquitous wall chalkings around the city incensed the Home Office, but there was no real way to combat them. In the past few months, Chase had seen many such protests directed at the roundly despised Orders in Council, a set of trade restrictions intended to combat Napoleon's blockade. These same Orders in Council seemed likely to provoke the Americans into outright war. The people's anger did not surprise Chase, nor did their contempt for the dissolute Prince Regent, who was vastly unpopular with his subjects.

Purcell gave a small smile. "No sir. 'Twas a gift like. I found it when I set up shop this morning. What can I do for you today?"

"I seek word of a man named Dick Ransom."

"I know of this man, but whether I would do right to speak of him to you is another matter. He is an agent of mankind, a warrior in the Cause of Truth. You and your kind do but seek to silence him."

"He is silenced already. If you wish to see his murderer brought to justice, you must help me."

"Murdered?" The lines around his mouth hardened. "Look to your Home Office spies. They'd think nothing of putting period to a man's life to save the Crown the trouble of locking him up."

"You may, in fact, have the right of it. I promise I intend to learn the truth, regardless. Will you help me?"

He waited while the print seller busied himself among his wares, as there between them lay the time Chase had saved gunner Purcell a flogging for some misdeed he had not committed. Chase understood full well that the man would not thank him for the unspoken reminder but that his rigid system of morality dictated its acknowledgment.

At length the stationer looked up. "Ransom heads a sort of debating society of shoemakers, printers, and other tradesmen, known as the Free Britons. They draw up petitions, sell tracts, and hold tavern meetings. Sing their songs, propose a few toasts to Natural Rights."

"Treason, you mean? Armed insurrection? I have heard that the Jacobins would even go so far as to countenance French delusions of conquering England."

"Nothing of the kind, so far as I've heard, though many see Napoleon as Liberator. At any rate, *you* may call it Treason." He surveyed Chase out of black, flashing eyes. "I am of a different mind, sir, for what allegiance does a man owe to a Government that betrays its citizens into want, neglect, and misery? Have we not the duty to take our axe to the root of this Corruption?"

"Know you anything further of Ransom's history?"

"He was journeyman tailor, as once was I before the hard times came," he said proudly. "Ransom was apprenticed to a breeches maker. Wild, liked to kick up a rumpus with the drink and prostitutes, yet they say he quieted down, found God and his convictions. They call him the Dark Prince, you know, like Lucifer, the fallen angel, who knew what it was to sin and could be counted on not to cut up too rusty with a fellow. The officers on his committee are known as the twelve Apostles."

"Where does this committee meet?"

The eyes fell. "Any number of places, I should imagine. Public houses. He is said to have raised divisions all over the metropolis, men to be called on when the time is ripe."

Ripe for what, Chase wondered, his unease growing. He had always been inclined to dismiss the Jacobins as so many loons, too full of their own importance, too disorganized, and too ineffectual to be of much harm, but perhaps he had been wrong. "Give me a name, Purcell. You knew of Ransom. You must have heard the name of at least one of these so-called Apostles."

"Can't say as I have."

Drawing a deep breath, Chase tried again. "You say Ransom found God. Are you aware of any connection he might have had to a female Methodist called Rebecca Barnwell? Ransom possessed one of her salvation seals. It may be that she is at the heart of these schemes and plots."

"The West Country Prophetess?" said Purcell, his face going still. "I wouldn't know about that either, sir."

Chase reached out to grip the man's arm. "These are dangerous times. A man like you can ill afford to bring down the wrath of the authorities on his head."

Shaking him off, Purcell bent down to retrieve a few prints that had been knocked to the ground. "What do I care? I have nothing to lose," he said bitterly. He met Chase's look with defiance. "I have helped you as much as I can, sir. You may consider my debt paid in full."

❦

Snarling something about Chase's lack of a warrant, the porter at the Westminster brothel slammed the door in his face. Clearly, the man had received his instructions, Chase thought, as he strode off down the street, ignoring the glances from passersby who took one look at his set face and gave him a wide berth.

Several hours later saw him no further along in his inquiries. Jaunts to several Barnwellian chapels in Southwark had yielded the information that Miss Barnwell's residence in the metropolis was a closely guarded secret, as her followers would give her no peace were they to discover the woman of God in their midst. When Chase had inquired about Dick Ransom, he had received responses varying from blank incomprehension to indignation to outright ridicule that God's handmaiden could be involved in something so sordid as murder.

Instead, he had been treated to glowing accounts of the imminent birth of the Savior and had shoved in his hand the tracts describing the "powerful visitation" of the Spirit that had quickened her womb. One woman attempted to sob down his coat, further exacerbating his sorely tried temper. And Chase's efforts to discover more of Ransom's debating society had met with no better success. After speaking to close-mouthed, suspicious tavern-keepers at half a dozen unsavory establishments, he was forced to admit defeat.

In the mellowing light of late afternoon when the soot-stained buildings were painted a temporarily brighter hue, Chase entered Bow Street office to find the veteran Runner John Townsend observing the proceedings with a benevolent air. Occupied with his attendance at Court, the Bank of England, the Opera House, and various haunts of fashion, Townsend was rarely to be seen at the police office, but liked occasionally to turn up and lord it over his erstwhile colleagues. Chase nodded and would have continued on his way to the Bench had not the older man lifted a peremptory hand.

"Mr. Chase. I hear you've been a trifle down pin. Feeling more the thing? I believe Mr. Read requires an officer to execute a warrant upon a baker or some such presumptuous insect who thinks to fight a duel."

Chase eyed the portly figure in its knee breeches, gaiters, and white hat. "You are too kind, sir. No doubt you find yourself too much engaged to attend to the matter?"

"I? Surely you jest, my dear sir. I who have the privilege of attendance upon dukes and earls, and who have intervened in many an *aristocratic* affair of honor? Let the baker fight if he likes it, but don't let me be so degraded."

"It is fortunate the rest of us aren't so nice in our notions. You will excuse me, sir?"

"Delay one instant, Mr. Chase. I have it in mind to impart a bit of advice regarding the footman with a knife to his heart in St. James's Square. You ought to have consulted me, bless you, sir, you really ought. 'Tis said the Home Office is not best pleased."

"What do you know of the matter, Townsend?"

He offered an unctuous smile that revealed his yellowed teeth. "I chanced to encounter a certain gentleman of fashion, shall we say, and he was kind enough to give me the hint. You are treading on some important toes."

Chase gazed into the other Runner's face as his hands clenched involuntarily at his sides. "I repeat. What do you know of the matter?"

"The proprietress of a certain…establishment had a word with my noble friend. Stupid of you. Gentlemen never wish their pleasures interfered with."

"I've traced the slain footman to that brothel, Townsend, and stumbled onto some sort of Jacobin plot."

"Nonsense. I cannot in all discretion say more, but you can take it from me that the patrons of the establishment in question are men of the highest order and respectability. Why, I have been there myself."

"That makes all square then," said Chase savagely.

"Surely, sir, there is business enough to share amongst the lot of you fellows? Why do you not seek it out and let the Home Office worry about its plots and counterplots. No profit for you and much danger of offending those whose favor a prudent man would do well to curry."

"As you have done, Townsend?"

He shook his head. "You ought to realize that your poor efforts in the profession can never hope to equal *mine*, my dear sir, but you might at least consent to take a lesson from the man who wrote the book."

"Excuse me, sirs," said a quiet voice, and Chase turned to find a man standing close enough to breathe in his face. His nose aquiline, his eyes large and intense, the owner of the voice had close-cropped hair and looked the gentleman in a light brown surtout and striped yellow waistcoat. Taking a step back, Chase gave a polite nod.

"Yes?"

"I am John Bellingham. I ask you to conduct me to the magistrate Mr. Read, who has had a letter of me to which I require my answer."

Chase glanced up at the Bench, where the magistrate was clearly occupied hearing testimony. "Perhaps you may leave a message, sir?"

Bellingham stiffened. "I will not be fobbed off. His Majesty's Government has endeavored to close the door of justice in my face, but, through the offices of Mr. Read, I shall once more solicit the Ministers to do what is right and proper on my behalf."

Before Chase could reply, Townsend stuck a finger in the man's neatly tied cravat. "Be off with you. Mr. Read has mentioned your name to me and showed me your letter. Beware, sir. It has been conveyed to members of the Government who will know well what to make of such as you."

"What's this about?" demanded Chase.

"He's a malingerer." Townsend took out his snuffbox and inhaled a large pinch with evident enjoyment. "He claims the government owes him redress for his own mistakes in business."

"Heed me well," said Bellingham, the dark blood staining his cheeks. "If I do not receive satisfaction, I shall hold myself ready to execute justice."

Townsend dusted the snuff from his sleeve. "My dear sir, you positively terrify me."

❧ ❧

Chase managed to exchange a few words with the chief magistrate, who, impatiently dismissing the subject of the murder in St. James's Square as well as any "crack-brained" fears about Jacobin plots, sent him off to execute the warrant on the baker. Chase could not know whether the magistrate's reticence stemmed from a word in the ear from above, as seemed possible.

Having bound over the strutting rooster of a baker to keep the peace and stopped at a chophouse for an extremely late luncheon, Chase decided to pay a call upon Mrs. Wolfe. It had been several weeks since he'd seen her, and he wanted to discover if her considerable powers of observation had turned up any information that might be of use in his inquiry. There had to be some reason Ransom had chosen Sir Roger Wallace-Crag's establishment to work incognito as a footman, for John Chase could not believe in the existence of a far-flung conspiracy amongst the London servants of the aristocracy.

"I cannot say if Mrs. Wolfe is at liberty to receive you," said Timberlake, taking the greatcoat Chase thrust in his arms with poorly concealed distaste. "Should you wish me to inquire?"

"Yes, I wish you to do precisely that."

The butler left him standing in the hall but returned about ten minutes later as Chase tapped one finger against a suit of armor that stood amongst the busts and marbles.

Timberlake frowned. "Come this way, sir. Mrs. Wolfe will see you in the morning room."

He led Chase into a pleasantly appointed chamber with faded but pretty hangings in floral silk, a matching sofa and chairs, and a lady's writing table. Apparently, Wallace-Crag had never attempted to implement his notion of interior décor here, as the room was obviously intended for the females in the family.

"Good afternoon, Mr. Chase," said Penelope, rising. Dismissing Timberlake with a smile, she poured Chase some tea from the service on the table in front of her and handed him the cup. While he took a chair, she perched on the sofa opposite.

"Where have you been, sir? I was afraid you had quite forgotten all about us. Other business keeping you occupied?"

"You might say so."

"I am glad you have come, for I have much to tell you," she said, her expression a curious mixture of trepidation and pride.

"Proceed." Chase's tone was more uncompromising than he'd intended, for his temper was still frayed.

"You don't seem especially interested, but it doesn't matter. What I have to show you will make you sit up fast enough."

"Why do I get the feeling you've been meddling?"

She looked down into her teacup. "You don't understand. Some situations are thrust upon one. There are opportunities that, once spurned, are forever lost."

"Some opportunities are meant to be spurned. Well, Mrs. Wolfe, let's not delay. Out with it."

Her hand went to the reticule attached to her wrist to extract a white handkerchief. She pulled back the material, but was careful not to touch the object inside with her bare fingers as, gingerly, she passed it to him. Nestled in the cloth was a smallish gold dagger.

"I believe this is the knife that killed Dick Ransom. It belongs to Sir Roger."

Launching into her story, she spoke rapidly, describing Buckler's encounter with the poor, mad Bedlamite and the barrister's rather unlikely theory that the garden intruder with the scarred wrists was none other than the prophetess Rebecca Barnwell whom all had read of in the newspapers.

This idea made Chase sit up, considering what he had learned of the prophetess. But once he had heard of Penelope's trip to the Market and absorbed the gist of her exchange with Wallace-Crag about his missing letter-opener, he was startled by a burst of anger so strong he felt his hands tremble. "You sought out this knife-seller when Sarah was with you?"

Guilt played over her mobile features. "I do assure you Sarah took no harm and was only a little frightened."

"By God, Mrs. Wolfe. Have you no sense, or are you too much the child yourself to realize what could have happened? The knife-seller might have turned nasty, so also the man who pursued you. What might he have done to you or your little girl had he wanted to play rough?"

"Really, Mr. Chase, as if a greengrocer would accost us at Covent Garden Market."

He was quiet a moment, trying to regain control. When he spoke, his voice was lower. "You don't understand, do you? You can't conceive of a world different from your own imaginings. It's a form of conceit, Mrs. Wolfe, and of sheer willful ignorance."

She stared at him, shocked, tears awash in her eyes. "You might never have recovered the murder weapon otherwise. The instructions were quite clear. I was to go, no one else. It is important, isn't it?"

Swearing inwardly, he handed her his handkerchief since hers was still wrapped around the dagger. She blew her nose loudly and turned again to face him, her back very straight despite pink nose and cheeks.

He said, "Never so important as your safety and that of the child. Leave the dirty work to me, Mrs. Wolfe. It is the job for which I am paid."

"I thought Bow Street Runners aimed to secure convictions at any cost. How else should they reap their rewards?"

Oddly, this remark hurt him. The Runners were London's elite force of constables. The public looked to Bow Street above the other seven public offices to solve the more complex crimes. Everyone knew a Runner worked for a profit, as his salary was in actuality only a retainer. The bulk of his income came from fees, the rewards for criminal convictions referred to as "blood money," and from gratuities. Still, these facts did not prove that greed was John Chase's sole motivator.

They gazed at one another in silence as the tea in their cups went cold.

Finally, Penelope said with obvious challenge, "You haven't said what you make of this woman, whoever she is, being in possession of Sir Roger's knife. Could she be the killer, think you?"

Chase held up the blade to the light. "I cannot say." Perhaps because he felt sorry for making her cry, he found himself describing his adventures since their last meeting and telling her of the Barnwellian seal, which, according to his fellow footman George, Dick Ransom had owned.

"Then Mr. Buckler may well be correct. You must locate this prophetess."

"I shall inquire again if anyone recalls seeing the woman in this vicinity. And I shall charge Sir Roger with his failure to report the loss of his dagger. Why should he withhold information that might help snare a murderess?"

"The woman is said to be simple," Penelope objected. "She didn't strike the knife-seller as dangerous in the least."

"Leave me to worry about Rebecca Barnwell."

Penelope stood abruptly. "As you wish, sir. You will excuse me?"

Standing to face her, he slipped the dagger into his pocket and gave her back her linen. She had not returned his. "Good afternoon, Mrs. Wolfe."

Her eyes did not waver. "One moment. You are correct that I was wrong to imperil Sarah, Mr. Chase, even if the danger was remote, but I've seen a great deal more than you realize.

I am, after all, a woman alone, answerable only to myself and responsible for my own and my daughter's well being."

"Nevertheless, you do expect, even demand, that the world be less squalid, less ugly than it is. And that makes you vulnerable."

Before she could frame her reply, he was gone.

Chapter XIII

Encountering the secretary Owen Finch in the corridor, Chase inquired, "Is your master at home?"

"No, sir. He is gone to Somerset House."

"Lord Ashe?"

"I couldn't say. Shall I inquire?"

He looked into the secretary's unsmiling countenance. "If you would, Mr. Finch."

When Finch ushered him into the library, Ashe glanced up from the letter he had been writing, nodded a curt dismissal at the secretary, and pointedly resumed his task. Chase stood some five minutes listening to the pen scratch across the paper. Deliberately, Ashe sanded and sealed his missive before he spoke. "Well?" he said coldly.

"I am come to offer my report, my lord."

"Save your breath. I have no intention of hearing it. In fact, consider yourself discharged, Mr. Chase. You may present your reckoning."

Placing both hands on the highly polished mahogany desk, Chase leaned forward. "What's this? There has been progress made, and I am not the man to leave a job half done."

"Your work is finished. We have no further need of your services. Now get out."

"I have discovered that your footman was a lying, treasonous Jacobin, my lord, guilty of some foul conspiracy against our government. He is entangled somehow with that West Country prophetess Rebecca Barnwell who anticipates an end to the world, a time when rich men like you will get their deserts. I should think you would wish to get to the bottom of this matter. To think of the taint touching your household, your womenfolk…your wife."

"You go too far, Chase," said Ashe, his brows snapping together. "I shall feel no compunction in reporting this insolence to your superiors."

Chase drew out the knife Penelope had given him. "The murder weapon, my lord. I'm told it belongs to your father-in-law."

As Ashe rose from his seat, his chair toppled to the carpet. He came round to grab Chase by the cravat. "Not another word," he ground out, yanking with surprising strength so that Chase lay half across the desk. Nostrils flared, Ashe stared into his eyes, then let go. Chase banged his cheek painfully on the corner of the desk and stumbled to his bad knee with a jarring thud. As a red rage clouded his vision, he listened to Ashe's labored breathing and imagined smashing his fist into the other man's jaw and disarranging that thin, sneering nose.

After a moment, he got to his feet. "I'll go, my lord, but be assured I am not through with this business."

Face white and strained, the secretary still hovered in the corridor. "Are you hurt?"

"Eavesdropping, Finch?" Chase was too tired to inject much heat into his tone.

"Sir, this conspiracy you spoke of. What does it portend? This…female, the prophetess. Do you believe a woman could be privy to a plot such as you describe?"

"You know of her?"

"Not really, just what anyone has heard. There *is* something, however. No, it is quite possible I am too fanciful."

The secretary shook his head, but as Chase merely waited, brows lifted in question, he at length stammered, "I heard what you told Lord Ashe about the prophetess. Could it be that Ransom had come under her influence?"

"What sort of influence did you have in mind?"

"I have often thought the authorities do not act decisively enough to put down religious enthusiasts, Mr. Chase. Such fanatics are a danger to everyone. Perhaps this female led Ransom to conspire against his master to further some wicked plot. And if it should be that the servants in other households are similarly vulnerable to corruption? We none of us would be safe."

Chase smiled wryly. "As Ransom was safe? That's the trouble with your theory, sir, for if Dick Ransom is the villain of this piece, who murdered him?"

⁂

As Penelope lifted her hand to knock at Lady Ashe's sitting room door, she heard raised voices and hesitated.

"Damn it, Julia. You will learn the behavior expected of a lady in your position, or I shall find a way to teach it to you."

"Keep away, you coward," came the reply, shrilly defiant yet with a genuine note of fear that crawled up Penelope's spine. "Oh, I learned what you are long ago."

"I'll kill you for humiliating me thus. How dare you embroil me in your sordid tricks. To think it was felt necessary to drop a warning in my ear about my wife. My *wife*."

Swift footsteps crossed the carpet, and Penelope heard a little cry, quickly suppressed. After a moment there was a sound as if something had toppled to the carpet. An ominous silence ensued.

Penelope backed away, intending to efface herself as quickly as possible, but instead found herself approaching the door again to knock. When Lord Ashe opened it almost immediately, she quailed at his expression, but forced herself to meet his gaze.

"I beg your pardon for disturbing you, my lord."

He bowed, standing aside for her to enter.

"Penelope," said Julia on a note of glad relief, "have you brought the flowers?" She was on her feet in the center of the room, an overturned chair at her back, embroidery frame at her feet.

Penelope glanced down at the basket she carried. "Yes, ma'am. Would you like me to arrange them now?"

"Do. This room needs a bit of color. You will excuse us, Ashe?" she added, pointedly avoiding his eyes. "I make no doubt you have many demands on your time today."

Without another word he turned on his heel and departed, closing the door with some force. Penelope and Julia were left staring at one another. Feeling hot color in her cheeks, Penelope crossed the room and righted the chair. Then she bent to retrieve the embroidery frame.

"Thank you," said Julia softly.

"'Tis nothing, my lady. I'll just go and fetch some water for the flowers before they begin to wilt."

"Wait, Penelope. I must just tell you—"

Feeling suddenly exhausted by all the emotional undercurrents in this house, Penelope could not bear for her to continue. John Chase had counseled her to mind her own affairs, and, at the moment, that seemed an eminently desirable notion. "Shall I ring for tea? I own I am thirsty after my battles with your gardener over which of his pretty blooms to cut."

Julia's hand came out to grasp hers. "I would have thought that you of all people would understand my difficulties," she said, her voice thickened with tears. "Yet you set yourself above me, judge me. You don't see, Mrs. Wolfe."

Just as abruptly, Penelope was ashamed. Julia knew enough about her companion's marital situation to realize this shaft would go home. And was it true? Did she keep the vain and frivolous Lady Ashe at arm's length because they were of such different worlds, or because they were, at bottom, much the same: two women who, having made unwise matches, lacked the moral constitution to make the best of them? Was that the source of Penelope's scarcely concealed impatience, her contempt that was, in truth, aimed at herself?

"I see you are unhappy, Julia, and, indeed, I am sorry for it."

"You have your Sarah, but I…I have nothing. Ashe reproaches me for seeking a bit of fun as if a few gowns and some debts of honor are anything to remark upon. He calls me barren, the barren wife who has failed in the one duty required of her." She laughed wildly. "How am I to bear a child of my own when much of the time he behaves as if I don't exist? The fool!"

"Ma'am?"

Julia shook her head, lifting one white, bejeweled hand to dash the tears from her eyes. "When I was small, I had a nurse who, I am certain, was the one person to love me. But she was sent away a year or two before my mother died in childbed. After that, there were only my father and Ashe who was always…there." She looked up. "You at least chose your fate, I believe, Mrs. Wolfe, so the responsibility for your marriage must be yours. I never chose mine. My father was determined to keep the property safe. I was to be brood mare to satisfy his desires and Ashe's. Never my own."

She dropped Penelope's hand. "Oh, I am so tired." Moving slowly to the door, she said over her shoulder, "I must go and have a rest. You will arrange those flowers?"

"Yes, I will. My lady, if I have failed to show proper gratitude for your many kindnesses…"

"You may keep your gratitude, Mrs. Wolfe. 'Twasn't that I asked of you."

The next day John Chase paid a visit to St. Mary of Bethlehem Hospital, despite the fact that he put little faith in Edward Buckler's theory. It seemed to him a wild supposition that Dora's visitor might actually have been the prophetess, and yet the significance of Barnwell's name cropping up yet again could not be denied.

Chase, however, was not granted an interview with the apothecary Haslam, dealing instead with the steward, a truculent individual who had no use for the Runners in general and no intention of allowing this one to address a patient. But Chase was able to wring from him Dora's surname, which was Lubbock, and also the name of the hospital in Islington where she had formerly been incarcerated.

This institution proved a pleasant surprise. Standing in the sun-bathed entry that contained a leather-bound book open on a table as well as an arrangement of fresh violets in a tall urn, Chase was kept waiting only a few minutes after he sent in his name. A surreptitious glance at the book informed him that this comprised a record of guests to the establishment, but he had time to peruse only the top page before he was joined by a portly, plump-cheeked gentleman in a black frock coat. He had round eyes alight with intelligence and good humor and a small, delicately molded nose and mouth.

"Good morning," said Chase, politely removing his hat.

"Ezra Broughty at your service, sir. I am physician at this establishment. Bow Street, eh? What can I do for you?"

"I understand you once had a patient called Dora Lubbock here. She is now at Bethlehem Hospital."

"Indeed, sir. Sad case. Why does she interest Bow Street?"

"Actually, it is another female, said to be her friend, whom I seek. She is another such as Miss Lubbock." Chase tapped his head.

"Her name?"

"Rebecca Barnwell."

The pleasant smile faded as Broughty tugged absently at his rather large cravat and lowered his rounded chin into its folds. "Is that not the name of the woman who claims the Last Judgment is upon us?"

"The same. Miss Barnwell's name has come up in connection with a murder inquiry, and I have reason to believe she may have visited Dora in Bedlam recently. Dora Lubbock may know something of the matter, though I was not permitted to see her."

Broughty's eyes had turned wary, and Chase was aware of the need to keep this man's feathers smooth, for clearly, the physician feared anything that would reflect poorly on his place of business.

"Nonsense," Broughty said. "Dora has been locked up for more than a quarter of a century. Besides, she is an innocent, no danger at all to anyone, except perhaps to herself. As for Miss Barnwell, she is a public figure and well respected, even revered."

"I was hoping to persuade you to consult your records, sir. But to start with, what can you tell me of Dora Lubbock? How long was she in your charge?"

"Oh, she came well before my time. Had God been merciful, she'd have ended her days here among those who knew her tragedy and pitied her."

He sent Chase a sharp glance that seemed to probe the Runner's motives and character. Apparently, whatever he saw satisfied him, for he continued without further prompting. "She is a woman who has lived for many years under a load of guilt so heavy it cannot be thought strange that it drove her mad. 'Twas the old story, Mr. Chase. When she was young and comely, she fell under the eye of some scoundrel who seduced her and left her to bear her shame as she could.

"The child was fostered out, but Dora found the load of opprobrium too heavy and was unable to resume her normal life. Eventually, her family sent her to us."

"From where, sir?"

"It was a long time ago. I'm afraid I do not recall the details. My predecessor was not one to maintain records, and in any event he destroyed any papers before my arrival.

Professional jealousy, I suppose, for he and I had very different notions as to the proper treatment of lunatics. Which brings us to your other request. I'm afraid I can tell you nothing of Miss Barnwell."

"You mean, don't you, that you could shed some light if you so chose?"

Broughty's tiny mouth drooped, and the lids came down over his bright, knowing gaze. Chase felt sure he was about to be dismissed, but then the physician said, "She visited Dora, always wearing a veil to conceal her identity. Dora told me who she was."

"They were friends?"

"Yes. Dora admired her deeply. She lived for Miss Barnwell's visits, though years would go by without us seeing her. I presumed she came as an act of Christian charity, yet I admit I wondered how it all came about unless she'd known Dora in her youth."

"Or had once been a patient here herself."

Broughty nodded. "I own I thought as much myself. You see, Dora made a remark I have not since forgotten." As if striving for the exact words, he paused, then lifted somber eyes to Chase's face. "She said that Miss Barnwell was the only person in the world who understood her loss."

At the faint, plaintive cry, Rebecca curled one arm over her ear to deaden the noise and burrowed deeper into the straw mattress. From this position, she could not lift her other arm, attached as it was to a heavy chain ending in an iron ball that nestled amongst the loose bits of straw, filth, and rat droppings on the floor.

She had long ago accustomed herself to the physical discomforts. The smell of human excrement, her own and Dora's. The raging thirst and numbing cold that left painful chilblains on every finger and toe. The bleakest hours of night when the voice of God deserted her, and the demons returned, howling. But it was the times when the child called for her, and she could not go to it, that tried her most. It was then she wanted to die, would have thrust the knife in her own breast, if only oblivion might be her reward. And yet, knowing that the Lord would hold her accountable, Rebecca did not believe in oblivion, and, for that reason, would never have taken her own life.

"Do you hear that?" she whispered as the cry came again.

Straw rustled as Dora turned on her mattress. "Hear what? They won't be coming with the gruel yet. The shadows are not thick enough."

"Not that. It's the child. He is lost somewhere. I must go to him."

"No," said Dora, the thin edge of panic in her voice. "You must not leave me, Rebecca. You said there is work to be done, that we must wait and watch and be patient. You said the Lord will reveal all to us one day. He knows our hearts. He will look after my child—and yours. And one day, the ungodly will burn and writhe in hell."

Tears pricked Rebecca's eyes. Those people had stolen her child and branded her a murderess. The keepers had told her she ought to be grateful for the mercy shown her, for she might have been tried and executed for her crime. She knew better. It was not a desire to show mercy that had motivated the Master, but instead a fear of scandal. Rebecca had seen no magistrate after Jack Willard had discovered her in the church, had simply been dispatched, nearly dead from her ordeal, in a hired coach. No doubt everyone had been told she died in childbed or that she had fled her shame.

Dora was right. The Master would pay for his sins. They would all pay. Lifting her head, Rebecca listened, then, sinking back, closed her eyes in relief. The crying had stopped.

≈≈≈

One wintry afternoon in February, 1794 the keepers allowed Rebecca and a half-dozen other women out of doors to pace back and forth in the yard. Rebecca had been an inmate in the asylum some seven or eight years and until then had found nothing whatever to interest her in the routine of days that followed one upon the last so that Time stretched before her, a vast desert.

It was a child who drew her attention. He stood to one side, observing the procession of ragged women with tattered blankets tied round their shoulders and blank faces fixed on their shuffling feet. Rebecca kept her eyes lowered too, but, when she thought he wasn't looking, she sneaked glances in his direction.

A fine, sturdy boy, she thought, old enough to have lost his plump baby cheeks and put aside his petticoats. Dressed with care in a neat suit, he carried a squashed cap in his lean, brown hand. Rebecca watched as the boy's mother, a young woman garbed in widow's black, approached to lay a hand on his shoulder, smiling down at him. His answering smile brought a tightness to Rebecca's throat.

After that, she saw them often, and cautious inquiry of the steward when he chanced to be in a good humor had revealed that the beautiful young woman was not a widow at all, nor was she a wife. It seemed that her lover, the boy's father, was a patient in the hospital.

As, gradually, the spring advanced and the bitter cold thawed to something that resembled warmth, the women were permitted to exercise for longer periods. And one morning, after a night of dreams in which Rebecca had trembled under her divine lover's hands, as perfect as ever woman knew the touch of a husband, she felt the Spirit, a draught of cool, fresh water, heady like wine, revive within her.

Climbing up on a bench, she began to exhort her companions, her words a mixture of scripture she did not recall ever committing to memory and of messages that seemed to well up from some source both within and beyond her. She was transported, made whole, and the women leaned forward to finger the hem of her gown with reverence, their expressions, for once, alive, full of hope and anguish. Crying for joy, Dora was shouting, and some of the women could not hold themselves up but fell to the ground in their passion.

And then Rebecca felt her arm seized in a cruel grip, and she was yanked from her perch. "What's this?" demanded a keeper, the one Rebecca dreaded and avoided whenever possible. "I see who be causing this uproar, and I'll make you sorry for it." He grabbed her by her lank hair and started propelling her toward the door that led to the wards. Too stunned to protest, Rebecca stumbled after him.

Suddenly, the woman and her son stepped into the keeper's path so that he came to an abrupt halt and loosened his grasp on Rebecca. Wriggling free, Rebecca stared at her rescuers, panting with fear and excitement, sure that momentous events were about to overtake her. The boy's mother stood tall, her black silk dress lending her dignity. Rebecca had always thought her lovely with her full lips and slumberous blue eyes, but now glimpsed a power that seemed beyond the reach of a mere female. The child too, young though he was, bore a look of determination on his small face, as he stood square, his feet planted on the path as if daring the keeper to object to his presence there. Rebecca had not noticed the mother and son before, so rapt had she been, but now she realized that they must have witnessed the entire incident.

"Leave her be," said the woman. "She has done nothing wrong."

The keeper nodded respectfully, but said in sullen tones, "Begging your pardon, mum, but we don't hold with troublemakers here. She was trying to rouse the others to mischief."

"No indeed, she was not. On the contrary, her words brought them great comfort. It was…quite extraordinary. Leave us now. I would speak to her in private."

He looked as if he meant to argue the point, but, thinking better of it, shrugged and turned aside. "Suits me, if you want to give the time o' day to a lack-wit."

When he was out of earshot, the woman said, "I am Mrs. Gore, and this is my son. Tell me your name, please. I've noticed you before, and I do not think you are quite like the rest."

Rebecca thought about this. No, perhaps she was not, though she didn't really want to set herself above her fellow inmates. She told the kind lady her name, then found herself speaking of her history. She could not bring herself to mention her own child, but she spoke of having been a nursemaid and of missing the little girl who had been in her charge. And she told of Dora and the cruel family who had ripped her infant from her arms and taken it away.

Bitterness twisted Mrs. Gore's lips. "I, too, know what it is to lose someone." She glanced at the boy, and Rebecca thought she meant to send him out of earshot, but instead she tugged him closer in a fiercely protective embrace.

"Ma'am?" said Rebecca.

"The boy's father. He was once a respected solicitor, but the authorities had him imprisoned for a six-month. Do you wish to know his crime?"

At Rebecca's grave smile of acquiescence, Mrs. Gore continued. "He joined a reform society, and, together with his brothers, composed a pamphlet pointing out that true equality for all Englishmen requires that we have no king, only men working together for society's betterment. For this he was locked up like a common felon. The disgrace and the barbarous conditions destroyed his health, and he has not since recovered. His wife does not visit him. He remains here, alone and ill."

"There is no kingdom, save that of God," said Rebecca. "I am certain he did right to speak the truth."

Mrs. Gore reached out to clasp her hand. "I should like to help you if I can, Rebecca."

Chapter XIV

A voice hailed John Chase as he strode toward Bow Street public office. "Will you step in, sir?"

Ezekiel Thorogood's portly frame hung precariously from the door of a hackney which, blocking the carriageway, had already incited a stream of shouts and curses from other drivers. The angle made the old lawyer's leonine head appear disproportionately large and heavy with its tufting wisps of white-gray mane, like a benevolent gargoyle with hair.

"A moment, sir." Stepping to the horses' heads, Chase instructed the jarvey to move the equipage to one side.

"No need," the man replied and smacked his lips insolently at his beasts.

Chase frowned at him, but climbed in the coach nevertheless. As soon as he settled in the seat opposite, the lawyer took up his walking stick and thumped the roof. Immediately, the coach lurched off, throwing Chase back against faded, dusty squabs.

Startled, he said, "What the devil? Where are we going?"

Thorogood regarded him placidly. "In good time, friend. What do you know of a Miss Rebecca Barnwell, the Virgin Prophetess?"

"Why do you ask?" returned Chase, a shade too evenly.

Undaunted, Thorogood chuckled, his blue eyes gleaming in their wrinkled beds of flesh. "I've my reasons. Do you intend to answer my question?"

"I think not, sir."

They exchanged a long look. Chase thrust aside the leather curtains so that he could see out the window. The carriage had turned off Bow Street onto Long Acre, heading for Drury Lane. Traffic was light. They made quick time, wherever they were going. But the weather had worsened, the sky suddenly a dirty, roiling gray with lowered clouds.

Thorogood said, "By Jove, I see why you and Mrs. Wolfe inevitably come to blows. You wore a softer aspect when you dined at my board on Christmas Day. In brief homage to the spirit of the season?"

Chase smiled. "How fares your gracious wife?"

An entirely new expression crossed the old lawyer's face. "She is hale, thank God. I shall tell her you inquired." He cleared his throat. "Well, I shall answer *your* question, sir, and willingly. I ask about Miss Barnwell for the simple reason that today was the third time in as many weeks that her name has been brought to my notice. I don't need to tell you that I sat up and took heed, for there is always significance in such coincidence, as I am sure you know very well."

"Go on."

"I read in the papers of her imminent intention to present the world with a Savior. Then my friend Buckler told me of a curious conversation he had with a lunatic in Bedlam."

Chase checked the window again. They now traveled east on High Holborn, heading in the same general direction from which he had just returned. He quelled his mounting exasperation with difficulty. "Do you intend to tell me where we're going?"

"I can't help but feel a certain curiosity about this matter, Mr. Chase. And I should like to help you get at the root of it."

"Oh?" he said with soft menace. "Is that why I am here, sir? Then I presume you have no objection to describing the third string in your chord of coincidence?"

"None at all. It was Buckler's clerk Bob who told me that Miss Barnwell plans to appear this afternoon at an assembly on Clerkenwell Green. I had thought you might wish to accompany me to see what knowledge we can glean of her. The opportunity seemed too good to disregard."

Gesturing with his stick, Thorogood added, "I see the weather's turned nasty. No doubt we are in for a good drenching."

❧❧

When the hack rolled onto Clerkenwell Green, Thorogood disembarked to pay off the driver. Jumping down in his wake, Chase stood gazing around. The promised squall had arrived. Water poured from the sky as if to deluge any faint balminess one might hope for on this chilly April day. Already slick under Chase's feet, the paving gave off that peculiar London odor, half coal smoke and horse droppings, half rain freshness. He pulled his greatcoat tighter and wondered how long it would take the damp to penetrate his knee.

Several hundred people, mainly women, had massed in the large open space in front of the sessions house. The grassless and treeless "green"—a storm had blown down the trees some years back—was hardly an inviting spot for human habitation just now. Yet the people near Chase, though dripping and miserable, remained patient as if they had waited a long time and were content to wait longer that they might be satisfied. Their yearning surged forth every so often like a vast, exhaled breath, then was indrawn as the watchers sank back.

"Did their mothers never tell them to come in out of the rain?" murmured Chase. As he spoke, he caught the hungry look of a woman who smiled into his eyes as if they shared a great secret. Hastily, he turned back to the lawyer.

"A good wetting rarely hurts anyone, sir." Obligingly, Thorogood angled his umbrella so that only half of Chase was subject to the elements. "If we are lucky, it shan't be long in any case. What say we listen to this prophetess and afterwards seek her out?"

Resigned, he nodded. North and uphill from Smithfield meat market, ancient Clerkenwell village was a place of brewers, gin distillers, and innumerable clock, watch, and mathematical instrument makers, set amongst the remnants of a medieval priory and nunnery. Once a fashionable retreat for those seeking fresher air, as well as the medicinal benefits of spring waters, the area had grown ever more begrimed by a terrible poverty. As they waited, Thorogood beguiled the time by musing on the prospect the inhabitants must once have had of verdant, wooded hills in every direction but that of the City.

Not ten minutes later it seemed they were to be rewarded for their patience, for a current ran through the crowd, the onlookers stirring and jostling for position. At first, Chase could not account for this shift in mood until, craning his neck, he noticed the open door of a house on the north side of the green. From this door had emerged a huddle of black-garbed figures that crept beetle-like toward the rough wooden platform erected next to the session house steps. Willingly, the crowd parted.

Once the men in neat suits had ascended to the platform with their charge, the attendants fell back, and the prophetess Rebecca Barnwell stood alone, a slight figure with a thick farm woman's neck from which fell a heavy cloak that shrouded the rest of her form. Even from a distance, Chase thought her slightly protuberant eyes looked like two smooth, wet stones. Apparently, the roar of her audience fell pleasantly on her ears, for she lifted one hand and smiled.

Initially, she stumbled over her words, appearing confused, though the audience remained quiet and respectful. But after a time, the thoughts poured forth, a curious mixture of scripture, exhortations to remain steadfast in faith, and finally a series of obscure references to the wise Virgins waiting to enter heaven with their Bridegroom, which Chase, at least, could not retrieve from his fund of Biblical knowledge gleaned in childhood. After a while, he occupied himself with studying her figure, trying to discern some hint of the supposed pregnancy.

At length, she pronounced, "As man once clamored for the blood of our Savior, so must we now join hand and heart to clamor for Satan's destruction. Be ready and watch for the Coming of the Lord, for it is imminent."

The spectators roared their approval, chanting, "Blood. Blood. Blood. Show us the Blood."

Smiling, she shook her head, but offered something else in return. Tenderly, reverently, she unfastened her cloak, pushing it back to expose her distended belly. Chase scrutinized her surprisingly frail wrists but could not see whether they bore the marks of restraint Penelope had noted. Barnwell threw back her head and lifted her hands.

"What the devil?" hissed Chase.

The lawyer spoke out of the corner of his mouth. "Stigmata. She has prophesied that she will one day be marked by Christ's wounds—and bleed. A miracle of faith. There are many such recorded cases."

"Of all the absurd, lunatic notions."

Thorogood only shrugged. On the platform, the covey of men had surrounded the prophetess to hustle her down from her perch. Again the crowd opened to receive her as she made her way back to the house on the other side of the green. When she reached the entrance, she turned and gave one wave of her hand before she stepped inside, closing the door behind her. The watchers groaned their dismay.

"Friends," shouted one of her honor guard who had remained on the platform, "disperse now. Miss Barnwell must take her ease before returning to her many duties. I know you would not disturb her for the world."

Chase glanced around with some anxiety, for a London crowd was always a chancy thing, especially when it had been thwarted of its will in some way. But here and there he could see the men in black circulating to call out words of reassurance as the dazed spectators mopped wet cheeks or remained talking together in low, exultant whispers.

"Come, Chase. Let us set about our inquiries," said Thorogood.

"Not just yet. It will be easier to make our way across the Green in a few minutes, and the prophetess will no doubt stay comfortably holed up in that house until the traffic has dispersed."

They waited perhaps a quarter of an hour until one of the attendants moved in their direction, and Chase stepped in front of him. "John Chase, Bow Street. Take me to your mistress."

Blinking, the man spoke in a broad country accent. "Well now, I don't rightly know."

"At once, if you please, sirrah," said Thorogood sternly. "Mr. Chase has urgent business with Miss Barnwell. I promise she will be most grateful should you do her this service."

The man didn't look as if the prospect overwhelmed him with confidence, but before he could respond a woman bustled up. Wearing a high poke bonnet with feathers that shielded much of her face, she was dressed in a blue gown that to Chase's eyes appeared expensive and fashionable.

"Go and bring the carriage, Robert. We shall be departing in a few minutes."

"Yes, ma'am." He escaped gratefully.

The woman would have swept on, but Chase said again for her benefit, "John Chase, Bow Street, madam. Would you be so good as to escort me to Miss Barnwell?"

"Bow Street? Take yourself off at once. We want no dealings with you." She drew back the fringe of her shawl as if he might contaminate her.

Chase stepped closer to her, allowing menace to surface in his voice. "Nevertheless, you will do as I ask. It's not for you to refuse an officer on the King's warrant." This, of course, was pure fabrication, but he wanted her to pause and take notice.

It worked. As she turned her head to gape at him in dismay, he got a full look at her countenance. Perhaps five-and-forty, she was quite astonishingly beautiful with heavy-lidded, startlingly blue eyes, a decisive nose, and a richly sensual mouth.

"Whom do I have the honor of addressing?" he asked after a moment when she still didn't speak.

"I am Mrs. Gore, sir," she replied with cold dignity.

Mrs. Janet Gore. The woman who had provided the character of the footman Dick Ransom and who, according to the prostitute Belinda, was madam at the Westminster brothel. Turning to Thorogood, who watched him with a puzzled air, Chase smiled. "You were saying about coincidence?"

Just then a tall man in a beaver hat shoved his way through the press, shouting something unintelligible as he went. As people apparently began to absorb his urgency, they let him through, and a moment later he stumbled up onto the platform.

Once there, he tore off his hat and cried out, "Friends! Miss Barnwell has been attacked! The devil has done his work. Our lady is most grievously injured…"

A cacophony arose as the crowd bellowed its horror and disapproval, every man or woman turning to his neighbor with the question "What of the child?" on everyone's lips. Bent over now as if gasping for breath, the man on the platform was so completely surrounded that nothing more could be seen of him.

Removing his baton from his greatcoat, Chase reached out to grip Mrs. Gore's arm with one hand and brandished the baton with the other. She went with him passively, her face reflecting a powerful astonishment and anxiety.

"Make way for Bow Street," he yelled over the din, nodding to Thorogood to follow and trying not to slip on the rain-wet pavement. After a few paces, Thorogood lowered his umbrella, which he used, as Chase did his baton, to help force their path through what seemed a solid wall of flesh. Slowly, they made their way across the green to the house.

"What has happened?" cried Mrs. Gore when they reached the door to find the black-suited men huddled together, conferring in whispers.

One looked up. "We've sent for the doctor, ma'am. The woman as owns this house is with Miss Barnwell. We thought it best to leave her to a female. You'll go in now?"

"No sign of the person who attacked your mistress? Where were the lot of you?"

The man turned bleak, terrified eyes on Chase, which widened when they dropped to the Bow Street ensign of office in the Runner's hand. "We were right here, sir, outside the door. Never stirred for a moment. No one could have entered without we should see him, except one o' course, and nothing we could do would stop *him*, I tell you. How can it be thought our fault, and yet for all that it's true that we have failed her."

"No, no," broke in Thorogood. "We do not seek to impute blame to Miss Barnwell's loyal friends. But who is this mysterious assailant?"

The old lawyer's measured tone had its desired effect, for the attendant sucked in air and cleared his watery gaze with some rapid blinks. But it was, after all, Mrs. Gore who spoke.

"Satan, sir," she said flatly.

❧◖☙

Chase did not await permission to enter the house with Janet Gore, and, surprisingly, she did not object. Leaving Thorogood to continue his conversation with the Barnwellians, Chase accompanied Mrs. Gore through a cramped entryway and down a narrow, mildew-redolent corridor into a parlor.

A female in a crumpled apron looked up as they entered, but did not pause in her ministrations to the prophetess, who lay, eyes closed, on the needlepoint settee. The injured woman was deathly pale, and now without the cloak, Chase could see her belly thrusting against the fabric of her gown. One limp arm held in place the blood-spotted cloth draped across her middle. Bending over her, Chase peered at Barnwell's wrists and was not surprised to discern a fretwork of scars, whitish with age.

Mrs. Gore rushed forward. "Has she spoken, Mrs. Croft? Rebecca, can you hear me? It is I, Janet." She gazed down upon the blood, turning so pale Chase feared she too might swoon. "The baby," she whispered. "Oh, dear God, someone must help the baby."

"Here. Sit down for a moment, ma'am." Chase led her to a chair some distance away, then turned back. "Mrs. Croft, is it? John Chase, Bow Street. I believe this is your house, ma'am? Tell me what you know of the attack."

"Why nothing, sir, beyond what you see with your own eyes. She came in smiling, pleased by her speech and the love of her people. I bid her step into my parlor while I went below to make tea. When I brought it up, I found her on the floor. I gave a little screech, and her men friends heard me and ran to help me lift her."

"Miss Barnwell never cried out?"

"No, sir, not so I heard."

As Mrs. Croft leaned over to rinse her cloth in a bowl, several drops of water splattered the gleaming wood box that sat atop the table. Veneered in costly Brazilian rosewood and inlaid in brass with a fleur-de-lis and dot design at the corners, it looked as out of place in this room as a peacock in a chicken yard.

"Does the writing box belong to Miss Barnwell?"

Mrs. Gore stirred. "A gift from a supporter of our ministry."

Chase jiggled the lid. "Where is the key?"

"The wound," she moaned hoarsely as if he hadn't spoken. "Is it mortal?"

"The gashes do bleed but little, mum," cried Mrs. Croft. "As to their being mortal, I shouldn't think so, but what do I know? I do know as I didn't bargain for the likes of this when I let my parlor to you. 'Tis clear some lunatic is after your lady, and me and my boy might have been killed for our pains."

Hastily, before Gore could repeat her absurd allegation about the Devil being the attacker, Chase began to inquire about the layout of the house, its entrances and exits. Satisfied on that score, he made a rapid search of the shabby parlor, poking behind cushions and checking under furniture. Mrs. Croft was not a careful housekeeper, and Chase's hands were soon coated with dust. Then under one of the matching needlepoint chairs near the settee, he found it: a silver and horn penknife. Only about four inches long, it boasted a metal carrying ring, which would attach to a belt. Chase ran a finger over the tiny retractable blade.

"Does this belong to Miss Barnwell, or to either of you?" he inquired, holding it up by the ring.

Mrs. Croft studied it with interest while Janet Gore merely looked appalled. But they shook their heads.

"Rebecca has a pen-knife, of course, but much finer than that," faltered Mrs. Gore.

Carefully, Chase wrapped the little knife in a bit of paper and put it in his pocket. Interesting that in both attacks the weapon had been a blade, in this case the sort of everyday implement many people possessed, often ready to hand. He wondered what that meant, whether this choice of weapon might perhaps indicate a lack of premeditation on the part of the assailant. He thought, too, that unlettered footpads and other such scum did not carry pen-knives.

"Does Miss Barnwell keep anything of value in her lap desk? The lock seems to be secure, yet could it be the attacker was after something kept inside?"

There was no reply. Judging that he had permitted Mrs. Gore enough time to collect herself, he crossed the room to her side. "I would inquire about another matter, ma'am. You once provided a character reference for a footman called Dick Ransom, who was, I believe, a frequent guest at your Westminster fancy house?"

She stared at him, her magnificent eyes blazing fire, but then the door banged open, and a gentleman wearing a frock coat and carrying a small black case entered. He went immediately to the settee to lift the cloth. "Ah. I had expected worse."

Janet Gore swept forward in a swish of skirts. "The babe, Doctor? May we hope it has not been injured? What with the terrible shock she has sustained, might not Miss Barnwell deliver the child before its proper time?"

"We shall see. You may stay to assist me." He nodded to Mrs. Croft. "Fetch a fresh basin and cloths."

The medical man barely acknowledged Chase's introduction, making it clear his presence was superfluous, so Chase accompanied Mrs. Croft into the corridor.

"I should like to have a look around while the scent is yet fresh," he told her and hurried away before she could resume her complaints.

Taking himself down to the kitchen, he surprised a young drudge at her scullery pots. In barely comprehensible English, she insisted that she had been there the entire afternoon and that no one had come in or out the area door. Afterwards, Chase made his way above stairs again and out the back entrance to a weed-choked garden. Patches of blue had appeared in the sky as a brisk breeze blew away the storm clouds. From somewhere close by, a thrush warbled cheerfully.

As he stood drawing in the fresh air and pondering his next move, he suddenly felt eyes upon him. A twig snapped, and he turned his head to peer toward an overgrown lilac hedge. Chase dropped to his haunches on the mired ground. In a small, raw hollow that looked as if it had been torn out of the hedge by sheer force huddled a child.

Two eyes regarded him, one hand curling around a dirty, tear-streaked cheek.

"Come out of there." Chase thrust out his hand, but the child shrank back. "I'll not hurt you," he added, not troubling to mask his impatience.

When the mite stood before him, Chase saw that it was a boy of seven or eight years. A wiry figure in nankeen trousers and a snug bottle green jacket, he was all knees and elbows, as was often the case with children that age.

"Your name's Croft, I believe."

In response, the boy threw back his shoulders and thrust out his sharp little chin. "Jimmy Croft," he said clearly, then, as an afterthought added, "sir."

"Well, Jimmy," he heard himself say in an over-hearty voice. "John Chase, Bow Street. I've been speaking with your mum. She is looking after a lady who's been hurt, and it is my duty to find the man who did it. I was hoping you could help me."

"I'll try, sir."

Chase felt himself curiously at a loss. He didn't wish to come right out and demand an explanation for the tears and the hiding place, for he thought that might wound the child's dignity. On the other hand, his business was pressing.

"Have you been in the garden for a bit, young 'un?"

"Mum told me to stay back here. She didn't want me in the Green with all the carrying on today."

Chase jerked a thumb over his shoulder. "Anyone come through that door?"

Color flooded the boy's sensitive skin. "Yes, sir. He near bowled me down, he did. I...I didn't know what to do, so I hid in the bushes...in case he would come back. I thought my mum would call if she needed my help."

"Were you hurt, boy?"

Jimmy shook his head, the misery on his face so acute that Chase wanted to swear. "That's all right then. If you were worried about your mum, she's fine, and it looks like the lady who was injured will come through as well. Tell me about this man you saw."

"Oh, he was tall. Tall as an oak tree. He wore a big black coat that covered him all up. And he had eyes that would burn you up if you looked in 'em, I guess. But I didn't look. I jus' kept my head down till I heard the latch on the gate shut."

Burning eyes? Either Jimmy's imagination had gotten the better of him or someone had been priming the pump. "You been talking to anyone? Maybe one of those men in black suits that accompanied the preacher lady?"

"No, sir, I stayed right here, as my mum bade me."

"Do me a favor," said Chase, getting to his feet. "Keep your tongue between your teeth about what you saw."

Chapter XV

John Chase went out the gate into a timber yard that ran along the rear of these houses, but, though he found several men at work with large axes, no one reported having seen anything out of the ordinary. He then penetrated some little distance into Clerkenwell Close, pausing at a rather ugly church built on the foundations of the nunnery, according to the garrulous clergyman to whom he spoke.

The clergyman gave him the name and direction of a retired brewer who took his constitutional in the close at this hour each afternoon and might have noticed something, but this fellow too was of no help.

When Chase hurried back to the Green, he found that much of the crowd still lingered awaiting news, singing hymns that seemed to float through the luminous air.

"What news?" said Thorogood.

"The doctor is with Miss Barnwell." Chase cupped his hands around his mouth. "Your attention, my good people. Give me your attention." It took a few minutes, but finally the noise died down enough that he could make himself heard.

"I am from Bow Street. I will seek Miss Barnwell's attacker, I promise you, but if there is anyone here who saw aught suspicious, let him come forward now. I am ready to listen."

He waited, and when after a long, uncomfortable moment no one responded, he continued, "In that event, I say you do no good here and may do harm if you provoke riot and rumpus in the streets. The prophetess is injured, true, but it is thought not seriously. It may be she will recover. Take yourselves off and hope to hear good tidings of her soon."

Their protest clamored in his ears. Half shrugging, Chase turned to Thorogood, who said, "You did your best, sir, but these people seem harmless enough, and I believe the local authorities are here as well. There was one asking to speak to you a moment ago."

"I would we had not lingered before seeking out Miss Barnwell after the speech. I might have prevented all this."

Thorogood eyed him keenly. "*Fata obstant.* The Fates oppose."

The door to Mrs. Crofts' house opened, and the doctor emerged. As soon as they caught sight of his frock-coated figure, the crowd surged forward to call out questions about his medical verdict and the state of the Messiah. Swishing his cane around him to clear his path, he at first did not choose to answer, but when several of the most determined interrogators surrounded his hack, he swung to face them, his countenance darkening.

"How dare you. Get out of my way, at once, you *hoi polloi.*"

"The child. The child," they moaned piteously.

Chase reached his side. "Your pardon, sir, for this inconvenience. Can you tell me how you find Miss Barnwell? Not in danger of her life, I trust?"

The doctor met his eyes and spoke in a lowered tone. "Nothing of the kind, man, though she has yet to rouse from her swoon. She'll do well enough, as I told that Mrs. Gore, so long as she is not disturbed for a day or two."

"No tragic consequences to be feared?"

"You refer to the pregnancy? I'll say nothing on that score, as her handmaiden outright refused me permission to conduct a thorough examination. Seemed to feel Miss Barnwell's modesty would be outraged."

Nodding briskly, he turned to mount the steps into the coach, but the knot around the horses' heads had tightened, and the doctor was swept away from his goal, his hat tipping over one eye. "Get away from me," he cried, practically foaming at the mouth in his rage. "You are all the biggest fools in Christendom. A simple woman of farm stock, and you lot credit this Banbury tale about a Messiah…"

Chase's heart sank as the doctor's words spread through the crowd like a bolt of lightning, no doubt becoming garbled in the process, as they were repeated from mouth to mouth. Then he heard the low cry of anguish that welled up from a hundred throats. "He says there's no child," said one bewildered woman. "The Devil has taken the baby. Satan, I tell you. Satan has stolen away our Savior."

This time when Chase wanted to swear, he did, long and with vicious pleasure, until Thorogood coughed gently. "Mr. Chase, I think perhaps we are at the end of our usefulness here. Let us just assist the good doctor to mount into his carriage and then locate some form of transport for ourselves."

"You go. I must first speak to Mrs. Gore. I've not had an opportunity to explain to you, but she is somehow involved in the business with Dick Ransom."

He cleared his throat. "Er…I spoke to the poor distressed lady myself and was able to satisfy myself on a number of points. You will be glad to hear—"

"You take too much on yourself, Thorogood, when you know nothing of the facts. I'm sure you'd be interested to learn that your lady in distress is a brothel madam who is likely up to her eyebrows in treasonous plots. But never mind that now. Where is she?"

One look at the lawyer's guilty expression told him everything he needed to know. "She's gone, isn't she, and you let her go? Hell and damnation, Thorogood, with friends like you, a man has little need of enemies. Unless you ask me to excuse you on account of her beautiful eyes?"

"She said she must make haste to employ a nurse to remain with the prophetess until she may be moved. You forget I had every reason to believe you had already questioned Mrs. Gore closely when you removed to the house together. I merely carried her box to the coach, detained her some few minutes in conversation, then bid her Godspeed. What would you have if you don't confide your plans to a trusted confederate?"

"Her box?" Chase echoed with foreboding.

John Chase waited in the flickering half-darkness at the arched entranceway to the George Inn yard. The night was blusterous, the cobbles beneath his feet slick with horse effluent and damp. Flambeaux, high on the wall, provided just enough light to make out fellow Runner Dugger Farley, who stood conversing with the local constable a few feet away.

Here just off the north side of the Strand, their quarry might have picked any number of bolt holes. Yet even in the heat of pursuit he had chosen well—a large inn yard with bustling traffic and innumerable places for a clever thief to hide such as bedchambers, pantries, wash rooms, stables, kitchen, attic, and nooks and crannies throughout. They'd be extremely fortunate to locate him at all, if he hadn't already fled.

Droplets of misting rain struck the brim of his hat as the earlier storm resumed. Chase glanced over at Farley, whose breath came in sharp white puffs. The thrill of the hunt had fired him, too. After posting a man at the back entrance, they had cleared the area of inquisitive patrons, serving maids, and ostlers, sending them all to the rightabout with instructions to keep their doors shut and locked. The landlord, bristling with indignation at this interference to his custom, had been persuaded to retire to his parlor.

Bending down, Chase massaged his bad knee. The rain always made it fiercely stiff, as if someone had strapped a board to the back of his leg. He hoped they would not have to pursue this fellow, for over-exertion, rather than loosening the knee, only seemed to freeze it and cause agonizing jabs of pain to shoot up to his thigh.

Not for the first time it occurred to him he wouldn't be able to do this job forever. The thought didn't trouble him overmuch, although he wasn't sure what he'd do with himself when the time came. Once, newly retired from the Royal Navy, he had tried country life and found it dismally flat for a still-young man, despite nearly twenty years in the floating wooden world. Maybe rural existence would strike him otherwise should he try it again. Nowadays, he lived frugally; he had almost enough savings for a small cottage somewhere where he could…his mind shied away.

After leaving Clerkenwell Green, Chase had stopped by Bow Street office to speak to Graham. The magistrate was intrigued by his tale of the West Country prophetess, who, it seemed, might have served as the catalyst of whatever fate had overtaken the Jacobin Dick Ransom. If the prophetess Barnwell had once been confined to a madhouse, might she yet be dangerously homicidal? After all, she had been in possession of the presumed murder weapon. But then who had attacked her this afternoon?

Graham had commented doubtfully, "She may have stumbled upon the presumed murder weapon the night she was apprehended by the parish authorities, that is if you your-self had missed it in your examination of the garden, Mr. Chase. It's possible the real culprit had dropped it there, eh?"

In the midst of this exchange a group of citizens erupted into the court with a prisoner, a well-known thief called Harper, in tow. With great excitement they reported that the neighborhood of Newcastle Street was in great alarm after a watchmaker's shop window had been broken into and robbed by a gang of four men. The watchmaker and his neighbors had pursued the thieves, taking Harper, but the others had escaped when one of the band had produced a pistol and threatened to "blow a hole in any fool who got too close."

The gang had dispersed, but a few minutes later one of the thieves had been spotted running into the George Inn yard near Little Drury Lane. Unable to locate him, the citizens had come seeking Bow Street's assistance.

Chase and Farley found themselves setting off hotfoot for the Strand, led by the watchmaker. About sixty years old and portly, he nonetheless set a spanking pace.

"They took a rope and tied the door knocker to the scraper and railing so I couldn't get out of my shop to follow," he huffed. "A neighbor saw and sounded the alarm."

"Lucky for you," said Farley.

"The sheer audacity of the villains. They first thought to break into the linen-draper's shop, actually knocking on the door and pretending to ask if their friend lodged there. When Jamison wouldn't open up, they smashed my shop window and made off with what they could carry."

"What was taken?" asked Chase.

"Fobs and seals. Two gold watches."

They had reached Little Drury Lane, where a crowd was gathered at the entrance to the George.

"This scum ain't gonna walk into our arms, Chase," Farley said now, "and I can't say I'm partial to the wet."

"I take there's something else you'd rather be doing tonight?"

"Only about a hundred things." The raindrops began to pelt down now, and the cobblestones grew even slicker.

Farley lifted his blunderbuss. "Let's go."

Chase drew one of his pistols. It felt cold and heavy against his palm. "Right."

Farley stepped under the arch, Chase dropping back a few feet to cover him as they proceeded up the narrow carriage-way and into the yard proper. The inn, including stables and outbuildings, sprawled around the courtyard on three sides. Rising several stories above the pavement in the galleried style, the main structure, solid and imposing, looked especially warm and inviting this evening. Apparently, word had spread, and it seemed as if every window in the place was lit up. Heads peeked over the banisters from above, and a suspicious number of waiters and yardboys had found excuses to linger in the court. *Perhaps our fugitive isn't yet to be congratulated, after all,* thought Chase, nodding politely to a bewhiskered gentleman who had edged open the taproom door.

"What next? Start knocking?" Farley flung out an arm to indicate the row of closed doors.

"Let's begin out here."

For the next ten minutes they poked into every corner of the yard, looking behind dustbins and piles of old boxes, even shining a torch down into the well. Nothing.

"How about I go inside and check the coffee room, the taproom, and the kitchens while you do the stables?" said Farley when they had exhausted the yard's possibilities.

Chase nodded absently. Yet as Farley sauntered off it seemed to him that the stables in a busy inn would be one of the worst places to hide. At any time of day or night, there would be arrivals and departures, people either requiring stabling for their horses and equipages or calling on the ostlers to produce transport.

He looked around. Where would the thief hide? In an out-of-the-way closet or trunk perhaps, or behind the bureau in an unoccupied bedchamber. Or, he thought, as his eye fell upon the entrance to the cellar, below ground. *Instinct,* he reasoned. *The hunted creature often goes to earth, burrowing down, forgetting he may thereby be trapped.* It was worth a look anyway.

The door opened easily, the combined smells of dust, stale air, and beery miasma hitting him like a wave. A stairway descended into total darkness. Before going in, he appropriated a lantern that was hanging from a nail by the door.

Afraid of presenting too tempting a target outlined by the light there at the top of the little landing, Chase did not linger, but, after closing the door behind him, moved as rapidly down the steps as his knee would allow, one hand clutching the lantern, the other his pistol.

He reached the bottom without incident. Stilling his breathing, he stood listening, without making a sound himself, for at least two or three minutes.

The lantern shed a small island of light in the immediate vicinity, but left the greater portion of the cellars in impenetrable shadow. He sensed this was a large space, low-ceilinged and narrow. As he swung the lantern in a slow circle, he caught glimpses of the enormous ale barrels and vats of wine and other liquors, but, fortunately, heard no scurrying of rats. The landlord kept a good house, it seemed.

Chase turned and approached the far wall, moving through the barrels, stopping to test their fastness and shining his light around them and in the corners. Then, turning, he came back, inspecting the opposite wall. It was then that he noticed the low cupboard.

Set into the wall was a door about four feet tall and two feet wide with a newly gleaming brass handle fastened by a stout little lock. The coal hole. No doubt the landlord was wise to secure it thus. Coal was expensive. He was about to pass on, thinking that the cupboard was too small to hold a man, when something made him stoop to examine the lock. And as soon as he put out his hand, the lock came away, and Chase saw that underneath it a round, precise hole had been cut in the wood.

"You may as well show yourself." He trained his pistol on the cupboard.

❧ ❧

A diminutive, coal-smudged figure emerged, its hands lifted in surrender. "Chase?"

Chase lowered the pistol. "Goddamnit, Packet. What are you doing in there?"

He grinned. "Obvious, ain't it? I have to say I'm right glad it's you what found me. Maybe that salvation seal is bringing me some luck for a change. I could use it. How'd you know I was there?"

"This is the second time this day I've discovered a little man hid in a little space. Empty your pockets."

Packet hesitated. Even in the dimness Chase could see his eyes flitting from side to side, to the stairwell, and back again.

"Empty them, Noah," he said again, inexorably.

Sighing, Packet complied, removing a gold watch and two seals from a pouch under his shirt. Then darting an inquiring look at Chase, he dug in deeper, this time emerging with a fob from which he took two small saws, about three inches long, of highly finished tempered steel. They were made to slice through chains or iron bars, silently.

Chase took possession of the hoard, putting the watch and seals into his greatcoat and slipping the fob and saws into his boot. "Where's the other gold watch?"

Packet looked pained. "One of them others had it." He pulled out his handkerchief and began to wipe the black streaks off his face, still avoiding Chase's eyes.

"This is it, you know. Nabbed in the act with expensive goods. One of your cohorts threatening citizens with a gun. You'd weigh forty for sure." He referred to the practice of waiting until an offender's crimes increased in scope until at last the Runner could be sure of a capital conviction and a portion of the forty-pound reward.

"I ain't worried you'll blow the gab. Ought I to be?"

Chase skewered the other man's gaze so that it couldn't slip away again. "I should have pressed you further that day at the menagerie. You'll tell me the whole now. I assume the 'misunderstanding' that sent you to earth is behind today's little foray?"

"I always said you was a knowing one," Packet said admiringly.

"Well?"

The single syllable had been harsh, uncompromising. Packet, perhaps beginning to feel the tingle of cold doubt, rushed into speech. "Started when I chose myself the wrong mark, one as no man would care to trouble. Bit of bad luck. Plucked what was in his pockets."

"The fellow didn't appreciate your attentions, I take it?" He studied his companion, noting the unshaven cheeks and gaunt filthiness under the superficial dusting of coal. "If you've had a bad time of it, you're well served."

Packet's gaze slid to his boots, a favorite trick he had when he wanted to look pathetic. "He come up with me t'other day and said either I march with his lay or else. No choice. I had no blunt to buy him off."

The story was probably true. If a local criminal had put on the clamp, only the foolhardy would resist. Besides, Packet's lay had always been lifting handkerchiefs, snuff-boxes, and the like from chubs on the street. More than that, he traded in the information he picked up, hoarding any tidbit against the possibility of future value. He had not been, to this point, a housebreaker.

"You've gone too far this time, Noah," said Chase.

"Last time, you asked me about that son-in-law of Sir Roger's. I picked up a bit o' hearsay that may prove service-able. He likes the little 'uns—girls, the younger the better. I had a word with a maidservant at a certain house of pleasure. She allows as this Lord Ashe is a frequent caller."

Chase's lip curled. "Charming people, these swells. And yet I don't see how Ashe's tastes matter unless perhaps Ransom had learned of them and was blackmailing him."

"Maybe I got something else for you," said Packet, watching his face anxiously. "You ever look into that other accommodation house?"

Chase folded his arms in front of him. "I did and discovered that the murdered footman was known there, so your information did not come amiss. I have unfinished business with the whore in charge."

"O'Callaghan, one Patrick O'Callaghan. You find him, Chase. You talk to him and see what's what. But best you be cautious like. He's a dangerous 'un."

"Who is he?"

Packet coughed. "He got me into this fix. The salvation seal I showed you belonged to him. I hear tell he's got some dealings with that house, owns a piece of it maybe. That's why I sent you."

"But conveniently forgot to mention this O'Callaghan's existence?"

"Smart cove like you, I figured you'd be on to him yourself and maybe do me a good turn and get him off my back. Kill two birds with one stone."

Chase gave a short laugh. "He's the man you robbed, isn't he? A common thief himself. Lord, that's rich, Packet."

"A thief, but he ain't common," Packet said dryly. "We met at a pub in Little Windmill Street to plan this little jaunt. It's a place where you find men of Jacobin leanings, something I don't hold with, I can tell you. Anyhow, I did pick up one interesting titbit. It's allowed as how this Dick Ransom was a known radical. They were busy toasting his memory." He shot a look at Chase. "I see I ain't surprised you none."

"Get to the point." Chase's interest had sharpened. He could always tell when Packet was about to cough up the real information, for his voice got even hoarser, his gaze fluttering like more than a dozen moths.

The little man shot him an injured look. "I heard talk of a meeting of a certain committee. I warrant O'Callaghan will be there."

"Oh? When is this meeting is to occur?"

"Tuesday week to be exact," he said triumphantly. "But I ain't mentioned the cream of the jest…" The eyes rested on his only momentarily. "You know how them secret societies got their codes and their handshakes and all that rot? These boys will have to show their salvation seal along with a password, of course. I didn't get that, of course, but I reckon it might be something as has a sort of Biblical flavor."

"Give it me then," said Chase. "The seal, I mean. I'll be needing it, and don't try to tell me you've restored O'Callaghan's property to him."

After Packet had placed it in his hand, Chase asked, "Packet, on the subject of the Jacobins, do you know anything about an underground conspiracy afoot in London? Men with nothing to lose plotting mayhem against King and country and giving sleepless nights to Home Office spies and informants?"

"You mean like the Luddites? It's true many would like to see the swells get theirs. Folk is tired of the rich taking all."

Before Chase could ask another question, the door at the top of the steps opened. Packet froze.

Farley's voice floated down. "You there, Chase? No sign of him, and I checked the bedchambers as well."

Reaching out to grip the top of Packet's head, Chase sent him sprawling to the stone floor. A subdued grunt told him he hadn't been particularly gentle about it either.

"Chase?"

"I'm just coming. We had best go see if the thieves dropped some of the booty in the lane as they fled. Worth a try anyway."

Chapter XVI

Julia and Penelope did not ordinarily breakfast with Sir Roger and Lord Ashe, who both came down early before departing for various pursuits, antiquarian or political. Julia never stirred until eleven o'clock after long nights spent dancing and drinking French wine at one Society gathering after another. And more often than not, she required Penelope to accompany her, not seeming to notice or care that her companion had not a word to say to the hard-faced, glittering throng of people who looked through her as if she were invisible. Nor did Julia seem to realize that Penelope rose with the sun to mind a four-year-old bursting with energy.

Today, however, Ashe had left instructions that his wife was to present herself at the breakfast table, so here they were, both heavy-eyed and listless, Julia sullen with resentment.

"Good morning, my dear." Rising, he bowed to Penelope. "And you, Mrs. Wolfe. You are looking well this morning, ma'am."

Julia did not reply, but Penelope thanked him and took her seat, smoothing her blue muslin gown, one of three given her to replace the ruined green sarsenet. At first, she had not wanted to accept the dresses, but had reflected sourly that, after all, she earned them and that pride should not require her to appear so often in public unsuitably clad. The mystery of who had destroyed the first gown had never been solved, though the outcry amongst the maids who had felt themselves under suspicion had been unpleasant. But Penelope was almost certain the culprit had been Mrs. Sterling, who made no secret of her dislike and resentment.

Immersed in his book, Sir Roger barely acknowledged their arrival, merely nodding to his daughter and offering Penelope an absent smile. As Penelope sipped her chocolate and nibbled at a roll, a prickly silence lay over the table, a silence that ought to have made everyone uncomfortable but seemed to be affecting only the one person who had nothing to do with whatever was brewing.

Seeming determined not to speak first, Julia sat in her chair, from time to time pushing back a stray lock of hair, which, undressed and flowing down her back, glowed in the morning light that streamed through the windows. Her face was uncharacteristically still, her skin like a smooth, brittle shell worn thin by the sea.

"You will be wondering why I troubled you to come down early this morning, my love," said Ashe conversationally after a time.

Julia stared at her plate, giving no sign she had heard him except for a faint tightening around her mouth and a clenching of white fingers around her cup.

"We leave for Dorset in the morning with your father. I thought you would like to know so that you may make your preparations."

Sir Roger looked up, surprised. "You mean to accompany me to Cayhill? I had thought you fixed here for the Season at any rate. What on earth will you do in the country? You know I shall be occupied with my excavations."

"We are content to remain quiet. No doubt Julia will benefit from the air and from some simple, wholesome food. She's looking a bit pulled, wouldn't you say, sir?"

"I suppose you're right," said Sir Roger, studying his daughter with puzzled eyes. "But she'll be sadly bored, you know, Ashe."

"As if you have ever cared how I felt about anything," said Julia in a low, passionate voice. She sent a contemptuous glance at her father, then turned to her husband. "You are mistaken, my lord. I have no plans to remove from London at present. You, however, may do as you please."

Lifting his coffee to his lips, Ashe smiled, and, replacing his cup deliberately, addressed his wife in the same pleasant, even tone. "You will do precisely as I bid you. You see, my dear, I've had my fill of you comporting yourself like Haymarket ware in every drawing room in London. You shall not return to Society until you have learned self-control and breeding."

Julia flinched as if he had slapped her. "My God, Ashe, you'd think I'd been carrying on like that silly cow Caro Lamb, yearning day and night over that insipid poet, following him all over town, and making perfect a cake of herself. I've done nothing of the kind. Why do you think I take care to keep more than one string to my bow? I do assure you 'tis out of consideration for you."

"Thank you, my dear," he replied dryly. "Nevertheless, you will make yourself ready to depart on the morrow. It is precisely the sort of situation in which my friend William Lamb finds himself that I seek to avert."

"If you are quite certain, Ashe," broke in Sir Roger, "I must tell Finch, who is engaged even now in packing up a number of my curiosities to be conveyed to Cayhill. I'm afraid there won't be much room in the baggage coach."

"Damn your monstrosities, Father," cried Julia. "I'll not travel with them or stay in that great ugly barn you've built as monument to the past, a filthy, sordid past that will pull you down and choke you if you let it. I won't have it." Her voice had risen dangerously, and Penelope, wishing herself anyplace but here, half rose as if to leave the room.

It was a mistake. Recalling her presence, Sir Roger said, "What of Mrs. Wolfe? I suppose you intend that she should accompany Julia, Ashe? I own I would find her services most welcome in setting some of my papers to rights."

"If she wishes," came the indifferent reply.

Penelope sat down again. "I rather think I had better stay in town. I encountered a cousin of mine in the Park not long ago. He mentioned that he and his wife would be glad to welcome Sarah and me for a visit. I have written to my father about the invitation, and, though he has yet to reply, I am sure he would approve this opportunity to mend an old breach in our family."

Julia's hand snaked across the tablecloth to grip Penelope's arm. "You couldn't be so cruel, Mrs. Wolfe. Please, you must accompany me. I cannot bear it alone."

"For heaven's sake, Julia, don't be so melodramatic," snapped her husband. "Mrs. Wolfe must do as she thinks best, of course."

"Penelope?"

With Julia's gaze fixed beseechingly on her face, she found it impossible to look away. She had never truly liked this woman, nor did she especially trust her. She half thought that Julia deserved her husband's scorn. And yet the expression in her eyes held Penelope immobile, for she had seen it before in her own mirror.

❧ ❧

On his way to the chambers of a barrister friend, Buckler caught sight of a lady in blue, who strolled along twirling a parasol that, he noticed inconsequentially, clashed with her gown. As she lowered the parasol, he saw her face for the first time and recognized Penelope.

"Mr. Buckler," she exclaimed with a bright smile as he approached. "I was just coming to find you. How do you do?"

"Is everything all right?" he asked sharply. He had grown increasingly worried since he had heard Thorogood's report of the jaunt to Clerkenwell Green and had, in fact, intended a visit to St. James's Square the very next day.

"Why, yes, of course, but I have come to take my leave of you. We leave for Dorset tomorrow to pay a visit to Sir Roger's estate."

"Dorset? This is rather sudden. Are you certain you wish to go, Mrs. Wolfe? With the murder business as yet unresolved, I don't think I shall feel easy in my mind."

"I didn't mean to at first. Do you remember my friend Maggie Foss? When I objected that I wouldn't have a proper person to mind Sarah, Lady Ashe said I should employ Maggie to accompany us, if you can credit that. At any rate, Mr. Buckler, I can't conceive why anyone would wish me any harm. We'll stay for a few weeks, a month perhaps, and then I shall have to look around for another position."

He chose not to inquire why she didn't write to her father for help. Penelope had grown up on the isle of Sicily, acting as her father's hostess after her mother died, but something had gone awry between Sandford and his daughter. Though Buckler suspected this rift had to do with Penelope's husband, she had never said so directly.

"I begin to regret I ever recommended you to Lady Ashe's notice." He reached for her arm. "Come. Let us walk in the garden, and you can tell me all about it. You know that my brother is Sir Roger's neighbor in the country. I shall write to him and tell him of your visit."

They walked down Crown Office Row and through a set of imposing iron gates. The garden was a pleasant place with its roses, elms, flowering shrubs, and neat graveled walks. Carefully cultivated beds of tulips and Dutch yellow crocus as well as peach, plum, lime, and cherry trees offered refreshment to the eye and a balm to the spirit. Penelope and Buckler strolled for a time, content to speak of commonplaces.

Some quarter of an hour later, he led her to a seat, saying seriously, "Thorogood has been telling me the strangest story about Miss Barnwell, the West Country prophetess." He described the events on Clerkenwell Green.

"What a terrible thing if she truly is to have a child. Is it believed she will recover?"

"Thorogood spoke to a Mrs. Gore, a sort of acolyte to the prophetess, who said the wound appears to be superficial. Mrs. Gore claims that neither she nor Miss Barnwell ever heard of Dick Ransom or his employer's house in St. James's Square."

"How then did Ransom obtain one of Miss Barnwell's seals?" said Penelope slowly.

"There are thousands about, if one is to believe the accounts one hears of the extent of the prophetess' following."

"Mr. Chase mentioned political meetings held in a certain house in Westminster."

Buckler didn't meet her eyes. "Yes, well, it seems the house belongs to Mrs. Gore, and she sanctioned the meetings, which, she admitted to Thorogood, may have been a trifle 'indiscreet' but nothing criminal. Men in their cups full of boasts and hot air was how she put it."

Penelope tapped her gloved fingers on the bench and stared into the distance, her gaze unfocused. "I feel certain that the woman who came to St. James's Square on the evening after the murder had a very good reason. After all, she had the knife. She had either witnessed the murder or committed it herself. If you could have seen her wild grief when they apprehended her…"

"I cannot like this, Mrs. Wolfe. You had best remain in town."

Smiling, she shook her head. "You worry too much, my friend. Now I must go, though an interlude in this lovely garden had done me good." Her glance took in the trees, now streaked with long shadows, and the path still crowded with clusters of black-robed lawyers. Buckler had been steadfastly ignoring the curious looks cast their way.

He took her hand, noticing with amusement that the fingertips of her gloves were smudged with dirt, and recalled suddenly how it had felt to hold her in his arms. "Penelope. You will take care?"

Her eyes flew to his, startled, then dropped. "Yes, of course. If there is any trouble, I shall call upon your brother for assistance. He is a Justice of the Peace, is he not?"

"Yes, and a very good fellow. I am glad you will have Maggie to bear you company as well. She seems a sensible young person." He willed her to look up again. "Penelope. I wish—"

Pulling her hand away, she rose to her feet. "I really must get back. Please tell Mr. Thorogood I shall write to him and Mrs. Thorogood as soon as I am settled."

Buckler sat up straight and willed her to look at him again. "No, wait. I *will* speak, Mrs. Wolfe, though I have no right. You are so alone, ma'am. I want you to know I am at your service whenever and in whatever fashion you should require. You would tell me?"

"Yes, I suppose so, but I am well able to look after myself, sir. I can't think why you should doubt me."

"It's not a question of doubt," he said gently. "Just know I would be honored by your confidence."

When she nodded as if she understood him completely, he found himself smiling at her, though his sense of loss was keen. "Good-bye then, Mrs. Wolfe."

"Good-bye, Mr. Buckler," she said and hurried away.

❧ ❧

Next morning, Penelope took Sarah to get some air before climbing into the traveling coach that would take them to the country. Anxious that Maggie, little Frank, and the baby would not arrive in time, Sarah wanted to be in the square where she could observe every approaching vehicle. There weren't many at this hour when a weak sun had dissipated only a portion of the lingering mist.

For a time they amused themselves telling stories about the statue in the center of the basin, but Sarah began to fidget and wonder over and over where Maggie and Frank could be. Penelope, engaged in a mental review of the contents of their various packing cases, could afford her only abstracted replies. At length, however, they were rewarded by the rumble of wheels as a shabby hack pulled up in front of Sir Roger's house.

"They're here!" shouted Sarah, running forward.

"Mind the horses."

As Sarah reached the hackney, Maggie, broad, freckled face beaming, jumped down on the pavement, a baby in her arms and a little boy clinging to her skirts. Frank released his mother and went to his playmate, who grabbed his hands and pulled him rather roughly to one side as if staking immediate possession. The two children began to chatter and cavort in circles.

Grinning, Penelope turned to Maggie. "Thank goodness you're here. Sarah was in a pucker you wouldn't make it in time."

Maggie smiled back. "We set off later than I meant. Frank would dilly-dally over his breakfast. Then a friend of mine come by to bring us a little farewell gift." She held up a rather crushed bunch of flowers.

After admiring the posy, Penelope helped Maggie remove her bags and paid off the jarvey. Maggie had managed to cram her belongings into a small valise and two large bandboxes. Helping her carry these to the door, Penelope rang and instructed George to take the bags to the traveling chaise, which was being loaded in the mews.

"Eh, but you know just how to talk to him," said Maggie admiringly when the door had closed behind the footman. "He jumped right quick to do your bidding."

Penelope laughed. "Why shouldn't he? I asked politely enough." She glanced at the timepiece pinned to her dress. "We have about twenty minutes. Do you want to come and have a cup of tea, Maggie?"

She parodied shock. "No, indeed, mum. That wouldn't do for me at all. What would all these fine gentry servants think? No, I'll take the children up to the nursery. I hear them hatching some scheme about fetching something Miss Sarah forgot. You best go stretch your legs, Mrs. Pen, and grab a moment's peace while you can."

"Thank you," murmured Penelope, a trifle ruefully, wondering how long it would take for her new "maid" to begin managing the entire household.

As Maggie moved away, shepherding her three charges toward the door, Penelope called after her. "Baby looks well today. Did you give him some of the tonic I sent?"

"Oh, yes, mum. You don't need to fret about him. He be fit as a fiddle and ready for his first carriage journey."

Left alone, Penelope strolled back toward the basin in the middle of the square, her thoughts a little pensive. Just as she had yet to receive a reply from her father, she had not heard from Jeremy in some weeks either. She felt increasingly uneasy about her position and now about this journey out of town. But at least she and Maggie would keep busy entertaining the children—and keeping ears perked for any bits of information or gossip that might help solve Dick Ransom's murder. Penelope had a strong notion that the key to this riddle would travel to Dorset with the household. If that was so, she could perhaps do more to solve the crime than could John Chase in London.

She had circumambulated the basin four or five times and was ready to go inside to relieve herself and don her hat when her ears caught the sound of footsteps, and she looked up to see John Chase himself approaching. He moved toward her leisurely, his partially buttoned overcoat undulating in the stiff morning breeze. He'd removed his hat, so that his graying hair, drawn back in an untidy queue, flapped in tendrils about his face. His expression was intent, a little cold, with no welcoming smile on his lips. Apparently, he still recalled the brangle they'd had at their last meeting.

"Good day, Mrs. Wolfe. You're off this morning?"

"Yes, Mr. Chase." She spoke with stolid formality.

He came right up to her. "A word with you. I wanted you to know I've spoken to all of Wallace-Crag's servants. Their movements are all accounted on the morning of the murder, yet I cannot be certain they aren't covering for one another. It appears that the person who last spoke to the victim during the prior evening was George, the other footman, but he noticed nothing out of the ordinary until he awoke to find Ransom absent from his bed."

"Why do you tell me this?"

Chase didn't answer her question, but instead went on inexorably. "The family and the upper servants are another matter. They all sleep alone so there is no one to say whether or not they were in their beds when Ransom was killed. Sir Roger was not roused, and that secretary fellow claims he had been working late and dozed over his papers. Oh, and Ashe says he caught some of the commotion below and was awakened, but his wife told us, you will remember, that her rest too was undisturbed."

She felt herself softening. "So you've come to warn me that the villain may very well be a member of Sir Roger's household, or, indeed, of his family?"

"Yes, though I suppose anyone might have broken into the garden. The gate is easily breached."

Folding his arms over his chest, he leaned back against the iron railing and continued in a low, musing tone. "Typically, there are a limited number of motives for murder. Murder within a family for reasons of financial gain or jealousy. Crimes of passion between two lovers. Murder of master by aggrieved servant or vice versa. And slayings committed in the course of another crime such as robbery."

"'Tis clear this wasn't a robbery." She hesitated, wondering if she should repeat that old cat Mrs. Sterling's slander of Julia. Could it actually be that a lady of fashion would so far forget herself as to engage in intimacies with her footman? Penelope feared she knew the answer to that question.

"There is another possibility," she told Chase. "How about murder so as to prevent the discovery of a secret?" She hesitated, then told Chase about Julia's reputed absences from her chamber at night and about the damp cloak found stuffed under the counterpane.

His gaze sharpened. "Do you suspect the husband anxious to avoid the scandal of an unfaithful wife? I have reason to think Ashe's attentions may be turned elsewhere, but perhaps, after all, this was a crime of passion. But where does Rebecca Barnwell come in? She had the murder weapon in her possession. By the by, when you saw her that night, did you not notice that she is with child?"

"She was wearing a heavy cloak. But I do not see how a woman such as Miss Barnwell should be roaming the streets of London and spending the night in the parish lock-up."

"I thought at first she was connected to Dick Ransom in some treasonous plot. Now I wonder if I had it the wrong way around. What if she was known to someone in this household before Ransom's time? What if Ransom came to St. James's Square *because* of her?"

Penelope frowned. "I have never heard her spoken of by anyone here, Mr. Chase."

"I have some reason to suppose that the virtuous Miss Barnwell may have a scandal in her past, possibly an illegitimate child."

"A child! How extraordinary. I have heard no reports of that nature. What will you do now, sir?"

Straightening up, he pushed a strand of hair from his face and thrust his hat on his head. "I shall seek out your Covent Garden knife-seller for one thing. Good-bye, Mrs. Wolfe, for the present."

She glanced at her watch. "Yes, I must go in. They'll be wondering what's keeping me." Looking over Chase's shoulder, she met the fixed gaze of the bronze statue, King William III as a Roman general. "Did you ever notice the molehill under the horse's hooves? It quite fascinates Sarah."

Chase swung around. "What?"

"The molehill. That's what killed William while he was riding at Hampton Court. Sarah wanted to know if the statue-king knows it's there. I told her that the statue captures the moment just before the king's horse strikes the molehill. He's quite safe really."

Long into the night, Rebecca listened to the voices that swelled in anger, then dropped to murmurs that seemed even more menacing. She sat, shivering, in the hard chair by the window, limbs cramped, eyes raw with fatigue. She had tried to pray, but the words failed her. She had thought of marching into the next room to confront the Committee, but was afraid and ashamed. What if they would not believe her?

Resting one hand protectively over her belly, she shifted her bulk to find a more comfortable position. In the years since Janet had secured her release from the asylum, Rebecca had labored to bring the word of God to the suffering, the despised, and the poor. She had transcribed the powerful voice of the Spirit into dialogues and pamphlets by the handfuls, rallied rich and powerful men under her banner, and traveled the length of England, mile after weary mile, addressing assemblies of her followers despite a paralyzing fear of public speech. It seemed unfair that now, even as the fruition of every hope, every promise of glory, hovered within reach, she must discover that the past had not loosened its grip after all...

She must have dozed off, for suddenly Janet was shaking her, bending over to whisper, "Rebecca. They're ready for you. Be careful what you say." In carrying tones, she added, "She is awake. Give her a moment to collect herself."

Rebecca looked up to find herself surrounded by a circle of faces. The light from the adjoining room was at the men's backs so that their features were mostly in shadow. But she read neither pity for her distress nor any hint of the reverence she had come to accept as her due in the way they loomed over her without speaking. Involuntarily, she shrank back.

"Do not crowd her," said Dick curtly. "I have no doubt she will satisfy us."

"Satisfy us? Let us hope she is able to do so," drawled the one called O'Callaghan, whom Rebecca feared above all the rest of the Apostles. She could never recall the time she had seen him lift his wine glass and pretend to be drinking Christ's blood in a mockery of the Last Supper without shuddering at the blasphemy. Dick, the boy Rebecca had watched grow to manhood, often seemed a stranger to her when in O'Callaghan's presence.

She forced herself to sit erect. "Ask what you will. I am ready."

O'Callaghan nodded at Dick, who went to turn up the lamp. In the stronger glow, Rebecca saw that the Irishman held a sheet of paper between his lean, elegant fingers, and her heart sank. Waving it to and fro, he said, "You wrote this letter today, Miss Barnwell. It is apparently not your first, as you chastise the recipient for not as yet favoring you with a reply."

"You have no right to intercept my correspondence, sir."

"Who is this man, this fine gentleman of St. James's Square no less, to you? Why should you, a woman of God beloved by thousands, write in such terms—" Here he broke off to refer to the sheet in his hand. "*I beg you do not fail me. I must know the truth before I face the coming ordeal, or I cannot answer for the outcome. So much depends on your mercy.*" He looked at her, one brow cocked, a sardonic gleam in his black eyes.

"Miss Barnwell has not been herself of late," broke in Janet with another warning glance in Rebecca's direction. "Her rest has been disturbed and her...spirits have become depressed. Great events will soon overtake us. She must be excused for showing the strain we must all feel. There is nothing serious to concern us, and I swear I will watch over her the more carefully."

"Can you stop her from slipping out in the dark to roam the streets? What do you intend to do, keep her under lock and key for the rest of her days?" A look flashed between O'Callaghan and Janet that Rebecca did not understand, just as she had never understood her friend's overly rich dress and seemingly bottomless purse when her lover, Dick's father, had long since died in poverty.

"We cannot afford any ill reports," one of the other men burst out, "not with the time so near. We must not call attention to ourselves."

"Be silent," snapped Dick, but it was too late, for Rebecca was on her feet, anger burning through her veins.

"You seek to use me for your own ends, but beware, gentlemen. The Lord acts in His own time and His own way. 'Tis folly to think He has need of you."

"No, but you do," said O'Callaghan and grinned. "For when the dust has settled, we shall be the ones to place the scepter in your hand and the cloth of purple on your back."

Dick snorted. "Oh, for Christ's sake. You know that's all a hum, and so should she if she's got any sense left. When we have declared a Republic—"

"Dick!" cried Janet. "You are offensive. I think you should leave, all of you. I will speak to Miss Barnwell myself. Nothing can be done tonight at any rate."

He looked sheepish. "I am sorry, Mother."

They turned to go, O'Callaghan with the rest, though he cast one more probing glance at Rebecca before he followed in Dick's wake. Suddenly exhausted, she groped for the chair at her back and subsided. The voices retreated, but Rebecca scarcely noticed, for her anger had turned to ashes, and the prospect of the hours of darkness ahead appalled her. There was a humming in her ears, and then, as if from a distance, another sound, faint but unmistakable. Rebecca moaned, rocking faster.

"Tell me, Rebecca," pleaded Janet. "Whatever it is, let me help you, or let Dick, if you require a man to act on your behalf. You would not see everything we've worked for jeopardized."

"My baby. I must go to it. Please. Make it stop crying." She gave herself to the rhythm.

"Baby?" Janet gripped her shoulders, forcing her to halt. "Look at me. Your child is safe. He is to be the Most High whose birth will usher in the millennium. Christ is your bridegroom, and you conceived His child when He poured the Spirit into your flesh."

Rebecca opened her eyes. "No," she whispered. "You do not understand. It was a...a long time ago."

Janet stared in shocked silence, and Rebecca watched her face twist in anguish as she seemed to grasp something of the truth. Her hands tightened on Rebecca's shoulders.

"You ignorant, ugly slut," Janet said viciously, shaking her so that her head snapped back. "What man would want you?"

With that, she slammed out of the room, leaving Rebecca to discover, almost two hours later, that Janet had forgotten to lock the door.

Chapter XVII

"You wish to claim the dagger as your property?" said John Chase.

The knife-vendor's bony chin thrust out, sending the strings of her yellowed bonnet dancing. Under the bonnet, a full set of suspiciously fat curls did not budge. "That addle-brain who give it me weren't coming back. I'll lay you odds she don't even recall what she done with it."

"It's a valuable piece. Your friend was generous."

"I told you," she cried as drops of saliva spewed. "She weren't my friend. I only had words with her two, maybe three times. She said it weren't hers, and she were afraid someone would have it off her. Wanted me to keep it safe."

"Meaning she'd be back to collect it one day?"

"Gawd only knows." She stepped away to attend to a patron.

Custom was lighter at the Market this afternoon than Chase, who lived close by, was used to seeing. Usually one did well to mind his pockets while mingling among the press in the square. Thieves, whores, and vagabonds were all too plentiful in Covent Garden, the innumerable taverns attracting a constant supply of undesirables.

Over their teacups, Chase's landlady Mrs. Beeks and her friends enjoyed abusing the Market; to them, it represented much of what was wrong with the world with its grasping after profit and its dirt and mess. The doorsteps of all the houses along the approach to the square were left covered with refuse, the pavement stained green with trodden leavings. And at the top of anyone's list of nuisances were the ragged waifs who slept beneath the stalls of the Market at night and woke to prey upon the merchants by day. According to the knife-seller, Chase's mystery woman had occasionally dossed down with these children.

She was back. "Where can I find the little beggars?" Chase asked.

"Come back tonight," she said sourly. "The devils is always here."

"Where now?"

"They is around. You can ask the orange-lady as they seem to like to fuss her." Her eyes were sharp on his face. "What about my knife? You mean to give it back?"

Chase turned to walk away. "It is material evidence in a murder inquiry. Besides, it was never truly yours."

"It surely don't belong to that fine lady bitch what took it off me neither," she shrieked after him. "You tell her I said so!"

⋙ ⋘

Chase located one of the children easily. Dressed in a pair of men's trousers, rucked at the waist and inexpertly turned at the ankles, a gaudy waistcoat embroidered with wide purple and gold stripes, and a shiny black tailcoat much too large for his slender frame, he was dogging the heels of the orange-seller.

Chase flipped her a coin. "Give him one."

Both of them gawked at him, but the woman took the coin and plucked a piece of fruit from the top of her stack. She offered it to the boy.

"I'll pick it meself," he announced with dignity.

Instead of lingering over his choice, as Chase might have done, the boy shot out his hand and snatched the first one he touched. This he thrust into his pocket.

"Thank you, sir," he mumbled, looking down at his feet and waiting, for in his world, and to some degree in Chase's as well, there was no such thing as kindness for its own sake.

Chase motioned him to one side. "Your name, boy?"

"Fergus."

"Where do you live?"

"Roundabout. Where I can."

"How do you get your bread?" he asked sternly.

Fergus sidled away. A dull, resigned expression had come over his face. There was a long pause before he replied. "I were a coster's boy, helping to push a barrow and cry out the wares. One day he don't want me no more, so I stay here and pick up what I can."

"At night?"

He stiffened with alarm. "Who's asking, mister? I ain't done nothing." Taking another step back, he glanced around surreptitiously as if seeking reinforcements.

"John Chase, Bow Street."

The dullness vanished. "Bow Street," he breathed.

Chase sighed. This boy was about the same age as Leo Beeks and a year or two younger than Chase's own Jonathan. The thought made him wonder briefly whether Jonathan too would look upon him with admiring eyes, or whether he would only see the man who had not been a father to him. "I asked if you slept here at night."

"Yes sir. Me and some others catch a few winks under the stalls. We don't hurt nothing."

"Did a woman seek shelter with you recently?

"You mean Dora?"

For a moment, Chase was confused; then he understood. Dora. It was the name of the woman safely confined in Bedlam, she who had once been an inmate at the Islington asylum. Could it be that Rebecca Barnwell had borrowed the name from her friend? He felt his breathing quicken. "Yes, probably," he said casually. "Tell me of her."

"Not much in her cockloft," said the boy, tapping his head. "But she's a right one. Once, when she had some blunt to spare, she treated me and me mate Joseph to a pint of porter and a pie."

"What is this female's appearance? Young? Old? Pretty? How dressed? Was she with child, by any chance?"

"I'd say she's too old for that, sir. Brown and gray hair pulled well back. Her face has lines, and it looks, well, sad, I think. She always wore a cloak, so I dunno what she had on underneath."

"When was the first time you saw this Dora?"

His face crumpled in concentration, but time would have little meaning to a child like this. "Some while back," he said after due consideration. "It was cold, and she were lurking round the Market. It got to be night, and she didn't have no place to go. We let her bide with us, and she loped off again in the morning. We figured she had a begging post somewhere."

"She never told you anything of her history? Where she came from, for instance?"

He looked surprised. "Naw. I didn't ask."

It would be a common enough phenomenon for young Fergus. People must move in and out of his life like ships with no berth. The rule of the streets demanded that a person mind his own business; it was the first requirement of survival. And possibly in this case an innate and delicate courtesy would have kept the boy from speaking out.

Reaching into his pocket, Chase retrieved a coin. "Much obliged."

But as he began to stroll away, the boy burst out, "Look here. Why you asking? She wouldn't do nothing wrong."

Chase turned around. "Oh?" he said softly.

"No, sir. She be a godly woman. Why, she told me the Savior would come again to take all the poor folk up to Paradise, and I should go too if I was good."

"You believed her, boy?" Chase heard the hard note in his voice and knew Fergus would think the anger was directed at him.

"Yes, sir. Salvation belongs to all, but as for them what don't turn away from sin…" Giving an eloquent shrug, he drew one dirty finger across his neck.

⚜

Laughter and rollicking song greeted John Chase at the Fleece on Little Windmill Street, the noise coming from behind a door that probably led to the inn parlor. The taproom itself was deserted but for the proprietor, a watchful man who stood behind the bar polishing a glass.

Tucking his cloth under one beefy arm, the barman said unsmilingly, "Evening, sir. What can I do for you?"

Chase gestured at the closed door. "I've come for the meeting. From the sound of it, you've a full house, landlord."

"It's the debating club, sir, and I'm afraid it's members only. May I inquire how you came to hear of it? I've not seen you round here before."

"A friend told me of the club. He said I should find both congenial company and an opportunity to make myself useful in a good cause."

"That so? Well, maybe I can pass on the word to the officers. I can't say as whether the club be open to new members, but if you'll leave your name and direction—"

Chase clapped a hand to his coat pocket. "How foolish of me. I had almost forgotten. He said I was to present this." Reaching in, he drew out the seal and laid it gently on the scarred wooden counter.

The mask dropped, and a look of greedy curiosity made the landlord seem for a moment like a goblin brooding over a nugget of gold. But when he turned the seal in his hands, his expression shifted again. "'Tis made out to a Noah Packet. That you?"

"My friend, as it chances," said Chase. From within came the sound of raised voices, then another song accompanied by what sounded like the stamping of feet and the pounding of tables. "It seems I am missing all the fun. I'll just go in now."

He turned away, but before he had gone more than a few paces the man was around the bar, blocking his path. Suddenly, the publican seemed much larger, and though Chase was tall, this man loomed over him. "I can't let you do that, sir. This is a private gathering. I'm only following instructions, see, and you wouldn't have me fail in my duty? There is procedures to be followed like."

Inspiration struck. What was that verse from the Bible Ransom had gasped out in the moment of his death? Chase took a step back. "You mean like a password to gain admittance?" He paused, then spoke clearly. "*The sun shall be turned into darkness, and the moon into blood, before the great and the terrible day of the Lord come.*"

When the landlord's jaw slackened, Chase knew his luck had not failed him. Quickly, he stepped around him and was at the door, relieved to find that the knob turned easily. Though he felt the publican's gimlet eyes on his back, the man made no further move to stop him.

Once inside, Chase sucked in a smoky breath and looked around. The parlor proved to be a long, narrow room dominated by an enormous fireplace opposite where he stood. The combination of the large fire and the close heat of about forty bodies piled willy-nilly on sofas, stools, and chairs almost overpowered him. He shook his head to clear his smarting eyes and retreated behind a nearby table strewn with penny and two-penny pamphlets, as if desirous of studying them.

It seemed no one had paid much attention to his entrance, for all were focused on a man who stood, wobbling glass in one hand, pipe in the other, declaiming a speech. Surreptitiously, Chase's eyes traveled from face to face as he committed to memory as many of the details of each man's appearance as possible. They were a crude, raffish bunch, but their faces glistened with enthusiasm, and here and there he saw the marks of tears, quickly dashed away. He wondered which of these men was the crime king who had hounded Noah Packet into hiding.

At length, when the speaker sat down to the usual claps and cheers, another took his place, delivering his piece in much the same style, a sort of meandering harangue on the topic which, as Chase slowly gathered, had something to do with whether the profligate expenditures of government may be said to cause the miseries of its people. Someone proposed a merry-making song, and Chase, dropping the Thomas Paine pamphlet he'd been pretending to read, listened in grim amusement as the gathering bellowed forth a lusty tribute to the Regent:

> 'Tis in Pall Mall there lives a Pig,
> That doth this Mall adorn,
> So fat, so plump, so monstrous Big,
> A finer ne'er was born.
> This Pig so sweet, so full of Meat,
> He's the one I wish to kill.
> I'll fowls resign on thee to dine,
> Sweet Pig of fine Pall Mall.

Gusts of laughter erupted, and a man in a shoemaker's apron cried out, "A toast, gentlemen. May the last of the kings be strangled with the guts of the last of the priests." The crowd roared its approval and lifted glasses of porter, Chase with the rest, for he had managed to commandeer a mug from a serving girl circulating through the room.

Looking around triumphantly, the shoemaker called, "Someone else. Give us one, Captain O'Callaghan."

All eyes turned toward a floridly handsome Irishman with snapping black eyes, so there was no one to notice Chase's involuntary start. He had already marked this man as being a cut above the rest, garbed as O'Callaghan was in a neat-fitting coat, dark breeches of good cloth, and polished boots, but now Chase studied the Irishman with renewed interest. When O'Callaghan heard his name pronounced, he smiled rather sardonically and bowed.

"May the skin of the Tyrants be burnt into Parchment, and the Rights of Man written upon it," he said quietly in a voice that nonetheless carried to the far corners.

Chase started, recalling the soft, cultured tones heard through a haze of pain while riding in a carriage. He was certain this was the man who had warned him to steer clear of the brothel—government informant, criminal, and Noah Packet's nemesis, rolled into one. Seeming to sense the intensity of regard, O'Callaghan gazed back at first questioningly, then with a kind of wry recognition.

Chase moved toward him, but, at his back, the door opened, and he spun round. A woman, heavily veiled, had come into the room. Looking neither right nor left, she walked forward with firm and purposeful steps as the men fell back in her wake. In the lamplight, her black gown had the sheen of a raven's wing, and her silk cloak swirled about her upright form as if she were a queen come among them. In her outstretched arms, she bore a large writing box.

The men shifted uneasily, muttering to themselves, but no one spoke out or moved to stop her. Reaching the center of the room, she set her burden on a table and faced them. Slowly she began to lift her veil, then, as if losing patience, shoved it back with rough hands to reveal a lovely face, ravaged by a desperation that trembled on her lips and glared from her eyes. Before she had even uttered a word, Chase felt the men's withdrawal as if they knew they looked upon something fearful.

"I have come to ask you but one question," said Janet Gore. "Are you men?"

Chase felt their confusion, their uneasiness, the dawning of a baffled anger, but Gore rushed on. "I have sacrificed my first born, my flesh and my blood, to the Cause. What of you? You sit here singing your songs and do nothing. Miss Barnwell has left us. Who among you will go in search of her before it is too late, and the child is born in captivity, or worse."

The murmurs increased in volume; here and there someone swore or pounded his fist in the air.

"What's she on about?" one man demanded.

"Lord, if I know," said another scornfully. He raised his voice. "Get you gone. This ain't no place for a female."

All at once the men were shouting and stamping their booted feet, while Mrs. Gore stood there, head unbowed. O'Callaghan called out, his words lost in the din. He strode forward, taking Gore by the shoulder. She shook him off, her face aglow with an expression of such malevolence that the Irishman shrank back.

She bent over the writing box on the table. "Get away from me. Do you or do you not want to know the Will of God? I will tell you. I *must* tell you," she shrieked. In a moment she had the little key in the lock, the lid lifted, and she was brandishing a paper in her hand. With one finger she broke the seal, and little bits of red wax fluttered to the floor. Rapidly, she scanned the lines penned there, holding the paper tightly against her body to guard against having it snatched from her grip.

"Death," she cried triumphantly. The men stared back at her, their protests silenced. "I thought it would be so. Soon there will be a death. The prophecy says 'twill be a man of stature, a man of power, and when he dies we will know the end is nigh."

She thrust her hand back in the box to pull out a sheaf of papers, some of which fell from her hand to flutter to the ground. "What will you do to pave the way for Glory? Will you shed your own blood if such is required of you?"

Breaking another seal at random, she unfolded a piece of parchment, almost tearing it in her haste. Before she could read it out, Chase was at O'Callaghan's side. Together they pulled the papers from her hands and took her by each arm.

The door slammed open. "Bow Street!" someone shouted, and Chase glanced over his shoulder to see about two dozen officers streaming into the room, some with truncheons raised, others waving a pistol in each hand. The Jacobins jumped to their feet to bellow their rage, but in those close quarters there was little they could do, their only exit blocked.

Chase caught one glimpse of the terrified publican in an officer's grip. All was confusion as the police swept through the crowd, slapping on handcuffs and hustling men out of the room. Though some struggled, many seemed too stunned by drink or sheer amazement to resist.

Tightening his grip on the woman, Chase looked at O'Callaghan, who gazed back as if they shared an amusing secret—as if, Chase thought, he had known this would happen and was as pleased as a cat with its dish of cream. When a constable motioned to the Irishman, he went without a murmur.

Left alone with Janet Gore, Chase turned her to face him, reflecting that much that had eluded him was now clear. "Ransom was your son. Why did Barnwell send him to St. James's Square?"

She looked back, contempt in her eyes, and he thought she would refuse to speak. But to dissemble would be beneath this woman, he realized, especially now when the game was up. She practically threw her words in his face.

"She didn't send him. Rebecca had run off as she often does, but this time she didn't come back for weeks. We were terrified. Dick was to intercept her and also to determine if there was any threat from that quarter."

"You mean a threat to your conspiracy."

"Yes, it seemed she would ruin everything."

"What is Barnwell's connection to Sir Roger Wallace-Crag and his household? And where is she now? I should have heard had she been arrested."

"You can't stop this," she said hoarsely, slumping in his grip. "Do not think you can."

Another constable had approached, and Chase was forced to display his Bow Street staff before he himself was dragged off. On this man's heels was a familiar rotund figure, the veteran Runner John Townsend.

"Remove this woman," he said to the constable, pointing with his walking stick.

"Yes, sir."

Chase bristled. "I've not finished, Townsend."

"I can't say I'm surprised to find you here," the Runner returned pleasantly, "though you might have heeded my advice and stayed well out of this bumblebroth. Leave the female. She's not for you."

Short of engaging in a wrestling match, there was little Chase could do. Inwardly fuming, he watched the constable escort Gore from the room.

≪✺≫

The news of Wellington's victory at the Spanish fortress of Badojoz had arrived on the same day as the police raid on the Fleece. As Chase made his way back to Bow Street, voices called out jubilantly in the darkness, and shadowy forms gathered on street corners to discuss the great tidings.

"So you swept up some rubbish, eh?" said Graham when Chase presented himself in the small office that all the magistrates used.

"Not my doing, sir. I was just along for the ride you might say, though in truth, no one had mentioned the prospect of such a journey this night."

The magistrate grunted. "We'll end up freeing most of the Jacobins, of course, but I'm told some incriminating papers have surfaced in the possession of the ringleaders. It seems they'd concocted a plot against the Regent, though how much of it was just bluster is anyone's guess. There is evidence, however: lists of servants and doorkeepers employed at Carlton House, household schedules, and notes on the Prince's habits and movements."

Shaking his head gloomily, the magistrate went on. "This at a time when the Luddite scoundrels grow ever bolder, more desperate in their villainy. Did you hear of the attack on that mill near Manchester? Several thousand men were there, and at least three in the crowd were killed by musket fire from the men protecting the place. A very bad business."

"Yes, sir. Is the Regent thought to be in any danger now that the conspiracy has been foiled?"

Graham stroked his upper lip. "I should hope not. If we are lucky, we have apprehended enough traitors for the present. Still, Townsend has been instructed to be particularly on guard to ensure His Majesty's safety."

"What of the prophetess Barnwell, sir? Surely, her disappearance is cause for concern under the circumstances."

"Indeed, especially as it seems she murdered the footman. A falling out among conspirators, it has been suggested. I had a man called Dobbin from the Home Office in here earlier to make arrangements to remove the Jacobins for questioning. A filthy little fellow, I must say, but he seems to know his business. He had nothing but good to report of your work in this matter, Chase."

"That's more than I can say in return," he replied, thinking of the blow to his knee.

"There's no question that this lunatic Barnwell must be found as soon as may be. It takes only one to pull a trigger. She is a dangerous woman, as is her handmaiden Janet Gore, who, by the way, has nothing to say for herself."

"Mrs. Gore has admitted that the footman was her son, who went to St. James's Square seeking the prophetess. But

I still do not know why. Sir, I should like to speak to Mrs. Gore again. Also, there was a man called O'Callaghan appre-hended tonight, a government informant."

Graham avoided his eyes. "That won't be possible, Chase. I believe the Home Office hopes Mrs. Gore will turn King's evidence, and you would do well to put O'Callaghan out of your mind as well. He may be a thief and an extortionist, but he has proven his use. He will be quietly released, I've no doubt, free to resume his unsavory career."

"Thief?" echoed Chase bitterly. "Yes, and double-dealing Jacobin to boot. A busy man, it seems, but his cohorts would tear him limb from limb if they knew the whole of it."

"No loss if that were to happen. Now if you'll excuse me, I must tackle this mound of papers before seeking my bed."

At the door Chase halted, his hand falling from the knob. Slowly, he turned back to face Graham. "Have you any objection to my leaving town for a few days?"

Chapter XVIII

When the chaise had rumbled through the last of the gray streets, Penelope caught her first glimpse of green vistas and felt her spirit quicken with an unexpected gladness. Meadows flashed by, flaunting clumps of red and yellow primroses, and blooming hedgerows lined their passage. She gazed out the window, thinking of a print Jeremy had hung on the wall of their rooms in Palermo when they were first married.

In it a fiery-haired, naked youth, arms flung wide in joyous self-abandon, stood poised on high ground against a brilliant sunburst. Below him was blackness, left behind rather like, it seemed to Penelope, her own escape from the London soot that coated one's skin and left its persistent ashy taste in the mouth.

Jeremy had looked up from his easel to point out that the print was probably inspired by the old Renaissance proportion diagrams demonstrating how the human form, with arms and legs extended, fit into perfect geometrical shapes like the square or the circle. But Penelope had said that she preferred not to confine that glorious youth to something so dull as geometry. Funny she should think of it now, even recalling Jeremy's answering laugh and tender smile, while riding in a coach on the Salisbury road.

Mr. Finch, Maggie, Penelope, and the children rode in the traveling carriage as the baggage chariot, piled high with its load of antiquities, made its stately progress at the rear. In the family barouche, Lady Ashe and her father and husband had pulled well ahead, though Penelope's party met up with them at the next change of horses, where they dined and slept at a coaching house.

The next morning they set off again, muscles sore from the constant jarring, eyes heavy after their night in the inn with ostlers shouting at all hours and the rattling of carriage wheels in the courtyard. But the children continued well behaved, thank God. Feeling only a trifle unwell with the motion of the coach, Sarah amused herself by playing games with her friend while the baby slept and woke and slept again. Mr. Finch commented on the passing scenery for Maggie and Penelope's benefit and described Sir Roger's home in north Dorset, which, of course, he knew well after so many years of service with the family.

"The original structure was Tudor with Jacobean additions." Absently, he bent down to pick up one of Sarah's marbles which had rolled under his shoe and restored it to the giggling children.

"Sir Roger had the house completely rebuilt?"

"Oh, yes. The results are rather…remarkable, as you will see for yourself, Mrs. Wolfe."

When Maggie gave him a puzzled look, he added, "It must be acknowledged that Sir Roger has spared no effort or expense with Cayhill. While some may quarrel with his taste, he is not a man to leave a thing half done."

"The house in St. James's Square has always struck me as a veritable hodge-podge. One can but admire all of Sir Roger's acquisitions, the crosses, daggers, stone tablets, and the rest. Still, there is no harmony or unity of design in the décor." Pausing, Penelope looked into the secretary's tired face and wondered if her remark might have offended his sense of loyalty to his master, though she'd really only meant to make conversation.

But after a moment he replied, his tone light. "I've often thought the same, Mrs. Wolfe. In matters of aesthetics, and possibly also philosophy and morals, it seems best to elect for the simple, even the austere. Otherwise, one is soon left in a sad jumble, I'm afraid. It should be most interesting to see what you make of the Abbey, ma'am."

"No doubt you are pleased to return there, Mr. Finch? It must be in some sense your home as well."

"My home? No, indeed," he said curtly. "I have not felt it so for many years."

There was a short, uncomfortable silence; then Finch, apparently fearing he had been discourteous, added, "There was a time when my late mistress Lady Wallace-Crag was alive when Cayhill did seem a place I could belong, but with her passing…" He shrugged.

At that point the children began to clamor for a snack, and Penelope had no further chance to continue the discussion. As the afternoon waned, conversation became ever more desultory, and at length they all lapsed into sleep.

Penelope did not awaken until the carriage entered a gateway under an entrance lodge and wound up a broad avenue lined by ancient oaks. When they emerged from the trees, she was given her first view of Cayhill Abbey.

Streaks of red tarried in the western sky, a paler, residual light illuminating the vale below. Sir Roger Wallace-Crag's country seat was built in the Gothick style in the shape of an irregular cross with minimal exterior ornamentation, carved pointed arch windows, and huge corner buttresses. Above a sea of chimney pots and fanciful turrets thrust a mammoth octagonal tower several hundred feet high. In actuality only a decade or two old, the structure was apparently meant to seem an ancient building that had been extensively altered over many centuries. Still, Penelope could not but admit that the atmosphere of brooding horror felt remarkably genuine, accentuated by the deep shadows across the enormous façade like slashes of black paint.

Before long they had rattled through an archway into a cobble-stoned courtyard to pull up abruptly at the entrance. After the coachman let down the steps, they disembarked, and the butler and the housekeeper came forward to greet them.

"Welcome to the Abbey, madam. Will you step in?" said the butler, who then turned to Finch with a polite greeting.

The housekeeper, Mrs. Dobson, was a heavyset, elderly woman with a richly tinted, porcelain-like complexion and exotic, slanted eyes that hinted of Spanish blood. Curtseying respectfully, she looked at Penelope. "Lord and Lady Ashe and Sir Roger arrived some time ago. They bade me welcome you, ma'am, and invite you to dine in one hour unless you be too fatigued."

Penelope smiled and thanked her, understanding the woman's not so subtle message. Her anomalous position in this household was not to be held against her; she was, in fact, to be treated as honored guest, rather than upper servant. It didn't hurt that Maggie had accompanied her as maid.

The butler had moved away to instruct a manservant about the luggage, but the indefatigable Mrs. Dobson prattled on to Penelope in her soft country tones that were so at odds with her unusual face. Shivering in the cold, clear air, Penelope made the appropriate responses, but was more than ready when the woman offered to conduct her to her room.

When Maggie tried to take Sarah's hand and follow a maidservant who had materialized to conduct her inside, the little girl clung to Penelope's knees and buried her head.

"I'll take her, Maggie," said Penelope, thinking ruefully that the Abbey might very well give the children nightmares despite the fact that it was probably a splendid place for imaginary games. She smiled at her friend. "Do you go with the girl and get Frank and Baby settled. I'll see you presently."

As the maidservant led Maggie around the side to another entrance, Penelope and Sarah followed Mrs. Dobson up one side of a double flight of steps and through a set of doors that must have been thirty or forty feet tall. She found herself in the great hall. Large terracotta figures of saints and biblical heroes occupied high niches. The windows, including a high rose window, were paned with heraldic glass, and a massive fireplace dominated one wall. Carved tables of yew matching a set of crude side chairs did little to fill the enormous space. Looking up, Penelope saw that various arms were emblazoned on the ceiling; whose she could not tell since they could hardly all belong to the family.

After crossing the hall, they paused at an archway. Running north from where they stood for a distance of several hundred feet was a series of dimly lit galleries culminating in a burst of light that emanated from a rear chamber. The effect was disorienting, to say the least. Penelope had the irresistible impression that she stood in the transept of a medieval cathedral looking toward a candle-lit high altar.

The housekeeper cast a swift glance at Penelope as if to discern her reaction, then led her to a circular staircase rising from the bottom of a turret in one of middle galleries. They climbed several flights to the second floor.

"I've put you in the red room," she said as they proceeded down a dim corridor. "There's no nursery wing at Cayhill. But in any event Lady Ashe said you'd not like to be too far from your daughter. I thought mayhap your dressing room would do for the child. There's a bed there. Or would you rather she be accommodated in the servant's quarters with your woman?"

Feeling Sarah stiffen, Penelope said quickly, "The dressing room will do admirably. Thank you, Mrs. Dobson."

Fortunately, the red room was large and comfortably appointed. A four-poster with canopy and crimson hangings had plenty of room for both her and Sarah, for Penelope knew her daughter would wheedle her way into the bed. The rest of the room held ebony furnishings, including a gargantuan wardrobe, incongruously set next to a delicate lady's writing table. Most importantly at this moment, a cheerful fire burned in the grate, quite banishing the lingering gloom from downstairs. In short, they would find this room a much-needed haven.

She turned to Mrs. Dobson. "It's lovely, ma'am. And the warmth is most welcome."

Sarah wiggled away, and, running to the fire, pulled off her mittens and muffler. "You're right, Mama. This is nice."

The housekeeper's face relaxed. "Surely you'll like it here, miss. Plenty of nooks and crannies round about. Watch you don't get lost playing hide and seek in the cloisters." Her lace cap bobbed at Penelope. "The head groom's young 'un was forever doing so when he was about your little girl's age, ma'am."

"Cloisters?" said Penelope in a faint voice.

"Yes, ma'am. Just east of the house. Sir Roger calls it his 'atmospheric walk.' One can promenade there in most any weather."

Pulling off her gloves, Penelope followed Sarah to the hearth and began warming her hands. "Mr. Finch told me I should find Cayhill remarkable and indeed he was right. I presume there's also a chapel, suitably medieval, of course?"

"Oh no, Mrs. Wolfe, no chapel, though there is an altar downstairs in the Sanctuary. If you be thinking of Sunday services, we go to the parish church in Buckland where the family has its pew and vault. That be where Lady Wallace-Crag is buried and the babes."

"Babes, Mrs. Dobson?" asked Penelope. Sarah had gone still, her eyes flying up to fix on their faces.

"Yes, ma'am. All her pretty ones laid in a row so that when she come to join them, poor lady, there they'd be waiting." Seeming to shake herself, the housekeeper gave a thin smile and reached out to ruffle Sarah's dark hair. "She died a few years after birthing Miss Julia. I should think she was fair worn out."

Penelope said casually, "What a tragedy for her and for Sir Roger. It must have been…difficult for him to have a wife in such delicate health and then to lose her thus. He was quite a young man at the time." She had been thinking about Chase's notion of an illegitimate birth in Rebecca Barnwell's past and wondering how best to probe Sir Roger's character without being too obvious. But the housekeeper appeared to misunderstand her innuendo.

"Indeed. My lady's health and spirits were never robust, but at least she enjoyed the comfort of her religion. And toward the end, her friendship with that young person who was Miss Julia's nurse brought her much solace…how curious, I've quite forgotten her name. That's what happens when you get older, my dear."

"Her nurse?" Dimly, Penelope recalled Julia saying that her nurse was the only one who had ever given her love.

Mrs. Dobson lowered her voice. "I'm afraid the girl got herself in trouble and took it in her head to tell tales to avoid the disgrace. If you can credit her brazenness, she claimed the good Lord had sent her a child as if she had nothing whatever to do with the matter. We never did discover who the father truly was, but Lady Wallace-Crag actually believed in her nonsense."

"How fascinating…what happened to the girl and her child?" To Penelope's ears, her voice sounded high-pitched and artificial, but she couldn't help it.

Mrs. Dobson shook her head sadly. "She went away. We heard later that they had both died."

❧ ❧

"Don't you fret, Mrs. Pen," said Maggie. "We'll have our supper and unpack, after which I expect the children will be ready for their beds. I'll settle Baby and Frank here on the sofa until you return."

Grimacing at her own face in the looking-glass, Penelope straightened her collar and smoothed her hair, which showed a tendency to sag out of its pins. No question about it, she looked fagged to death with a dazed look about the eyes, a sallow cast to her cheeks. Moreover, her gown was sadly creased.

She bent down to kiss Sarah. "Be good, love. I shall be back shortly."

Penelope stepped out into the corridor, hoping she'd be able to find her way to the dining parlor. After the brightness of her bedchamber, the corridor, lit only by sparsely placed candles in wall sockets, gave her the momentary illusion of being in some sort of underground tunnel. Instinctively, she reached out one hand to the wall as if seeking an anchor and walked on, trailing her hand against the faint roughness of walls painted to look like stone. Reaching the dark, circular stairway, she started down. Really, she thought crossly, atmosphere was all well and good, but it would be far too easy to break one's neck in this house.

Perhaps it was, after all, hunger or fatigue, or perhaps merely the ambience of the house, but Penelope felt reality weakening its grip to slide into some corner of her consciousness. She knew she was descending a stairway in Sir Roger Wallace-Crag's house and that her dinner and the company of other people awaited her below. But those were just facts, far less powerful than the almost vertigo-like sensation of her feet striking each step and her hand swimming along the smooth oak of the banister. It was as if, having once started a course, her body had been caught up in an eddy that moved it inexorably downward almost without her volition.

But as she attained the first floor landing, a figure loomed in her path. Feeling the sudden presence like a jarring blow, she halted.

"Good evening, Mrs. Wolfe," said Ashe. "I shall do myself the honor of escorting you down to dinner." He gave one of his glinting, empty smiles and bent closer, crowding her in the confined space.

Looking into his black eyes, Penelope discovered the solution to a puzzle that had long troubled her. A woman knows, she thought, when a gentleman likes her, enjoys her company, and even if she doesn't reciprocate the feeling, she can't help but experience a tiny thrill of conquest. Yet while Lord Ashe might choose to treat his wife's hired companion with complaisance, she realized in that moment that idle flirtation, or even mere kindness, was not his aim.

He took her arm to guide her down the stairs. "I am pleased that you decided, after all, to accompany Julia, Mrs. Wolfe. I cannot but acknowledge you a steadying influence on my wife."

Nonplussed, she replied, "Thank you, my lord. Possibly a sojourn in the country may do us all some good. I shall not be sorry to enjoy quiet nights and go early to my bed."

"Quite sensible. If you will only convince Julia to do likewise, I shall be grateful. I do believe that business with the footman has distressed her more than she realizes."

She murmured something noncommittal, schooling her expression to remain impassive. Ashe took another step, then stopped, turning again to face her in the narrow space.

"The matter is behind us," he said softly. "I feel at liberty now to confide that I have been most uneasy in my mind. You see, this Ransom was not what he seemed. That he should insinuate himself into a gentleman's residence…but it might have been worse, Mrs. Wolfe, much worse."

Penelope's heart gave a painful thump. "How so, my lord?"

He bared his teeth in a mockery of a smile. "Need you inquire, my dear? You have come to know Julia so well."

❧❧

Edward Buckler pulled up the gig to survey the rolling downland he'd once called home. Over a sleepless night, he had decided to leave London and set out after Penelope. Usually, he strove to make calculated decisions; he was not used to acting on the spur of the moment.

But while tossing and turning in a futile battle with his covers, it had seemed to him that she would be too alone, too isolated not knowing anyone in Dorset. Though he'd written to ask his brother to look in, Buckler could not feel at ease thinking of her in that strange, remote house.

In the morning, after asking Bob to reschedule his paltry few appointments, he packed a bag, left a note for Thorogood, and booked passage on the stage. An outside seat, for, of course, the guard refused to allow Buckler's dog inside the coach, and even to secure a place on the roof had required a substantial bribe. Two, in fact, since he'd also had to shell out to still the outcry from the assorted riffraff who were to be his travel companions.

After a chilly, jarring, interminable ride during which he never had time to bolt more than a few morsels of food at various coaching inns, he rented a gig at Salisbury and set off down the turnpike for the last sixteen miles to his brother's home.

By now, afternoon was deepening to evening, less than an hour of daylight remaining. He'd best get on. The high road beginning in the miry, low ground of the Ebble valley had ascended to a throat-catching expanse of land and sky that continued until Blandford. Traffic was light at this hour, and the horse seemed to know the road well. Buckler had plenty of leisure to think, to observe the flocks of purplish-green lapwings, and to listen to the hoarse shrieks of rooks.

There was something about this place that both stirred and depressed him. It was beautiful yet somber, even eerie, rich with endless variety, and always endlessly the same. Occasionally, the grassy swelling of an ancient earth mound, so much a part of the landscape as to be accepted without thought, broke the ground's contour. It was said that somewhere existed a barrow which held a magnificent golden coffin awaiting discovery. Near Woodyates, one observed evidence of a later presence when the high road joined briefly with a stretch of the old Roman thoroughfare. And it was in this vicinity that the royal bastard Monmouth had been captured at the conclusion of his ignominious bid for a crown.

Curled at his feet apparently sound asleep, the dog missed the greater part of this journey across the downs. It did not stir until they stopped to pay the toll at Cashmore, at which point it rose slowly to its haunches and looked around without much interest. Aged and of indeterminate breed, Ruff was the most lugubrious, inert animal Buckler had ever encountered. The dog neither fawned nor groveled, but seemed curiously independent of humanity, his master included. Still, in recent days it seemed that Ruff had come to view him with some measure of partiality, as evidenced by a weakly thumping tail whenever Buckler approached with food.

Thus, he was astounded when a few minutes after they left the turnpike, Ruff, having seemed to lapse again into a doze, reared up from his place on the floorboards to peer over the edge of the seat.

"Hell and the devil," said Buckler.

His response was a distinctly baleful look out of watery eyes and a growl. Ruff turned his gaze back to the road and maintained a low rumbling, punctuated by short, furious barks. Buckler looked also, but saw nothing; they were alone on the road, which led to Buckland village and the manor where his brother was squire. Unless the damned mutt had decided to bark at the lengthening shadows, Buckler had no notion what there was to trouble him.

"Easy, boy," he said soothingly and placed a hand on the dog's head, trying to nudge it down.

Ruff shoved back, hard, thrusting his body up so that his forelegs scrabbled up and across Buckler's lap, nearly overbalancing him. Lifting his head, the dog gave a wild, inconsolable cry.

Before Buckler's ears had time to register this fearful noise, he had his hands full of plunging horse. Swearing fluently, he yanked the gig to a shuddering stop. Ruff subsided at his feet, trembling.

Rebecca waited until the gig had disappeared in a cloud of dust before rising from behind the gnarled tree. When she was sure it was safe, she set off in the same direction, thinking of the bewilderment on the man's face, the piercing strangeness of the dog's howl. Somehow, the creature had known she was there, but she did not know what this portended. Why should it fear her? Perhaps it had sensed the shadow of evil and death that was her constant companion and had merely sought to warn her.

For a moment she wondered if she'd done right to run away again and shivered remembering Janet's anger when she had crept back the last time after that terrible night in the parish lock-up. Sobbing out the story of Dick's death, Rebecca had thought Janet would strike her. Janet had purpled with rage, then turned so white that Rebecca had started forward to prevent her falling. But Janet pushed her away, and after that, they no longer spoke of Dick.

This time was different. Rebecca had suddenly known where she must be to finish it all. No matter that the demons would follow her; it might be that she would get there first. Repressing the urge to glance over her shoulder, she forced herself to go on, though her feet felt as if they were rooted to the earth and had to be ripped up for each step she took. Oh, she was tired. She'd had nothing to eat since morning when a kind farmer's wife had given her a hunk of bread and a dipper of milk, and despite the mildness of the spring evening, she felt cold.

Clear, reddish light washed the sky as the day offered up its final burst of glory. There was a fullness in her womb and a dark blood haze coloring the edges of her vision. It will soon be over now, she thought.

Chapter XIX

"You didn't meet Sir Roger and his party on the road?" asked Henry, offering Buckler a brandy.

"They are to spend one night at an inn, and I imagine I got a far earlier start on the stage. No, the only event of any note on this journey was when my dog took violent exception to thin air and nearly overturned us."

"Do you suppose he saw something?"

"How the deuce should I know? I was too busy controlling the blasted horse." Buckler raised his brows. "Why, what do you suppose we came across on the Buckland track? A hare? Or do you mean something rather less corporeal?"

"No," said Henry, his cheeks getting rather flushed. "I was just thinking of the old tales about travelers on the downs encountering monstrous, saucer-eyed dogs and the like."

"Ah." Buckler was the least superstitious of men except when it suited him to indulge fancy. Even his worst enemy could not have called him a *believer*; his mind hadn't the necessary tone. Henry was much the same.

"We'll go together to church on Sunday," said Buckler's brother with an abrupt change of subject, "and you can satisfy yourself about your Mrs. Wolfe."

They were in the library, whence they'd retired after dinner to dismantle the formality of a long separation, but

Buckler was finding it increasingly hard to hold up his end of the conversation. It felt as if a great weight like Henry's monstrous dog had decided to flop upon his chest.

From the depths of the shabby, comfortable easy chairs that had furnished this room as long as either of them could recall, Henry Buckler watched his brother with a worried expression. Ruff, keeping his distance ever since they'd arrived, also eyed his master narrowly from his spot by the fire. And yet all of them, servants included, always kept up appearances. His brother would say little if anything, even should Buckler retire to his room and stay there for the duration of his visit. It wasn't that Henry didn't care, Buckler knew. Quite the contrary.

In truth, Henry's reticence was meant to show that he respected his younger brother's privacy and trusted him to come about as he always did. Still, sometimes Buckler wished that this reserve were not so impenetrable and that his brother were more forthcoming about the needs and feelings at the center of his life. Buckler might thus find it easier to acknowledge his own. Why now, he thought with something approaching despair. *Why must it happen now when I've just come home and this ought to be a time of happiness?*

"How are things in the village?" he asked, hearing the forced cheer in his own voice. "I found my welcome a trifle restrained when I rode through this afternoon. They greeted me right enough, but there was none of the usual raillery."

Henry frowned. "'Twas a hard winter. You know the last harvest was a disappointment, so some belt tightening proved necessary. Our people came out all right, but I'm afraid Wallace-Crag's tenants are feeling the pinch."

"Yes, I'd heard he lost his bailiff. A shame. A good man. Who'd they get to replace him?"

"A grasping, money-sucking here-and-thereian."

"That bad, eh? I don't suppose matters will improve now that Sir Roger has returned to the estate. He's never taken much interest in the welfare of his people."

His only answer was a snort, and the brothers lapsed into silence, each busy with his own thoughts. Even in the gentle firelight, Henry's face looked more lined than it had the last time they'd been together. He was a well set up, modestly handsome country gentleman, a dozen years Buckler's senior and a good half a foot taller. He had never married; why no one knew. He ran his hounds, oversaw his land, and lived what was obviously a busy and fulfilling life as a trusted and permanent fixture in the lives of his dependents. When the thought chanced to occur, Buckler was vaguely troubled that as his brother's heir he would someday bear the responsibility for the estate. He doubted he would make near as good a job of its management.

After a time Henry picked up the conversation where they had left off. "Wallace-Crag's nonsense about digging up that old abandoned church isn't helping matters any. I tell you that man has windmills in his head, which no one is inclined to doubt considering that medieval horror he had built."

Buckler actually laughed, feeling a momentary lessening of the gloom. "He's excavating around that ghostly wreck in the Druid's circle? What does he hope to find?"

"Dashed if I know," said Henry, grinning at him in obvious relief at this indication of a lighter mood.

"I have heard of an antiquary in Wiltshire who's been opening up every barrow in sight. He's found bits of a coarse pottery, small bronze and iron pieces, some Roman coins. And several urns of human bones. You have to admit, Henry, that it's time someone investigated the prehistoric remains in this area. Jupiter, there are enough of them."

"I'm not so sure. Not when the villagers are so quick to fly up into the boughs about it. Besides, there ain't a burial barrow just there, just an earthbank."

The gloom resettled. Beginning to think longingly of his bed, Buckler put down his brandy glass on the side table.

Spirits wouldn't help the headache that throbbed at his temples.

"Why should the villagers care? It's been years since anyone used that church. The roof fell in, didn't it?"

"Yes, at least two score years ago."

Buckler got to his feet. "Then what's the problem?" he said, impatience creeping into his tone.

Henry looked at him. "You had better ask Mrs. Thomas for a dose of laudanum to help you sleep, Edward. You look done in."

"I am," he replied, trying to speak pleasantly. "I believe I'll take your advice."

"Good." Henry rose too, and for a strangely awkward moment the brothers faced each other across the hearthrug.

"I'll see you at breakfast," Buckler said finally.

Bells, liquid and soaring, summoned the parish to Sunday service. Afterwards, as Lord and Lady Ashe waited to exchange greetings with the clergyman, Penelope scanned the crowd of farmers and local gentry until she spotted Edward Buckler standing alone by a low stone wall, coat-tails flapping in the breeze. At his back sprawled a large farm, an expanse of corn fields, and a cluster of cottages. Beyond that, there was only a country track that dipped down the valley, accompanied in its course by a stream swollen with the spring thaw.

She had been astonished during the service to see Buckler sitting across from her, an older gentleman at his side. Penelope had liked the look of Sir Henry Buckler on sight. The two brothers did not much resemble one another, though some indefinable similarity revealed their shared blood.

But what to make of Buckler's presence here? Thinking of their last meeting, she had felt the prick of unease. He had seemed so…determined, but on what she could not be certain. He must know that any real intimacy between them was impossible given her circumstances. And yet, she could not be entirely sorry he had come. It would be a comfort to be sure of having a friend in the next village, for as much as she liked Sir Roger, he was not the man to turn to in any difficulty.

Now, as Ashe exchanged courtesies with the vicar, Julia lingered, clearly feeling out of place, but seemingly unsure of what to do with herself. Penelope assayed a smile in her direction, which was not acknowledged, and excusing herself with a brief gesture, walked away.

"Hello, Mrs. Wolfe," said Buckler.

She gave him her hand, thinking he looked weary and that his smile lacked spirit. Even in the intermittent bursts of sunshine, his red-brown hair, which he kept pushing out of his face, appeared dulled, quite without its usual glint of fire. His eyes, a darker gray than normal and shadow-ringed, met hers without ostensible interest.

"I did not expect to see you, sir," she said brightly. "I had thought you fixed in London."

"How is Sarah?"

"She's fine. She and Maggie and Frank are exploring the cloisters at Cayhill this morning."

"Have a good journey?"

"Yes, thank you. And you?"

"Uneventful."

Suddenly shy, she couldn't think what more to say. There was something in his manner that constrained her, prevented her from behaving naturally. She turned with relief as Buckler's brother joined them.

"Good morning, ma'am," Sir Henry said courteously, bowing.

As Buckler performed the introductions, Penelope studied the two men. Where Buckler was slight of stature and build, Henry had the sportsman's tall, well-formed figure. Dressed with propriety and simple elegance, he was yet attractive, though gray powdered his dark hair.

"A pleasure to make your acquaintance, Mrs. Wolfe. I hope you'll find time to see something of our county whilst you're here, ma'am. We have much to offer whether your taste runs to the ancient, or to the picturesque. I suppose Cayhill might be said to fall into the latter category," he added dryly.

Smiling at him, she had framed a suitable reply when Buckler interrupted. "You do not know but that whatever menace struck down that footman has followed you here to Dorset, Mrs. Wolfe. Be on your guard at all times in that house."

Her eyes flew to his. "Is that why you've come?"

He didn't answer, and Sir Henry stepped into the breach. "You've only to tell us if we can be of any use to you. Buckland is not far, a mile or so distant. Send a message anytime."

Penelope was still looking at Buckler, a cold pit of dread forming in her gut. "What is it? Your manner seems so odd today. Are you unwell?"

"Mrs. Wolfe," called Sir Roger. "Would you care for a tour of our little church? The vicar has kindly granted us permission to do some poking around."

"Go on, Penelope," said Buckler in a low tone. "I'll ride over and see you in a day or two."

She shook her head at him uneasily, but there was no time for more. Perforce, she made her farewells, and taking Sir Roger's arm, walked with him up the path toward the chapel.

Julia still loitered near her husband, who was engaged in earnest discussion with the vicar.

"Accompany us, my dear," said Sir Roger.

After an uncertain glance at Ashe, Julia curtsied. "I own I shall be grateful to remove from this wind."

Penelope and her companions stepped inside, pausing in the nave. This was an unadorned flint structure with no arches and a roof of rough-hewn timbers. Its few windows were narrow, making candles necessary even in broad day. The church was a modest, aged structure with no tower or steeple, only a humble wooden casing to house the bell.

"Such austerity is oddly appealing," said Penelope. "It frees the mind for contemplation."

"Indeed, Mrs. Wolfe," said Sir Roger with approval. "Some disparage our old church as no better than a barn, but I cannot agree. Its very age must commend our veneration. Norman, you know, originally of Saxon origin. It was once the chapel of a nunnery founded by a daughter of King Alfred, who was Abbess of Shaftesbury. The nunnery sat just below us where the farm is now." Seeing that Penelope was looking at the murals on the wall, he added, "Those are of a later period, Mrs. Wolfe. Thirteenth or fourteenth century."

"I daresay you find all this rather tedious, my dear," he said, turning to his daughter.

Her lip curled. "No more than usual, Father."

Suppressing a smile, Penelope interposed. "I was noticing this font earlier. I can't quite make out the carving, however. It's rather worn."

Sir Roger joined her. "Julia was baptized from this font, as was I." He lifted one finger. "The carving's of a female figure. Can you distinguish her against the pattern of chevrons, those inverted V's?"

Penelope ran her fingers over chill stone. "Yes, I see now. Here is her head and torso." She looked more closely. "Are those her outstretched legs? What is it she sits on, sir?"

"A spray of vegetation, Mrs. Wolfe. She's not sitting on it. She gives it birth."

Julia stared at him, her cheeks losing color.

Sir Roger hadn't noticed. "Curious, isn't it? The theme is common in medieval church architecture. Our good vicar would probably say all these unclothed females are meant as a warning against the evils of concupiscence, a moral pitfall that seemed to so exercise the medieval mind. Not that we're all that different today as far as that goes."

"Are you all right, ma'am?" asked Penelope.

"Perfectly, Mrs. Wolfe," Julia said coldly, "but if you don't mind, I'll sit down a moment." She perched on one of the pews and made a big business of fishing around in her reticule.

Shrugging, Penelope turned away. The topic interested her, and besides this might prove a good opportunity to guide the conversation around to Rebecca Barnwell. She said to Wallace-Crag, "Wouldn't you think, sir, that the woman is an advertisement of the very thing the church most wishes to decry?"

He laughed outright. "I would, except that strangely enough there is a tradition that such exhibitionism actually sent the devil to the right about, as if there is such power in the image that it would ward off even Satan."

"Why vegetation, sir? Why does she not give birth to a human child? She doesn't look like she quite belongs in a church."

"Doesn't she?" There was a touch of wry regret in his voice. "But you see, Mrs. Wolfe, the Holy Mother Church was wise. Where it could not stamp out early forms of worship, it appropriated them, absorbed them into its very fabric. This female carving reminds us of a time when Nature, not God, reigned supreme. Of a time when one looked for evidence of the divine in the continuous rotation of the seasons."

"In this district," he went on, "one feels that the ancient ways have refused to surrender their hold entirely. Their power still hums beneath the surface. There are the visible reminders, of course, the barrows and earth mounds."

"You've long wanted to investigate these sites, have you not?"

He gave a short laugh. "Many would have it God does not approve of such inquiry, that it is an affront to Him to disturb Nature's sleeping secrets. Some of my colleagues believe these mysteries are to be contemplated by recourse to the wisdom of the ancients and to religious texts. Perhaps even by miraculous revelation, but certainly not by mucking around in the dirt, stirring up dangerous notions."

"And you, sir?"

"I shall first occupy myself with a look at the pagan earth circle and ruined church. I've often thought it logical there would have been some kind of offering made to consecrate the original site. Who knows but that the men who erected the church built over a burial chamber that had been on this site from time out of mind, enclosed and protected by an interior ditch, itself encircled by the earthwork. Or I suppose it is equally possible that the ancient Britons would have buried their treasure round that ditch, possibly to guard the margins of this sacred ground."

Penelope struggled to put a thought into words. "But what is the purpose of this ditch, sir? If intended for defense of the site, wouldn't they have placed it on the outside?"

His head snapped up. "An intelligent question, my dear. I don't know the answer, though I can hazard a guess that it had to do with keeping any potentially powerful spirits contained within."

Taking up his pencil, he began a swift sketch in his pocket-book. Penelope fell silent, not wishing to disturb him. After a moment or two he ripped out his drawing and handed it to her. It was a rough but vivid rendering of a crumbling church surrounded by its circular earthbank. He had even added a few trees at the margins.

"As the villagers remain convinced the site is ill-omened," said Sir Roger after a moment, "I wouldn't care to advertise any work planned there."

"You mean haunted?"

"You know how these tales spring up. As a matter of interest, there's quite a fascinating one told about a baby at the time of the Black Death. Seems this child's mother was asked to sacrifice her newborn son to propitiate the gods and save the village, which, as is hardly surprising, had reverted to a sort of primitive savagery after the plague struck. She refused, ran away, and that was the end of the village.

"There's a different version of the story, this one supposed to have happened sometime later in another village. There was a poor harvest, and a cruel bailiff who increased the rents. Another woman was brought to bed. This time she voluntarily sacrificed her infant there in the church. Voilà, the bailiff was turned off without a character, the village saved, prosperity to reign for decades." He broke off, looking at her quizzically.

"That's dreadful."

"I suppose it is. In any event it reminds one irresistibly of the Irish legend of Crom Croich. Do you know it? The gold idol that demanded the slaughter of one-third of the healthy children in return for a bountiful harvest of corn. It's an ancient and venerable practice, Mrs. Wolfe. Caesar, writing of the customs he observed during his campaigns, said that the Gauls believed the immortal gods could not be appeased unless one man's life be paid for another's. The Gaulish priests, the Druids, were supposed to have presided over these rites. Make no mistake. They were rites in every sense of word, for the Druids understood the power and sanctity of blood, both animal—and human."

Penelope's imagination was fired. "Those beliefs yet linger. It's just like the female giving birth to vegetation on the font, isn't it? Christians erected the church over the Druids' circle in order to appropriate the sacred site of an earlier belief, impress their creed upon it. Oh, I should greatly like to see that church, sir."

"You will, Mrs. Wolfe," he replied, pleased at her enthusiasm. "I'll show it to you myself in a day or two."

"I shall take you there tomorrow, Penelope," said Julia abruptly.

Penelope and Sir Roger spun in surprise. They had forgotten she was there.

Without their noticing, she had risen from her seat in a back pew and come forward to face them.

"Shall we make an outing of it?" she said with more eagerness than Penelope had heard from her all day. "We'll ride over, maybe have a picnic? You do ride, don't you, Mrs. Wolfe?"

Thrown off balance, Penelope stammered that she had been used to when she lived in Sicily.

"Well, then," said Julia.

Later, walking home, Ashe and Julia seemed absorbed in their own conversation, so Penelope felt herself able to indulge thoughts that had been stirred by the conversation in the church and by the events of the last few days.

Sir Roger professed himself a seeker of Truth and rejected any kind of presupposed intellectual, or moral, framework by which to judge it. But was Truth to be found by unearthing urns, fragments of pottery, and old coins? Penelope didn't know. She did sense that the man at her side, though charming and erudite, lacked a certain openness to others, a capacity for caring. He reminded her a bit of her father, now that she came to think about it, which was probably why she had immediately liked him.

But what had his relationship been with the young Rebecca Barnwell, who, Penelope now believed, had once served in his employ? Recalling his reluctance to speak when Penelope had raised the matter of the woman apprehended in the garden, she could not help but to wonder. And yet when she had inquired further of Mrs. Dobson just this morning, Penelope had discovered that Lord Ashe had been a frequent visitor to the house at the relevant time. Could he have been Rebecca's lover, or might the man have been Mr. Finch, the secretary?

She stole a glance at Sir Roger, who walked sedately at her side, lost in his own ruminations. "The stories you told in the church were most intriguing, sir," she told him. "But it doesn't work, the principle, I mean," she told him, knowing he would be able to follow her idea. "The shedding of one person's blood for another can never confer a long-lasting blessing. Blood only calls for more blood. There's always a price exacted for the loss of even one life."

A sudden gust of wind lifted his hat to deposit it on the ground in front of him. After they had exchanged a startled look, Sir Roger replied, "It seems someone agrees with you, Mrs. Wolfe."

Chapter XX

Arched over by clear sky, the day proved temperate with enough warmth to firm the ground so that the horses' way was made easier. They had proceeded up an incline toward a dark, glimmering belt of trees glimpsed around the bend of the track.

Penelope rode an old cob, recommended to her by the head groom at Cayhill, who'd muttered something about a "Lunnon" woman's ability to manage a horse. Her sidesaddle was so stiff and old-fashioned that she suspected it must once have belonged to Sir Roger's wife, dead these twenty-five years. Mounted on a splendid bay, Julia, in her stylish riding habit and hat with enormous plume, cut a much more impressive figure, and today, at least, she seemed bent on being an entertaining companion.

"Once, not far from here, a keeper walked home, having made his Easter communion in church. Poachers accosted him, bludgeoned him to death, in full day, mind you, but of course, this was in the last century."

"How dreadful," said Penelope.

Behind her the groom stirred restlessly as if he wanted to say something. Penelope made encouraging noises and asked another question.

"Hauntings?" Julia said. "At another gate a few miles north there's a mound of earth said to be inhabited by the local fairies called gappergammies." She broke off with a pretty shrug. "Just a silly superstition. Still, people in these parts don't always distinguish between fairy tales and reality. My maid tells me that a cross is kept cut in the turf near that barrow to ward off evil."

"A sensible precaution."

"There's also a tale about a lady in white hung by her hair from an ash tree over a well. I'm afraid I don't recall why. She was rescued, though some say you can still hear the hunting horn of her pursuers."

After slanting another glance at Penelope, she guided her mount forward, using the whip in her right hand. As the path had narrowed, Penelope followed behind with the groom riding at the rear of their little cavalcade. They were to skirt the wood and approach their destination from the south. It wasn't far, a mere mile or two, and once there, they would spread a blanket in the adjoining meadow and picnic with the ruins as backdrop.

"What have you in your basket, Lady Ashe?" Penelope was beginning to feel hungry after having had almost no breakfast. She'd been holed up in Sir Roger's study, trying in vain to restore order to innumerable notes, bits of paper, and pieces of years-old correspondence. Though she'd sensed that the secretary Finch did not especially welcome her presence, Sir Roger had seemed grateful for her assistance.

"Oh, any number of local delicacies." Julia pulled up abruptly. "Ben, open the basket. I'd like to check that Cook remembered the round of Dorset cheese. I made sure you'd enjoy that, Mrs. Wolfe."

Obligingly, the groom pulled up his horse, leaning forward to open the basket strung to his pommel. Peering inside, he gave a muffled exclamation.

"What is it?" asked Julia sharply. "Did she forget the cheese, after all?"

Flushing, the young man didn't meet his mistress' gaze. "Some sort o' mistake, my lady. There's naught in this basket but some old dusting cloths and a tin of polish."

"How can that be unless you picked up the wrong one, Ben? I pointed out the luncheon basket to you myself."

"Yes'm," he said, clearly miserable.

Julia opened her mouth to scold and closed it again. "Go back for it at once and meet us at the old church as soon as you can."

Resigning herself to a delayed meal, Penelope said, "Perhaps we can picnic another day, ma'am. Shall we ride to the church and have a quick look around?"

"No indeed. Go on, Ben, and make it quick."

Wheeling his horse around, the groom set off back the way they'd come.

"Wouldn't Lord Ashe be made uneasy by you dismissing your groom?" asked Penelope after a moment.

"No, why should he be? It won't take Ben but thirty or forty minutes to rejoin us."

They rode on up the track, Penelope admiring the oak and ash, their new-green buds like tiny jewels on the branches. From somewhere above a thrush sang, and a sweet breeze lapped gently against her cheeks. How different it was to welcome the spring here in this land that melded rolling hills of down with ancient verdant woodland. How utterly different from London, she thought.

Julia's voice roused her. "Mrs. Wolfe, would you care to ride into the forest a ways? There are the wildflowers, and we might catch sight of a doe with her fawn."

"I imagine the shade is lovely, especially in summer. Even now it will be welcome."

"Is the sun too bright for your eyes? Let us go in at once."

"No, it isn't that."

But Julia had already set off, her big bay picking its way delicately down another dirt track which branched off through the trees. When she reached a gate, she climbed down to open it and, after holding it politely for Penelope to pass through, nimbly used the stile to remount.

For a time all was silent, except for the calling of birds and the muted thud of hooves on damp leaves. Feeling curiously at peace, Penelope almost wished she were alone. The first thing she noticed was the quality of light here, dappled, shadowy, pooled warmly in some spots where blooms had appeared.

Julia dismounted again. "Oh, how lovely," she exclaimed, bending over a clump of yellow flowers, her back to Penelope. "I had forgotten all about the celandines at this season. Do get down and look."

Neither so tall nor so agile as her companion, Penelope shimmied down awkwardly from the cob and looped up her full riding skirt over her arm. Though wondering how she would ever climb up again without a mounting block, she clambered gamely behind Julia, who was beating through the tall grass at the side of the path with her riding crop.

After a minute or two, Julia abandoned this project. "Come with me," she said, her eyes glowing. "I've a notion."

"Where to? Won't the horses…"

"A little glade I know. There's something I'd like to show you."

She stepped off the main path, sidestepping shrubs and clumps of overgrown briar, trampling through them without hesitation when she couldn't avoid it. On she went until it seemed the path must be very far behind them indeed. And Penelope came after, her heart beating with a curious kind of anticipation.

"Hold a minute, Julia," she called as the skirt of her habit got entangled in a shrub. "Let me free myself."

Julia smiled back over her shoulder. "Of course, Penelope."

Bending to disengage the material from the clutches of the greenery took but an instant. But when Penelope glanced up again, it was to find she was alone.

❧ ❧

"Lady Ashe? Julia?" Walking to the spot where her employer had been standing, Penelope peered through the trees. Nothing. She stood still, listening. Surely she'd be able to hear her moving through the underbrush, but again there was nothing but the murmur of trees and the birdsong.

"You've had your joke now," she shouted, at this point wryly amused. Was Julia really such a child as this? Tell the credulous London visitor a host of country stories, then abandon her to the forest like some lost maiden of fairy lore. Only this lost maiden was thoroughly sensible and modern, not at all a fitting candidate for enchantment.

Which is rather a pity, when you come to consider it, said Penelope to herself. Nor was she really lost. She had only to retrace her steps to the path and find her horse. No doubt Julia would be waiting, her thirst for fun, it was to be hoped, quenched. In any event, this wasn't a particularly big wood.

Penelope set off, soon discovering that her plight was not so simple as she had imagined. For a short distance she followed the flattened bushes and grasses. But all too soon these signs of their earlier progress ceased, as if to illustrate an essential truth that the forest is quick to erase all signs of human blundering. Either that or she was heading in completely the wrong direction.

She wasn't really alarmed, only tired and hungry, yet as the minutes passed, she grew blindingly angry. Once or twice, hoarsely, uncertainly, she tried calling Julia, to no avail. Her fury mounted even higher as she found that hard as she tried she couldn't distinguish one clump of trees from another. Then as she paused to catch her breath, she heard it, a faint crackle, as if a twig had snapped beneath someone's foot.

Julia at her tricks, or possibly an animal, she told herself firmly, but she remained still, trying to quiet her breathing in order to listen. If a stranger were in the wood, no doubt it was only a local laborer. If he looked congenial, she would ask the way home. If not, she'd stay hidden and follow him out.

For a minute or two she heard nothing more and, reassured, was about to press on. But the rustling resumed, closer now, and this time a low, sobbing breath came to her ears. It was a desolate sound, full of urgency. She froze, the skin on her arms prickling with horror, palms braced against the rough bark of a tree. Whoever, whatever it was would be on her in a moment.

Penelope did not wait. Taking to her heels, she fled through the forest. Low branches tore at her clothing and slashed at her face. Several times, she tripped on roots, nearly falling headlong, the noise of her own progress covering any sounds of pursuit. Finally, she emerged from the undergrowth to see a path before her and waited a tense minute or two before she stepped out. Moving as silently as possible, she set off again.

She knew at once this wasn't the track she and Julia had used. The other had been wide and straight, obviously a main route; this one, smaller, wound sinuously, at times almost swallowed by overgrown scrub. Still, it must lead somewhere, she thought.

Whereas before the trees had all appeared much alike, now for the first time Penelope began to notice their variety. It was as if each one imprinted itself vividly on her mind's eye, almost against her will. There were beeches and majestically tall oaks, formidable with their naked branches; thick, curtaining evergreens; and other trees she didn't know the names of, some ancient and twisted, others tall and straight like young princes. All of them, or so she fancied, seemed to feel her there, though they were neither welcoming, nor overtly hostile. Rather they reserved judgment, watching to see what she would do, whispering amongst themselves.

It began to rain, a light patter that trickled down to dampen her hat. She lowered her head, shutting out everything but the squish of her boots on the mossy ground. Then some instinct made her look up. At eye level not three feet away, a leafy face hung among the branches.

The figure sported a dark, leaf-studded beard, dotted by scarlet berries. Above, like the spread wings of a bird, a fretwork of green needles fanned out over brown cheeks. Her gaze traveled up. Two eyes met hers. They weren't cruel or unkind, yet she shivered. Drawing herself up, she addressed him.

"Would you kindly direct me to Cayhill Abbey, sir?"

The man who stepped out from behind the tree was perhaps sixty. Rather stooped, he was not much more than Penelope's own height. Now that he had moved away from the obscuring greenery, she could see his skin, cracked and weathered like old wood, from which his dark eyes gleamed, shiny and mysterious like a snake's.

"Lost, missus?"

She agreed.

"Come then," he said.

"So you met old Jack Willard?" said Sir Roger. "That was fortunate, Mrs. Wolfe. You couldn't hope for a better guide in these parts."

They had gathered in the Rose Saloon, a chamber of paneled walls, rose-colored hangings, and Oriental lacquer furnishings. A graceful, if slightly dusty harp reposed in one corner. Penelope had told Sir Roger and Owen Finch of Julia's spiteful trick, the motive of which still eluded her, and of her own conviction that someone had been stalking her in the forest. Jack Willard had merely shrugged laconically when she'd mentioned the matter to him.

"Perhaps a poacher, my dear," was Sir Roger's verdict, "though the fellow would have to be fairly brazen to come out in daylight. He wouldn't have intended you any mischief."

"What did you make of Jack, ma'am?" inquired Finch. "I've not set eyes on him in years."

Feeling the effects of her unaccustomed exercise, Penelope attempted, discreetly, to shift her weight to a more comfortable position on her rather hard chair. "He barely spoke to me the entire way home. A most unusual person, though I was glad of his presence."

"No harm in Jack," agreed Sir Roger. "His father was park-keeper and warrener at Cayhill."

"Mr. Willard is employed on the estate?"

"In a manner of speaking only. I'm afraid he and Ashe don't see eye to eye in regard to modern modes of hunting and game preservation. Jack favors the old ways. He lives in a cottage in the wood and keeps to himself."

"That doesn't surprise me," said Penelope slowly. "One senses he's gentle, yet there's something hidden and…and alone about him. It was a little frightening somehow. And to burst out with that warning right at the end."

Finch spoke. "What warning, Mrs. Wolfe?"

"He told me I should stay out of the wood. When I said I'd meant to visit the ruined church, he said I must not, that it was 'needful' I keep away."

Sir Roger snorted. "I do trust the local people aren't going to raise a dust when I begin my survey."

Finch said, "They say that place has been accursed ever since the Black Death wiped out an entire village there in the fourteenth century. The disease took all the children first, or so the story goes. Then their elders began dropping by the score." His voice dropped. "Until no one was left."

His employer smiled, but his reply sounded impatient. "My dear fellow, you ought to know by now that tales of that nature do but add a fillip to an antiquary's interest. If anything—"

The door opened, and Ashe came into the room, accompanied by Julia. Breeches creased and dirt stained, Lord Ashe held his hands and arms stiffly, almost clenched. His black eyes, glittering and unfathomable, swept around the room and lighted on Penelope's face.

"Mrs. Wolfe. Thank God, you're safe home." Reaching back, Ashe hauled Julia to his side.

"What do you know of the matter, Ashe?" demanded Sir Roger.

He didn't answer, merely giving Julia a little push. She looked equally disheveled and miserable. The jaunty habit was quite ruined, the lace at her wrists torn and filthy. Her hair had escaped many of its pins to fall in untidy wisps about her shoulders. But it was her mute, white face that riveted Penelope. She looked like a terrified animal, or a tiny child, cringing as a hand lifted to strike her down.

"I've come to apologize, Mrs. Wolfe," she said in a low, dazed tone. "'Twas a foolish thing to do."

"Why did you? What has happened to my horse?"

Finch had risen to lead Julia to a chair. Flashing the secretary a grateful look, she accepted the glass of cordial he put in her hand, yet her eyes followed Ashe as he draped himself across the sofa opposite, paying no attention to the clumps of mud dropping from his boots.

"The horse made its way back to the stable," he said curtly. "And is perfectly sound. You yourself suffered no mischance, Mrs. Wolfe?"

Penelope hesitated. "No, my lord."

"It was foolish of me," Julia stammered. "A joke. I thought to give you a start."

"It doesn't matter." There was a great deal Penelope didn't understand here, such as where Julia had encountered Ashe, and why this undercurrent of thick emotion swirled about the room.

Sir Roger, as was his wont when losing interest, had retreated to private speculations. Finch and Ashe both observed Julia narrowly, the one she thought with pity, the other with a kind of predatory alertness that Penelope found most unsettling.

"Never mind, my dear," said Sir Roger vaguely. "I'm sure all's forgiven now."

"Of course, ma'am," put in Penelope, hoping to reassure her. "Perhaps we might attempt our excursion another day? I am still eager to see the church."

It was Ashe who replied. "I think not, Mrs. Wolfe. My wife had best remain at home until she learns not to give the world a disgust of her."

This was a piece of ugliness, and Penelope rushed in to gloss it over, smooth it away. "No, no. As a matter of fact, I rather enjoyed my adventure."

Julia looked up from contemplation of her glass, a queer light coming into her eyes. "Do you mean it, Penelope? Shall we go upstairs then? There is much I would wish to say to you before it is time to dress for dinner."

"Yes, let us go," replied Penelope, making sure Julia saw that her agreement was ungrudging.

Ashe frowned, but before he could speak, the door opened, and Maggie entered. One glance at her white face was enough to make Penelope catch her breath, her heart squeezing with a terrible fear.

Chapter XXI

There had been very little warning except that Sarah had seemed subdued and a little tired during the afternoon. Maggie said that the child hadn't wanted to play at spillikins, or take her doll for a stroll in the cloisters. At luncheon she had managed only a few bites of soup. By late afternoon, she blazed with fever.

Penelope began with determined cheerfulness. While little Frank stood by, she and Maggie sponged the tiny, hot body over and over, all the time watching the door for the arrival of the doctor Sir Roger had summoned. For several hours Sarah had done nothing but thrash in her bed and moan that she ached everywhere. When they'd tried to give her water, she cried out that her throat ached and she couldn't swallow. Eyeing the untouched tray sent up for her dinner with revulsion, Penelope understood.

"She'll be more the thing now," said Maggie without much conviction after they'd just completed one of the sponging baths.

Penelope nodded briefly, thinking that Maggie didn't look so good herself, her freckled cheeks pale, her eyes dark pools of fear. Penelope's eye fell on Frank, hovering near the door kicking his toe at the carpet, and the brittle shell of composure with which she'd armed herself exploded into fragments. They had tried to send him away with the servant who had taken charge of the baby. He wouldn't go. Perhaps he feared that if he left his playmate, she might not be there when he returned.

Penelope pulled herself up with an effort. Stop, she thought fiercely, such morbid rot. But more and more as the hours crept by and Sarah did not improve, she found that her mind played these cruel tricks. That was hardly bearable, but when she looked at Sarah, tasting the child's bewilderment at why no one "made it better," Penelope knew what it was to doubt her own sanity.

As the bath's brief respite of coolness ebbed away, they had to work hard to still Sarah's restless lunges that continually yanked the coverings loose. The bitter complaints had finally ceased, as if the child had now turned inward. Penelope alternately stroked and sponged with one hand, the other remaining anchored across her daughter's middle.

After a time, Maggie straightened. "Where's that doctor?" she said wearily. "He ought to be here." She looked at her son. "Frank, go see if he's coming. Ask a footman if there's one lurking about."

"Maggie, go with Frank and put him to bed. What if he were to take the contagion? It isn't safe for him to be here."

"I reckon as we'll have a time keeping him away, mum." Still, Maggie followed the boy out.

When they were gone, Penelope glanced around the bedchamber with its cheerful crimson drapes and elegant furnishings. At least Sarah would have a pleasant room in which to make her recovery. Mrs. Dobson had already proved helpful, commanding a large fire to be built in the grate and sending up various concoctions and remedies from the kitchen. And Sir Roger had conveyed messages and reassurance through Owen Finch, who'd also expressed himself at her service. Her eyes traveled to the clock on the mantelpiece. It was nearly ten o'clock, she saw.

Some twenty minutes later, she jumped to her feet as the door opened, but it was only Maggie again. "Frank's asleep, poor lamb. How's Miss Sarah? Any change?"

"No." Penelope had given up the sponging for the moment as it only seemed to fret the child further.

Maggie approached the bed. "A shame that her dad ain't here to comfort her. A sick child wants both its parents."

Penelope flinched as if she'd been struck. Funny how the thought of Jeremy had been with her all this interminable evening. Maggie was right. He had the duty, the right, to share this burden, not the nursing itself, of course, but rather the decisions that might have to be made. Sarah hadn't asked for Jeremy in some weeks, had given up asking. But, young as she was, she'd remember and be glad to know her own father was near.

Looking up, Penelope saw that Maggie was gazing at her with pity and a kind of wry comprehension, for she, too, had a wandering husband.

Steps and voices sounded in the corridor outside. "There's the doctor now," Maggie said, not troubling to disguise her relief.

❧ ☙

Maggie went to open the door, but it was only Sir Roger come to see how Sarah did.

"I'll only disturb you for a moment, ma'am," he called softly. "The doctor sent to say he was a trifle delayed but will be along. I thought you could do with a glass of wine to keep up your strength."

She approached him and, seeing the worried expression on his face, felt her throat tighten. "Thank you, sir."

"How is the little girl?"

"Much the same, though I believe she has slipped into a light sleep. I will come out to you if you don't mind."

She allowed him to usher her to a seat in the window embrasure and to hand her the heavy silver goblet that he had himself carried up the stairs on a small tray. A quick glance through the window told her that no light lingered in the sky, nor were there any stars visible, and the glass itself felt cold against her back, a deep, empty cold that seemed to emanate from the house itself. She shivered and, taking a long, warming sip of the wine, forced herself to smile.

"This will do me good. It was kind of you to bring it."

Perching next to her on the seat, he patted her hand. "Your woman is there. You will be summoned if the child needs you, and I shall sit with you for a few minutes until you drink this down. Have some more, ma'am."

Obediently, she sipped the wine. "You will think me very foolish to make so much of what will no doubt prove to be a trifling ailment."

"Not at all. I quite see she is everything to you. You are more fortunate than you know, Mrs. Wolfe."

"Yes, I realize that. It's just the thought of…well, Mrs. Dobson told me of your wife's many bereavements. You know what it is to face the loss of a child, sir. Your lady must have been a brave woman. I know I could not have endured it."

He was gazing at her oddly. "She was determined to give me an heir."

There was a short silence, then Penelope said, "People often speak as if the heavens keep a kind of scorecard, as if when one somehow offends, the gods must and will strike back. Tit for tat. But your wife had not offended. She had done nothing to earn such a death."

"Perhaps it was not she who deserved it. She may have been the instrument of someone else's fate. But you have articulated the essential philosophy well. *This even-handed justice commends the ingredients of our poisoned chalice to our own lips…*"

Suddenly, the wine tasted sour in Penelope's mouth, and she set down her goblet on the window ledge. It was fantastical, of course, yet the idea of Sarah suffering for the faults of others did present a horrible logic. When had Jeremy provided a stable home for her as a father should? And what of Penelope's own stubborn refusal to bow her head and honor her marriage vows, however much of a mistake it had been to make them in the first place?

"You mean, don't you, that fate had decreed *you* should not have a son?"

"Yes, I suppose that is what I meant. And there's the true reason I never attempted a second marriage, Mrs. Wolfe, for, against all reason, I was convinced the outcome would remain the same. Still, if Julia will only give me a grandson, the slate will be wiped clean."

The certainty flashed into Penelope's mind with such luminous truth that she could no longer doubt. "Mr. Chase of Bow Street is sure the woman apprehended in your garden was the prophetess Rebecca Barnwell. I believe she is not unknown to you."

"Rebecca was once a servant in this house, and even then a most unusual young woman."

Penelope nodded, unsurprised. "Mrs. Dobson has told me something of her history. It may be that Rebecca witnessed Dick Ransom's murder or perhaps was driven to commit the crime herself." She felt the heat rising in her cheeks. "Do you know of any reason why she should bear you or anyone in this household ill will?"

It seemed at first he would not answer her, but at length, he said, "She was called Rebecca Barton then. I was a rash and impetuous youth. From the start of my marriage, it seemed my wife had been breeding and consequently always ill. Rebecca and I became...friendly."

"She had a baby, didn't she? A son?"

"The old story, ma'am. But in this case she was driven to destroy the infant in a moment of anguish. The poor thing spent some time in the madhouse and eventually was released, cured. For all that, she has made something of her life, so perhaps it was for the best."

Appalled, Penelope said, "I suppose Ransom knew your secret, and that is the reason for his death? But surely—"

"You are most astute, Mrs. Wolfe." Getting to his feet, he gazed down at her, a gentle smile playing on his lips. "Whatever the truth of the matter, none of this could have come about had I not wronged an innocent maid. The gods are indeed just."

❧ ❧

It was called the English Malady. Some in the medical establishment still believed the affliction stemmed from an imbalance of the four humors. An excess of black choler, black in Greek being "melan," thus *melancholer*. Melancholia. That the English were particularly prone to the disorder was borne out by the startling number of suicides reported yearly in London. Above all, the weather was blamed, the curse of fog, rain, and a bleak chill that besieged the city much of the year. Added to these were the manmade scourges of smoke from fire and industry, the Thames' stench, the crowds, and the noise.

Here it was quiet but for the birds that trilled outside Buckler's window in the bright May morning. He lay sweating in bed in the room where he had spent his childhood before being dispatched first to school, then to university, and finally to London and the career chosen for him. Maybe he should have taken orders instead and flaunted his melancholy in an epic tussle with the devil, not that a good Church of England man would countenance such enthusiasm.

Buckler's spells had begun in his youth, to continue with such unremitting regularity that he sometimes considered them a bane laid upon him by God. This time, as usual, he had not been able to pinpoint the root of his trouble. Hours of reflection, of self-prodding and scolding, had brought only one fact to light: his life, in aggregate, failed to satisfy. He had found neither a true vocation in his career, nor deeply satisfying fulfillment in personal relationships, for of what use could it be to dangle after a married woman? He didn't suppose she cared for him anyway.

Although he had the curtains drawn, the rich sunlight slipped through the gaps to collect in warm pools on the faded rug. His chamber, furnished years ago by castoffs from the public rooms below, had never changed. It was stolid, reassuring…suffocating. He stumbled to his feet. He would take out the horse that Henry kept for his brother's use and ride the downs, letting the fresh air rout his lethargy. Perhaps he would be in time to accompany his brother as he ranged over the property in his stylish curricle, accompanied by his hounds and a groom to open the gates.

Buckler strode to the washstand and, lifting the ewer, poured out water to wash. The coolness refreshed his hot brow and cheeks, and when he looked in the glass hanging on the wall, a surge of strength swept through his veins. Bemused, he stared at his dripping face in the mirror. Yes, he thought, the day awaited him, and he did not intend to miss his appointment.

When he had made himself presentable, he descended the staircase to the hall, where he encountered the household's single footman.

"Where is my brother?"

"In the library, Master Edward. A local man has called to speak to him," the man replied cheerfully.

The library was one of the few rooms that had been redone since his mother's time. The young female cousin who had raised both boys after their mother's death had always wished to redecorate, but had only succeeded in convincing Buckler's father to "freshen up" the one chamber in which he practically lived. But that had been twenty years ago. Today it bore the same comfortably inhabited atmosphere as the rest of the house.

Henry was seated in his favorite ancient armchair. He had really only one manner of disposing his long frame, whether he sat his horse, his carriage, or this chair inherited from their father. It was a sort of relaxed ease, as if he knew himself always to be in the right place at the right moment.

Buckler did not at first recognize the man who stood on the hearthrug opposite Henry but noticed immediately that, though the visitor looked singularly out of place, he was not overawed by his surroundings. Bent and stooped, he wore a woodsman's smock over woolen leggings and leather gaiters. He held a misshapen hat in front of him, his stern face composed.

"Edward," said Henry, catching sight of his brother lingering in the doorway. "I was about to send for you."

Buckler was gazing at the visitor. Old Jack Willard, he thought, as he finally placed him. In Buckler's youth, the neighborhood boys had gone in terror of this man who had confiscated the slingshots they used to shoot at birds and shouted at them for disturbing the deer during the rutting season.

Buckler went forward to offer his hand. "Good day, Jack. You are looking well. It's been many a year since I've set eyes on you."

Willard gave a regal nod. "Master Edward."

"Sit down, brother," said Henry. "I've asked Jack to do likewise, but he won't."

"I be best as I am."

"Well then, I'll ask you to start from the beginning, Jack. My brother will want to hear your tale, especially as it concerns Mrs. Wolfe, who is a friend of his."

Willard nodded. "The London woman. Yesterday I carried eggs to the Abbey, and Cook told me the child was took terrible ill."

"Sarah? What's amiss with her?" demanded Buckler harshly. He did not take the other armchair Henry had motioned him to, but remained facing the woodsman across the hearthrug.

"The fever, I reckon. That's what was said. I mentioned the matter to Rebecca when I reached home last night, and this morning, she'm gone again. That be why I come."

"That's the odd part, Edward," broke in Henry. "Jack says this prophetess Rebecca Barnwell was once a local woman, a nursemaid at the Abbey. I seem to recall something of her. She went by a different name then—one Rebecca Barton. Was that it, Jack?"

Willard nodded slowly, his unfathomable gaze on Buckler's face. "That be it, Squire. She were a pretty little thing in those days, but full of herself, you might say. She landed herself in difficulties."

"You mean, in the usual way?"

"Yes, Master Edward. After all these years, I found her in the wood t'other day, wandering all lost-like. Well, it put me in mind of finding her before, so I knew who she was. I gave her shelter."

Buckler was thoughtful. John Chase had discovered that the prophetess was mixed up in the murder in St. James's Square. Now it seemed she had surfaced at the same time as Wallace-Crag's household was in residence.

Willard continued. "A day or two later I came home for dinner, and she was gone. When I went looking, I found that London woman with some story about being stalked in the wood. It were Rebecca, of course, though I can't say what she wanted with the lady."

"The prophetess has disappeared again? I assume you think she may still be seeking Mrs. Wolfe?"

"Well, Master Edward, she did before. You see, she's been speaking so wild. I don't feel easy in my mind."

"Jack and I have an understanding," said Henry gravely. "He knows to turn to me when in trouble. He did very right to come."

Buckler and his brother exchanged a long look, and Buckler said, "What of finding the woman in the wood all those years ago? What were the circumstances?"

For the first time, Willard looked uncomfortable. Lowering his eyes, he stared at his boots.

When Buckler looked a question, Henry shook his head warningly. "You've kept your secret well, Jack, but now it is time to speak." He turned to Buckler. "This was a year or two before Sir Roger's wife died. You are too young to remember, brother, but there was some talk that things weren't quite right at Cayhill. When the girl was sent away, the matter was quickly forgotten."

Willard burst out, "It weren't in the wood but in that old church t'other side of it. I was nearby, and I heard her call out. She were there lying on the stones, staring up at the sky. Her dress was all…bloody, and she were white as if near to death."

"Good God," said Buckler. "She had given birth out there all alone?" A cold horror trickled down his spine at the thought of it.

"Alone? Maybe, Master Edward. But, you see, there was no baby, and she were crying for it, heart fit to break. Her wits went a-begging that day, and I don't suppose she's ever found 'em again. So I took her home and sent a message to the Abbey. Next day Sir Roger sent someone to take her away. I never see her more until t'other day."

"But the child…what was its fate? Did no one ever discover?"

"I reckon 'twas born dead, for when I went back to the church, I saw some freshly disturbed soil along the earth-bank. I warrant the babe is laid to rest there."

"Surely the woman was in no condition to wield a shovel," objected Henry. "Someone must have removed the corpse before you arrived, Jack, and buried it."

"I reckon so, Squire. There was something not right about the business. And I reckon it isn't finished yet."

Yes. Buckler knew. He had been feeling the gathering storm clouds ever since he had learned that Penelope meant to travel to Dorset. Perhaps that partially explained his melancholy. It felt good now to throw it off and to know what to do.

"I shall go at once to the Abbey and make sure Mrs. Wolfe and young Sarah are all right," he told Henry.

"Yes, I think that would be wise."

"Jack," said Buckler, "Rebecca Barnwell is said to be pregnant. Does she seem to you to be near her time? Perhaps that is why she has returned to her home, to bear her child at the scene of her earlier shame. To atone for her sin, erase it with this new life?"

Willard avoided his eyes. "All I know is she says she must find that child from long ago. If she don't, the babe she carries is doomed and the rest of us along with it."

"Madness," said Henry. "Didn't you tell her the baby was dead?"

Willard smiled without humor. "That I did, Squire, and took her to see its resting place."

Chapter XXII

Morning came, brilliant and still but for the birdsong and the far-off bleating of sheep on the downs. On the elm tree outside, the tender leaves and reddish clusters of flowers trembled with an unearthly joy, and the sky above the monks' cloister glowed a clear, sweet blue. Penelope had been standing at the window a long time, struggling to master the yawning fear that threatened to swallow her whole. The beauty spread before her eyes like a feast seemed unreal, the stuff of dreams, and she was sure that if she closed her eyes for an instant, it would all be snatched away.

At her back, she heard Maggie enter. "Has the letter gone?" she asked without turning.

"Yes'm. The man did ride for Salisbury a quarter-hour since, but Mrs. Pen, a strange thing—"

"She is quieter now, sleeping I think."

Penelope heard a rustling noise as Maggie approached the bed to adjust the covering, then a gasp. Her breath catching in her throat, she turned. "My God, what is it? Do we need to change her nightgown again?"

Maggie did not at first reply, but stood with her reddened, toil-worn fingers cupped around Sarah's cheek as tears slipped unheeded down her face. She said, "Sorry, mum, I didn't mean to frighten you. Come see. Look, she'll do now. The fever has broken."

Penelope was at her daughter's side in an instant, thrusting out her own hand to touch her. Sarah's forehead was cool, and there was a faint, fresh color under her skin. Penelope looked at Maggie and tried to smile. "Yes, she is better."

"I don't mind telling you I was right worried." Maggie reached into her apron pocket to retrieve her wipe. Loudly, she blew her nose. Then she asked curiously, "Be you sorry you sent that express?"

Penelope plucked a few strands of sweaty hair from the child's eyes. Her hand drifted over the small form, patting and stroking, checking to make sure everything was in its proper place. There was no doubt. She was better. "No, I'm not sorry. If Jeremy comes for us, well, Sarah will be glad to see him."

"I warrant you too after a shock like this."

"I shall make sure you and the children can return to London if you like, or maybe you can stay on here. I'm afraid I won't be able—"

"Don't you worry, Mrs. Pen. We'll be fine."

"Yes, of course," she replied, smiling at Maggie with a rush of affection. "Go now and see to the children. They'll be wanting their breakfast."

"Yes'm. Mrs. Dobson will be glad to hear Miss Sarah is on the mend. Shall I tell her, mum? And old starched shirt and the maids as well. Why, that child is a favorite with one and all. 'Tis a pity I couldn't have given a better account of her to that poor country woman as inquired."

"One of the local people, Maggie?"

"I reckon so. A pitiful, strange creature, she was. Stopped me when I went outside to speak to the post boy. She laid her hand on my arm and asked me how the little girl did. When she saw my worry, she told me not to fret about Miss Sarah, that the end be near when the Lord will come in glory to take all the little white souls up to heaven. And she patted her belly."

Penelope's heart, which had slowed to a reassuring, solid thud, suddenly accelerated again. "This woman was with child? Oh, Maggie, it must be she, but what could she want here? I must find Sir Roger at once."

"You've no call to fear that one, mum," replied Maggie, bewildered. "She's weak and ill, and it'll go the worse for her when her time comes, which is nigh, I can tell you."

"I must ask you to stay with Sarah a while longer. Bring Frank and Baby in here and let the children stay together. I don't suppose they will take infection from her now."

"You're never going out without changing your dress?" cried Maggie, scandalized, as Penelope shoved her feet into her boots and began to lace them.

Dragging a brush through her unruly hair, Penelope only shook her head. She tore off her soiled gown and donned another, hardly stopping to see which it was. She felt a driving urgency, yet she had no clear notion of why.

Ten minutes later, she was tapping at the door of Sir Roger's study. She knew his habits well. In the country he breakfasted even earlier and should be at his desk by this hour. But it was Julia who answered her knock, throwing open the door so abruptly that Penelope took a step back in alarm.

"Penelope. How is Sarah?"

"The fever has abated. I came to speak to your father."

Julia gaped at her. "He isn't here."

"It is most important I speak to him. Where is he?"

Slowly, Julia extended her right hand towards Penelope and, uncurling her fingers, revealed three small, unripe hazelnuts nestled against her pinkly delicate palm.

⊷ ⊷

As the wind roared over his head, Chase snatched at his hat and tugged it closer. He slapped the reins. The old horse ignored him, merely continuing its sullen plod up the track.

Many would find the country air clean and invigorating. He could well imagine Ezekiel Thorogood, for instance, voicing a running panegyric on the scenery. But Chase felt exposed in this low, boundless landscape. And buffeted. A London wind, wafting its odors of spices, oranges, oysters, sewage, baking bread, and coal smoke, snaked through alleyways, crept around buildings, and nipped at one with icy teeth. Here any true gale would flatten all that came before it.

This was just one element of the country that disconcerted him. Everything was too spread out, even if only a mile or so separated the various tiny villages. Mired byways. Lonely stretches of woodland that might easily harbor the last bastion of thieves and other malcontents. The so-called beauties of nature were lost on John Chase.

He cracked the reins a second time, but with much the same result. Clearly, the landlord's "third best horse" possessed more stubbornness than wind. Moreover, the trap to which the beast was hitched was poorly sprung and rickety.

Slipping a hand into his greatcoat pocket, Chase fingered the little Celtic letter knife that he still carried. In spite of Graham's belief that the arrest of the Jacobin conspirators had neatly resolved the matter of Dick Ransom's murder, Chase knew otherwise. Rebecca Barnwell had not been taken with the others, and she, he was convinced, was the key to the whole.

Caught up in his musings, he was startled when a man on horseback thundered down a rise in the road to pass the trap with a bare inch to spare. As Chase gave the reins a hard yank to the left, he was already opening his mouth to call out in recognition. The rider, it seemed, had recognized him too, for he pulled up in an impressive display of horsemanship and turned back, his mount dancing over the track.

"John Chase! What brings you here?"

Occupied in trying to avoid the ditch at the side of the road, he growled in reply, "I imagine the same thing that has brought you. How is Mrs. Wolfe?"

"I was on my way to inquire. It seems young Sarah has taken ill, perhaps seriously."

Chase felt a pang of fear at the thought of Penelope's little girl in danger, but all he said was, "It seems I have arrived opportunely. Let's go."

"By all means, but not in *that*." Buckler abandoned his inspection of the ancient equipage, adding, "I'm afraid there's more you should know." Chase listened as he related Jack Willard's story of the nursemaid giving birth in the abandoned church.

"Strange, isn't it?" Buckler finished. "A disgraced young woman transforms herself into God's mouthpiece on a divine mission and manages to persuade thousands of other people to embrace her nonsense. But I cannot tell you what any of this has to do with the footman's murder."

Chase was thoughtful. Wallace-Crag had mentioned his plan to survey an abandoned church, remarking upon misplaced correspondence that had held up the project. Was it possible someone in the household had not wanted the site disturbed? "Janet Gore alleges that Ransom went to St. James's Square to intercept the prophetess, who had run away. Now, according to this woodsman, we learn that the prophetess seeks a child dead these five-and-twenty years. A young man died, and Barnwell herself was viciously attacked because of this old tragedy."

"Do you believe Wallace-Crag killed the footman, that is if he was the one to father Barnwell's babe?"

"It may be so, yet he doesn't seem the sort to care overmuch about a youthful folly." Chase picked up the reins. "We had better go."

"Yes, of course. You will allow me to mount you on one of my brother's horses?"

A short distance up the road, they swung onto a broad, graveled sweep opening to a fair prospect of a two-storied brick house, which looked at once commanding and gracious and so much a part of the landscape as to be unremarkable.

A solid but never a brilliant rider, Chase, soon provided with his own rather mettlesome mount, eyed its prancing with some misgiving. He was exhausted, and his knee still felt the effects of yesterday's long coach ride. The thought of the ride to Cayhill, the return trip to Buckland, and the three-mile journey back to the inn seemed daunting.

But when they were on their way, Buckler said, "Henry will send a groom to return the trap and collect your luggage. Of course, you will stay at Buckland."

Embarrassed, Chase spluttered a protest that was waved aside. "Henry looks forward to making your acquaintance. He says you must not deprive him of the opportunity to crow over the neighbors. No one in this district has ever entertained a Bow Street Runner."

"Most people would not deem that a distinction. Still, I thank you both." He thought it strange that a baronet should show so little height in his manner.

The contrast between Buckland and Cayhill Abbey could not have been greater. As they approached, Buckler, observing Chase's bemusement at the spectacle of turrets, pointed windows, and vast tower, remarked, "I shouldn't be surprised if it tumbles down about their ears one day. I don't suppose anyone around here would shed a tear."

Buckler fell silent as they both caught sight of a man, hat in hand, descending the shallow steps to cross the cobbled courtyard. Glancing up, the man stopped, clearly startled, and with calculated rudeness, turned his back, continuing toward a shiny phaeton hitched to one of the best bits of blood Chase had ever seen.

Buckler dismounted. "Good day, Ashe," he called. "May we have a word?"

Slowly, Lord Ashe pivoted, an upright figure in his leather breeches, blue tailcoat, and top boots. "I am expected elsewhere." He looked at Chase. "I told you your employment with us is at an end. Get out."

"My lord, we must speak to Mrs. Wolfe on urgent business." Chase swung himself down to join Buckler.

"Get out," Ashe repeated, but Chase had seen the fear flicker in his eyes.

"Take a damper, Ashe," said Buckler with cold authority. "We were told that Mrs. Wolfe's daughter has the fever. Naturally, we are concerned."

"Mrs. Wolfe ain't here." He gave an unpleasant smirk. "She and my wife have gone riding, and before you ask me, I haven't the vaguest notion where they may have gone. Nor do I much care, if you must have the truth."

"I cannot credit that Mrs. Wolfe would have left Sarah," said Buckler.

Ashe shrugged. "Why not? I understand the child has improved. The doctor has already been with her this morning. Anyway, I know the ladies like to play at being devoted wives and mothers, but I find they generally put their own pleasures first."

"As your wife did when she made a mere footman her lover whilst you were off taking your pleasure of children," said Chase softly. "I suppose such behavior is perfectly acceptable in the gentleman, but she risked your good name and made sure ridicule would be your lot if anyone learned the truth. Only you soon discovered the possibility of far worse consequences. My lady Ashe's lover was a Jacobin, a traitor plotting against our Prince Regent, no less. Far, far beyond the usual *peccadilloes* one expects of Society matrons."

"You're mad." Though Ashe spoke with his usual arrogance, it seemed a hollow defense, like the coward who blusters when caught in a lie, aware that the façade can easily be ripped asunder to expose a yawning hole of shame. Buckler sent Chase a curious look but did not comment, and Chase went on.

"Perhaps it was one of your political friends who whispered in your ear about a certain brothel the Home Office spies had been watching and the young man often seen there who turned out to be employed in your father-in-law's establishment. Would this be enough, I wonder, to drive you to murder?"

"If you know so much, why ask me?" said Ashe, taking a step toward his phaeton.

"Chase, I think we must go after Penelope," said Buckler. "God knows what that Bedlamite woman wants with her."

Chase held up a hand. "I think my lord may be of some use to us on that score. At the very least, I am certain he can tell us of Rebecca Barnwell and her connection with the family. He and Wallace-Crag are friends of long standing."

"What of it?" demanded Ashe. "I have not the vaguest notion what you blabber on about."

"One Rebecca Barnwell, prophetess," said Chase. "I believe you knew her by a slightly different name—Rebecca Barton. Once nursemaid to Lady Ashe, she got herself with child, then disappeared to resurface later in a lunatic asylum. Only no one seems to know what became of the infant, least of all Rebecca herself."

Ashe absorbed this information, becoming abruptly thoughtful. "So that's it. She was the woman in the garden that night? Strange I did not know her, but she is altered almost beyond recognition."

"Your wife recognized her, for I have little doubt it was she who bribed the night-beadle to secure Barnwell's release from the parish lock-up the next day."

"Julia? After all these years, why should she care?" He seemed shaken, honestly bewildered.

"The nursemaid's babe?" pressed Chase.

"I cannot tell you. Look, I didn't like the chit overmuch, had a score to settle with her on my own account. And it was clear Roger was heading for disaster. He was the father, you know, but once the damage was done, he should have acted to remove the girl before his wife caught on. He let matters go until the bitch was ready to drop the brat at any moment. The situation became intolerable."

"What then?" asked Buckler. "I presume you advised your friend to abandon the girl."

Ashe pressed his lips together to repress an involuntary smile. "I did more than that. I tricked her into coming out of doors one night and bundled her off in a coach, which was to convey her to an establishment for such creatures. I never saw her more. But the answer to your little mystery is patent to anyone with a grasp of human nature. She bore the child and did away with it herself to avoid the shame. If she is stirring up trouble now, no doubt she thinks to bleed poor Roger."

Chase had despised Ashe from the moment he met him, for this was the sort of specimen who gave the ruling classes their well-deserved reputation for callous blindness to the realities of the world. Chase had wished for the chance to get the viscount alone, man to man, to see what he was made of, this creature that preyed upon helpless little girls. Now, he merely wanted this confrontation over.

"Where did you take her, Ashe?" he said wearily.

He laughed. "You fool. I wasn't the one driving the coach."

❦

Following Julia on her big bay, Penelope was mounted on the cob again. This time, riding in silence, each busy with her own thoughts, they skirted the wood and met only a girl picking flowers and storing them in her apron. The girl looked at them curiously and informed them in a thick accent that she had encountered no one else this morning but for an old tinker who had tried to sell her a skin lotion.

They thanked her. When they had moved out of earshot, Penelope said in halting tones, "You once wished to honor me with your confidence, and I refused you. Will you speak now?"

An enigmatic smile touched Julia's lips as she turned her head, the long crimson feather in her hat wafting in the soft May breeze. "You feared my wickedness would corrupt you."

"I hope I am not so foolish as that. It was mostly that I was unhappy and felt I did not belong," said Penelope, adding in a carefully neutral tone, "The woman they call Rebecca Barnwell, the prophetess, was once your nurse whom you dearly loved as a child. Was that why you allowed yourself to be drawn in, or was it because of Dick?"

"It's true I had agreed to help Dick. He came to me soon after he entered my father's employ and told me...a story. Well, I believed it. Then there came the day when Rebecca left a letter for you at your solicitor friend's chambers. Dick went to retrieve it."

"He smashed the window and broke in."

She nodded. "Dick asked me to watch for Rebecca whilst he was gone, for he was afraid she might show herself in St. James's Square. And she did, very late, close to morning when I had almost given up the vigil. I was standing at my window when I saw the glow of her candle drifting across the lawn. I went down and led her to the shrubbery to await his return."

"So you *were* in the garden. Your maid found your dampened cloak stuffed under the counterpane the next day."

"She told you that?" Julia said, shooting Penelope a look of surprise.

"Why should Miss Barnwell attempt to correspond with me? I have never met her."

"She'd been lurking around the square for some days, apparently, and had seen you out-of-doors with young Sarah. I think she hoped you might intercede with my father on her behalf. She wouldn't have wished to involve me."

"Your father has told me she bore him a child many years ago. I do not understand what she could desire of him now."

Julia looked her full in the face, then, reassured by whatever she read there, said, "Justice and an end to the pain of not knowing the truth of her past."

The horses had slowed to a stop. As the cob lowered its head to nip at some grass, Penelope, curiously at a loss, stroked its rough coat. She had the feeling that Julia spoke as much of herself as of Rebecca Barnwell.

"How did Dick die?" she asked at last.

"I stayed with Rebecca for a time. She was pleased to see me once she could be brought to understand who I was. After a time, I heard Dick call out, softly. We had been absorbed in our conversation and failed to hear his approach. I was so relieved, but Rebecca ran away before I could restrain her. He told me to go back inside and started after her.

"But someone else had heard us. He must have noticed the light, as I had, or caught the sound of voices. And Rebecca ran straight into his arms before Dick could catch her. They struggled. I saw Dick go to her aid. He cursed once, and I saw him fall. Steps retreated. I wanted to go to Rebecca, but I couldn't get my feet to obey me. I think she must have knelt at Dick's side to remove the knife, for I caught the gleam of metal as she held it to the sky. Then that unearthly cry. I…I wanted to help, but I couldn't see, and I knew I must escape before I was discovered. I slipped in the side door and went up the back stairs to my chamber."

When her voice died away, Penelope sat back, thinking. She could so easily imagine the two women waiting in the dark and the men who found them there, one of whom, it seemed, had tried his best to protect them. "So you did not identify the assailant?"

"No. No, I didn't."

"You say Rebecca sought justice. And I think perhaps you yourself have not been displeased to see your husband and your father suffer unease in this matter."

Her eyes fell. "I've served them a bit of their own, at any rate. Ashe has not had a moment's rest since he decided I'd taken a common footman for a lover. As for my father— him I merely drove to murder."

"Oh, Julia," said Penelope with horrified pity, "why should an old scandal drive Sir Roger to such measures? He is not so bound by convention as that, quite the contrary."

"What else can it be? Nothing makes any sense. He would have been deeply shocked to see her. Perhaps he thought she meant to attack him. Ashe told me Mr. Chase recovered my father's Celtic knife. You see, Father must have had it in his hand when he came out that night. I'm sure Dick took the blow meant for Rebecca."

Something Julia had said finally penetrated. "What do you mean Lord Ashe *decided* you had taken a lover. It's not…true?"

She laughed. "Is that why you've been so starched up, Mrs. Wolfe? You believed that of me. But it wasn't like that. He told me he was my brother, the son of my childhood nurse, the son my father never had. Still, I'm sure he was handsome enough for the thought to present itself, and such dalliance would have added a delectable spice to the whole situation. Can you imagine my father's horror? I see I've missed my chance."

"He lied to you," said Penelope flatly. "Sir Roger says Rebecca destroyed her child in a moment of despair. Dick was not your brother."

"If she did, she is not to blame. Yes, Dick lied. He and his friends needed Rebecca for their nasty plots, and they couldn't be sure whether the old story would surface to harm her. Oh, Dick was clever. He played the long-lost son for my benefit very well indeed. It was the perfect excuse for his probing questions about the family and his touching concern for his 'sick mother' who had run away."

"Those nuts you found this morning. What do they mean? Mr. Chase found a bit of hazel greenery in Dick's pocket."

"Rebecca must have crept in and left them for my father. When I was little, she used to make me hazelnut chains. I think she meant them as a sort of signal. Do you realize that she was in the wood with you that day?"

Penelope gaped. "Is that why you abandoned me? If she wished to speak to me, why didn't she approach?"

"She is not quite…rational," said Julia, shrugging. "I had encountered her near the lodge the day before and promised her I would bring you along. I would have waited for you to find your way out again, but Ashe came upon me and took it in his head to be angry I was on my own."

"Something is wrong, Julia. Don't you feel it? We must find Sir Roger at once."

"Wait, there is one thing more I must tell you," she said, a fresh note of constraint in her voice. "The dress I gave you. It was I who destroyed it. I have no excuse but that you had spurned my offers of friendship, and my maid told me you'd been overheard gossiping about me with that harridan Mrs. Sterling." Her head drooped. "I am sorry, Penelope. I was sorry as soon as I did it."

Penelope reached out to clasp the hand she extended. "Your maid had it wrong. I didn't gossip about you, but never mind all that now, Julia. There has been fault on both sides."

❧ ❧

After they rounded the edge of the wood, they continued north, heading, by unspoken consent, toward the ruined church. Soon Penelope caught her first glimpse of the church, rising from the center of an encircling, grassy rampart. In truth, the mound of earth, immeasurably ancient, had survived the years much better than the structure built to supplant it. How bereft the remnant is, she said to herself, with its roofless walls and misshapen form like some crippled beast hunched over the land.

The only sound was the quivering of the thick grasses, which flowed toward the earthwork, a living carpet. At the center of the circle, the church was of flint and dark red sandstone, an ivy tree winding shriveled branches round the tower. Two old yews, flanked by a small copse of hazel, stood guard to the east. Beyond the enclosure stretched fields, aglow with ripening corn, and sparsely treed meadows. In spring's fullness, the land appeared gently swollen like a woman's belly.

She was reminded of the sketch Sir Roger had drawn for her in which he had captured something of the brooding loneliness of this spot. Glancing at Julia, she saw that she too looked apprehensive, though there appeared to be no one else around.

They dismounted, Penelope with some difficulty, and looped their reins around a bush before walking up the slope until they gained the top of the ramp. Below was an inner ditch that followed the enclosure's line.

Julia said, "Mind the ditch. I'm afraid it's muddy. Look, why not wait here a moment, and I'll walk round the other side and take a quick look. There's no point in both of us soiling our shoes."

Nimbly, she jumped across the gap and, sweeping her train over her arm, strode toward the church, but Penelope was too restless to wait. Instead, she toiled through the long grasses at the side of the ditch, feeling the dew soak through the skirt of her habit. The sun was stronger now, almost hot on her back and shoulders. Overhead a lark sang, a liquid chirrup fading even as she listened.

She followed along the edge, seeking a spot to cross that looked less muddy. The recent rain had poured down the little gully, washing away rocks and large clumps of earth. In places the water stood in puddles that came halfway up the tufts of thick turf and red-flowered thistle. She glanced over her shoulder. Julia was out of sight.

Gathering up her skirt, Penelope launched herself, but at the other side she staggered, her ankle twisting as it slipped into a declivity she hadn't been able to see. Cursing silently, she leaned in the opposite direction and grasped a tuft of grass to prevent herself from falling. She was balanced at the edge of a small, irregular hole, perhaps three feet wide and only a foot or two deep. Her first thought was that Sir Roger must have begun his explorations, and carefully, she took a step back, not wishing to disturb them. She stared at the ground, and this time her eye caught sight of a grayish-white fragment sticking out of the bank just above the hole.

It looked like a bit of cloth.

Something made her bend down, pick up a long stick in her gloved hand, and lean across the ditch to poke at it. Gingerly, she scraped away, trying to catch the stick around the cloth. But after she had freed perhaps two inches, the cloth stuck fast in the mud.

With a grunt of annoyance, she shifted back on her heels and removed her right glove. Reaching out her hand, she gave a yank. The cloth tore. Threads unraveled in her fingers as a few more inches came free. With her stick Penelope dug out more dirt and tried again.

This time a bigger piece came away, and she was able to examine the cloth. For an instant she was excited, wondering if by chance she had stumbled on some genuine archaeological discovery. She recalled that when Sir Roger had spoken of the possibility of a burial mound under the church, he had mentioned that the ancient Britons might have chosen instead to bury their dead with their artifacts out here on the margin, perhaps to guard the boundary.

Common sense asserted itself. This was cloth, by all appearances once a piece of coarse homespun. It certainly couldn't be that old. Still, Penelope was curious enough now to remove her other glove and keep digging, heedless of the muck getting all over her clothing.

Finally, after she'd created a little hollow in the side of the earthen circle, she thought she had most of the cloth exposed. Afraid to pull too hard, certain it would disintegrate if she did, she began to slide it out. When she had most of the fabric in one hand, she probed the earth warily with the other to find the end. But as her fingers encountered something hard and strangely textured, she drew back, surprised.

Taking up her stick, Penelope dislodged still more earth. Slowly, several clods rolled down the incline into the gully. Another object followed in their train. Her eyes tracked it down and stopped.

"Penelope, come quickly," came Julia's voice on a high note of panic.

Penelope turned slowly toward the sound and attempted to frame an answer through the roaring in her ears. Slowly, she bent down to make certain of what she had seen, and there it was.

A tiny skull lay in the ditch.

Chapter XXIII

The trees shivered, whispering low. Though bright sun illumined their tops, the forest floor seemed dim, mysterious. As his feet sunk into a patch of muddy ground, Chase found himself thinking with some chagrin of his trousers and boots. He'd brought very little in the way of clothing on this journey. It would be just his luck to spoil a good portion of it on the second day.

But he kept moving doggedly down the track behind Edward Buckler, who set a rapid pace, glancing back over his shoulder every so often to meet Chase's eyes. Does he think I'm too old and feeble to keep up with him, Chase wondered, irked. Then he realized that Buckler was driven on by the same feeling of dread that pressed against his chest like a stone. Where were Penelope and Lady Ashe? Buckler thought they must be with Barnwell at the ruined church where the prophetess had once borne her baby, and something told Chase he was right. It would end where it had begun.

Suddenly, he collided with Buckler as the other man skidded to an abrupt halt. Smothering his cry of pain as the barrister trod on his toe, Chase said in a low voice, "What is it?" and tried to peer over his shoulder.

Buckler rushed forward, calling out, "Dear God. Chase, help me."

They stood in a small clearing, ringed with oaks that had trunks the size of cathedral pillars. The light streamed down; the dark, rich smell of earth mingled with the sweetness of wildflowers. A single butterfly, gold and green and blue, hovered lazily in the air, then drifted down to a branch.

From this tree dangled a man, noose knotted round his throat, his booted feet rotating in a slow half circle as the branch swayed. As Buckler reached out in a futile attempt to support the body's weight, Chase gazed upon the dead man's blackened, swollen features, easily recognizable as those of Sir Roger Wallace-Crag.

❦

Rebecca Barnwell had crawled into the niche formed by the remains of the chancel, a close space open to the sky. Crouching beside Julia on the red-gray stones, Penelope couldn't tell at first if the prophetess were aware of their presence, for she seemed locked within her pain, a caged animal.

"I think the baby is coming," said Julia, raising terrified eyes to Penelope's face.

Penelope regarded the mound of the woman's belly straining against her simple gray gown. Her gaze traveled lower, and she saw that the lower half of the dress was darkly wet. Blood, so much blood that its sharp tang filled the air, and Penelope imagined it soaking into the patches of earth between the stones. Nearby, a shovel leaned against the archway, upright, with gleaming blade.

Penelope opened her mouth to speak, trying in vain to keep her voice steady. "Go and fetch help, Julia. I'll stay with her."

Rebecca struggled to lift her head, but fell back. "No, no…please. No earthly aid can be of use to me now."

"You need a doctor." John Chase had not believed this woman was truly pregnant, but something was causing her to bleed. If they did not act, she would die and the child, if there was one, along with her.

"No," the prophetess said, and her hand shot out to grip Penelope's with surprising strength. "Too late. It won't be long, and I should like to talk to you."

"Julia, the water in your saddlebag. Can you bring the bottle?" Gently freeing her hand, Penelope whipped off the jacket of her riding habit and slipped it under the prophetess' head. Next, she enfolded Rebecca's hand in both of hers, turning it over to chafe the skin gently, fingers tracing the faint, whitish scars along her wrist. Penelope thought of the intense sorrow this woman had experienced. No wonder it had sent her mad to be shut up behind stout walls like that pitiful creature in Bedlam of whom Buckler had told her.

"Did you leave the nuts for Sir Roger this morning?"

A ghostly smile played over Rebecca's lips and vanished. "All one year we were lovers. I used to go to him in his study at night when the house was abed."

"You discovered you were to bear his child."

"*She* couldn't give him a son," Rebecca whispered, weaker now, but Penelope heard the thread of exultation in her voice and was chilled. "He said I must go away, that he would care for me and the babe. Slink away like some Jezebel branded by her shame? No, I couldn't do that. I didn't mind the whispers, for the Lord was with me."

Julia was back with the flask of water. Carefully, Penelope slipped an arm under Rebecca's shoulders and raised her so she could drink. Penelope looked at Julia, confirming the imminence of death, a tangible presence that hovered over the three women like a foul smell in an airless room.

Penelope grasped the frail hand again. No time. If she didn't speak now, Rebecca would die with this dreadful secret on her conscience. Suddenly, Penelope did not want that. "Your baby, Rebecca. Tell me what happened."

"They tricked me into the carriage. But when it stopped, I ran away through the trees to this church, an unlucky spot. But my pains were too strong, and I could go no farther. I don't recall much more. But I'm sure I saw a man's face, the Devil himself ablaze with hatred and evil, swimming before my gaze. When I woke up, the babe was gone, and Jack Willard stood over me."

"Whose face did you see?"

"He came again these many years later to try to take this babe from me too. He told me he'd intercepted my letters to the Master and said he'd kill me if I didn't keep silent, stay away, and stop telling tales to the world. When I said I only wanted the truth, he thrust his…knife to my belly."

Her fingers fluttered in Penelope's grip. With what seemed an almost superhuman effort of will, the prophetess managed to turn her head so that Penelope was looking into pools of despair.

"Where is my child?" she said, barely audible. "Please, you must help me."

Penelope glanced at the shovel. Had Rebecca dug just a little deeper, she might have discovered that tiny skull. Penelope did not know whether to be glad or sorry she hadn't. "The child has been found, Rebecca," she heard herself saying. "You mustn't worry anymore. Everything will be taken care of."

"He…must be…baptized or he will be lost, condemned to wander until Judgment Day. I have heard his voice… crying in the wind."

"Yes, I promise. I'll see to it." Penelope was crying herself, but she saw that Julia sat mute and stiff as if waiting for the axe to fall.

Penelope bent back to Rebecca, whose lips were moving again. "That's…good," she whispered against Penelope's cheek. "You are a mother yourself."

It was over. Gently, irrevocably, Penelope closed the dead woman's eyes and looked up. "We must go back to Cayhill. They will need to bring a litter for her."

Julia nodded and got to her feet, staggering slightly. Suddenly, there was movement behind her, and someone rushed forward, crowding them, a figure in a long black coat with a hat pulled low so that his features were not visible. He seemed to take in the woman lying on the stones; then his attention shifted to Julia, who cowered, whimpering with fear. He plucked her up in his arms and shook her like a dog worrying a bit of rag, so that her head lolled from side to side in an odd jerky motion. With one hand, he slammed her body against the stone and clamped his hand over her mouth and nose, squeezing, squeezing. As Penelope watched in horror, Julia's lovely white skin began to purple.

"No!" Penelope cried, "stop it at once." It was as if he hadn't seen her yet, as if there were only room for one at a time in his red-hazed vision. She looked around wildly, her gaze lighting on the shovel still leaning against the archway. Snatching it up, she swung it in a wide arc, praying she wouldn't hit Julia. The shovel struck the side of the assailant's head with a sick thud. His hand dropped away; he fell to his knees and crumpled to the ground, face down. As Penelope stood over the man, panting, Julia stared at her, the marks of the man's fingers already standing out in livid bruises.

"Penelope?"

Slowly, as if half asleep, she turned toward the sound of this new voice. It was Buckler, she realized, and glad relief filled her heart. In a moment she was safe in the circle of his arms, shedding tears down his coat. As he patted her back soothingly and murmured nonsense in her ear, she clung tighter, until, gathering herself with an effort, she took a step back and noticed his companion for the first time.

"Mr. Chase! Where did you come from? Thank God you are here to help us sort out this disaster."

He looked up from his examination. "I'm afraid it's worse than you know. Are you hurt?"

Penelope felt her stomach drop, and she moved farther away from Buckler. "Do you mean I've killed him?"

"Him?" Chase prodded the figure with one booted foot. "No, Mrs. Wolfe, but he'll wake up to wish you had." He looked with compassion at Julia, but went on unflinchingly. "I'm afraid I have dreadful news. Your father is dead, my lady. He was knocked out and hung from a tree. Come," he added with rough sympathy, "you had better sit down for a few minutes."

Chase nodded at Buckler, who took Julia by the arm to guide her toward a low wall. Like a doll, she allowed herself to be positioned there, saying not a word.

Stooping over the limp figure, Chase again prodded it. "Do you know who this is, Mrs. Wolfe? Shall I show you his face?"

She thought of a man who had lived his life in shadow, observing and assisting others, often treated with contempt or, worse, indifference. One woman had shown him kindness, even in the midst of her tragic struggle to bear her husband a child, an heir.

For her, this man had committed a crime, the most terrible of all, the murder of an innocent. But he had known that the very existence of this child would be a reproach to a woman he admired deeply if she discovered the truth and would bring scandal down upon his master to whom, in his own way, he was loyal. Perhaps he had believed that the sacrifice of the one might serve the greater good.

"He was working late on the night of Ransom's death," said Chase. "He must have heard or seen something outside the window and gone to investigate."

At Chase's feet, the man stirred, giving a low groan. Reaching into his pocket, Chase removed a pair of handcuffs and bent to pull back his arms roughly. "Do you know who this is, Mrs. Wolfe?"

"It's Owen Finch," said Penelope.

"I baptize thee in the Name of the Father, and of the Son, and of the Holy Ghost," said Sir Henry Buckler. Dipping his fingers in the vessel of water, he sprinkled glittering drops over the cloth-wrapped bundle cradled in his other hand. Penelope felt something inside her ease, and she saw that Julia's expression had lightened too as she and Buckler exchanged queer, sad smiles.

It was the third day after the deaths of Roger Wallace-Crag and Rebecca Barnwell, and while services for Sir Roger had been held this morning, the prophetess had already been interred without fanfare, her grave marked with a humble wooden cross. The murderer Finch had been taken away to be incarcerated until the payment of his debt should finally end his misery.

Grieving over her father, Julia seemed to have cut herself off from the world, though she had been unusually gentle with Penelope and openly regretful of her companion's imminent departure. Ashe, however, Julia ignored, as if he had ceased to exist. For his part, Ashe seemed deflated somehow, unmanned perhaps by his old friend's death and his wife's open contempt.

"What will you do now?" Penelope had asked her this morning when they were alone at the breakfast table.

"Perhaps I shall take a trip to Scotland to visit some of my father's people...or travel abroad, if there is anyplace left to go with Bonaparte still on the loose."

"And Lord Ashe?"

Julia looked up. "I've a little money of my own from my mother. Ashe may go to the Devil for all I care. I can't imagine why I've been afraid of him so long. Do you disapprove?"

"It seems for the best," Penelope had replied, and Julia had smiled that same smile she had just given Buckler— sad, yes, but also aware and alive.

For Penelope, all packing complete, there remained only this duty, a promise she had not known how to redeem until Buckler had hesitantly voiced his idea. She remembered how strange, even macabre, it had seemed, though now she was conscious only of its rightness.

A local doctor had examined those tiny bones they had been able to recover, but it had not required his expertise to determine the infant's original cause of death. The skull provided the answer, the back of it crumbling away like sand, marked indisputably by the crushing blow that had ended a life almost before it had begun. The same doctor had also performed the autopsy on Rebecca Barnwell.

Penelope knew that in her nightmares she would see Owen Finch dashing the infant against the stone wall, and she often imagined his fastidious distaste at the blood splattering his hands and clothing. Was that why he had worn the voluminous greatcoat to attack Miss Barnwell on Clerkenwell Green and then again to murder Sir Roger and attack Penelope and Julia in the church?

Sir Henry was speaking again, barely glancing at the paper Julia held up in front of him. No doubt he had attended many a christening, or for that matter, many a wedding or funeral, in his tiny parish.

"They brought young children to Christ, that he should touch them; and his disciples rebuked those that brought them. But when Jesus saw it, he was much displeased, and said unto them, Suffer the little children to come unto me, and forbid them not; for of such is the kingdom of God. Verily, I say unto you, Whosoever shall not receive the kingdom of God as a little child, he shall not enter therein. And he took them up in his arms, put his hands upon them, and blessed them."

Sir Henry nodded to his brother. "Dost thou, in the name of this Child, renounce the devil and all his works, the vain pomp and glory of this world, with all covetous desires of the same, and the carnal desires of the flesh, so that thou wilt not follow, nor be led by them?"

The sun struck fire on his bent head as Buckler took a step closer to the tiny grave they had dug in the center of the circle just outside the ruined church. Placing a hand on the cloth bundle in Sir Henry's arms, he said clearly, "I renounce them all."

Sir Henry turned to Penelope. "Ah, the child's other sponsor. Wilt thou then obediently keep God's holy will and commandments, and walk in the same all the days of thy life?"

Throat tight, Penelope placed her hand next to Buckler's, and though their fingers didn't touch, she was deeply conscious of him at her side. "I will," she murmured.

After Sir Henry made the sign of the cross over the bundle and laid it in its resting place, he and Buckler filled in the earth, then carefully placed the small marker Sir Henry had commissioned from the mason. In silence, Penelope and Julia decked the gravesite with bluebells and scarlet geraniums.

Afterwards, as they lingered near Sir Henry's curricle to say their farewells, Penelope said softly to Buckler so that Julia, whom Sir Henry was tossing into the saddle, would not hear, "Of what avail was it to murder Sir Roger? Finch must have realized he couldn't hope to keep his secret any longer."

"Revenge, I should say. Had it not been for his master, Finch would never have been driven to murder in the first place. Barnwell should not have been driven to madness and treason. And Ransom would still be alive. I suppose Finch saw it as closing the circle. For that, he needed Wallace-Crag to die as well as Barnwell and her unborn child along with her."

"Only this time there was no child," said Penelope sadly. "Merely some sort of internal growth, a monstrous tumor that killed her without any interference from him." She put out her hand. "I have had word. My husband comes for me and Sarah tomorrow, sir. So this is good-bye for a while."

Buckler clasped her fingers briefly, his expression shuttered. "Godspeed, Mrs. Wolfe."

"Has Edward been telling you of his plan to stand for Parliament?" said Sir Henry, coming to pump her hand. "I vow I shan't know what to make of my care-for-naught brother."

❧ ❧

Pipe in hand and a mug of ale at his elbow, Graham sat over his papers in the private chamber at Bow Street office. "You're back, Chase."

"Yes, sir." He had arrived back in Town yesterday and had hurried home to discover if a letter from his son Jonathan had arrived in his absence. None had.

"Any luck catching your culprit?"

"Yes, in fact. I located Rebecca Barnwell, who is dead, and apprehended Dick Ransom's murderer, though unfortunately not until he had taken Sir Roger Wallace-Crag's life as well," he added, quelling the sense of regret and guilt that the thought of the baronet inevitably evoked.

Graham's bored look vanished. "Indeed?"

When Chase had finished speaking, a silence fell which Graham broke. "Your friend Ezekiel Thorogood has been retained as solicitor to Janet Gore. She will turn King's evidence, it seems, and handily escape the gallows for her part in the plot against the Regent's life."

"My friend?" Chase began, but just then the door burst wide, and a young boy employed by the office to carry messages and run errands burst in without ceremony. "The Prime Minister's been shot in the House of Commons! Perceval is dead, and they've got the assassin."

Chase stared at Graham, watching the blood drain from his face so that he looked for the moment an old man. For an instant, Chase too felt lightheaded and ill as a sense of unreality overcame him.

"What villain did this?" said Graham hoarsely.

"They say a man called John Bellingham lodging in Milman Street," the boy replied, almost dancing in his eagerness to tell his tale. "Bellingham hid himself behind the folding doors leading into the house and burst out upon Mr. Perceval. Shot him through the heart, he did."

Back in the stuffy inn parlor of the Fleece, Chase could hear Janet Gore's voice saying, *You can't stop this. Don't think you can,* and he wanted suddenly to smash something for the pure pleasure of it. The plot to assassinate the Regent had come to nothing, but somehow Barnwell's prophecy had come true, after all. Was the world peopled with lunatics, awaiting their hour upon the stage, their bloody opportunity, or was there some pattern in this Chase couldn't see?

"Bellingham was here in Bow Street, sir," he told Graham. "I saw him myself when he came seeking a response to his letter of grievance. We sent him away."

Lowering his head to his hands, Graham shuddered, then raised red-rimmed eyes. "Is it thought this man acted in concert with others? A treasonous plot?"

"No one knows," said the boy. "He says he acted alone. The mails are to be stopped and a Cabinet Council called. They are examining Bellingham now abovestairs in the House. A crowd has gathered outside."

"Let me go there at once," said Chase urgently. "I will position myself in the throng and help to keep the peace."

"Yes, yes," said Graham, waving a distracted hand. "We will need to remain calm, only show our force as necessary. Leave me now while I go to Mr. Read and we ponder what is to be done."

Chase found that the boy had offered no more than the simple truth, for the street outside the Commons was full of people. But having expected ugliness, even violence, he was not at all prepared for the mood of the people, which astonishingly was celebratory, even joyous. They stood shoulder to shoulder, from time to time breaking out in songs, cheers, and ear-splitting whistles.

"Down to hell with the Devil, and may the rest of the damned scoundrels go the same way," Chase heard one man call out.

"God bless John Bellingham," others cried. "Let all the Devil's brood go to Hell so that poor people may live!"

Waiting there the rest of that endless evening until finally about one o'clock in the morning when the assassin was brought out under guard to be transported to Newgate, Chase felt that he had stumbled into an unrecognizable world. The gulf between rich and poor, the powerful and the weak, had never seemed so wide. Could they be stopped, these faceless masses who nourished hatred and revenge in their hearts? In that moment he doubted it. They had been injured; they would strike back, again and again. Here was the pattern.

The crowd pressed around Bellingham's coach, their shouts clamoring, their bodies a heavy wall of flesh. Chase, who could not have moved, watched helplessly as men crawled over the coach like insects, perching on the wheels and mounting the box. Several managed to get the doors open and push their hands inside to wring Bellingham's. The police struggled in vain to beat them back so that the coach could move, eventually resorting to whips, which they wielded with a strength born of fear.

When the coach, finally, was gone, John Chase allowed himself to be swept away down the street, one man alone in the laughing, cheering crowd.

Author's Note

In my portrayal of the prophetess Rebecca Barnwell, I have "borrowed" biographical detail from the life of Joanna Southcott, born 1750. Southcott was a domestic servant, who at the age of forty-two felt the call of the Spirit to fulfill a great destiny. She established a ministry, wrote dozens of books and pamphlets, and attracted thousands of followers.

When she was sixty-four years old, she suddenly announced she was to give birth to a messiah "by the power of the Most High." People showered Joanna with costly gifts like lace caps and silver cups and, believing that the Millennium approached, flocked to the metropolis to be on hand for the big moment. As the story goes, Joanna did appear to be pregnant, but as a year went by and no baby came forth, it became obvious her health was failing. She died a few days after Christmas in 1814, an autopsy later attributing her symptoms to "biliary obstructions" (whatever those are!) and the mass of her stomach to ordinary weight gain.

Of course, my version of Southcott/Barnwell's history, including the love affair with Sir Roger Wallace-Crag and her later association with Jacobin conspirators, is purely fictional. Nonetheless, I am indebted to James K. Hopkins' *A Woman to Deliver Her People: Joanna Southcott and English Millenarianism in an Era of Revolution* (University of Texas Press, 1982).

The profligate Prince Regent, whom the radical Leigh Hunt described as "a man who had just closed half a century without one single claim on the gratitude of his country or the respect of posterity," was indeed the target of threats around the time of this novel, though I don't know of any actual conspiracies. And certainly Prime Minister Perceval had a strong inkling of the mood of the people before his own life became forfeit to John Bellingham's bitter grievance. Perceval had received many threatening letters from the Luddites during the spring of 1812, such as this one about the frame-breaking bill that Lord Byron had ineffectually opposed:

> The Bill for Punish'g with Death has only to be viewed with contempt & opposed by measures equally strong; & the Gentlemen who framed it will have to repent the Act: for if one Man's life is Sacrificed, !blood for !blood...(qtd. in Sale, *Rebels Against the Future*, Addison-Wesley Publishing, 1995)

Finally, readers might find it interesting to note that on May 18 Byron rented a prime spot in a house overlooking Newgate Prison to see the assassin John Bellingham "launched into eternity" to the accompaniment of applause and congratulatory shouts of "God bless him!" I cannot but reflect that sentiments of this nature seem terrifyingly familiar these days.

December 18, 2002